Praise for *All of Us with Wings*

A Barnes & Noble Most Anticipated #OwnVoices
YA Book of the Year

A Book Riot Most Anticipated LGBTQ Read of the Year

A Book Riot Must-Read Debut Book of the Year

A She Reads Best YA Book of the Year

A Hip Latina Best YA Book of the Year

A Paste Best Young Adult Book of the Month

"Keil's ambitious debut is jam-packed with twists and depth
and froth and function . . . [this is] a book about embracing
everything—people, lifestyles, beliefs, experiences—and, in so
doing, finding your own distinct power."
— *The New York Times Book Review*

"Michelle Ruiz Keil's strange but original premise gives fresh
perspective to the ways pain and rage can manifest themselves
as toxic elements that threaten a person's well-being and
endanger those around them." —**NBC News**

"In her debut novel, Michelle Ruiz Keil crafts a fantastical ode
to the Golden City's postpunk era." —*Entertainment Weekly*

"A spellbinding tale about finding magic in the mundane
and hope in the unknown. Filled with dizzying danger and
electrifying music, *All of Us with Wings* left me breathless."
—**Ruth Ozeki,** *Los Angeles Times* **Book Prize–winning
author of** *A Tale for the Time Being*

"Michelle Ruiz Keil creates a vivid and original novel full
of music, rage, and characters that sing with purpose. Keil
is a new voice to keep an eye on." —**Zoraida Córdova,
award-winning author of** *Labyrinth Lost*

"Keil is at her best playing with the magical realism element . . . using lush, imagistic prose to cast a dreamy (sometimes nightmarish) pall over the scenes."
—Bulletin for the Center of Children's Books

"Michelle Ruiz Keil has crafted something of astonishing radiance with *All of Us with Wings;* it's not always easy or pretty, but it's a novel with real staying power that will reward all who succumb to its magic." *—Locus Magazine*

"The writing soars . . . This tale of found family and recovery weaves an unforgettable punk rock-infused spell."
—*Kirkus Reviews*, Starred Review

"[An] atmospheric debut . . . Keil plays with prose and imagery, interweaving the dreamlike language of Francesca Lia Block with a Latin-American sensibility. The frank inclusion of sexual exploration and drug use adds an extra level of maturity to this thoughtful story about trauma and vengeance, adult decision making, and recovery." *—Publishers Weekly*

"This intricately constructed urban fantasy is complex and beautiful, blending folklore, San Franciscan history, the music scene, vampires, magic, and the intertwined lives of characters, including a cat named Peasblossom who sees and understands more than the humans . . . Fantasy fans will find this book appealing, fun, and hard to put down."
—School Library Journal

"*All of Us with Wings* is unapologetically queer, sexy and colorful. It doesn't pull its punches, but it also examines narratives of rape recovery in an as ethical a manner as possible. There is hope, it says. There is family. There is life beyond the trauma."
—Young Adulting

All of Us with Wings

All of Us with Wings

Michelle Ruiz Keil

Published in the United States by Soho Teen
an imprint of Soho Press, Inc.
227 W 17th Street
New York, NY 10011

Library of Congress Cataloging-in-Publication Data
Keil, Michelle Ruiz, author.
All of us with wings / Michelle Ruiz Keil.

ISBN 978-1-64129-135-4
eISBN 978-1-64129-035-7

1. Governesses—Fiction. 2. Supernatural—Fiction.
3. Revenge—Fiction. 4. Musicians—Fiction. 5. Mexican Americans—
Fiction. 6. San Francisco (Calif.)—Fiction. I. Title.
PZ7.1.K41513 All 2019 | DDC [Fic]—dc23 2018049992

Wing art: by SuicideOmen

Interior design by Janine Agro, Soho Press, Inc.

Printed in the United States of America

10 9 8 7 6 5 4 3 2 1

For my nana, Luciana Ruiz Smith Dudley.
And for Carl, my true love.

All of Us with Wings

A Note from the Author

THERE ARE SCENES IN this book that discuss sexual abuse, the use of hard drugs, and the loss of a loved one. If these might be triggering or harmful to you, please be mindful of that and pause, stop, or even forego reading the novel as necessary. Here is a little bit about why I feel these scenes were important to include:

All of Us with Wings is my first novel. For years, I learned to write within its imagined San Francisco in time stolen from my daily life as a caregiver, glowing with the secret of the story in my pocket. As the years went on, I wrote to heal myself, to bring my own hidden histories to light.

As an abuse survivor and mixed-race Latinx, I have long struggled with empowerment and identity. Though promising and bright, I found myself unable to follow the traditional path of high school, college, and career as the effects of my childhood trauma manifested in adolescence.

For many years, I longed for a life that seemed unattainable: the ivy-covered college campus, the cap-and-gown graduation ceremonies, the fabulous career in theater or law teachers and family assumed I would pursue. But as I grew older, I began to see the value of a different sort of education—the one I'd given myself. I had to find my own rites of passage, my own path to adulthood. I wanted to write a story about this kind of life, both its struggles and its gifts.

Like Xochi, the heroine in *All of Us with Wings*, I ran away to San Francisco at seventeen and fell in love with the city. There was something about the sky's watercolor blue, the sun-faded pastel of the houses, the pearly sheen of fog that woke me to the world's magic. I wanted to write about the way art and music and long talks and fast motorcycle rides can heal. About the bookstore I once worked at with a wise and cranky Siamese cat.

As the daughter of a teen mom, I wanted to write a story about young parents and their kids raising each other, and what it means to be on your own in the world at an age when most of your peers are still living under their parents' protection. I wanted to tell a story about found family and complicated love. Finally, I wanted to write about a girl who has been sexually abused and works to reclaim both her power and pleasure.

Writing such a book proved to be a difficult and dangerous journey. When I felt lost during the first draft, I found the Brothers Grimm story "The Maiden Without Hands," a fairytale roadmap to healing from the worst kinds of betrayal. In researching the name Xochi, I learned of the goddess Xochiquetzal, patron of lovers, embroiderers and sex workers, who lives in a verdant heaven where the winds blow glittering obsidian knives and the trees bleed when their jeweled blossoms are plucked.

To my astonishment, I also discovered that, just like my Xochi, the goddess's story includes the piercing of tongues. In *All of Us With Wings*, this act creates a space for magic to enter the ordinary world. On Xochiquetzal's feast day, supplicants are pierced, passing straw after bloody straw through their perforated tongues, one for each of their sins, to emerge clean, forgiven. Free.

This moment of synchronicity led me to wonder what it takes for survivors of abuse to reclaim their power, and whether perpetrators can ever really make amends. I wanted to explore the ways we so often unintentionally inflict pain as we make the mistakes it takes to grow up, and how complex that dynamic becomes for survivors as we create imperfect heavens of blades and blood and found family and poetry.

I also discovered tales from all over the world of dangerous, powerful child-sized creatures who protected streams, lakes, forests and hot springs. In the danger and power of these beings, I saw a path for our broken bodies to connect with earthly powers, a way to draw parallels between the mistreatment of women and children and the degradation of the planet herself.

But most of all, I wanted to tell my own story and the story of the other lost young people I've known and loved.

Abuse can make us self-destructive. Sometimes, we blame and want to hurt ourselves.

It can cause us to be comfortable in dangerous situations because they feel familiar.

It can drive us to do dangerous things because we long for relief and want to feel good.

Sometimes, we can avert danger by avoiding it.

But when we can't, danger must be surmounted, outsmarted, survived.

Because *All of Us with Wings* is that sort of story, the characters sometimes make mistakes. There is drug use and sex and very real danger, both emotional and physical. But there is healing, too—a thread leading out of the labyrinth.

In the end, I wrote *All of Us With Wings* for the girls who are smart, but not in school because life has gotten in the way. For the mixed-race kids already exhausted by the ubiquitous question, *What are you?* For the motherless, the fatherless. The queer kids. The ones who retreat into sleep. The ones who scream and throw stones. The ones who survived and remember how it was.

For all of us who grew up too fast with only ourselves to rely on:

I want you to know that everything you did, you did to survive.

And you made it. You are here, reading these words.

You are strong. You are beautiful.

I can't see you, but I know you're there.

I.

Low, low, deep and low, the sibling pair sleeps
Hands clasped, hair entwined
They share a dream of springtime

They dream music
They dream of a girl
Of tears
And heat and honey

The mudpot stirs
Dreaming, they drift
Honey, heat, tears, springtime

Earth exhales her fumarole breath
How long have they slept in their aquifer nest?
Lithium bubbles, lighter than air

Eyes open, obsidian bright
Birdsong?
Thunder?

Together, they feel
Together, they listen
Together, hands clasped, they begin to rise

1

All Tomorrow's Parties

Pallas sat sidesaddle on the kitchen counter, velvet ankle boots resting daintily in the deep porcelain sink. Pressing her nose against the dark kitchen window, she glared at the hulking cyclops creeping steadily toward Eris Gardens, its single working headlight illuminating the carriage house and steep gravel drive.

"No one's supposed to park back there," she said. "Can't they read?"

"Maybe they're too tired." Xochi yawned. "I mean, who starts a party at midnight?"

"It's an *after*party." Pallas swirled a perfect cursive *P* in the steam her breath had made on the window. "Midnight counts as after."

"Midnight counts as bedtime." Xochi downed the rest of her coffee.

"Maybe for you."

Pallas had never had a bedtime herself, not even as a baby. Certainly not now that she was nearly thirteen.

She giggled. "You claim you're not governess material, but listen to you—so prim and disapproving."

Xochi rolled her eyes and reached over Pallas to pull back the lace curtain. Exhaust poured like fog from the old car's tailpipe. "Who drives a hearse?"

Pallas sighed. She had a pretty good idea of who the boxy

eyesore belonged to. "Some people get one song on the radio or open for Lady Frieda a few times and suddenly they're above parking on the street like everyone else."

She held her breath as the rusty behemoth lurched past the collection of vintage motorcycles parked behind the kitchen and shuddered to a stop. Four doors opened and five girls emerged. Like a line of paper dolls cut from the same pattern, they were thin and pale, with long white muslin dresses and waist-length blonde hair. They came in single file without knocking and passed through the kitchen without a word. The last one spared a head movement toward Pallas that might have been a nod and followed the others into the hall.

Rude, Pallas thought. But they were just bitter. That wannabe coven of undead schoolgirls had spent all of last summer trying to infiltrate Eris Gardens. They learned soon enough: sleeping with the band did not make you part of the family. Pallas slid off the counter with a thud.

"Wow," Xochi said. "So are they a cult, or what?"

"Just a band. *Filles Mourantes*," Pallas said. "Dead Girls. They sing in a made-up language and never eat. They want people to think they're, like, vampires or Parisian or something."

Pallas wasn't about to admit that their music was actually good. It was easier to have compassion for the not-so-gifted who tried to make up for it with attitude, but those attractive, talented girls had no excuse for being mean.

"They're gorgeous, though," Xochi said. "And those dresses are amazing."

"Please. You're way prettier." Pallas opened the industrial-sized refrigerator, the only modern thing in the large, drafty kitchen, and took out a platter of sushi and a bowl of chocolate-covered strawberries—Equinox food. "And your hair is perfect, especially with that dress. I'm so glad you listened to me and Kiki."

Xochi touched her newly bare neck. "It's not too short?"

"Of course not!" Pallas's godmother Kiki had bobbed

Xochi's hair perfectly. And this after magically producing a sparkly ashes-of-roses flapper dress when Pallas had worried Xochi wouldn't have anything nice to wear for the concert. The dress had once belonged to Pallas's mother–Io was too thin for it now, but it fit just right on Xochi. She looked so glamorous.

Like a storybook governess, Xochi was from a small, uneventful place where the most exciting happenings were potlucks and school dances. Although she was almost eighteen, she had never been to a real concert, let alone an after-party for one.

Pallas sighed. It would be selfish to keep Xochi cooped up in the attic all night reading.

She took a deep breath. "You know," she said, "you could stay down here and check out the party. If you want."

"I thought we were finishing *Villette*."

Taking turns reading their favorite books aloud had been Pallas's idea; she'd chosen *Villette* because of its governess heroine. Xochi was usually into the story as much as Pallas was. But tonight, there was a tiny hint of reluctance in her voice.

Before Pallas could answer, a disgruntled yowl sounded from the patio.

"More vampires?" Xochi's eyes were brighter now, the way they always got when her coffee kicked in.

"Not this time." Pallas hurried to open the back door. "Just one grumpy old sphinx."

Peasblossom strolled in, looking pleased with himself as usual. Pallas reached down to pet him.

"Wait a minute," Xochi said. "Is that the bookstore cat?"

Pallas couldn't help but laugh at the look on Xochi's face. "He comes over to keep me company during parties."

Peas trotted past Xochi and leaped onto the counter, suspiciously close to the covered party platter of sushi.

"In your dreams!" Pallas scooped him up and set him back on the floor. His tail twitched. "Nora said no sushi—it gives you gas."

Peas washed his shoulder in disdain, clearly insulted.

"Nora—she's the bookstore lady, right?" Xochi's brow furrowed. "She knows about these little visits?"

"Of course," Pallas said, stroking Peasblossom's velvet nose.

"But how does he know when there's a party?"

"I tell him," Pallas said.

The front door banged. Laughter. Voices. The thud of music gear. The mayhem was about to begin. Pallas steeled herself. It wouldn't be so bad now that Peas was here.

She feigned a big yawn, put a few pieces of sushi into her Hello Kitty bento box, and looked down at Peasblossom, her best and oldest friend. "Come upstairs, hungry thing. Maybe I'll give you *one* bite of my yellowtail." To Xochi, she said, "Reading's going to be pointless when the music starts. Why don't you go freshen up your lipstick? You should experience the full catastrophe at least once. In the morning, I'll say I told you so."

Xochi's eyes narrowed. "Are you sure?"

Now it was Pallas's turn to roll her eyes. Of course she was sure. Wasn't she? She'd always loved the feeling of being alone in her attic bedroom during a party. She'd imagine her bed was a ship in a storm or Dorothy's house spinning through the tornado toward Oz. That kind of imagining was harder these days; she wasn't sure why.

"Totally sure! I'll probably just go to sleep." She yawned again, this time for real. She *was* tired. And honestly a little peopled out, as her mother would say.

From somewhere in the front of the house, a speaker made a catfight screech, putting Peasblossom's fur visibly on end.

"You can sleep through this?"

Pallas shrugged. "I have earplugs. I've been at this since I was a baby, you know. Every Solstice and Equinox and Samhain and Beltane—a concert, a big afterparty. I have it down to a science."

"Maybe I'll just go check it out for a minute . . ." Xochi was already pulling the red lipstick Kiki gave her from the pocket of her leather jacket. She looked so beautiful with her warm brown skin and minky waves. The kind of girl flapper dresses and fishnets and combat boots and leather jackets were made for.

"Come on, Peas," Pallas said, heading for the attic staircase. She bit her lip against an absurd welling of tears. There was no reason to be upset. Nothing was different about this Equinox from any other—nothing except Xochi. And now that Xochi was going to the party and Pallas was alone, nothing was different at all.

2

Rite of Spring

Xochi perched at the top of the grand staircase, watching the party below. The partygoers wore their wildflower crowns with tattered Victorian picnic clothes or spiderwebbed layers of black, eyes painted like Egyptian royalty. The music wasn't Lady Frieda, but something from the same section of the record store—hypnotic and velvet dark, the soundtrack to a dream.

Xochi touched the rose at her ear, plucked from the bucket of leftover flowers in the kitchen. In the thick of things, she spotted familiar pink curls and a sparkly silver mermaid dress—definitely Bubbles. As usual, she was laughing, surrounded by boys. She paused to hug a tall dark-haired guy, his mouth beside her ear. The strobe light illuminated his face: Leviticus, Pallas's dad. Uncrowned, his long, wavy hair was wet. He must have showered after the show. Earlier that night, onstage with his guitar, his presence had been the source of gravity, his voice a replacement for air in the sold-out art-deco theater. Now, in the middle of the crowd, he went unnoticed.

Xochi had read something once about Marilyn Monroe, how she could turn her star quality on and off whenever she wanted. Leviticus seemed to have the same power, floating in his own quiet eddy, a river inside a river. She watched as his black T-shirt disappeared into the crowd.

Before meeting Pallas, Xochi had never heard of Lady

Frieda. She might have never moved in if she'd known the band was more than just "named after a British aristocrat who painted tarot cards," "pretty good in a gloomy art rock sort of way," and "kind of famous."

After seeing them perform for the first time tonight, it was clear they were more than *kind of famous*. As for *pretty good*— no, they were Bowie good, Patti Smith good. The real thing.

From the moment Xochi had met Pallas two months earlier, a lonely girl eating black licorice on free admission day at Steinhart Aquarium, she'd felt like she was living someone else's fairy tale. *Once upon a time, there was a white castle on a green hill, overlooking a city by the sea.* And tonight, there was even a ball.

She rolled her neck, already stiff from thrashing around at the concert. When was the last time she'd danced? Had it really been the bonfire after her grandmother's wake? Xochi touched her throat, where a pair of carved jade hummingbirds held a glowing opal between their two beaks. The necklace had been Loretta's favorite. Xochi rarely took it off.

Laughter floated up from the party. Whatever heaven Loretta was in must be a lot like the swaying chaos in the ballroom below. That woman lived for parties. She would celebrate anything: a full moon, a perfect sunset, the first day of fall. Xochi wished Loretta could have heard Lady Frieda at least once.

The music changed, slinking and heavy with the bass so low Xochi felt it in her tailbone. She recognized the song from the concert—Lady Frieda covering the Beatles. The rhythm took off, coming apart at the seams in a way Xochi's hips understood. Loretta would have been all over this. *Get off your ass and dance*, she'd say. Also: *fake it till you make it, kitten.*

Down in the ballroom, Xochi closed her eyes and surrendered to the tide of bodies as Lady Frieda sang about doing it in the road. A set of arms wrapped around her waist. It was Bubbles, electric pink ringlets bouncing around rum-and-coke eyes. At twenty-four, she was the youngest person in the band and claimed the rest of them were less and less fun the closer they got to thirty.

Bubbles took Xochi's hand and pulled her toward the cluster of people around the DJ. The only familiar face was Pad's. Xochi had been surprised at how efficient he'd been at the concert, running everything backstage with his clipboard and walkie-talkie. Now he was back to looking purely ornamental with his lilac-and-ivy wreath, shorn dark hair and jay-blue eyes, the mermaid tattoo on his forearm a warning most girls failed to heed: beware the siren song.

The day Xochi moved in, Pallas made sure to tell her, "Watch out, Pad is a rake." Now she'd seen it for herself almost every morning at the crack of dawn when Pallas dragged her out of bed and Pad's night was just ending—the Pretty Girl Parade from his bedroom to the front door.

"Happy Equinox!" Pad hugged Xochi, something he'd never done before. "You look gorgeous tonight, love. Did you cut your hair?" He reached over to touch it, wrist grazing her collarbone. His normal hint of an Irish accent was thicker than usual. A sure sign he was either flirting or drunk, according to Pallas.

"Kiki did it."

"Well, that explains it. Kiki's a genius."

"What about you? That set was incredible. And those lights! I had no idea you were so talented."

"Don't you flatter him, Xochi," Bubbles said. "He's conceited enough."

"You wound me!" Pad clutched at his heart. "Really, I'm quite insecure. It's why I need so much encouragement." This was directed to the girl beside him. Tall and haughty, she resembled the others Xochi passed in the hallway outside his bedroom most mornings. *Hair ponies*, Pallas called them, the same thing she called the long-maned model horses she'd collected when she was little.

A pale, slender boy with a lavender Mohawk and a blue

crescent moon tattooed on his forehead emerged from the crowd with a gilded water pipe. He handed it to Pad with a kiss on the cheek and danced back into the crowd.

"Is that a hookah?" Xochi asked.

Pad took a hit and passed it to Bubbles. "It is," he said. "Not something you'd expect the governess to know, though, is it?"

"Depends on the governess," Xochi said.

Pad laughed and the hair pony glared.

"It's hash," Bubbles said. "And a little tobacco."

Growing up on a pot farm, Xochi had inhaled enough secondhand marijuana to last a lifetime. The few times she'd consciously imbibed, the plant had not been her friend. But the hookah smoke smelled nice and it wasn't exactly weed.

She put the tube to her mouth as Bubbles leaned down to light the bowl. She was halfway through her inhale when the smoke changed direction, exploding out of Xochi's lungs in a fit of rasping coughs. Laughing, Pad handed Xochi his beer.

"You have to go slow. Here." Bubbles inhaled and brought her lips to Xochi's, blowing the hit gently into her mouth. Xochi had never kissed a girl—not that this was a kiss. But the plush lips, the soft hand on the back of her neck—it was something to consider. Bubbles's breath must have cooled the smoke. It slipped down Xochi's throat like a sip of water.

"Better, right?"

The smoke penetrated the tight muscles in her neck and shoulders, the start of a nice, civilized buzz. "Way better." The hash was different from weed, but related. With the familiar dissolving of limbs came an added electricity, a psychedelic edge. The first wave of high hit gently enough, but it kept on coming. The music was so loud. Her heartbeat competed with the hammering bass.

"I'll be right back," Xochi told Bubbles.

"You okay?" Bubbles was almost too shiny with her sequins and coppery eyes.

"Fine," Xochi said. "I just need some air."

Anxiety shot through her body in time with the music, now a mindless surf-punk pound. The dancers had abandoned rhythm for contact, bashing into each other like dogs in the park. Xochi made her way to the foyer and stumbled over the smokers clogging the front porch and stairs.

The night was uncommonly clear, with icy stars and an almost full moon. She walked past chalky pastel houses lining the street like beads on a candy necklace. Streetlights uncloaked the occasional bat.

The breeze lifted the thin fabric of Xochi's dress. She should be cold, but she wasn't. She was hungry, though. She would go back and eat some food. Go to bed.

Xochi stopped. How long had she been walking? If she was near the park, Eris Gardens couldn't be far. But . . . wait. This wasn't Buena Vista. This was a different park, one she'd never seen before. Her usual tactic of jumping on a bus and asking the driver for advice was useless this late at night. She spun in a full circle. Continuing downhill was the only logical move. She began to walk again, shivering now. She should have grabbed a jacket.

She heard the bar before she saw it, hunched between two shabby Victorians, its cinder-block façade stained red by a flashing neon sign. A man was outside smoking, muttering, looking at the ground.

No. Not the ground. He was looking at her, but not at her face. Xochi crossed the street.

"Hey, princess," he rasped. The word leaked out around his cigarette as his gaze lifted, now on Xochi's chest. "Where's your boyfriend?"

Xochi walked faster. The end of the block was just a few steps away.

"Bitch, I'm talking to you. Don't make me chase you now."

Xochi meant to keep walking, putting squares of dirty sidewalk between her and the greasy threat in his voice, but the air was too thick, the ground tilting and unstable.

Some sane part of her rose from her body and hovered under the streetlamp, shrinking away from the figures below—hers in its thin beaded dress and his in a crusty army jacket and stained jeans. She saw herself turn and walk back until she was directly across the street from him.

"Say it again," she said, her voice unrecognizable. "Say it to my face." What did she think she was going to do? Her blood buzzed and her skin crawled, slug damp with something that should have been fear.

"Crazy bitch." He laughed and dropped his half-smoked cigarette in the gutter. "Go back to the psych ward, cunt."

He stepped back, spat and pushed against the battered door of the bar. It opened wide, spewing speed metal and smoke, inhaling him into its dark, rank guts.

3

Pandora

Pallas stomped down the attic stairs, bare feet cold on the wooden treads. She took the final flight on tiptoe, willing herself transparent—a ghost girl, nothing but a flicker of light on the periphery of any wasted partygoer who might pass by.

Where was Xochi? With Bubbles, maybe, but then what? Just walk up and say hi? Pallas wasn't supposed to be down here on her own. For the last several months, she hadn't come down during parties at all. She tiptoed through the front hall, keeping close to the wall, the bumpy plaster cool under her hand.

The dining room was dark, the table a wrecked memory of the beautiful spread Kiki had arranged. Two boys leaned against the wall, one with burgundy hair and black eyeliner, the other a time traveler from the Summer of Love or *A Midsummer Night's Dream* with his leafy garland and fringed leather vest. They were younger than most of her family's friends. Teenagers, maybe—an undignified word. In three months, Pallas would join their ranks. Her childhood would be over.

She slipped into the kitchen, ducking under the breakfast table just in time to avoid her godmother. All she could see of Kiki were the tattooed vines that climbed up the backs of her shiny brown legs, disappearing under the hem of her black silk shorts.

Pallas held her breath. Kiki was extremely observant, sure to find Pallas out. Not that she'd do anything, except worry. But no—she went to the pantry.

"Sorry it took me so long." Kiki said quietly. "I think the coast is clear."

"It's no trouble," a man answered, stepping into the room. "My next client isn't due for another hour." Pallas placed the voice immediately. It belonged to James, a performance artist who owned the piercing shop up the street. But why was he hiding in the pantry? And was he really planning to see a client at two o'clock in the morning?

Pallas pulled the tablecloth up an inch. James looked the same as ever, with his horn-rimmed glasses and silver-streaked hair. He used to come over once in a while for family potlucks, but never to big parties. Just like her mom, he avoided crowds.

"I could do without the subterfuge," James said. "But I do respect her need for privacy."

Who needed privacy? And why?

"Right," Kiki said. "Such a delicate flower."

Io, then. People always said Pallas's mother was sensitive. But Kiki's tone was strange tonight.

There were more footsteps. Pallas's dad's beaten-up motorcycle boots appeared in the doorway to the stairwell leading up from the basement recording studio.

Kiki inhaled a bit too quickly. James stuttered a moment before saying hello.

"I'd better be going," he said. "Happy Equinox!"

The back door squeaked open, clicked shut. There was silence. Finally, Kiki spoke.

"Hey," she said. "You okay?"

Huddled perfectly still, Pallas thought of the three monkeys—see no evil, hear no evil, speak no evil.

"Lev?"

"I'm fine." Her dad's voice sounded like pages in an old book, crackly and stiff and easy to rip.

"Full of surprises, our girl," Kiki said, her voice almost too quiet to hear.

Their family was always talking things over, checking in. It was exhausting, really. Her dad and Kiki were clearly headed for a long, heartfelt talk, and Pallas would either be trapped or found out.

Fabric rustled. Kiki's shoes approached her dad's—a hug! Perfect. Pallas made her escape.

In the parlor, party guests lounged on the antique furniture, drinking wine and passing around a joint. A tall, shirtless man covered in rose tattoos tuned his violin. In the corner, a gnomish girl took out a silver vial and tiny spoon. She'd be kicked out if anyone from the house saw. Hard drugs weren't allowed, but people did them anyway.

The violinist began to play a slow, eerie snake-charming melody for a curvy, dark-haired dancer, his bow keeping time with her hips. As she danced, the fur around her shoulders shifted— not a piece of clothing after all, but an actual animal, possibly a ferret. It cocked its head toward Pallas, button eyes bright. She felt the pull of her younger self, a whimsical person she could no longer respect. A younger Pallas would have danced with the woman and her ferret, and she'd never have noticed the drugs. Kiki said it was temporary, this unforgiving eye. A symptom of puberty—another awful word, almost too grotesque to think about, let alone say.

Pallas stepped back into the hall and scooted up the front stairs under the velvet rope that cordoned off the private part of the house. The quickest way back to the attic was through her mother's wing, to the old servants' staircase. Maybe Xochi was back. Maybe they could read together after all.

The library door was ajar. Last year at Solstice, they'd found puke on the fluffy sheepskin rug by the fireplace. Pallas turned on the light, but everything looked fine. Along with Leviticus's enormous record collection, the library also had one of the best secret compartments in Eris Gardens. At the age of seven, Pallas had scoured the house to find them all.

To the left of the early Americana shelves was a piece of

paneling that was really a door. It opened when she pressed, quiet thanks to the olive oil she'd used on the hinges back then.

She stepped into the cramped space with its rusty metal bucket and pile of rags, maybe as old as the house itself, and pulled the door closed behind her. Something metallic twinkled in the darkness, a pile of wrappers from the chocolates she used to eat here when she was forlorn. Now her head nearly touched the top of the compartment. The party noises were muffled, but a haunted, romantic piano piece filled the small, dark space. It was Schubert, Io's music, the record scratchy from constant use.

At the back of the compartment, down by the floor, was a hatch of sorts leading into Io's large walk-in closet. Unlike the other secret passageways in the house, it was shabbily constructed, a square cut into the wall with an unpainted wooden flap on rough hinges and a scarred handle that might once have belonged to a chest of drawers.

Pallas opened the flap an inch but couldn't see a thing. She tried to stretch flat on her stomach, but her legs had gotten too long. She curled on her side and tried again. Her nose itched from the dust. She pulled the knob carefully, expecting a second darkness.

Instead, the closet door was open and Pallas saw her mother.

Io stood naked in front of her gilded, full-length mirror, peering over her shoulder like a nude in a famous painting. Pallas looked quickly from her mother's small breasts, concave belly and ballerina thighs to her dreamy green eyes, pink cheeks and wavy champagne hair. Io was always beautiful, but in this moment, she was so perfect she hardly seemed real.

Pallas's hand shook with the effort of holding the flap open just enough to see without being seen. With a little laugh, Io turned to face the mirror and Pallas saw what her mother had been admiring.

Embedded in the flesh in the small of Io's back was a set of small silver hooks, much like the fasteners on Pallas's own Victorian boots. A black ribbon crisscrossed her mother's bird-boned spine, connecting the hooks like laces on an invisible corset. Pallas almost gasped, shoving her fist into her open mouth to stop the sound.

Now she understood: the kitchen, the pantry. Kiki. Her dad.

These were piercings. Done tonight. By James.

Pallas closed the flap and sat up. There was a momentary silence, a mechanical whir and click. The Schubert was on repeat. She heard the rasp of the needle as it searched for the right groove, the opening chords of the Trio in E-flat.

Pallas had once flipped through a book of photographs of outlandish piercings and tattoos she wasn't supposed to look at. Io's disturbing new hooks and ribbons weren't attached to some unimaginably painful private place, but like the piercings in the book, they were definitely sexual—frightening, powerful and secret.

Pallas sat doll still, eyes closed. She imagined she was made of porcelain with a painted face and glass eyes and real human hair. She waited until the Schubert was over and the dressing room door creaked and clicked.

She opened the hatch again, the darkness in the cupboard combining with the dark of the dressing room, scents mixing: rose water, old wood and L'air du Temps, Io's special-occasion perfume. Her legs cramped as she crawled out of the cupboard, her nightgown smeared with the fine black dust the house seemed to exhale.

The grand staircase was littered with empty bottles and forgotten jackets. A lone couple argued in a corner. Tears streamed down the girl's face, but the boy could have been a statue with his folded arms and bored expression. Pallas flicked on the hall light. It wouldn't be so easy for him to ignore his girlfriend now.

A burgundy rectangle perched on the newel. A box of clove cigarettes. Pallas hesitated, then palmed it. The edges of the box dug into her hand. It was small, but it was something.

She trudged back to her attic. Not a ghost girl after all, but still completely invisible.

4

Persephone

atch the animals, Loretta always said. *How do they get over a fright?*

Xochi walked. Slowly at first, then faster and faster, her long strides pushing past the barred windows and trash-filled gutters into a neighborhood where the Victorians had better paint jobs and greenery softened the city streets.

Don't make me chase you.

Crazy bitch.

Psych ward cunt.

She sat at a bus stop. When Xochi was small, she and her mother had had a cat, a war-scarred tabby abandoned by the previous tenants of their apartment. He came home one night with a hot lump of pus bulging from his shoulder. There was no money for the vet, but Xochi's mom knew what to do. She wrapped the cat in a towel and made Xochi hold tight as she opened the abscess with a sterilized knife. What swelled in Xochi felt like that.

It wasn't being called a bitch or a cunt. Those words were nothing, bouncing around her head like half-filled balloons. She sat there and breathed, in and out. She let herself shake. A car passed by, breaking the quiet of the street. A memory hovered: a clothes-strewn airless room; a still life of a girl lying rigid on an unmade bed; eyes wide, uncrying.

Of course, Xochi thought. *Of course it's that.*

There was a book she'd read once, a fairy tale about a girl without a tongue.

How do animals get over a fright?

First, they get away.

Xochi had done that.

Then, they take stock.

She stood. The familiar Walgreens at Haight and Fillmore was on the next corner.

What was next? She rubbed her bare arms, sticky with spilled beer and sweat. The blunt ends of her hair grazed the back of her neck. *It's over,* she told herself in Loretta's voice. *It's over now and you're okay.* Eris Gardens was just a few blocks and one insanely steep hill away. All she had to do was walk.

Xochi set out, but her bladder screamed mutiny—another disadvantage of city living. If she'd been out in the woods, she could've just squatted, problem solved. The hill was going to be murder, but there was no getting around it.

Across the street, a man unlocked a storefront. She'd read a profile on the owner of Pagan Piercing in the free weekly paper, but the middle-aged man at the door looked more like a college professor than an underground legend.

"May I help you?" he called out, noticing her stare.

Xochi hesitated, but the thought of the hill made her bolder than usual. "Sorry to bother you, but may I use your bathroom?"

He stepped aside and gestured for her to come in. Bells trilled as the door closed against the night.

The bathroom was clean and painted black. Xochi ran warm water over her cold hands and fixed her smudged mascara. Back in the reception area, she stopped at a framed photograph of a human skull with an oddly shaped hole, tracing the wound with her finger. The piercer glanced up from the counter.

"Trepanation was one of the first surgical procedures. It was also used for shamanic purposes. This is the oldest example they've found."

That explained the puncture, too clean to be accidental. "Why did they do it?"

"It makes sense for a head injury with brain swelling. And if you're a shaman, it's your job to communicate with the divine. Why not open the door and invite her in? They used it for mental illness, too. Crazy out, divinity in. It was practiced for centuries. Some people see it as valid, even now."

Other photographs decorated the bloodred walls, images of bodies in every shape and shade, perforated a thousand ways. "Is that why people get pierced? I mean, beyond the way it looks or feels?"

"It's why I do it," he said. "But what about you? Have you got any piercings yourself?"

"Just my earlobes." Xochi pulled her hair back. "Done at the mall when I was seven." She blinked back a forgotten image of that day, her seventh birthday. Ones and fives from her mother's tip stash paid for the fourteen-carat gold studs. "Don't want your ears turning green," Gina had said.

"My first piercing was also an ear. My left." He tapped the silver dollar–sized disc distending his earlobe. Xochi blinked. She hadn't noticed it before. "I was nine. My parents were not amused. Afterward, I confined my experiments to less obtrusive places." He turned to the clock on the wall. It was after two.

"I'm sorry to keep you." Xochi eyed the dark street through the shop window. "I didn't realize how late it was." She walked toward the door, ready to face the windy night.

"Oh, not at all," he said. A brass ring now hung from the center of his nose, more satyr than professor. "I can't always accommodate the nocturnal, but I do try, especially around Solstice and Equinox."

"It's worked out great for me! You're a lifesaver. It's been a weird night."

"I imagine it has. It's a long, strange walk back from Hades, young lady."

Xochi suppressed a smile. "I might be wrong, but I'm pretty sure I just came from Hayes Valley?"

"Call it what you like. But I, for one, am extremely grateful. It's not every year Persephone appears on your doorstep the night of her return."

"Her return . . . from the underworld?" Xochi recalled her childhood book of Greek mythology: a dark-haired princess, ruby pomegranate seeds, endless winters in hell.

"Of course," he said. "An offering is in order. I'm James. And I'm at your service, if you'd like."

"You mean a piercing?"

He nodded.

"I don't know where I'd want it." Xochi touched the twin hummingbirds at her neck.

Once, when she was fourteen and deep in a phase of hating her own face, she'd asked for a nose piercing. Loretta had called her bluff. "I've done ears before," Loretta had said, brandishing a long surgical needle, "and stitched up my fair share of lady parts after births. How hard could it be?" Xochi smiled at the memory.

"Just ask yourself," James said, rolling up his sleeves. Bright green snake tattoos curved around each forearm. "I'm sure you'll know. I'll go wash up and give you a moment to think. Come back when you're ready."

Xochi went back to the waiting area, sat, and closed her eyes.

Crazy out, divinity in. Where do I need some of that?

ONCE SHE DECIDED, IT happened quickly. She sat on a high table and stuck out her tongue. James touched a spot near the tip with a Magic Marker and held the meat of her tongue with metal tongs. Xochi's throat burned as her mouth dried out. His hands were graceful as he performed the fluid steps of the ritual, but after a glimpse at the needle, Xochi closed her eyes. Ice shot through her mouth and fire raced up her spine to meet it. The pain was clean and jolted her awake. She tried to stand, but another wave of heat rolled up her body, crashing into the new metal in her mouth.

"Careful," he said, handing her a pamphlet about aftercare. "You may feel a bit euphoric for the next few hours. Many people do."

5

Witches' Song

Xochi trudged up the servants' staircase. The etched metal bar weighed heavily in her mouth, unfamiliar, yet already a part of her. It was too early to know how much the piercing would hurt. In the moment, it had been like flying from a rope swing into an icy river. She'd emerged alive in her skin. Heroic. A punk rock Joan of Arc.

The attic door was unlocked, the sitting room dark. Pallas sat hunched on the window seat, feet tucked under her long white nightgown, a lit cigarette in one hand, a teacup in the other. A real, live smoking twelve-year-old.

Xochi switched on the light. "What are you doing?"

"What does it look like?" Pallas dropped the barely smoked clove cigarette into the gilded cup. It hit the liquid inside with a hiss.

"Are you okay?" Xochi came in slowly and closed the door.

"Great. Perfect. How about you?"

Pallas's voice was a dare and a plea. Xochi thought of her old stray cat the second time that night—his plaintive cries and threatening growls as Gina had dealt with his wounds. She kept her eyes averted, her voice even.

"Me? Fine. Tired, though." So tired. Xochi forbade herself from glancing at the door to her room. Her bed was so soft . . . She yawned, opening her mouth wide.

"Oh. My. God." Pallas stood, fists clenched. "What did you do?"

"Huh?" Then Xochi understood. "This?" She stuck out her tongue.

"Why does everyone insist on maiming themselves!"

"It's not permanent. If I take the stud out, James said it will close right up—"

"*JAMES?*" Pallas stomped her bare foot. Hard.

"I left the party to take a walk. It was the middle of the night, but he was opening up his shop. 'For the nocturnal,' he said. Maybe he meant vampires." Xochi smiled, but Pallas just glared. She wouldn't be able to distract her with a joke, that was clear. And this wasn't about her new piercing. It was three in the morning, late even for night owls. A badly made fire sputtered in the grate. A few books lay open on the coffee table. "Was the party too loud?"

"What do you think?"

"I don't know, Pal. Why don't you tell me? And why are you so mad about my tongue?" Xochi went to the mirror over the mantel and stuck it out. "I think it's cute."

"What are you talking about? It's not even legal," Pallas said. "You're supposed to be eighteen."

"James never asked," Xochi said. "Anyway, I'm close enough." She plopped onto the sofa. "Also, hello—you're supposed to be eighteen to smoke, too." She unlaced her boots, wincing at the blister where they had rubbed at her toes through her fishnets.

Pallas was quiet. A siren howled.

"I'm sorry," Pallas said. "About the cigarette. I didn't enjoy it."

There was a smallness to her voice Xochi had never heard before. Xochi's stomach clenched. "Did something happen? Did you go downstairs?"

"No!" Pallas said, too quickly. "No. I'm just sick of it. I used to think the parties were fun. I didn't get what people were doing. Now I stay up here." She blinked, too stubborn to cry. "I'm not trying to ruin your night. I know I'm lucky."

"It's okay to be mad."

Sloppy laughter drifted through the open window. Car doors slammed, music blared and faded.

"Xochi?" Pallas raised her head, gaze finally meeting Xochi's. "It's hard to stay mad at them."

"I know," Xochi said. "Curse of the charming parents."

"Are yours charming?"

"I only had my mom." Gina did a lap inside Xochi's brain— there and gone, just like real life. "She was charming, all right. Charming as fuck."

"Xochi!"

"I'm just being honest. I know from experience—you can love them and also be pissed."

"I guess . . . I mean, yeah. But the concerts and parties and everything are kind of their job." A single tear escaped. Pallas brushed it away. At that moment, she looked far younger than twelve.

"I should have stayed," Xochi said. She grabbed Pallas's hand and squeezed.

Pallas pulled away. *Not a hugger,* Xochi reminded herself.

"I told you to go to the party," Pallas said. "I wanted you to."

"Maybe I shouldn't have listened."

"Maybe." Pallas blinked hard.

"As your nanny-companion-governess-thing, I promise to do better. Okay?"

Pallas nodded. "Me too."

"And in my esteemed role as whatever-it-is, I decree we need music," Xochi said. "No—step away from the stereo. Now is not the time for show tunes. We need violence!" She dug through the clutter of music next to Pallas's stereo until she found what she wanted. Furious industrial stomped out of the speakers. The bookstore cat shot from under the sofa, ears pinned in disgust. He retreated to Pallas's bedroom, tail in the air.

"*Fates*," Xochi sang, flinging herself to the nail gun beat. "*Fates and FURIES!*"

Pallas closed her eyes. Clenching her fists, she slammed her feet on the wood floor, swinging her head side to side like an elephant Xochi had once seen at the zoo, finished with gentleness and complacency. They spun and pounded, Pallas in her white cotton nightgown, Xochi in her ripped fishnets and borrowed flapper dress, singing at the tops of their voices. When the song ended, Xochi turned the music down, lit all the candles in the room and turned out the lights.

"What are we doing?" Pallas asked.

"Your family thinks they're witches, right? But it's us. *We're* the witches!"

"And they're the *bitches*!"

Pallas cursing was almost as shocking as her smoking. Xochi saw the opening she'd been waiting for since she'd moved into the attic with Pallas. "We have to make a potion!" she said. "Haven't you ever done that? With flower petals and crushed-up leaves and perfume and stuff?"

"*Please*." Pallas rolled her eyes.

"Right, too woo-woo. Who cares? Run the water!"

Pallas stared at the tub. "I already had a bath today."

"I know that, Miss Literal. It's our cauldron, okay?"

"Oh. Okay, I guess . . ." Pallas rolled up the sleeves of her nightgown.

"You need to play, kid," Xochi said. "They've done studies. It's a proven fact."

As Pallas turned the dolphin-shaped knobs to fill the enormous clawfoot tub, Xochi appreciated the attic for the little-girl utopia it was. The sitting room was circular, perched in the tower that topped the huge Victorian. Windows arched around the room, studded with wavy stained glass. Cupids danced on the coved ceiling in a blue sky strewn with fluffy clouds.

Crammed bookshelves lined the north wall and continued

into Pallas's bedroom, a large chamber complete with gilded princess furniture and a truly fabulous canopy bed.

In the center of the sitting room was the largest bathtub Xochi had ever seen, midnight blue with lion's paws for feet, toenails painted gold.

"All you need now is a magic wardrobe," Xochi said. "Or perhaps a Pegasus?"

"They gave you drugs at the party, didn't they?"

Xochi didn't answer the question. "It's called having an imagination. Watch and learn." She broke off a piece of aloe from the plant by the window. "Goblin blood!" She squeezed the goo from the leaf into the steaming bathwater and dropped the slimy mass into the tub. "Guts!"

Xochi found her backpack. Grabbing her brush, she pulled out a clump of dark hair. "What's this?" she asked Pallas, dangling it over the tub.

"Fur of . . . a she-bear killed by hunters?"

"Excellent!"

Pallas snatched her Mighty Mouse Pez dispenser and poured the pellets into the brew. "Teeth of murdered toddler."

"Nice one."

Next came the Hello Kitty bento box on the side table with the remnants of Pallas's dinner. Xochi grabbed the tea basket.

"Demon breath!"

"Mermaid scales!"

"Traitor's heart!"

"Ferret's eye!"

Xochi paused, a crusty voice sliding into her mind like an unwanted tongue. *Crazy bitch. Psych ward cunt.* She unwrapped a pack of Pallas's scented bath cubes, clutching one in each fist. They broke with a visceral crunch. "Bridge troll testicles!"

"So gross!" Pallas grinned. "We've lost it!"

"Never had it!"

"Now what?" Pallas's eyes sparkled.

"I don't know. I think we need to meditate. Let the potion

tell us." Xochi sat in the center of the oriental carpet. Pallas followed, mimicking her cross-legged posture.

Xochi inhaled, the steamy air from the bath reminding her of the forest she left behind in Badger Creek. Loretta was buried there in a grove of old-growth redwoods. In the mornings, the sun through the branches made an intricate pattern, geometric like the weave of Pallas's rug, like the quilts Loretta made from scraps, natural and also mathematical.

Memories crashed in, wave after wave: a refrigerator snapshot of freckled Gina and brown baby Xochi one long-ago summer; Loretta kneading bread in the kitchen, the afternoon light shining through the bones of her hands; Xochi and Evan, fixing a flat tire on his ATV with too much between them the day after Loretta died; Xochi's best friend Collier driving over every morning after the funeral, his Cheerio breath in her face as he tried in vain to get Xochi up for school; the stacks of college catalogs Xochi had finally used for kindling; the shoebox in the back of Loretta's closet with Xochi's name on it, stuffed with small bills; the numb terror on the side of the road the moment before a sweet college girl stuck her head out and said, "I'm headed for San Francisco. Want a ride?"

"Fates," Xochi whispered, the tang of the metal bar in her mouth exotic and pleasurable. "Fates! Fates and Furies! Open, open, open up the door!"

The mist thickened as Xochi pulled Pallas up to dance in the now-silent attic. Their feet pounded a primal rhythm. They were spirit girls, priestesses, fiends. Pallas danced faster, fueled by the coiled fury of twelve, the hope and terror of almost thirteen. A feeling Xochi couldn't name—not anger, not exactly fear—pushed through her body in a hot swell. Her tongue throbbed. She opened her eyes as Pallas whipped past her, socks sliding on the hardwood floor, skidding to a stop in front of the tub.

"I've got it!" Pallas said. "It's perfect! We have to hover

over the bath—I mean the cauldron—okay? It has to be *super* spooky or it won't work."

Xochi grinned. It was already working.

Pallas grabbed Xochi's hand and began to chant. "Double, double, toil and trouble. Fire burn! Cauldron bubble!" Slowly at first, they circled the tub. Pallas repeated the spell with unerring rhythm, joined by Xochi's hissing harmony.

"Fates! Fates and Furies!"

They chanted louder, circling faster and faster around the tub.

"Trouble!"

"Bubble!"

"Fates!"

"Furies!"

"Open up!"

"Open up!"

"Open up the door!"

Xochi and Pallas collapsed onto the soft carpet. The breeze from the open window cooled their faces as they listened to the fading party below, a lullaby of heavy doors and hushed goodbyes. Minutes passed, then half an hour. Blurred voices murmured up from the street as the final party guests hurried to beat the sunrise. When the house was silent and the last motorcycle sped down the hill, Xochi and Pallas drifted into a deep and dreamless sleep.

6

Slippery People

Peasblossom woke under Pallas's easy chair. He yawned and stretched, extending his claws one paw at a time. Why was he awake? He customarily enjoyed a long morning doze in the post-party quiet of Pallas's home. Today, he needed that more than ever. The pair of amateur witches had woken him up several times in the night with their punk-rock chanting.

He raised his hips, working the kinks from his spine. The windows were purpled and the air was warm, scented like the redwood grove in Golden Gate Park, a deep narcotic perfume. *Rest,* it seemed to croon. *Go back to sleep . . .*

Suddenly, his fur was on end.

He blinked.

The room had become dense with fog.

He streaked from under the chair to Pallas. The girl was still sleeping, curled on the rug like a snail in its shell, feet tucked into her white cotton nightgown. The governess snored lightly, her beaded dress sparkling in the unnatural mist. Peasblossom circled the room twice before he understood: something was terribly wrong with Pallas's bathtub.

He inched forward, pelt screaming alarm. In his youth he could have managed a slow, unsupported rise to his hind legs, allowing him to see inside the tub without getting too close. Now, bravery would have to substitute for agility.

He approached and rose quickly, bracing his front paws on the tub's porcelain lip. Thicker than water, the liquid inside hissed and spit as it struggled toward a roiling boil. Peasblossom held his ground as scalding liquid splashed his shoulder and every instinct told him to run. The scents of cedar and sulfur filled the room as the liquid gathered mass and two creatures emerged from the bathtub brew.

Hand in hand, they stood in the tub like a pair of small children waiting to cross the street. *No,* Peasblossom realized as the mist cleared. *Not children. Something else.*

Their eyes were wide and dark, their features fine boned and beautiful. They were unclothed but not visibly gendered, their bodies leanly muscled and compact. Water droplets clung to their sleek hides like moonstones in the predawn light.

The taller of the pair had deep brown skin and ink-black hair. Its companion was green skinned and more delicately made, with hair like the inside of an abalone shell, iridescent rainbow pale.

Peasblossom now found himself under the sofa, his mind and body at war. Every hair on his coat longed for the fire escape, the open air. He gritted his teeth and crept out a few inches until he could see Pallas. She still slept, none the wiser. The cat's pulse soared as the pair exited the tub in an effortless leap, hands clasped, landing softly.

They lifted their faces to the open window to meet a sudden breeze, eyes shining as their hair snaked along the hardwood floor. Unfurled, the strands were longer than the creatures were tall, floating to dance around them like seaweed in a slow current. As if sentient, the pale tresses reached for the dark, sliding together and moving apart in a series of shapes that struck Peasblossom as a form of greeting or celebration—now flower, now feather, now honeycomb, now moon.

Peasblossom tensed, ready to spring as they moved toward Pallas, but found he could not move. The smaller of the pair hovered near the sleeping girl, hands spread above her forehead. In the moonlight, Peasblossom could see the fine webbing between its fingers. The creature closed its eyes. Suddenly, Pallas was rising! She floated up from the floor like a helium balloon, her skin lit with the same lunar intensity as the creatures', her hair alive like theirs, a golden cape around her shoulders. After an interminable moment, Pallas exhaled, coming to rest on the floor as if rising and descending were the most natural processes in the world.

Peasblossom's pelt twitched with the painful need to go to his young friend, but he remained pinned where he was, unable. His frustrated meow came out a strangled croak. The larger of the pair acknowledged him with a neutral glance and returned its attention to Xochi, resting brown fingertips lightly on the young woman's forehead.

Minutes passed.

The creatures were utterly still.

Birdsong and garbage trucks announced the coming morning. Pallas and Xochi slept on, unaware of the newly formed beings beside them.

When the creatures finally sprang back to life, their speed was uncanny, taking them from the center of the attic to the window seat in the space of a single breath. They paused on the sill, silhouetted against the paling sky, their lashless eyes reflecting the streetlight's final glow.

Suddenly able to move again, Peasblossom reached the window in time to see them balanced on the highest branch of the hawthorn in the side yard. He slipped out the open window to the fire escape as the creatures joined hands and stepped into the air, hair billowing above them like parachutes as they floated to the ground.

It was a shock to see them outside the attic—a confirmation that, against all logic, Xochi and Pallas's nonsensical ritual had summoned these very real otherworldly beings. Peasblossom climbed down the dew-slicked fire escape with the speed of a much younger cat and leaped onto the damp grass as the duo rounded the corner toward the street. Panting, the cat reached the front yard. Hand in hand, the creatures approached the curb, their hair still streaming behind them as if they were moving through water, not air. A bank of fog lumbered up the hill to meet them and rolled to a stop. The pair embarked, melting into the soft gloom of the San Francisco morning.

7

Predictions

Xochi woke on the sitting room floor. She vaguely remembered Pallas shaking her sometime in the early morning, telling her to go to bed. She should have listened. She rubbed the kink in her neck and yawned, metal grazing the roof of her mouth.

According to James, her tongue was supposed to be too swollen to eat or talk, but it felt almost normal. She tried to remember her last physical injury. Had she healed especially quickly when she'd cut herself on her pocket knife last year? She'd broken her arm when she was thirteen, but that had taken forever to heal. In her small bathroom, she examined the piercing. A little redness, but that was all. She yawned again, then groaned, remembering the mess in the bathtub, but when she returned to the sitting room, the tub was spotless. Pallas must have cleaned it, the little neat freak.

Pallas's bedroom door was open an inch. All that was visible under the creamy pile of comforters was a bare foot. The mattress was so thick, Pallas needed a step stool to get into bed. *The Princess and the Pea*, Xochi thought. Grinning, she remembered the bookstore cat. Was he asleep somewhere in the pile?

A shower worked out the knots in Xochi's back. She pulled on jeans, a T-shirt, and red high-tops and drew a sooty outline around her tired eyes. A comb was her one concession to last night's makeover. She had to admit it—Kiki and Pallas had been right about her hair. Taking a final look in the mirror, she put on some cherry lip gloss, messed up her bangs and clasped Loretta's necklace closed at the back of her neck.

Her stomach growled, and the ache in her temple told her it was hours after her usual morning coffee. Checking her jeans for money, Xochi headed down from the attic. On the second landing, she stopped. The narrow stairway widened, and it was a short flight down to the main floor if you kept going straight. If you veered left, there was an unexpected passage leading to a door. "Kylen's Lair," Pallas had explained during Xochi's grand tour of Eris Gardens. "I almost had his room myself. We flipped for it, and Ky won. I'm glad now, but back then I was all about the secret passages. His room used to be the butler's. I guess butlers needed to sneak around a lot."

"Does Kylen?" Xochi had asked.

"Ky likes a mystery. And he eats secrets for breakfast."

"What do you mean?" Of all the people at Eris Gardens, Kylen seemed the least thrilled about Xochi's presence and the hardest to figure out.

"He just kind of . . . knows stuff," Pallas said. "I used to lie to him to test it out, but all he has to do is touch you, and *bam*! Game over. He *knows*."

THERE WAS A SOUND coming from Kylen's room now like the purr of an enormous cat. Xochi walked closer until she stood pressed against the heavy door. It vibrated under her ear, the old wood breathing like part of a living tree. She closed her eyes, every sense engrossed in sound. It took her a second to realize the door was giving way. She stumbled inside.

Kylen sat naked in the center of the cluttered room, a cello between his legs, his skin washed in watercolor reds and blues by the light filtering in through a pair of intricate stained glass windows. His long, dark hair was loose around his angular face. His eyes were rolled back, unseeing, as he slid the bow over the strings.

Backing away as silently as she could, Xochi was nearly through the door when she bumped into a table sending a stack of tarot cards flying. They fell like cherry petals in a windstorm, settling around Xochi's feet, all facedown except one.

Queen of Cups, she read, gazing at the image of a woman obscured by rippling water. Xochi blinked as a second card made a belated fall. "The Tower." Xochi said it aloud before she could stop herself. It was ominous looking, with a dove fleeing a burning ruin. *What does it mean?*

"You'll know soon enough."

Xochi jumped at the sound of Kylen's voice. His dark eyes were all pupil.

"I'm so sorry," Xochi said. "It was the music—I was listening and the door just opened." Kylen's blank expression stopped her. "I'll go."

He pulled his bow away from the strings, bending gracefully to dislodge a card wedged under the end pin of the cello, his muscles as defined as a dancer's. He seemed to not care at all about being naked. He held the card out. A man and woman stood before a priest, a white and a black cherub on either side of them. The card was labeled *The Lovers*.

Xochi took it. "I have a feeling this isn't about falling in love."

"If you have to ask, you'll never know."

Xochi opened her mouth to thank him, apologize, something—but his eyes were closed, the bow poised again against the strings. Xochi backed out of the room, shutting the door behind her.

She wanted to sit on the landing till her legs stopped shaking, but the idea of Kylen leaving his room and finding her there kept her moving.

In the front hall, she collided with Bubbles. Her curls were secured atop her head with chopsticks. A ruby sparkled in her belly button, peeking over her pajama bottoms. Aaron was behind her in an unbuttoned plaid flannel with polka dot boxers and wool hiking socks, the Tibetan death mask tattooed over his heart glaring under his friendly face.

"There you are!" Bubbles hugged her, giving her shoulders an extra squeeze. "Where'd you go last night?"

"It's a long story."

"I know what you mean." Aaron rubbed his temples. His knuckles were scratched and swollen from drumming.

"Rough night?" Xochi asked.

"Wait a second." Aaron squinted. "You didn't have that before. Let's see it."

Xochi stuck out her tongue.

"You got it last night?" Bubbles leaned in closer. "But it's already healed."

"I know," Xochi said. "Weird, right?"

"Damn!" Aaron said. "Who did it?"

"James."

"James at Pagan? I tried to make an appointment to get my ears redone and they put me on a waitlist for June! Can I see one more time?" His eyes widened as he studied Xochi's tongue. "Nice jewelry, dude. Most tongue bars are plain, but there's engraving on yours, some kind of Celtic knot." He elbowed Bubbles. "The babysitter's got connections."

"Pallas is too old to have a babysitter," Bubbles said. "Didn't we decide on 'governess'?"

"I don't know," Xochi said. "I'm not sure I'm the governess type."

Pad emerged from the guest bathroom wearing a towel and a smile. Besides the mermaid on his forearm, he had a half sleeve on his muscled upper arm, a watery Japanese collage of waves and seaweed and tentacles. His nipples were pierced with small silver hoops.

"Why are you down here?" Bubbles asked. "Too many models in your bathroom upstairs?"

"Water pressure," he said, his accent milder than it had

been last night, more a lilt now than a brogue. "Why are you two accosting the governess?"

"She wants to be called something else," Bubbles said. "She says she's not the governess type."

"But she is," Pad said. "Like Mary Poppins, only hotter." He grinned.

Beware the siren song, Xochi thought.

Bubbles frowned. "Mary Poppins was so strict. Xochi's more of a Fraülein Maria, don't you think?"

Aaron nodded. "Totally, dude."

"I used to play the guitar," Xochi said. "But I'm not a nun. Also, I can't sew."

"Not a nun?" Pad draped his arm around Xochi. It was warm and slightly damp. He smelled like Ivory soap and breakfast. "Good to know."

"Stop!" Xochi laughed, pushing Pad away. "I'm going out for a bagel. Do you guys want anything?"

"What are you talking about?" Bubbles took her hand. "It's blueberry pancake day, sweetie. You follow me."

"I already ate about fifteen of them," Pad called, heading back upstairs. "Better hurry before they're gone."

"I'm still not over your tongue," Aaron said, shaking his head.

"I got too high and took a walk, and then I had to pee. Pagan was the only thing open. James let me use the bathroom. He kept calling me Persephone, saying it was a long walk back from Hades. He said the piercing was an offering to the goddess."

"Unbelievable," Aaron said.

"I believe it," Bubbles said. "I think the governess is just getting started."

8

Los Banditos

S unshine steamed the dew off the shrubbery in a neighborhood of well-kept bungalows. Peasblossom's stomach grumbled. He'd skipped breakfast to follow this hunch, and now it was easily past lunchtime with nothing but water. He sighed and found a likely shrub. As he finished his business, laughter and bird droppings pelted him from the trees.

Cherry-headed conures! A pandemonium of parrots—rogue pets and their descendants—shook the blades of the date palm overhead.

Tail in the air, Peasblossom turned and walked stiffly away. He wanted information from the garish, gossiping little clowns, but he was no spring kitten. They'd toy with him all day if he betrayed any sign of weakness.

He left the cul-de-sac and walked down Chestnut as it curved to face the bay. Before he turned the corner, the flock followed, settling into an overgrown fig. Whoever said cats were the curious ones had never met a parrot.

"Here, kitty kitty kitty," they called. He'd heard somewhere that conures weren't great talkers, but that was only what the clever little monsters wanted people to believe.

"Kitty kitty kitty kitty!" The flock tossed the taunt back and forth like kids playing keep-away. Peasblossom crossed the street.

"Hey, Cat, what gives?" The intonation was brusque and

mannered, classic old-time gangster. The parrot who landed on the sidewalk before him had clearly been raised with the television on.

"Just out for a stroll," Peasblossom said. A car door slammed. The bird startled. Peasblossom walked away.

A green youngster with yellow markings, smaller than the others, possibly an escaped parakeet, grazed Peasblossom's head and landed on a bush behind him. She wolf whistled, high and clear. Not a talker, perhaps. A breeze from the sea held a hint of cedar and sulfur, a teasing reminder of the bathtub creatures.

The parakeet flew to a tree behind the cat. Peasblossom followed and the bird flew on, retracing the path he'd taken an hour before, down Grant Street. The bird stopped again at a staircase, one of the many jungled paths leading through the maze of residential North Beach. Again, a wolf whistle. The rest of the flock invaded the canopy. Peasblossom dodged their droppings.

At the top of the stairs, he found the scent he'd been searching for all night—mossy and fungal and overly ripe, with a strong marijuana overlay. Emerging from the foliage, the view opened on a paper-white sky and inky water. The wind was shrill with gulls. On a bench with a cigar-sized spliff in her hand sat the object of Peasblossom's search.

At first glance, she appeared to be a drugged-out refugee of the sixties in dirty tie-dyes and a series of unraveling shawls, but in her natural state, the Mushroom Hag was much smaller, older and odder than she appeared to be aboveground. Unlike the majority of strange folk haunting the forgotten corners of San Francisco, the Hag was no European transplant.

"How's it hangin', Cat," she said. "Long time, no see."

"You're looking well," he said. In truth, she was more ragged than the cat remembered, with layers of dirt-spattered finery and twigs and debris in her long, tangled hair.

"Don't sweet-talk me, amigo," the Hag said, glancing

sidelong at the cat. "I'm looking pretty rough, baby. I got *down* last night. If I'm lying, I'm crying. But hey, man! Happy Equinox. Winter is over, baby. Here comes the sun!"

"Happy Equinox to you." Peasblossom bowed. They sat in silence. Alcatraz emerged from the fog. The Golden Gate Bridge was poppy-bright against the gray of the sea and sky. The Hag took a long drag of sweet herbal smoke. She offered the spliff to Peasblossom, but the cat shook his head.

"I need to ask you something," he began.

"Not here," the Hag hissed. "The feds, man. They got the whole joint bugged. Let's make like bananas, baby." She stood, swaying. She set the half-smoked marijuana cigarette on the bench. "Some high-heeled rich girl on the wharf floated me that kind bud last night, put it right in my hand wrapped in a five-dollar bill. The next freak that sits here— happy birthday, merry Christmas!" The Hag cackled. "It's karma, baby, you dig?"

"Of course," Peasblossom said.

The Hag teetered down the steps. Peasblossom followed her up Kearny Street to the abandoned reservoir that had been a neighborhood eyesore since the forties. Her coordination improved as she ducked under a gap in the chain-link fence and slipped into an opening in a blackberry thicket.

The tunnel was old and hard packed, swept clean of debris. She was closer to Peasblossom's size now. Her skin had tightened around her face, making her ears and eyes seem alarmingly large. "The pink pill makes you larger," she sang. "The kind bud makes you small . . ."

After several forks and turns, the Hag stopped at a doorway hung with a beaded curtain. "Mi casa is su casa, baby," the Hag said, throwing off a layer of shawls and rolling up her sleeves. Peasblossom hunched on a braided rag rug as she plucked foul-smelling herbs from various scavenged containers and dropped them into a dented pot, adding water from a corked glass bottle that looked less than clean. After making a neat fire in her round-bellied stove and putting the pot on the burner to boil, she sat in her twig rocker and listened to Peasblossom's story.

In the firelight, her sharp features softened, and Peasblossom was surprised at her almost regal bearing. Her moment of calm ended before he could finish his tale.

"They're coppers!" she hissed. "Pigs, man! The fuzz! If they're here—like for real, baby, not like you got dosed in the park—that means trouble, Cat. Bummer days, man. Bum-*mer* days." The Hag began to giggle, then cackle, dissolving into raucous laughter as she twisted the hem of her filthy skirt. After drinking a cup of acrid-smelling tea and warming herself by the stove, her black eyes went from hazy to sharp once more.

"How did they act with the chicas? You told me already, didn't you, Puss? Humor an old lady and tell me again." She dropped into her rocker and began to move back and forth at a furious pace, causing her chair to inch toward the fire. Peasblossom flicked his tail out of range and discreetly rescued the trailing end of one of her shawls.

He recounted the creatures' actions toward Xochi and Pallas. The Hag's wild brows rose on her mossy forehead. "They were scanning 'em, man! Running their priors. They know who's naughty and nice, like Santa Claus. They can tell." The Hag was silent for a moment, working her long gray hair into knots with sharp-clawed hands. "But why, man, why? Why'd they come? Those freaks never show up anymore, but they used to, baby, once in a blue moon. Weren't even calling it California back then." She snorted and sat back in her chair. "What do you think those babies want? What's their angle, Cat?"

"Babies?" Peasblossom purred—to calm himself or the Hag, he wasn't sure which.

"You know, man. Tlaloques, Chaneques. Waterbabies." Seeing Peasblossom's confusion, the Hag snorted. "You been hanging out with the squares too long. They're fey, right, but came outta the water? Hella old school. I'm surprised you even saw them. They're slippery, baby. Here one second, gone the next. But the freaks you saw sound a lot like the ones I remember—big-eyed kids with hair down to the ground."

"That makes them sound so . . . harmless."

"Harmless, my ass!" she said. "They're the bill collectors, baby." The Hag rose and began to tidy her madly organized burrow, moving things inexplicably from one location to another. "One girl floats, one girl sinks," she singsonged. "One smells like a rose, the other one stinks!"

Peasblossom had been careful to keep the urgency from his voice, but now it broke through. "Is it significant that Pallas was levitating?" His mind raced to witch hunts and inquisitions—situations in which floating was not ideal.

"Levi-what? Speak English, baby. We all had to learn it. But you mean the floating, don't you, amigo?"

Peasblossom nodded. Just discussing those uncanny children raised the fur on his spine.

"Wish I could tell you, Cat. Who knows why the oldsters do like they do? But I'll tell you what: somebody did somebody wrong. Somebody's jive, and someone's gotta pay. Banditos, baby. It's an old story, Cat. Old as it gets." She stopped suddenly and returned to her rocker, exhaling noisily. "Don't get me wrong, baby. Lo siento about the rock stars' kid and the foxy señorita. I see 'em around sometimes. They feed the birds, pet the dogs, look at the sky. Good energy. Me gusto, you dig?"

"My greatest concern is for the girl, Pallas," Peasblossom said. "She's under my protection. It did seem to me that the creatures were most interested in the young woman, Xochi."

The Hag rocked faster. "She's a little long in the tooth. Those coppers usually work for kids, man. But the señorita's not a kid, is she? Not a grown woman, either. In between, baby. No-man's-land. But they stayed with her longer than they did with the kid, isn't that what you said?"

"Yes, several minutes." Peasblossom's head ached. The room was stuffy, the Hag's odor intense.

She turned away from the fire and met Peasblossom's eyes, something she'd never done in all the years he'd known her. "You be careful, amigo," she said. "Those narcs are old school. Not like the candy-ass airy fairies we got around here now."

"So you think someone might have hurt one of the girls?" Peasblossom said. "And these . . . Waterbabies . . . are here to take revenge?"

"Cat! Listen, baby. They're the fuzz, not the mob!"

"So they're operating by some sort of moral code?"

"That's how they used to do. They were righteous, you dig? Like the Alcatraz Indians, baby! Like Martin and Malcolm. Like Cesar Chavez. Power to the people, Cat! Right on." The Hag raised her small brown fist in the air, suddenly young, her eyes fierce and bright.

Peasblossom purred in solidarity. After a moment he asked, "So the creatures are dangerous? You're sure about that?"

"Does a hippie spare change in the park?" The Hag spat into the fire. "Those creepy little cop kids lay down the law, baby. Anybody in their way better pull over fast. You better hope it was just some good acid you had, baby. Kickass acid and too much smoke."

9

Our Heaven

Xochi hadn't seen Leviticus in the kitchen since the first time Pallas brought her home to Eris Gardens. Leaving the aquarium, she and Pallas had stepped into the cold, clear light of Golden Gate Park, talking nonstop. It had been windy and bitterly cold that day, so they'd stopped at The Unbearable Lightness of Reading to warm up.

Loretta's stash of money had gotten Xochi from Badger Creek to San Francisco, but it was dwindling fast. Xochi worried about browsing when she couldn't buy, but Pallas seemed to think it was fine. She introduced Xochi to Peasblossom, inquired after the owner, and used the bathroom like she was the one who owned the place. "I come here a lot," she said.

Back outside, Pallas announced, "It's family dinner night. You have to come!"

Xochi felt weird accepting the invitation, but she'd been living on peanut butter sandwiches for almost three weeks. Her anxiety raced as they climbed the small mountain Pallas claimed was her street and the houses changed from apartment buildings to ornate, colorful houses, like the toys of some lucky child giant.

Pallas stopped at a brick stairway bordered by a tangled hillside garden. Above it loomed the gabled roofline of an enormous picture-book Victorian.

"You *live* here?"

Pallas had only laughed.

The steep stairs went on forever. After a switchback, the second flight was shorter, landing Xochi smack in the middle of Wonderland. A wrought iron gate covered in winter-dormant vines demanded a pause, providing theatrical timing for the big reveal: a tall, *Swan Lake* ballerina of a house, complete with ornate floral moldings and elaborate lacy trim, white on white like the prettiest embroidered lingerie, its tower crowned with an onion-shaped dome straight out of the *Arabian Nights*.

Through the gate, another set of steps led to the front porch, flanked by two stone lions with marigold wreaths around their necks. Above the door was a painted crest: a flaming, sword-pierced heart, the words ERIS GARDENS printed in gothic script across its blood-bright surface.

Pallas opened the massive wooden door without a key. After nearly a month of walking the city, longing to see inside one of its fabled Victorians, Xochi couldn't quite make the journey across the threshold. Pallas had rolled her eyes and grabbed Xochi's hand. "I smell dinner," she said. "My dad's an excellent cook."

The light-flooded foyer opened into a ballroom. A filigreed grand staircase arched to the second floor. Xochi imagined turn-of-the-century ladies making velvet-gowned entrances, their jewels outsparkling the chandeliers.

Pallas stomped past all of it, unaware of the bits of dirt her turquoise cowgirl boots left on the gleaming wooden floors. She led Xochi past a formal living room and dining room. "We only use them for parties," she explained.

The cluttered kitchen was deliciously warm and smelled of candles, incense and curry. When Xochi closed her eyes, it could have been the cramped Badger Creek kitchen, with random neighbors dropping by and Loretta sending Xochi to the garden for extra veggies to stretch the stew.

Pallas introduced her to everyone that night, their names a blur as they bustled around, setting the table, filling water glasses, opening bottles of wine. If they were surprised Pallas had brought home a stray girl she'd found at the Academy of Science, they barely let on. Only Kylen seemed suspicious, his eyes narrowed and his too-firm handshake held slightly too long. The rest of them acted like she was a family dinner regular, filling her wine glass without asking, making sure she had enough to eat. They invited her back the next week for Indian takeout and board games and out for pizza the week after that. Then one day, there was a message at the front desk of her Tenderloin hotel: *We have a proposition for you. Please call ASAP.*

"Don't bring your tricks in here," the clerk said, smirking. "I don't want trouble with no underage hoes."

An hour later, Xochi had packed her things and said goodbye to the cockroaches and her moldy window with its heating duct view. She'd spent five of her last eighty-six dollars on a taxi to Eris Gardens and never looked back.

THAT FIRST EVENING, LEVITICUS stood barefoot at the stove, yellow curry bubbling in a big enamel pot, humming along to Billie Holiday. Today, it was blueberry pancakes and old-timey gospel with a sin-voiced singer and tricky rhythm guitar. He sang along, tapping the rhythm with a spatula on the side of the cast-iron griddle.

His voice was deeper than the one on the record, but just as raspy—probably from last night's concert. Then, his songs had been spells, enveloping the crowd like the thickest liquid, the softest smoke. Xochi had been as starstruck as anyone. But now, he was a regular person again—still gorgeous, of course, but contained, private and untouchable.

"Good morning," he said.

"Good morning." Xochi sat at the massive yellow kitchen table.

"You're my hero," Bubbles told Leviticus, coming up behind him to press her head against his back. She handed a glass of water and a bottle of painkillers to Aaron, settling between him and Xochi and angling her chair so she could rest her bare feet in Aaron's lap.

"Who's first?" Leviticus asked.

"Better do Aaron and his monster hangover," Bubbles said. "Oh, but Xochi, are you okay to wait?"

"I'm fine," Xochi said. And she was. Relaxed, surprisingly well-rested. It felt like a good day, almost normal.

"Anyone else want bacon?" Leviticus opened the refrigerator.

"Um, yes," Bubbles said. "Duh."

"None for me," Xochi said. "I'm vegetarian."

"Me too." Leviticus turned to her and smiled.

Xochi got the feeling he'd just seen her for the first time. He'd always been nice, but distant. But then, so had she, with all of them. This morning was different. Warmer. Leviticus set her coffee down, a perfect frothy café au lait. "I should have asked—is milk okay?"

"It's perfect. Thanks!" Xochi blew on her coffee and took a small sip, testing her fresh piercing. It tingled, that was all. She sat back in her chair.

Kiki stood at the counter in a paisley bathrobe, her curls knotted at the nape of her neck. Her skin was a flawless beach-sand brown, a shade darker than her eyes. She looked like she'd been to an all-night spa instead of an all-night party. She hummed a harmony with Leviticus, her highs to his lows, as she pulled the lever of a large silver contraption, filling a pitcher with tangerine juice. Io stood at the center island, preparing a tray for a solitary breakfast, her normal routine. With her hair in two messy braids and cat-eye glasses, she was even prettier than she'd been onstage. She smiled at Xochi. "Did you have fun last night?"

"It was great," Xochi said, suddenly shy.

"How about you?" Kiki asked Io, something pointed in her tone.

Io didn't seem to notice. "Same as always: peopled out. Not

really the party girl. I read for a bit and went to sleep, but I had a weird dream. I think I'd rather have a hangover."

"Tell," Kiki commanded.

Io frowned, butter knife poised over a pancake. "First, Pal and I were in a city—London, I think—but then it became a forest. I was wearing this wild floral nightgown, sort of like the one I used to have, the one from my mum?"

Kiki snorted. "I can't believe you lost it. It was early Pucci, for fuck's sake! I've never seen another one like it."

"Can we please let go of the Pucci?" Io said, "It's gone, love. Ancient history."

"Fine," Kiki said. "Go on. What happened?"

"Well, for a long time, we just held hands and walked. The woods were completely quiet, kind of spooky. Then we came to a stream, and Pallas basically melted away and turned into a big fish—a salmon, I think? I reached down to touch her, but she jumped out of the water and transformed again into an owl. I kept jumping, trying to catch her. I finally jumped high enough and could almost touch her, but then I fell. Cue my classic nightmare ending—fell forever, hit the bed, woke up sweating. The birds were chirping and the bus started running. I never got back to sleep, just laid there, feeling terrible. I need a nap." She yawned, her tight-shut eyes and pink tongue reminding Xochi of a kitten's.

Bubbles dipped her finger in the syrup on the edge of Aaron's plate. "What do you think it means?"

"I don't know. Most of my anxious dreams are about losing people I love." Io sighed, tucking a stray hair behind her multiply pierced ear.

Without deciding to speak, Xochi heard herself say, "My grandma used to tell me that a lot of cultures see the salmon as sacred. When you eat them, you're absorbing part of the collective soul."

"But what about the owl?" Bubbles asked. Everyone in the kitchen was listening, curious.

"I thought they just represented wisdom," Leviticus said. Xochi remembered the owl tattoo on his bare arm at the concert, wings lifted, ready for flight.

"Owls are interesting," Xochi said. Her piercing hummed in her mouth. "They can mean wisdom, but some stories say they're bad luck. Others say they aren't necessarily bad, but if you see them, you better pay attention. An owl sighting in the daytime can signal deception, usually deceiving yourself. They're also known to carry the souls of the dead. I used to see them a lot, which my grandma said meant I was wise beyond my years and prone to being haunted."

"Your grandma sounds cool," Bubbles said. "How does she know that stuff?"

"Animal stories were her thing. Herbs and animals and babies."

"I was thinking," Io broke in. "If everything in your dream is you—"

"—or the parts of you Pallas represents," Kiki interrupted.

"Right," Io said. "The collective soul, family, motherhood, the band—the salmon. The owl is the solitary part. Pal and I are alike that way. But you're right. It's easy to get too isolated. I've usually got at least half my head up in the clouds."

"That's *one* way of describing it," Kiki said.

"Shut up!" Io laughed, bumping Kiki with her hip as she reached for the container of blueberries. Pallas said they'd been best friends since they were little girls—practically sisters. Xochi wondered about the rest, how they'd come to live here and love each other. Their connections enveloped the room with a deep, complex comfort.

"What about the silence in the forest?" Bubbles asked around a mouthful of food. Her plate had arrived, a now-dented stack of pancakes dusted with powdered sugar. "That seems important."

"Dude, look where she lives," Aaron said. "Of course she dreams about silence!"

"And that ending," Kiki said. "The way you fall and can't react. I've often thought it was about not speaking your mind."

"Or speaking your mind and not being heard," Leviticus added, meeting Io's eyes for a short moment before turning back to the stove.

"Maybe it's just hard being a mom," Aaron said. "One time, we found my mom down in the laundry room chanting, 'God hates me' while she sorted a massive pile of tube socks. We felt so bad we made her lunch, but then we burned the grilled cheese and the kitchen stank for a week."

Everyone laughed but Io, who loaded a second plate, smearing jam on the pancakes, and quietly left the room. Xochi knew who liked jam instead of syrup. Io was going to have breakfast with Pallas.

"Just to get you started." Leviticus handed Xochi a plate of perfectly stacked pancakes. They were golden and fluffy, with blueberries so dark they were purple. "Let me know when you're ready for seconds."

"I think this'll be more than enough." Xochi breathed in the sweet steam. "Thank you so much for making these."

"It's tradition," Kiki said. "Kitchen service the day after a show. Helps him shed any leftover god complex from the whole rock star business." She sat on a stool at the counter, flipping through an oversized fashion magazine, stopping to cut things out with a pair of nail scissors and arranging the scraps on the counter beside her.

Bubbles and Aaron were on seconds of pancakes, sharing the Sunday comics. Xochi was still working on firsts. Leviticus piled a towering stack for himself and sat down across from Xochi, drowning his plate in maple syrup. "I have a sweet tooth," he said when he noticed her looking. "I'm always starving the day after a show."

"You guys fast beforehand, right?"

"Io and Ky and I do. I don't know about the rest of these slackers."

"I do," Bubbles said. "Aaron is another story. Four double cheeseburgers, a six-pack of crappy beer and he's ready to rock."

"Dude. You want a grounded rhythm section. When I drum, I need my chakras connected to the earth, not the freaking ether. That means meat."

"Well, whatever you did, it worked," Xochi said.

"You liked it?" Bubbles pounced.

"I know those guys sucked," Aaron said, "but the drumming was awesome, right?"

"Give it to us straight," Leviticus said. "What'd you think?" His expression was open and curious, like he actually cared about her opinion.

"It was amazing. I danced my ass off," Xochi said. "I'm such a huge fan now, I can barely eat breakfast here without asking you guys for autographs." She laughed. It was the opposite, really. It was suddenly easy to be with them, like she'd known them forever. She took a big bite of pancake.

"Seems like you're managing," Kiki said. "And at the risk of spoiling them completely, I have to agree. It was a great show."

"What was your favorite part?" Bubbles asked Xochi. "Besides the costumes," she said, blowing Kiki a kiss.

"The end," Xochi said. "It was all great, but the end was magical." She closed her eyes, reliving Leviticus and Io's final ode to spring the night before.

She turned to Leviticus. "When I saw you and Io up there, it made perfect sense that Pallas is so special."

Leviticus blinked, his coffee cup paused mid-rise. "Thanks," he said. "I was kind of worried you thought we were shitty parents."

"What? Of course not!"

"But?" He held her eyes like it was a test.

"But . . . twelve can be brutal. Don't get me wrong. Pallas is amazing. She's like a cross between a Jane Austen heroine and a pirate."

"Kind of makes you proud to be a father," Leviticus said.

"I want some credit for the pirate part!" Aaron grinned.

"The Jane Austen is all me and Io." Kiki nodded. "Good thing we have you boys and Bubbles to even things out."

"See?" Xochi said. "You're good parents, a good family. But she's growing up fast. Maybe she needs something different right now."

The kitchen was silent. Sunlight streamed out from behind a cloud, turning the room gold.

Leviticus exhaled. "I guess we've got some work to do for our girl."

"I remember when she was born. So tiny." Kiki sighed, tucking a curl behind her ear. She got up and started collecting the glasses and plates strewn around the kitchen.

"I remember being twelve," Bubbles said. "It sucked so bad."

"I always knew we'd be in trouble when she started calling us on our shit." Aaron rolled up his sleeves and headed for the sink. "Twelve or not, that kid is smarter than the rest of us put together."

"Tell me about it," Xochi said. "I can't even get around without her. Every time I go out on my own, I'm totally lost."

Leviticus leaned back in his chair. "What are you doing today, Xochi?"

"I'm not sure. Seems like Pallas is hanging out with Io? I'll probably just wander around the city and get lost again."

"Want a tour?"

Aaron groaned. Bubbles pantomimed a yawn behind Leviticus's back. Kiki mouthed *boring*.

"Don't listen to them, kid," Leviticus said. "My city tours are famous."

"You could come shopping with me," Bubbles said. "After I take a nap . . ."

"It's too late now," Kiki said. "Look at him."

Leviticus was paging through the newspaper. He stopped

at the weather report. "It's supposed to be perfect. Sunny now, cloudy later. Great weather for a ride."

"You don't have to humor him," Bubbles said, "but if you say no, he'll pout."

"I don't know what could possibly be boring about a tour of San Francisco," Xochi said in her best governess tone. Suddenly, she realized what she was agreeing to. But Kiki was right. It was too late.

"I'll meet you out back," Leviticus said. "Make sure to dress warm and wear your leather jacket."

10

I Left My Heart in San Francisco

The afternoon was cold and clear. Colors pushed for attention in the fogless air, wide awake and ready for spring. Xochi's body remembered what to do after the first few awkward moments on Leviticus's motorcycle. Her hands found a reasonable place to rest around his waist as he cruised through Golden Gate Park, heading west toward the ocean. A remote wooded area Xochi had never seen opened into a field. Leviticus parked and hurried toward a chain-link fence; Xochi pulled off her helmet and followed.

Behind the fence was an improbable sight: a herd of giant horned animals calmly grazing.

Xochi yelped. "Are they buffalo?"

"Bison."

"They're beautiful!" Their rusty coats reminded her of the shaggy bark on old-growth redwoods back home. She gazed at one of the massive regal creatures. It returned her scrutiny, lumbering closer until it was a few feet from the fence. "I can't believe they're just . . . here. Who takes care of them?"

"Technically, they belong to the zoo. Look." Leviticus motioned toward Xochi's imposing friend. "See how broad her shoulders are? You can tell she's female. They're burlier than the males."

"Hi, beauty," Xochi called. The lady bison came closer. One

of her horns was longer than the other and slightly chipped on one side.

"I love these guys." Leviticus's face was boyish with excitement. "I have to say, your reaction is much more satisfying than Pal's was."

"Was she upset because they were fenced in?"

"She was upset about the European conquest of the Americas. It was my fault—I was reading her *The People's History of the United States*."

"Do you think it's possible to be *too* smart?"

"I've been living with too smart for almost thirteen years."

They watched the bison again in silence. The curious herd member nosed the fence, then snorted and trotted back to her family. Xochi and Leviticus got back onto the motorcycle.

The wide, curving roads of the park led back to city streets and into the wooded lanes of the Presidio. Breathing in the green, Xochi started to relax. The forest was one of the only things she missed about Badger Creek. That and motorcycles. She used to bully Collier, her best friend and then sort-of boyfriend, into letting her ride his beat-up Honda. Collier always said Xochi liked his motorcycle at least thirty percent more than she liked him. She denied it, but Collier had always been good at math. Racing away from their crappy town after school, it was easy to pretend she'd never have to go home. Now she was glad she knew how to be a good passenger, moving with Leviticus into the turns, holding on firmly, but not too tight.

Leviticus rode well. Xochi laughed every time they picked up speed until he finally revved the engine and really took off. They scaled the steep hills along the cable car route, zooming down at an almost vertical angle and cresting another hill to see the bay spread out before them. As they maneuvered down the famous roller-coaster twists of Lombard, slowly this time, Xochi had a chance to look around. The parts of the city she'd explored on her own tended toward seediness with the faded beauty of an old lady dressed up to ride the bus, but the houses in this neighborhood had always been prosperous.

"I wouldn't be the same person if I'd grown up in a house like that," Xochi said, gazing at a Spanish stucco mansion flanked by towering manicured palms.

Leviticus twisted to look at her. The light changed and they rode away, backtracking down Van Ness and stopping in front of a crowded restaurant on Mission Street.

"This is where I grew up," he said. "Right around the corner."

"Are we eating?"

"We are. There's no way you're missing this."

Floral plastic cloths covered the tables of the cafeteria-style restaurant, and Day-Glo paintings of the Virgin Mary and Elvis crowded the walls. An oldies station blared from the kitchen, a backbeat for the big spoons clanging against metal tubs of rice and beans.

A team of brown-ponytailed soccer girls in red uniforms scarfed silver-wrapped burritos, switching seamlessly from Spanish to English to tease each other between bites. A large family ate together at a long table, everyone smiling at the toddler dancing in his grandmother's lap. Xochi's stomach rumbled as they stood in line. Leviticus ordered in Spanish.

"How do you know Spanish?" Xochi asked.

"My dad. He's Mexican."

"Mine too. I never knew him, though."

Before Badger Creek, Xochi and Gina had lived in an endless string of suburbs. In some schools, it seemed like Xochi was the only kid without blonde hair and freckles. Her experience with Mexican food started and ended with Taco Bell. Even after two years of high school Spanish, she was hopeless. What would it have been like to know her dad's family? To grow up bilingual? Leviticus's skin was a shade lighter than hers, but here, among other Latinos, his features made sense.

The restaurant was already full, so Xochi and Leviticus ate their burritos outside, leaning against the wall.

"This place is the best." She slurped the final sip of her soda. "It's nice seeing other brown faces."

"Huh," he said. "I hadn't thought of that. Probably not much variety up north?"

"There's some. Native Americans mostly, at least in my town. People always ask if I'm Native. Or Hawaiian. I've also gotten Greek and Chinese. But no one ever guesses Mexican."

"I could tell right away," Leviticus said.

"Really?" Xochi grinned.

"Uh, yeah. Ever look in the mirror?" He grinned and took her trash, crumpling it with his. "I know how it is being mixed. Not one thing, not the other."

"Exactly." Xochi sighed and zipped up her leather jacket.

"So," he said, "how you doing? Up for more sightseeing?"

"Absolutely," Xochi said. "I don't know what those guys were talking about. This tour is the best."

Leviticus laughed and put on his helmet. Xochi was glad it was time to get back on the motorcycle. She needed a break from looking at him.

They rode quietly for a while, cruising up narrow alleys and down hidden side streets. Her helmet muffled the noise of the pedestrians, but Xochi's ears still tingled with the buzz and flow of the Spanish she'd heard at the restaurant. Her eyes were drawn to the words on shop signs along Valencia Street: BODEGA, TIENDA, BOTANICA.

Leviticus braked in front of a rickety duplex that might have been nice a century ago. He pulled off his helmet and gazed at the run-down building, its yard strewn with trash.

"You used to live here?"

Leviticus looked like Xochi felt when she thought about the past.

"Yeah," he said. "Sorry, this isn't usually a stop on my tour."

"It's okay. I like knowing where people come from." Xochi tried to remember if she'd ever seen him touch Io, ever seen them kiss.

"One more stop, all right?"

"I'm up for anything!" She put her hands back on his waist, the leather of his jacket still warm from her grip.

Leviticus drove through the financial district and headed for the narrow streets of North Beach. He parked in front of City Lights Bookstore.

"I tried so hard to find this place when I first moved here. I took three buses and never even got close!" Xochi swayed as she got off the motorcycle, legs stiff from the ride. Leviticus grabbed her shoulders to steady her. The street was oddly quiet.

"Come on." He steered her toward the entrance. For the first time, he was a little awkward, pushing the door a few times before realizing he needed to pull.

Alone among the shelves, Xochi fought the urge to pick something designed to make her seem smart or sophisticated. She settled on the poetry section, an honest interest.

"Find anything?" Leviticus's voice tickled Xochi's ear like a polite, velvet-nosed animal.

"It's hard to know where to start. I'd like to read some female poets."

Leviticus walked with purpose. "Do you know Sandra Cisneros or Diane di Prima? Or how about Sylvia Plath?"

"I've read *The Bell Jar*," Xochi said, careful not to add that it had been for a high school English class.

"Here." Leviticus handed Xochi a thin volume titled *Ariel*. She opened it at random to a poem—"The Rival." Startled, she closed the book. The poem's lines evoked an image of Io the night before, her pale face a bright moon on the dark stage.

"I have a first edition I'm saving for Pallas," he said.

"It looks great."

At the register, Xochi took a crumpled wad of money from her jeans pocket, but Leviticus already had his wallet out to pay. He took the book from Xochi's hand and sniffed. "You guys have the best bookstore smell," Leviticus told the clerk.

"It's the mold," the clerk said. "Nothing ever dries out this close to the bay."

"Thank you," Xochi said as they walked out of the store.

Darkness had transformed the neighborhood. Neon signs advertised BIG AL'S PLAYBOY CLUB, THE GARDEN OF EDEN, and THE LUSTY LADY, where a topless cartoon redhead danced, the words "LIVE NUDE GIRLS" blinking on and off below her high-heeled shoes.

"Back in the day, this street was crawling with pirates," Leviticus told her. "They'd drop anchor in the bay and come here to spend their doubloons."

"Seems like it hasn't changed much."

"Yeah. We traded our brothels and saloons for punk clubs and peep shows." He gestured to the bar across the street. "Wanna see where all the beat poets used to drink?"

"Um, sure," Xochi said. With luck, she wouldn't be carded.

She followed Leviticus into the bar, its wooden tables and mismatched chairs filled with people talking and laughing. The bartender greeted Leviticus by name and gave Xochi a long look, but didn't stop them when they sat at a table in the back.

Xochi's eyes adjusted to the light. The narrow elliptical room was taller than it was deep, with a curved staircase leading up to a second level. She recalled a block from a shape sorter she'd had as a small child. She'd played with that contraption longer than she was supposed to, but the satisfaction of fitting the solid wooden blocks into the right holes never faded.

"What'll it be?" Leviticus shrugged off his leather jacket.

"A pint of Guinness?" It was Xochi's favorite, considered more medicinal than alcoholic in Badger Creek. Loretta swore it was the best cure ever for cramps.

A few heads turned as Leviticus went to order their drinks, but they turned away quickly. He was handsome, of course, but not as pretty as Pad, who probably wreaked havoc just walking into a bar. There was a calm, bearlike energy about him Xochi appreciated.

She watched as he and the bartender bantered, Leviticus's laugh a pleasant growl. The bartender gestured toward Xochi. *Crap*, she thought. *I'm gonna get kicked out after all.* But then he pounded Leviticus on the shoulder and waved him away with their drinks, two pints of Guinness and a shot.

"The whiskey is for you." Leviticus set the drinks down between them. "Compliments of the house. You don't have to drink it. It's Leo—he says you look like a whiskey girl. He thought about carding you, but he changed his mind. Pretty girls are good for business."

Had he just called her pretty? No, it had been Leo who'd done that. Pretty and not quite legal, like a bad country song.

Xochi glanced at the bar. Leo raised a glass in her direction. What else could she do but raise her own shot and drink?

"Well," Leviticus said, "underage or not, I see you're no stranger to the bottle."

"I grew up with a bunch of guys. I learned to keep up." Xochi made sure to keep her voice light. *It's not like I lied*, she told herself. *No one ever asked how old I was. I doubt most of them know my last name.*

"So," Leviticus said, stretching out his legs and putting his feet up on the chair beside her, "what's your story, kid?"

Xochi tried to ignore the proximity of his boots, resisting both the urge to move closer and the urge to scoot away. "My story?" She took a long drink of beer.

"What brought you here?"

There were so many ways she could answer, none of them good. "I was traveling." It was what she always said, an explanation that could mean anything. She thought of Collier for the second time that day. She should have left him a note, written a letter. She imagined his face when he called and called. When he came to the door. When he finally understood she wasn't coming back.

"I was hitchhiking, actually." She was slipping, too relaxed. She waited for the look of horror on Leviticus's face. She wouldn't blame him—it *was* horrible. If Xochi hadn't gotten a ride from those college kids on their way home from Humboldt State, who knew where she'd be now. She searched his face, but there was no judgment. He was just listening. "I ended up at a crappy hotel in the Tenderloin. An SRO? I don't even know what that stands for."

"Single room occupancy," he said. "And cockroaches."

"Yep."

"Then what?" He leaned back, seeming certain she'd spill her secrets. But what else was there to say? That she'd spent her first two weeks in the city huddled under the scratchy bedspread either crying or asleep? That she'd lived on two-dollar pizza slices and peanut butter sandwiches? That she'd filled out application after application but not one place had ever called to offer her a job?

"I walked a lot," she said. "I fell in love."

Leviticus leaned forward slightly.

"With the city," she finished. "I fell in love with the city."

"What about it?" His boots were still distracting her. She imagined resting her palm on the worn black leather, feeling the warmth of his foot inside. She'd lost track of the silence. Had it been too long? *No,* she thought. *Just a sliver of time. A wingbeat or two, that was all.*

"I think it's the light," she said. "When it's overcast, the air is so soft. Everything glows like moonlight in the daytime. And then the sun comes out, and it's like Dorothy opening the door to Oz. The other day, we had fog and sun at the same time. Everyone on the streetcar started whispering, like it was a spell they were afraid to break."

"Monday." Leviticus smiled at the corners of his eyes. "Ky and Aaron took me surfing in Bolinas." That explained the strong shoulders, the gorgeous arms. "The bridge looked detached, like it was about to float away."

Xochi slid off her leather jacket. Twisting so she could hang it on the back of her chair, she was oddly conscious of her body.

"So," she said, slouching down in her seat, "what about you?" Her voice sounded weird, too. Was she drunk?

"What about me?"

"Your story."

"Which one?"

"You and Io. How did you meet?"

"Ah, that story," Leviticus said. "You ready? It's kind of long."

"I'm ready." Was she, though? It was so nice here in this moment, just the two of them, her body vibrating with the honeyed fatigue she felt after a summer day at the river.

"The first time I saw Io," Leviticus began, "she looked just like the decoration on my cousins' birthday cakes—strawberry whipped cream with a plastic blonde ballerina on top. They make them in the Mission, at the bakery we passed on Valencia."

"Did you get that kind for your birthday, too?" Xochi leaned back, stretching her legs out in front of her, parallel to his. "Or are you a chocolate person?"

He cocked his head, one eyebrow raised. So that was where Pallas got it.

Something shifted between them—cooled. Xochi was suddenly lost, the bar too loud. She replayed the last few minutes, and there it was. She'd been flirting this whole time. She knew from exposure, rather than experience. Flirting had been her mother's specialty and her gift.

Xochi rewound to the fluttering lashes, the languid slouch, her teasing tone when she asked if he liked chocolate. All Gina's moves. Xochi imagined her mother's lithe body superimposed over her own.

The silence was growing awkward, but Leviticus remained quiet. "It's weird," Xochi said. She had no idea what to say next. She thought of the tattoos she'd seen when he was shirtless onstage last night, the owl on his bicep and the tiny typewriter script curling around his neck and back and arms.

"What is?" Leviticus glanced at his watch. Was he bored?

"Seeing you here and remembering you onstage," Xochi said, relieved that the words had emerged. "It's like you sort of switch back and forth between two different people."

"Yeah, that's what it feels like. Me and that onstage guy? People confuse us all the time. The scary thing is when *I* get confused. You've been with us—what? A month?"

"Almost." It had been twenty days since Xochi had moved into her attic bedroom.

"You haven't seen much of anyone, then. It gets busy before a big show. I love rehearsal, but the rock star thing—not so much. But then when it's time to go onstage, I change completely. It's been like that since the first time I played a real show. It used to take me weeks to come down. Ky says I'm a bad transitioner. Now, if I'm chill at the parties and remember to eat and sleep, it's a lot quicker. So yeah. Dr. Jekyll and Mr. Hyde."

"I wonder if that can happen other times, to anyone."

"What do you mean?" Leviticus put his boots on the floor and leaned on the table with both elbows. Xochi seemed to have gotten herself out of groupie territory and back on solid ground.

"You just said it. Jekyll and Hyde. It's like a different being climbs into your skin and hangs out there for a while. What if it happens to all of us sometimes, and we don't even know it?" *Like just now.* Xochi suppressed a shiver. Had she really momentarily channeled her slutty runaway mom?

Leviticus's eyes gleamed. "There's a shamanic aspect to performing. Rock and roll has always played with that. But I think it's a part of yourself you're connecting with, not some outside force."

"It could be both. Like the collective unconscious—maybe there are times we tap into it."

"Right. Like the walls between you and the world around you evaporate. I like that feeling a little too much. That's when the trouble starts."

"Trouble how?" Xochi blinked away a sudden image, the invisible wall between her and Leviticus dissolving, skin on skin.

"Almost every way you can think of, lady." He took a sip of beer. "But not these days. At some point, I got it. I want something real, and that takes focus. So no drinking, no drugs. It's why we fast. Most of us, anyway."

"I think I saw some of that last night. At first it was about the spectacle, but then something changed." Xochi recalled the moment the energy shifted. The lights turned greenish and hazy. One by one, the instruments fell away until the bass drum was all that remained. Xochi's eyes had grown heavy, her body downshifting to match the perfect regularity of the drum's giant heart. "It was like . . . an initiation. Like you opened the door to this magical world and invited us in."

"But do you think it's too much?" Leviticus's forehead wrinkled. "I worry the spectacle makes it seem unattainable—the gods onstage, the mortals below. I don't want that."

"I get what you're saying, but not everyone can do what you guys do."

"People always talk about talent—I don't know if it really exists. Our thing is about ritual, about being in the moment, not some perfect end result. Sometimes I think we should just pare it down. Acoustic guitars. No eyeliner. No glitter. What do you think?"

Xochi laughed. "Well, some of us like the eyeliner and electric guitars. People need a little magic in their lives."

He smiled, the edges of his eyes crinkling again. How old was he, anyway? Thirty? Thirty-one? Xochi sat up straight, her posture mirroring his. A restlessness droned in her belly. She sent it a lullaby—*no mission to accomplish, no sweet stuff to want.* Just two people sitting in a bar, possibly becoming friends.

"So," Leviticus said, "where were we? You wanted a story of some kind, didn't you?"

"I think we digressed at birthday cake." It was good to be

back in a world where cake was innocent and things were perfectly fine.

"Right," he said. "Strawberry or chocolate."

Xochi knew this look, one dimple almost showing, deadpan eyebrows over sparkling eyes. It was the same one Pallas wore when she was teasing, waiting for Xochi to take the bait. Was *he* flirting now?

"The answer to your question is that most of the time, I'm a devout chocolate person. However, in the case of birthday cake, the strawberry whipped cream from that particular bakery is my favorite." He lowered his lashes.

Xochi's piercing tingled. She took a long breath. Leviticus was her boss. He was Pallas's *dad*.

He drained the last of his beer. "Sadly, I was never allowed to have one myself. 'Too girly.'"

"Wait, how can a cake be girly? I mean, yeah, I guess the pink and white—but come on. It's *food*. Couldn't they just swap out the ballerina for a race car and call it a day?"

"You'd understand if you met my dad."

"What's he like?"

Leviticus paused. "Macho. Religious. A bad combination." Something flashed across his face. Anger? It disappeared too fast to tell. "I left home at fifteen. Eventually, I made it all the way to London. I used to busk for money, and Io did ballet by my favorite spot. Later I found out dancing wasn't even her main thing. It was horseback riding. She almost made it to the Olympics."

"Why didn't she?" Xochi took a sip of her beer.

"Her mom caught her climbing in the window one morning, and that was it. Sold Io's horse and signed her up for boarding school."

"She was in high school?"

"Turned seventeen a month before Pallas was born."

My age. "My mom was young, too. Sixteen. We don't look anything alike, so people always thought she was my babysitter."

"Sixteen? That's how old I was. We used to lie about our age. The second people knew how young we were, all they did was look for mistakes."

"I know what you mean." Xochi pictured Gina in her Van Halen shirt and cutoffs, hurrying down the beige hallway of yet another new school.

"It was hard for Io at first, but she refused to go back. People in England talk about class way more than we do here. It took my friends a long time to accept her. After she inherited the money from her dad, she was almost embarrassed. She still keeps it on the down low. People think the way we live now is all because of Lady Frieda, but it's not. A lot of it is her."

"She got kind of upset the other day when she found me doing the dishes. She said I shouldn't feel like the hired help."

"She's right."

"Yeah, but . . . I *am* the hired help."

A protest rose to his lips, but Xochi interrupted. "I mean, I know I'm not the maid. But you guys pay me. I don't know how it works with other people in the house, but with me, it seems pretty straightforward."

He fiddled with his empty glass. His cuticles were ragged, his nails painted the same blue as Pallas's bathtub. "I don't know," he said. "I mean, we pay Pad for set design and stage managing. And the band splits everything."

"And Kiki?" She paused. "It's none of my business, I know. You shouldn't give me whiskey if you want me to stay polite."

Leviticus laughed outright. People at other tables glanced over. "I prefer honest to polite. And I don't remember any whiskey at the breakfast table."

Xochi looked down.

"Don't be embarrassed. You want to know who you're living with." He put his open hand on the table, a gesture to draw her in.

Wait, Xochi thought. *If he was sixteen when Pallas was born, that makes him—what?* She pushed her brain to do the simple math. *Twenty-eight?*

"Kiki has her own money."

"Like Io?" Xochi asked.

"Yes and no. Kiki's grandma is a duchess or something. She and Io met at this school where even having a banker for a stepdad made Io one of the poor kids. By the time Pallas was born, Io was broke and disowned. Then, after we moved to New York, Io's dad died, and it turned out he'd cut her into his will. He was a music producer and Io's mom was a backup singer. She got sick of waiting for him to leave his wife, so she ended up with the London banker. To look at her now, you'd never guess she used to party with The Rolling Stones."

Xochi tried to picture Gina dressed like a regular mom with a grown-up hairdo and sensible shoes. Maybe that was how she looked now. Six years was a long time.

"So yeah," Leviticus said. "Io's dad—he hadn't seen her in years. But he left her the house in San Francisco and a pile of cash."

"Wow."

"Our place in New York was smaller than the pantry at Eris Gardens. One minute we're street kids, the next we're parents with two jobs apiece, then all of a sudden we have this outrageous house." He sipped his beer. "When Kiki moved in, it got better. She organized us. She was the one who found Pad. They shacked up until their infamous breakup a few years ago."

"Wait a second. Those two were together?"

Leviticus nodded. "Star-crossed. Pad's a young soul. They may be the same age, but Kiki's got at least a couple of lifetimes on him."

"How about everyone else?"

"I knew Kylen when I was a kid. When we started the band and needed a drummer, Ky tapped Aaron. They go way back. After that, Pad became our set designer and stage manager, Kiki made costumes. It all fit."

"What about Bubbles?"

"Io and Kiki met Bubbles at Mitchell Brothers."

"Wait, the strip club with the dolphin mural? That was right by my SRO. I thought it was a pet store till I went around the corner and saw the sign. So Bubbles was a stripper?"

Leviticus nodded. "She was headlining, doing her burlesque thing. After Ky and Aaron were done fighting over her, she joined the band and moved in."

"Interesting. I didn't think Kylen felt that way about girls . . ."

"It's complicated—there's history there. Ask Bubbles if you want the entertaining version."

"Wow," Xochi said. "At first I thought the house was full of these set couples . . . then I realized I was probably wrong." Her color rose.

"I never thought about how it looked from the outside. Most of us don't really do monogamy."

Xochi nodded. "Bubbles explained polyamory to me. I see the logic behind it, but I can't really imagine it working."

"It's hard at first." Leviticus picked at the corner of a paper coaster. "When I was young, I wanted Io to myself. But for most of my friends, marriage was political—capitalism with jewelry."

"But what about jealousy? I mean, it's natural. Even animals feel it."

"Io didn't speak to me for three weeks once because I fought a guy for hitting on her. It's how I was raised—defend your woman's honor. Io said her honor was her own business. Can't argue with that."

"So I guess you came around?"

Leviticus hesitated. "We used to talk about it a lot, trying to figure out the best way to live. We tried a ton of crazy stuff. In the end, I guess it boils down to loving each other and telling the truth. Live and let live."

Xochi leaned forward, catching a flash of uncertainty in his voice.

"It's definitely a process. But so far, it's been worth it." He stopped, an easy silence. "So that's us," he said, stacking their empty glasses. "How about you? What were you up to before you hitchhiked to San Francisco?"

Xochi clenched her hands under the table. "Not much." She made herself hold his gaze like she had nothing to hide. "My life's been pretty boring up to now."

"Somehow, I doubt that." Leviticus stood up. "Come on." He grabbed Xochi's jacket and held it out for her. "I know the perfect way to end the day."

11

Six Bells Chime

The sky was clear and the stars were out as Leviticus zoomed back through the financial district. Back in the Haight, he stopped outside a huge red Victorian-turned-movie-theater. A poster in the entry advertised "*WINGS OF DESIRE*." A woman swung on a trapeze as a winged man in a trench coat sat on top of a building, gazing down at her. Underneath, it read, "*THERE ARE ANGELS ON THE STREETS OF BERLIN.*"

The movie was screened in a large front room with mismatched couches instead of regular seats and baked goods and hot tea for sale at the snack bar. Leviticus got them a plate of brownies and a bowl of popcorn. They claimed a faded sofa close to the screen. Xochi had checked her coat, and when she shivered, he laid his leather jacket over her like it was the most natural thing in the world. It smelled like rosemary and clean fur, a scent she'd come to know during their ride. The animal comfort of it made her want to close her eyes.

"You okay?" Leviticus frowned. "I should've told you to wear long johns."

"I'm fine."

"I'm getting you some tea."

"No, it's fine, I'm—"

She was cut off by his hand lightly touching her cheek.

"I knew it. Freezing. Sit tight."

Why is he being so nice? Xochi pulled her knees up under his jacket, making herself as compact as possible in spite of her long legs and big feet.

"Here you go." His hands shook as he passed her the steaming cup. Chamomile with honey.

The couches filled as more moviegoers arrived. The music in the background switched from classical to rock. *"Wild Horses,"* Xochi registered. *Gina's favorite.*

"Xochi?" Leviticus's voice was calm, but Xochi sensed something else underneath. "How old are you?"

Her stomach dropped. "Nineteen," she said. It was her stock answer. The only person in the city who knew the truth was Pallas.

"You're not nineteen." He tried again. "Did you run away from home?"

Xochi looked at her hands and sipped her tea. She reminded herself to breathe. The lie took forever to make its way to her constricted throat. Finally, she exhaled a single syllable into the charged air between them. "No."

She traced a pattern on the arm of the old sofa, a trail made by other fingers, people waiting for something to start. Taking another shallow breath, she met his eyes. "No one's looking for me. It's a good thing I left. I should have done it sooner."

"It's okay," he said. "It doesn't change anything here."

Xochi closed her eyes. Janis Joplin was singing now, a song about having nothing to lose.

"Want a brownie?" Leviticus's voice was uneven.

"Sure." Xochi took the brownie and began to pick at its edges. "So what's the movie about?"

Leviticus hesitated. The lights dimmed, and the screen came to life. Under the low strains of a cello, he answered. "It's about love," he said. "True love."

12

The Starlit Mire

At the Red Victorian, Xochi sat in thrall of the creamy black-and-white images on the flickering screen. Filled with the swelling strings and gravelly punk of the movie's soundtrack, her pulse followed the fortunes of the old man, the new lovers, the brooding musician, and the fallen angel. She let her tears and sighs come unguarded, Leviticus's shoulder pressed against hers. They stayed through the credits without looking at each other. They didn't have to. Xochi knew it would be like looking in a mirror.

Emerging from the blanket-fort darkness of the theater, she zipped her jacket against a blast of wind that smelled like the sea. Their easy silence relaxed into custom as they got on the motorcycle. Swaying with the wind, she, Leviticus and the motorcycle moved as one graceful being. Xochi closed her eyes and rested her head lightly against his back.

The moon shone silver over Eris Gardens. The house was dark, the curtains drawn. Leviticus parked behind the kitchen. Xochi's limbs were stiff, her hands numb from cold. Following the sound of laughter down to the basement, they found the family gathered around a grainy home movie.

"There you are," Kylen said from the recliner in the corner. "I thought we'd have to send a search party."

"Dad, you have to see this!" Pallas called. "Xochi, look what Mom and Kiki found!" Pallas scrambled to make room for

Leviticus on a low couch. The room was so different from the rest of the house, a 1950s version of modern with shag carpet and tweedy, angular furniture. Io looked gorgeous in her simple blue dress and messy bun. Snuggled between her parents, Pallas completed the picture, a perfect family.

Still standing in the doorway, Xochi turned her attention to the screen: a cottage garden in spring. A boy with a Mohawk—Leviticus?—struggled to erect a white canvas tent. A gorgeous Amazon with a mass of multicolored waist-length braids—Kiki!—helped a tiny girl with cropped hair and a hippie skirt walk around the garden.

Kylen glared at Xochi from his recliner. "Are you staying or going? There's a draft."

"Be nice," Pad said.

Bubbles patted the cushion next to her. She squeezed Xochi's hand when she sat down. "Isn't Io cute?"

Of course. The luminous girl with the pixie cut was Io, adorable and extremely pregnant. Here they were, the Romeo and Juliet Leviticus had described.

"I forgot we did this," Leviticus said.

"So did I. Kiki's mum found it." Io smiled at him.

"I can't believe that's Pal in there," Aaron said. The younger Io was striking silly poses with long-haired Kiki, playing up her enormous belly. Her laughter pealed into the room. Whoever had been operating the camera had figured out the sound. When the laboring girl in the movie yelped in pain, real-life Leviticus reached over Pallas to hold Io's hand.

Now I've seen them touch, Xochi thought.

Everyone was so relaxed and happy, and they seemed to expect Xochi to feel the same. They'd installed her in a pretty room, loaned her books and given her clothes, fed her delicious meals, sat her in the front row at their concert, introduced her to their friends. Most of all, they trusted her with their most precious member, the single person who made them more than a group of friends and lovers, a real family.

Blood pounded in Xochi's ears. She closed her eyes and tried to relax, but opened them to Kylen's cool stare. He knew something, or thought he did. Whatever it was, he didn't approve. He broke their contact with an eye roll worthy of Pallas, turning to give Leviticus a pointed look as he passed him a bowl of popcorn. Leviticus refused the bowl with a snort, nudging Kylen's slippered foot with his boot.

These people were too close, knew each other too well. How long had it been since they'd been like Xochi—truly alone?

When everyone was laughing at something in the movie, Xochi went for the door. She looked back at Leviticus one more time, drawn in by a gravitational pull toward the impossible, but there was only Kylen, watching her go.

II.

The city sings strangeness to Sister
Trees with pinecone-petal skins
And leaves like long green teeth

Gull-bright wind leads to the bay
The bridge arches land-to-land, a great bathing animal
Brother knows bridges. He knows the sea, a cold deep singer

Together, they whisper flame to sand
Daylily tongues lick the moon
Heat-filled they dive, pistil and stamen

Deep, deep, cold and deep, sea gives way to shoreline
Redwood memory, story forest
Mink-deep girl

The moon sinks to her repose
Brother takes Sister's hand
Together, they run North

13

Just Like Arcadia

Pallas opened the door. It had been years since Xochi's bedroom had been her playroom, but she still knew the creaky spots in the floor. Moonlight shone on Xochi's face.

"I knew it," Pallas said, padding to the foot of Xochi's bed. "You're sad."

Xochi could only nod and turn away.

"Scoot over." Pallas climbed in. "Did your butt get bigger?"

Xochi snorted. "There's a bed in your room, you know. Twice this size."

"It's cold in there." It wasn't, really. But Xochi knew that.

"Fine." Xochi scooted toward the wall.

"Xochi?" Pallas rolled onto her back. "Where were you born?"

"Concord." Xochi's delivery was deadpan, designed to put Pallas off. Obviously, she'd forgotten who she was dealing with.

"Like where they lived in *Little Women*?"

"What?"

"Louisa May Alcott. They lived by Concord, in Massachusetts. On a transcendentalist commune. Io told me about it when we were having breakfast. *Little Women* was based a lot on Louisa May Alcott's real life."

"That's fascinating. Now go to sleep."

"But you never told me where you were born."

"I did," Xochi said. "Concord, *California*."

"Where's that?"

"About an hour east of here. Way out in the suburbs."

"Xochi?"

"What?" Xochi sounded completely exasperated. But Pallas pressed on.

"Where do your parents live now?"

Xochi exhaled, the sound of defeat. "I don't have parents, Pal. I never knew my dad. And my mom—I haven't seen her in a long time."

"But who took care of you?"

"I lived with my mom till I was eleven," she said. "Then my grandma—well, kind of my step-grandma—she raised me for a while. She's the one who gave me this."

Xochi took off her necklace and handed it to Pallas. A pair of green hummingbirds touched their beaks to a central opal of midnight black. "My grandma said they were lucky. Protection from harm and a charm for good luck."

Pallas tilted the pendant into the moonlight. "Where did your grandma live?"

"I told you that, too. She lived up north. In the redwoods."

"Yeah, but *where* in the redwoods? There are a lot of them, you know."

"Can we please go to sleep?" Xochi rolled over.

"I'm sorry," Pallas said in her best animal-taming voice. "I know I'm being a pest. I just want to know. We're friends, right? Kindred spirits."

A single tear gleamed down Xochi's cheek, but when she spoke, her voice sounded normal. "I lived in a town in Southern Humboldt," Xochi said, "about six hours from here. My mom met this guy, and we moved there so she could be with him. I was nine. She left when I was twelve. My grandma—"

"Wait," Pallas said. "What do you mean, she left? Like, without you?"

"Right. Then I lived with my grandma. She was technically Evan's grandma, but—"

"Who's Evan?"

"My mom's boyfriend." Xochi's voice had changed. Maybe she didn't like the boyfriend. "Anyway," Xochi continued, "Loretta was his grandma, but she sort of adopted me. She had a cabin on the property. When my mom left, I moved in with her. But Loretta died last summer. It wasn't home without her."

"And then you came here, to San Francisco?"

"Yes," Xochi said. "And that's it, okay?"

"Okay. I guess." Pallas sighed and rolled to her side, her back against Xochi's. She tried to imagine Io or Leviticus leaving her and never coming back, but it was impossible. Wind chimes trilled in the garden and rain beat a happy song on the roof.

"Xochi?" Pallas asked. "Does this feel like home?"

Xochi was quiet. "I don't know," she said finally. "I'm not sure what home feels like anymore. But if I could pick, this would definitely be the place."

14

Going to California

Dear Xochi,

You were snoring, so I disabled your alarm. I'll be downstairs when you're ready. The crêpe place is open all day.

xoxo
Pallas

XOCHI DROPPED PALLAS'S NEATLY printed note and lay back in bed. She'd had a vivid dream of running through the forest on the heels of a brown-skinned boy with streaming hair and silent feet. His sweet voice perched in her ear, soundless yet somehow clear.

"This way, little sister."
Xochi follows, loping through the undergrowth.
A bird wings through the canopy: black feathers, red head, pale sky.
Trees give way to a road, the blacktop oddly comfortable under Xochi's bare feet.
A sign on a rough wooden post, the gray of a gravel parking lot — the entrance to Richardson Grove State Park.

XOCHI SAT UP, BLINKING in the cranberry light from the stained glass windows that circled her little room. Since leaving Badger

Creek, she'd only allowed herself thoughts of home in strictly measured doses. Surely now, she could grant her mind a little leeway.

She retraced the dream, traveling the section of Highway 101 that ran through Richardson Grove, then slipping back to the first time she'd seen a redwood.

Xochi had been nine, almost ten, and spent most of the drive from Oregon lying down, mourning what she'd been forced to leave behind. Gina had met Evan three nights before at the Oregon Country Fair. She and Xochi were supposed to be there with Gina's boyfriend, Adam, helping sell the silver jewelry his dad had made all winter.

Adam was nice. He liked kids and talked to them like regular people. His big hippie family was nice, too. They'd caravanned to Southern Oregon in a line of beat-up Volvos and colorful VW buses. Adam said the country fair was like a village out of a fantasy book—music everywhere, delicious food, and booths full of beautiful wares for sale, all handmade. Children could run wild, eating cream puffs and berry pie with painted faces and bare feet. Every evening, a special parade came through the fair to honor the famous dragon. When he passed, Adam said to chant, "Make way! Make way! Make way for the magic of the dragon!"

The day the fair opened, Xochi spent most of her time alone. All the kids in Adam's family were either much younger and had to stay with their parents or teenagers who wanted to find their fair friends without a stray ten-year-old tagging along. Xochi also got the feeling the three older girls didn't approve of her and her mother. She heard them saying Gina was just using Adam. Xochi hoped they were wrong.

Walking the figure-eight path that curved around the main fairgrounds, she was happy to wander alone. Performers danced on stilts, played old-time music on washboards and accordions, did acrobatic tricks on a trapeze, and told silly, slightly dirty jokes.

There was a drum circle with so many drums that Xochi couldn't count them all. How did they all know how to play in rhythm? Sweaty muscular boys jerked their arms and tossed their heads. Big-hipped women in long skirts and halter tops swung in sexy spirals. A boy of four or five pulled Xochi into the circle of bodies. She held his hands and danced until they had to rest, sprawling on hay bales and drinking the herbal iced tea his brown shirtless mother bought for both of them.

On the second day, Xochi found a secret theater tucked in a grove of trees, the dusty ground lined with rugs and cushions, the stage hung with silver stars. As she sat down, the most mesmerizing women Xochi had ever seen shimmered onto the stage. Moving like they had liquid under their skin instead of bones, their made-up eyes held secrets she needed to understand.

They reminded her of her mother, in a way. Gina was like a slinky cat everyone wanted to touch. The belly dancers were similar, with everyone under their spell. Xochi sat in the front row as troupe after troupe performed. At the end, a single woman took to the stage. She was older than many of the other dancers, curvy and soft and absolutely regal. She looked right into Xochi's eyes, her gaze like a present without strings attached.

Xochi imagined being a woman like that, strong and free. She saw herself listening to music and reading lots of books. She would love someone who liked animals and could be a friend. Other women would want to hug her, laugh with her, share their dreams and tell her their problems. They wouldn't be jealous or afraid like they were with her mom.

As GOOD AS DAYS were at the fair, nights were even better. When the heat of the afternoon waned and all of the regular fairgoers went home, the workers and vendors had their chance to play in the fairy-lit village. Music rang from every corner and food booths kept producing their delicious specialties, but the lines were short and the damp night air settled the fine dust on the paths into a velvet carpet under Xochi's bare feet.

On the final night of the fair, Gina took Xochi, who was filthy with dust and all the sticky things she'd been eating, to the communal baths called The Ritz. While they waited in line to get in, Gina explained that inside, past a dressing room, there was a wooden deck with open-air showers and a big redwood sauna. Men, women, and kids all cleaned up together. Xochi worried a little about the nakedness, but once they were inside, it was wonderful—clean and calm, lights low so you could see the moon and stars, gloriously hot water and happy faces everywhere you looked.

The fair was having a great effect on Gina. It was the first vacation she'd had in years. With no tables to wait, no orders to take and enough sleep, Gina was an entirely different person. She shampooed Xochi's hair and scrubbed her back with almond-scented soap. Surrendering to the delicious feeling of her mother's hands on her scalp, Xochi thought she must be imagining the music. Of all the wonderful, crazy storybook things Xochi'd seen at the fair, the grand piano in the bathhouse was the best. Xochi and Gina took their time getting dressed, staring up at the dazzling stars and enjoying the rich music. By the time they left, Xochi was clean and warm, her usual rat's nest of tangles flowing in silky waves down her back.

After dinner, Gina took Xochi to see the fire show in the meadow. In the rosy light of the flaming batons, Gina was a fairy princess. Her blonde hair and light eyes made it hard for people to believe she and Xochi were mother and daughter. The gauzy clothes she'd gotten from the fair suited her more than the tight jeans, tank tops, and high heels she wore at home. She looked way too young to be anyone's mother.

When Evan saw her, it was like a barn owl and a mouse. Xochi knew what was coming from the second he said hello. Her mother knew the owl-and-mouse dance very well. Only Evan probably had it backward. Gina was never the mouse.

They left Adam without saying goodbye. All of Xochi's things left at Adam's were forfeit. All she owned in the world now were five stuffed animals, three days' worth of clothes and a mother who had dragged her through at least four different lives on the way to the perfect fairy-tale ending Xochi knew would never come.

Evan and Gina wanted her to ride in the cab with them, but Xochi refused and climbed in the back. The camper shell was old and leaked in the corner, Evan said, but it wasn't likely to rain. He'd opened the side windows so she'd stay cool, duct-taping a ripped screen to keep out the bugs. Lying on a bed of their three sleeping bags, Xochi tried to ignore the sweaty man smell of Evan's things and pretend she was someplace else.

When the truck stopped, Xochi expected to see another gas station in some stupid, ugly town, but she climbed from the tailgate into a world of branches and green light. Forgetting to give Evan the silent treatment, she whispered, "What is this place?"

Unlike most of Gina's new boyfriends, Evan hadn't tried to get in good with Xochi to impress her mom. It was usually so gross and fake, a total waste of time. Xochi was determined to hate them all on principle, and Gina wanted a man for herself, not a father for her kid. But now Gina was in the restroom, and Evan joined Xochi on the tailgate as she craned her neck to see the tops of the trees, savoring the spicy redwood perfume.

"Smells good, doesn't it?" Evan said. His voice had a Northern California lift, sort of like a surfer guy from Santa Cruz, but not quite. Evan was so tall—"six foot four!" according to Gina—but even he seemed puny under those gigantic trees. "See the sign over there?" He pointed to the entrance of the gravel parking lot. "It says Richardson Grove State Park. But I've always thought this looked more like Middle Earth."

Xochi looked directly at Evan for the first time. His Tolkien reference wasn't much, but it was a start.

"You're right," she said. "It does."

15

All Cats Are Gray

The string of bells above the door announced a customer. "Hi!" Pallas's musical voice pierced Peasblossom's exhaustion.

"Hey there," Xochi said.

"Hi, girls," Nora called from her perch behind the cash register. Peasblossom raised his head at the happy note in her voice. Nora was wearing his favorite dress and long beaded earrings. She'd been his for many years, but he never tired of the details that made her beautiful. "How's it going?"

"Great," Xochi said. "I can't believe how nice it is outside today."

"Where's the kitty-man?" Pallas asked, irreverent as usual.

Pallas joined Nora in the children's section. The girl was rosy and calm, her scent sharp with exercise. Curls like summer grass spiraled out from under her customary furry cat-eared hat. "For solidarity," she'd said the first day she appeared in it. "We're in this together, Peas."

The cat purred, thinking of when the pale girl had befriended him two years ago. It had been during the worst time in Peasblossom's life. The winter Ron died, the entire city was in mourning. Lover after lover, friend after friend, beautiful man after beautiful, beloved man, lost.

Ron and Nora had been best friends since childhood. Nora, baby Anna, Ron and Peas had lived happily together for seven years. So happily that Peasblossom often forgot the yellow-fanged menace in Ron's blood, waiting to take him away from them.

In the heavy, joyless days after Ron's funeral, Pallas's company was the only contact Peasblossom truly enjoyed, a fact he hid from Nora and Anna the best he could. Pallas had never experienced death, but she seemed to understand. After hearing of the family's bereavement through the neighborhood grapevine, she visited the bookstore most mornings with a pastry for Nora and salmon jerky for Peas. She wisely avoided all overt expressions of sympathy. She was simply present, holding her ground a few feet back from the abyss.

By spring, the cat found himself sleeping less and eating more. He raised his head when customers came in and resumed his rigorous grooming schedule. By early summer, Peasblossom was back at work.

Nora's well-curated mix of new and used books made the shop a neighborhood favorite, but it was Peasblossom's uncanny knack as a bookseller that made the shop a Bay Area legend. The cat's picks were as profound as his methods were strict.

The process began with a certain quality of human yearning, a need for story that penetrated the cat's sun-drenched shop window meditations. Listening with some internal apparatus he could not name, Peasblossom would wander the store.

At times, the draw to a title was languid. He'd stretch, yawn, wash and stroll to a certain shelf, rubbing his cheek against the appropriate book. Other instances required assertiveness, even haste. Then Peasblossom would streak to a book, sometimes pouncing on top of it or biting its spine. Customers learned to listen as Peasblossom's selections gained a reputation for being spot-on, even life changing.

The only person who remained nonplussed was Pallas. Even a "Shouts and Murmurs" profile on Peasblossom in *The New Yorker* had failed to impress. With her cynicism, excellent fashion sense, and advanced skills in feline massage, Pallas's visits remained one of the highlights of Peasblossom's week.

"Look at him!" Pallas said. "He's like a pasha prince, all stretched out in the sun. He's taking up the entire table."

"He's kind of dirty for a prince," Xochi said, running a hand down his spine. "Look at this fur."

Peasblossom's tail twitched. He'd already washed as well as he could, considering the condition of his back. He'd limped into the bookstore only a few hours earlier after his interview with the Hag, and had hardly eaten or slept since Equinox. Peasblossom allowed a rare uncensored meow to escape his parched throat. Pallas responded quickly, scratching his chin and ears as he'd trained her to do.

"He looks tired," Xochi said. "I wonder what he's been up to."

Peasblossom suppressed a snort. If Xochi could manage even the most rudimentary of cross-species communication, she'd know that if the cat was tired, it was from attempting to clean up *her* spectacular mess.

The bell on the door chimed, and a group of tourists crowded the shop. Xochi paged through a book on Frida Kahlo while Pallas absently scratched Peasblossom's shoulder.

"Here," Pallas said to Xochi, "can you take over cat massage while I look for a book?"

Xochi's nails were short, likely bitten, but they found the perfect pressure on Peasblossom's tight shoulders without any coaching. "You're such a handsome cat," she murmured in her pleasant feline alto.

"Oh!" Pallas groaned. "I can't believe it."

"No good books?" Xochi inched her strong fingers down Peasblossom's aching spine.

"No. It's this." Pallas indicated a label on the shelf marked YOUNG ADULT. "There's a show tonight, some unplugged thingy with a band from LA. My dad and Ky are sitting in. Everyone's going, and they want you to go, too. I was supposed to tell you this morning."

"I don't get how that reminded you." Xochi's tone was light, but the cat sensed a change in her.

"I was talking about it with Io," Pallas said. "We've been having breakfast together." She was trying to sound casual, but it was obvious how happy she was with the new arrangement. "You know how you're always saying I should do more 'age-appropriate' stuff and act like a real kid? Well, Io and I realized we all have some developmental stuff we need to do. And you're, like, a 'young adult.' Which means you need to go out and hear bad music and drink beer and flirt. That means taking some nights off. Seriously, Xochi. You deserve to have a little fun."

"I don't know," Xochi said. "You were pretty bummed last time I did that."

"Yeah. But I feel better now. I'm glad you're my governess, but come on, can you imagine Jane Eyre if all she did was take care of the little French girl? No Mr. Rochester, no big mystery? Bo-ring!"

"You have a point," Xochi said. "I'm kind of tired, though. Not like I got much sleep last night with you hogging the covers."

"They all want you to go. They said to be ready by nine-thirty."

Xochi's change in scent made Peasblossom sit up. "Who's going?" Her voice revealed an inner turmoil. Peasblossom braced himself for the leap off the low table and rubbed against her ankles. When she stooped down to pet him, he inhaled. Nutmeg and basil, her natural scent. Cherry lip gloss. The musk of pheromones. The bitter-dandelion reek of fear.

"Everyone." Pallas reached down to give Peasblossom a goodbye pat. "Except my mom. She says she's had enough socializing for one week. But everyone else, except possibly Pad. Kiki has a date with the LA band's drummer and Bubbles says Pad is going to stay home and cry, but Pad says he's for sure going because the band has groupies who are, like, triplets or something."

Their voices faded as they said goodbye to Nora and left the store. Peasblossom inhaled again, the air still thick with Xochi's scent. He tasted her fear, teased out its parts.

In between, Peasblossom thought. *That's what the Hag called Xochi. Not yet a woman, but no longer a child.* He sighed, settling back into the sun. As he recalled the Hag's final words, the fur rose along his spine.

Those creepy little cop kids lay down the law, baby. Anybody in their way better pull over fast.

16

Mad Girl's Love Song

"I love that poem," Leviticus said.

Xochi looked up from her book. She'd been reading *Ariel* on the patio—silently at first, but when she reached the poem "Lady Lazarus," the words' bitter chocolate had refused to melt on her tongue until she read aloud.

Leviticus set two mugs of coffee on the table and sat across from Xochi.

"It's my favorite so far," Xochi said. "I can feel her voice in it, like a sort of command. Like she wanted it to be read out loud."

"Yeah," Leviticus said. "She has incredible rhythm."

Xochi sipped her coffee. "Why is this so good?"

"Organic whipping cream. My secret weapon." The words could have echoed yesterday's flirtation, the stupid thing with the cake, but they didn't.

Xochi had been tired all afternoon, but now she was shaky. It couldn't be the coffee; she'd only had a sip. Leviticus picked the book up from the table and set it back down, his hand resting just inches from hers. The garden was suddenly silent: no birds, no traffic, no wind.

All her life, Xochi had been a back-seat witness to the trouble a person could make in the small fraying seconds between things. If she moved an inch, raised her eyes, brushed his wrist with her fingertip, everything would change.

A car alarm broke the silence. The crows cawed on the power lines. Leviticus reached for his coffee and the moment was gone. Maybe she'd only imagined it.

A CLOUD SLIPPED IN front of the sun. "I should get my gear together." His voice was distant and polite now, the way it had been before their ride.

"Okay," Xochi said. "See you later."

He left. His coffee sat next to hers, still steaming. The Hollywood palms hissed at the sudden wind. Xochi gulped the rest of her coffee, scalding her mouth.

17

Precious

"Fräulein."

Breath tickled the back of Xochi's neck. She tried to
wake up, but the dream forest held her tight.

*She follows her brother through briars into a stand of fir, bare
feet tender with cold. As if for luck, he touches each trunk as they
pass. Xochi does the same, the bark rough under her small green
hand . . .*

"Xochi! Come on!"

*Moonlight shocks through a break in the trees. A golden tub
stands in the distance. Every part of her longs for it, but it is so far
away. Worry furs the edges of her mind. She is so cold. So tired . . .*

"Fräulein! Time to go!"

". . . Pad?" Xochi tried to snuggle back under the blankets,
but Pad yanked them away.

"Bubbles sent me to collect you. She's in a mood—let's not
make her wait."

The dual phenomena of Pad in her bedroom and Bubbles
being anything but cheerful made Xochi sit up. Half asleep,
she put on her boots, grabbed her leather jacket, and followed
him downstairs.

"Meet you at the van," he said, pushing Xochi out the kitchen door toward the carriage house, home to Aaron's pampered Volkswagen bus.

The sliding side door was already open. "Hey," Aaron said, smiling.

"About time," Kylen said from the passenger seat.

Xochi blinked, transported for a millisecond to the cold forest. What was it with these dreams? Inside her boots, her feet were freezing. She zipped her jacket up to her chin.

Bubbles and Leviticus sat on the bench seat in back. The obvious place for Xochi was between them. Even if the window seat was colder, there was no way she was squishing in next to Leviticus, not after the weirdness with the coffee and the poem.

"Can I sit by the window, please?"

"Of course, sweetie. Are you okay?" Bubbles scooted closer to Leviticus and patted the seat beside her, bad mood nowhere in sight, although her oversized sunglasses were an odd choice for nighttime.

Kylen shot a glance over his shoulder, sneaky antennae probing for information. Xochi forced herself to meet his eyes. They were pretty—pure black, with delicate, almost transparent lids. Xochi remembered the hematite bracelet Loretta wore to births. "It draws everything to ground," she always said. "Helps you tap into the earth." Maybe that's how Kylen did whatever he did—drawing in people's secrets with those hematite eyes.

"Where's Pad?" Kylen reached in front of Aaron to lean on the horn.

"Stop it," Bubbles snapped. "Not everybody's on their way out to a show at ten o'clock on a Wednesday. Our neighbors actually work."

"Whoa, girl," Aaron said. "Come on, now."

"Don't." Bubbles pulled up her dark glasses and met Aaron's eyes in the rearview mirror. He blew her a kiss. She mimed throwing it back at him and slammed her glasses back over her eyes. Kylen reached over Aaron and hit the horn again, lightly this time.

"Sorry, B," Kylen said. "We gotta go."

"Anything I can do?" Leviticus sounded like he was worried Bubbles might bite.

"Only if you have a quaalude, sweetie." Bubbles said.

Pad rushed into the carriage house. "Sorry," he said. "Had to get the phone. Should I take my motorcycle?"

"Get in," Bubbles said. "We're running late. Sit on the floor."

"Xochi needs the window," Kylen said, "and Pad gets carsick. She should sit on his lap."

"Awesome," Pad grinned.

"Fine." Xochi got up. "I don't mind if Pad doesn't."

"Right this way, fraülein."

Xochi settled onto Pad's lap. Kylen meant to embarrass her with the seating arrangement, but Pad's arms around her waist were surprisingly comfortable and so warm. She exhaled, tension draining from her shoulders. Pad sighed, too, a sadder exhalation.

"What's wrong?"

"Just missing my sisters. You remind me of Sam. She's the youngest."

"How many do you have?"

"Five. I'm second to the oldest, the only boy. How about you?"

"Only child." Xochi had once longed for a sister or brother. Now she wondered, had she wanted a companion or a witness? Pad squeezed her elbow, and Xochi leaned her head against his, watching the city pass by outside the window.

Aaron turned up the stereo. The Beastie Boys' bratty rap spat from the speakers. "She's Crafty," Xochi's favorite. By the time the guy in the song woke up naked on the floor with all his stuff stolen, even Bubbles was smiling.

The van slowed in a neighborhood Xochi didn't recognize.

Aaron drove around the block to the alley and everyone got out and started unloading except Bubbles, who stomped to the door marked STAGE and went inside. Xochi hesitated. She'd expected a music hall, but the sign over the door said RAY'S BAR.

"Don't worry," Leviticus said, "no one's going to hassle you backstage. Wait till it gets crowded before you go out front and you'll be fine."

His tone was nice but distant, like this morning. Nothing like the day before.

"So wait," Kylen said, helping Leviticus unload his guitar rig. "She's not twenty-one? How old is she, then?"

"She's seventeen." Xochi grabbed a mic stand and followed them through the stage door. "And she's right here." Saying it felt good.

"Why did I think you were older?" Aaron asked as he headed back to the van for a second load.

"Because she lied," Kylen called after him. "We've been through this."

"Who lied about what?" Pad moved carefully into the narrow hallway with Kylen's stand-up bass.

"Me," Xochi said, meeting Kylen's eyes. Did she see a twitch of humor? No, just irritation. What had she ever done to get on his bad side? Was he still mad about the naked tarot cello thing? She turned back to Pad. "I'm not exactly twenty-one."

"She's exactly seventeen," Kylen said. "Which makes her underage for *everything*, not just booze." He said it slowly, staring straight at Leviticus.

"Damn!" Pad grinned. "That was a close one the other night."

"In your dreams," Xochi said.

Pad poked Xochi in the ribs. "Hey, Lev," he called, "I'll go talk to the sound guy."

"Good," Leviticus said curtly. "Thanks." Did he really think something had happened between her and Pad? Would he even care?

"I—" Xochi began, but before she'd even finished the word, Leviticus was walking away.

Bubbles slouched against the wall in the hallway. Xochi stifled a giggle at her tank top, FUCK OFF printed in sparkly pink across her chest.

"The Rabbit Hole guys are here." Aaron put his arm around Bubbles and gave her shoulder a squeeze. "I'm gonna help them unload."

Bubbles shrugged him off. "They didn't even ask you to play tonight. They have the star dressing room, too. They should use their big egos to get their stuff inside."

"Those guys aren't so bad. And you know what my mom always says—two rudes don't make a polite." He planted a kiss on Bubbles's forehead. "See you later?"

Bubbles rolled her eyes but accepted a final hug. "C'mon." She grabbed Xochi's hand. "Those assholes take forever with their precious gear. Let's go drink their booze."

Yawning, Xochi followed Bubbles into a room with a faded red star on the door. A bare bulb threw shadows at the peeling skin of band posters and graffiti covering the walls. Streaky pink carnations drooped in a martini shaker on the makeup counter. A dented bucket held fresh ice and a bottle of champagne. There was a space heater in the corner, already on, adding a hint of stale plastic to the reek of beer and cigarettes.

Bubbles uncorked the champagne with professional ease and took a swig before launching into the saga of her doomed relationship with Dylan, Rabbit Hole's lead singer. "Goes to show you, if you have to date a musician, avoid lead singer-guitarist types at all costs. The only one I've ever met who's not a total misogynist asshole is Leviticus, and he's one of a kind."

"I've noticed," Xochi said. Bubbles passed her the bottle. Xochi took a sip. She shook off her jacket and sank into the vinyl couch, resisting the urge to lie down.

"Sweetie," Bubbles said, "what are you wearing?"

Xochi looked down at her usual uniform of jeans, a T-shirt and combat boots. "I fell asleep. I didn't have time to change."

"I'm going to tell you something."

Xochi raised the bottle to take another sip, but Bubbles intercepted it.

"I don't know what happened to you before you came to us, but I know it wasn't good."

Xochi opened her lips to deny it, then closed them again. Bubbles pulled her up so they stood before the mirror together, a short, curvy Tinkerbell and a tallish Lost Girl with dark under-eye circles and ragamuffin clothes. "Close your eyes," Bubbles commanded.

Xochi obeyed. Hands moved over her back from her neck down to her waist, as if scrubbing away a stain. When the pressure subsided, long nails marched up her spine, inch by inch, a slow procession of fairy feet. The steps came faster and faster until suddenly, they stopped. Bubbles lifted up Xochi's T-shirt and traced a careful shape on her back.

"Wings," she said. "Right here."

Xochi imagined brown feathers, a long, forked tail. She opened her eyes.

"When I was little," Bubbles said, "I was really cute. Like, ridiculous. Everyone said I looked just like Shirley Temple." Bubbles pulled at one of her curls. "I was totally into it. Wore little dresses, sang for company. There was this one time I was doing cherry drops on the monkey bars. I was wearing a dress. My underwear showed when I did the part where you drop back and flip to land. A lady on yard duty—a *grown-up*—called me a slut.

"When bad shit started happening at home, I thought it was my fault. I stopped playing on the monkey bars. I stopped wearing dresses. I stopped being cute. But here's the thing: it didn't work. No matter what I did, shit kept happening. So I decided—from now on, I'm going to be as cute and shiny and slutty as I want. That's what I'm talking about, Xochi. You don't have to hide. You get to be fabulous. Anyone who has a problem with it can fuck off." She stuck out her chest, underlining the words on her tank top with a product-model flourish of her hand.

Xochi sat down, the metal chair beneath her not quite stable. Her heart constricted around the image of Bubbles as a little girl; Xochi folded the snapshot away inside her body, even though it was too late to keep that little girl safe.

She considered the Bubbles standing beside her and the Bubbles in the mirror. Double trouble. In theory, Bubbles was totally right: stop hiding, be seen, shine. Like the directions on a shampoo bottle. But in practice? Xochi had no idea where to begin.

Bubbles sat on the counter, patent leather boots dangling. Their silver skull-and-crossbones buckles, stiletto heels and vicious pointed toes combined with lace-trimmed ankle socks to illustrate her point: the past doesn't own you.

"Well?" Bubbles said.

"I get what you're saying." Xochi gazed into her own tired eyes in the mirror. "I just don't know if it applies to me. I mean, I'm naturally sort of quiet. It's not like there's a secret extrovert in here trying to get out."

"So you're quiet—that's fine. I'm just trying to say that all of *this"*—Bubbles motioned to Xochi's body—"is yours. You get to do whatever you want with it. You can be quiet without being invisible. Invisible is a coping tool, and it becomes a habit—a bad habit we're going to have to break."

Xochi remembered herself in a red dress, drunk off her ass at Loretta's wake. She wasn't invisible that night. She'd hurt Collier. Made a spectacle of herself. Slept with a boy she hardly knew. "I don't exactly feel qualified. My past attempts at visibility have not gone well."

"Never fear." Bubbles handed the champagne back to Xochi. "You're talking to an expert." She started digging around in her bag.

Xochi took a long swig. Bubbles patted the back of the rickety folding chair. "Stand up on this." She brandished a pair of scissors from her makeup bag. Kiki had already cut off Xochi's hair—what was next?

The chair creaked as Xochi's weight shifted from one foot to the other. Cold metal brushed her leg as the denim gave way near her upper thigh. The room was warm now, almost too hot, but the draft from the door slid under her skin, snaking up her spine.

"Stay still," Bubbles said. "These things are for fingernails, not fabric."

Xochi closed her eyes and willed herself motionless as the scissors bit into her jeans. The sounds of people and music from the front of the club clashed with feedback as the opening band tuned up. Deep voices and bursts of laughter came from the dressing room next door.

"Almost done." Bubbles made the final snip, turning Xochi's nondescript jeans into short-shorts. She stood back to survey her work. "Here, sit and I'll pull the legs off."

"Let me get my boots," Xochi said. Laughing, she untangled her leg and stood in front of Bubbles.

"Rats!" Bubbles yanked at the hem of the shorts. "They don't show under your shirt." She pulled Xochi's oversized Led Zeppelin shirt in at the waist. She knotted it, a classic trick of Gina's for a too-big top, but the fabric was too thick for it to hold. Bubbles reached for her scissors.

"Wait! Don't cut this up. It's sentimental." Xochi had worn Collier's old T-shirt because she was out of clean laundry. It didn't smell like him anymore, but if she closed her eyes, the ghost scent of him was there, tree sap and SweetTarts, motorcycle grease and sweat, a comfort to her lonely skin.

Bubbles was right, though. The shirt was so long and the shorts so short, it looked like she wasn't wearing any pants.

"Let me think." Bubbles touched her own tank top and miniskirt, but there was nothing extra there. "Give me your shirt. I'll see if I can trade with one of the guys, and we can cut up theirs instead."

"Wait, take this off and give it to you? That's the plan?" Xochi's voice rose an octave.

"Come on!" Bubbles tugged the hem of Collier's shirt. "I'll tell them to be careful and make sure to get it back to you. Lock the door and finish the champagne. I don't want those Rabbit Hole losers getting a single sip."

18

The Seventh Dream of Teenage Heaven

Kylen tuned his stand-up bass with his eyes closed. Even if this gig was Rabbit Hole trying to cop some Lady Frieda gold dust for their tired-ass band, it was nice to take the old girl out for a spin. The all-acoustic show had been the drummer's idea. You knew the whole band was ass-backwards if the drummer was the brains in the operation. The guy even played smart. He was always right there under Dylan with a catch in his beat that changed the standards they were playing into something new. He was clever all right, but screw clever drummers. The rhythm section called for balls, not brains. He'd take Aaron over this guy any day.

The first song started without a hitch—tasteful, bordering on comatose. Kylen scanned the crowd for Bubbles. She was a dignified distance from the stage in her FUCK OFF tank top and tight little skirt, sure to make Dylan the Douche regret the day he scorned her.

Kylen listened for Leviticus, trying to find a hook to latch onto, but Lev's riff was off. He followed his friend's gaze into the crowd. Leviticus was distracted, all right. He was staring straight at Xochi. Whatever fun there was to be had with *that* girl, it was gonna end in tears. Way too young and way too messed up. Even if his cup-half-full housemates couldn't see it, he could.

He cast his net into the room again, searching for someone

to connect with. There was always a dancer whose body naturally conducted energy, who plugged into the rhythm of his bass like old friends talking or great sex.

He probed the crowd but kept landing on Xochi. She looked close to legal after Bubbles's little makeover, but her eyes were heavy. The kid was exhausted, not a good choice to get the lagging music up to speed. Still, something had to be done before the crowd went looking for cheaper beer and a band that rocked. Gritting his teeth, Kylen dug into the bass line, and Xochi's hips began to move. He had to accept it—tonight, it was her or nothing.

He plucked the strings harder, lagging the slightest bit behind the drums to create the necessary tension. Xochi was instantly in the pocket, her body moving in counterpoint to his groove. Kylen focused his inner eye and forced himself to relax. It was always like this, a psychedelic trip down some stranger's yellow brick road. There was usually light and color, and sometimes a scent. But Xochi's inner world was completely different.

Instead of a dreamy swim in her subconscious, Kylen found himself smack in the middle of a detailed allegorical dream. Well, okay, then. The music took care of itself, eating up the images as if they were pure energy. The crowd was perking up. Giving in, he turned his attention back to Xochi's dream space.

Ky is high in the trees, looking down. He grips a branch with his toes, which are not his toes at all, but the rough clawed feet of some other animal.

He shakes—no, he flaps.

A jet-black feather drifts down from his perch into the little green palm of the weirdest kid he's ever seen. A second kid creeps through the underbrush, this one dark brown with hair as black as Kylen's current feathers.

Under a massive fir, there's a trickle of steaming water dripping down some rocks into a large golden bathtub.

*Kylen blinks at the incongruous image as the tub becomes a
steaming pool.*

*The two weird kids are shivering, palpably cold, but the taller
one stops short of the water's edge. Little Green crashes into his
back.*

*He demonstrates the proper technique, submerging each limb
slowly, watching her closely to make sure she does the same.*

The green girl trembles as she enters the murky water.

*Acrid steam fills Kylen's nose with a rotten-egg mineral funk,
but discomfort becomes pleasure as the girl sinks deeper into the
water.*

HIS EYES JERKED OPEN. How long had they been closed? He
checked the music. The band was pushing toward the bridge
of the second song. Heat seeped from his belly to his fingers
as he refocused on the crowd. When his eyes landed on Xochi
again, he almost missed a beat.

She was wearing the same jeans Bubbles had tarted up into
shorts, the same similarly tricked-out wifebeater, but a few
minutes ago, she'd just been a moderately attractive girl who
needed some sleep.

But no more. Uninhibited and sexy, infused with fresh heat,
Xochi was a kick-ass song, a whiskey shot, a treasure map.
Kylen would bet his stand-up bass that her mid-song trans-
formation had everything to do with those weird kids in their
creepy forest. There was no doubt about it: those fey little long-
hairs were pulling Xochi's strings. Worry clenched Kylen's
muscles, speeding up his groove.

This was exactly the kind of trouble that loved to follow
Kylen around. He'd been born this way: queer as fuck and just
as uncanny. Over the years, he'd found his mantra: just say no.
Now he wasn't even tempted by other people's Ouija-board
after-school-special dramatics.

But damn, you had to hand it to the governess. All this time,
she'd passed herself off as grade B trouble—just your basic

ingénue in the right place at the right time to mess with Leviticus's head. Lev had been clean almost three years now. He'd kept it fast and loose with the chicks and a few choice guys— but not a single drop of drama. He was writing songs, surfing, healthy, happy and taking care of business. What should've been nothing but a bump in the road, a mere distraction, was looking more like a big-ass, road-blocking, steaming pile of crap.

The Queen of Cups. The Tower. The Lovers.

Sometimes, it really sucked being right.

19

Freeze Tag

Xochi leaned against the wall in the alley behind the club. The cool air was delicious against her sweaty skin, and the stars shone brighter than she thought possible through the veil of city lights. What Bubbles had said about not having to hide wasn't like hide-and-seek with everything normal once you stepped back into the light. It was more like an old drawing fading in reverse, the disappeared lines turning slowly back to black.

The stage door opened.

"Hey," Leviticus said.

"How's it going?"

"Great." He came over and leaned against the wall with her, following her gaze to the stars.

"That was pretty great," she said. "'Sweet Little Angel' is one of my favorites."

"Yeah," he said. "Me too."

The silence in the alley was comfortable, the concrete wall cool against Xochi's back.

"Sorry I lied about my age."

"No," he said, "I get it. People either try to take care of you or they take advantage. Pretending to be older is a good strategy."

Xochi glanced sideways. "You sound like you know from experience."

His eyes were on the sky. He closed them, a gesture she was coming to know. A sign he was thinking before he spoke.

"My dad—well, eventually he kicked me out of the house. I hooked up with a bunch of street kids. If you got caught, the cops sent you home—unless the people at home wouldn't take you back. There was no way I was doing a foster home. I stopped hanging around people my age, said I was older. Being a kid is overrated."

"My mom grew up in foster homes, but she always ran away. She said she was like Houdini, great at escaping but bad at not getting caught. Every time they found her, they put her someplace worse."

"Where is she now?"

"I don't know. She took off when I was eleven. Guess old habits are hard to break."

"Yeah." He reached for Xochi's hand, but as his calloused fingers touched her palm, the stage door swung open.

A woman in tight jeans, tall boots and a gangsterish fedora strode into the alley. She carried a violin case and set it on the ground so she could hug Leviticus with both arms.

"Hey, stranger," she said, her pouty lips in sexy contrast with her other features, which were strong, almost masculine. She wasn't conventionally pretty, but Xochi couldn't stop staring.

"Hey," Leviticus said, obviously happy to see her. "I thought you were in New York."

"I'm on my way to LA to record with these fools." She shrugged toward the club. "You should come down, too."

"That's what everyone keeps telling me. Are you sitting in for the second set?"

"If you want me." She took off her fedora, releasing a mane of dark hair, and put the hat on Leviticus, stepping back to appreciate the effect. Xochi felt like she'd been shoved a few feet off the ground and pinned to the wall behind her.

Leviticus put the hat back on the woman's head. "This is Xochi," he said. "Xochi, this is Andi."

"Hey. I heard about you inside. Pallas's nanny, right?" Xochi didn't bother to correct her. "I think Dylan's in love."

"Dylan's an asshole," Leviticus said. "I mean, he's an old friend, but I wouldn't wish him on my worst enemy."

"Yeah," Andi said, picking up her violin, "but figuring that out yourself is half the fun." She threw a conspiratorial smile at Xochi and headed inside. Leviticus hesitated in the doorway.

"You coming?" His voice was off, a half-note sour. He shifted his weight from boot to boot.

"I'm gonna stay out here for a while," Xochi said.

"Are you cold?" Leviticus unbuttoned his faded flannel, ready to keep her warm again, and there it was—Coll's Led Zeppelin shirt. It fit him loosely, the way it had fit Collier before he started playing football in tenth grade.

"You're wearing my shirt."

"Yeah. I guess I am."

"Be careful with it. It was a gift."

"I will." Leviticus leaned toward her like he was going to say more, but he didn't. The door closed behind him.

20

The Teardrop Collector

Xochi forced herself to go back through the stage door. The band was tuning up. Perfect. The dressing room would be empty. She'd rescue her jacket and stash it with Pad, put some money in her shorts pocket, and get Aaron to buy her a real drink. She'd find Bubbles and dance, not caring how gorgeous Andi looked onstage.

Xochi recognized Dylan in the haze of smoke in the dressing room. He was leaning over a mirror, chopping up some white powder with a razor blade. He snorted it and stood up. She hadn't realized how tall he was.

"Hey," he said, "want a line?"

Why wasn't he onstage? "Aren't you late?" Xochi said. *He's so tall*, she thought, but she'd already noticed that. His cherry Kool-Aid hair fell over hazel eyes and a boyish mouth. There was a buzz of something between them, but when Xochi stepped back an inch, the feeling dissipated.

"I'm not on till the third song." He came closer. There it was again, heat rising, a pull below the navel. *Shoo, fly.*

"I left my jacket in here."

He stepped in her path—playful, not threatening, but Xochi felt the power of his size, his belonging. Dylan picked up her jacket and dangled it out of reach, a bully move disguised as flirtation. Or was it the other way around?

"Trade for a kiss?"

Xochi blinked. Behind her lids, the bathtub from her dream bubbled. The image blurred, replaced by Leviticus following Andi's twitching behind back into the club. It was the way of the world: her mother's way. She'd seen Gina do it a hundred times. A surge of heat rose from her belly to her chest. The golden bathtub simmered. *Like mother, like daughter?*

She tilted her head the way Gina would, came a few feet closer. He held her jacket higher. Standing on tiptoe, Xochi planted a kiss on his cheek. It was that easy. Properly confused, he lowered his hand and Xochi pulled her jacket gently from his grip. Was this what Gina meant by getting flies with honey?

She'd planned to walk past him, go back into the club, and find a way to get quickly drunk, but his hand was on the small of her back and he was pulling her close. His mouth tasted like beer and weed. The kiss was loose and rambling. Xochi felt herself respond to his hands on her hips, the hardness under his jeans, unwanted but also hot.

A sound registered behind her. She knew what it was before she turned around.

"Hey, babe," Dylan said to Bubbles, his hand on Xochi's ass. "Gotta go," he said to Xochi. Before he reached the door, Bubbles was gone.

XOCHI STOOD OPENMOUTHED. MEMORY hovered, wingbeats stirring images she wanted to stomp and squash and kill: a different tall man, a different unwanted kiss. Desire, betrayal. Too familiar. "Shit!" She said it out loud instead of crying. "Shit, shit, shit!"

There was her jacket, in the corner. She picked it up and put it on. She needed to find Bubbles, but what would she say? Her feet were glued to the floor. She gripped her stomach, a useless gesture. The pain was old, a tattoo inked with poison. She tried to breathe—five counts in, six counts out—but her body was going into lockdown. Pure shame. So this was what it felt like. No wonder Gina never called, never wrote. How did you face such a colossal mistake? Where did you even start?

Xochi scanned the room for her abandoned body. Her eyes found the mirror with its neatly chopped line. She picked up the straw. White powder, speed or cocaine. Gina had done it once in a while with a friend from her foster care days. They'd lock themselves in the bathroom and come out pin eyed and sniffing. Once, Xochi caught them when they thought she was asleep—the mirror, the razor blade, the powder. Dylan's mirror was right in front of her. She looked down at her white-dusted, distorted face.

She aimed the straw and sniffed, gagging at the chemical reek. The effect was instant, a bitter blast of awakeness. Xochi's sinuses burned and her eyes felt huge in her head, but she could think again. She could move. She left the dressing room to find Bubbles and the "fuck you" she so richly deserved.

"Hey." The doorman put a hand on Xochi's arm.

Shit. Her blood raced with drugs and adrenaline.

"Bubbles is outside."

On the street, Xochi felt fully awake for the first time all day. And there was Bubbles, coming out of the liquor store.

"Come on," Bubbles called. She headed around the corner, away from the club. Aaron's van was parked at the end of the block. They walked in silence. Bubbles unlocked the van and climbed inside, motioning Xochi to the passenger seat. She yanked the paper bag from her bottle of Jack Daniels and pulled out a pack of cigarettes. "Time for girl talk."

Xochi accepted the bottle. Drinking didn't seem optional. She took a series of tentative sips. A cop car passed, siren flashing red but silent.

"Xochi? I shouldn't have to be the one who starts."

"I'm sorry." Xochi's hand shook as she passed the bottle back to Bubbles. "I don't want to make excuses, but they're all I've got."

"Oh boy." Bubbles took a swig of whiskey and lit a cigarette.

"Dude. You don't have to apologize. I'm not asking for that. You get to sleep with whoever the hell you want."

"Bubbles, I wasn't—I wouldn't do that." *You would,* said a voice in Xochi's head. *You have.* "He was flirting, and then he kissed me. I don't know why I let him."

"He's a good kisser, that's why. Kinda all over the place, but it works somehow. And his dick is huge."

"Bubbles!" Xochi grabbed a cigarette, even though she didn't smoke.

"Come on—you must have noticed. He's like zero to boner in three seconds. Unfortunately, that's about how long he lasts. It comes right back, though. Not bad for an old man."

"Old?" Xochi tried to remember his face, but all she could think about now was the hard-on pressing against her stomach.

"Pushing forty. Maturity-wise, he's about fourteen. The music thing is all he's got going for him. That and his dick."

Was it official? Did she have some sort of fetish for older men? Cigarettes usually made Xochi dizzy, but this one calmed her down. She accepted the bottle and took a small sip, then a big gulp. Too sweet, but the burn was good.

"Just to be clear"—Xochi rolled down the window so she could ash—"are we still talking about Dylan's penis?"

"It was the icebreaker." Bubbles took the bottle back and screwed the cap on tight. "We're here to talk about our feelings, sweetie."

"Okay," Xochi said. "I think I get it. What happened was weird, so we're doing this instead of you breaking my face?"

"Right. Which is easier said than done. But it's the only way."

"So . . . ?"

"So?"

Bubbles wasn't going to make this easy. Xochi took a drag from her cigarette. She touched the whiskey bottle on the dash, peeling at its label, and started again.

"So. Bubbles, how did you feel when you walked into the

dressing room and found me making out with your ex-boy-friend?" Xochi's stomach twisted as she said it.

"Good girl. Now you're owning it." Bubbles grabbed the bottle, unscrewed the lid, took a long drink. "I'm closing this now," she said, managing it after the third try. "To answer your excellent question, I was jealous. I don't want to be jealous. Not about Dylan—the guy's a joke. I know that. At least my brain does. So then I felt stupid. Because, when you think about it, it's kind of awesome. I mean, Dylan is a great beginner boy toy, so on that level, he's perfect for you. Because Xochi? I really, really think you need to get laid."

They both laughed. Bubbles snorted.

"I really do," Xochi said. "But not Dylan! He doesn't deserve either of us."

"We gotta drink to that! Just one more."

They drank. A bus jolted past. Rain fell softly on the wind-shield. A couple walked by, holding hands.

"Xochi?" Bubbles's voice was suddenly serious. "You know I've slept with Leviticus, right?"

Xochi's ears filled with static. Bubbles's voice was so gen-tle, her eyes so kind. Xochi wanted to rewind, to unhear her words, make her unsay them, but there was no going back.

"I'm so sorry, sweetie," Bubbles said. She scooted to the edge of the driver's seat and straddled the gear shift, pushing in next to Xochi in the passenger seat. She leaned her head on Xochi's shoulder.

"Of course you're smitten," Bubbles said. "Who wouldn't be?"

"Are you?"

"With Lev? Oh, sweetie, no. Not now. We don't have that spark. I wish we did. He really is a prince. Not like the guys I usually fall for."

"I feel like an idiot. I don't know why I'm so freaked out."

"Because it's confusing, that's why. It's impossible to know who's got history with who. Beyond Pallas as evidence of Io and Lev, it's anybody's guess—I remember what it was like when I first moved in. I'm so sorry for springing it on you like this. I just didn't want you to find out some other way and feel like I was keeping secrets."

"Thanks," Xochi said. "I'm sorry. I know this is stupid. I didn't mean to be such a cliché."

"Don't do that to yourself. It's not just you, I saw Lev out there. You made him mess up a few times. Ky was pissed. But you guys are star-crossed for sure. Leviticus has a thing about age, a strict policy. I barely made it through myself."

Xochi nodded. He *had* been looking at her during the show. And, policy or not, if Andi hadn't come out, what would have happened?

"Can I bum another cigarette?" Xochi was enjoying smoking like never before.

"In a minute." Bubbles shoved Xochi over with her hip. "Scoot! I'm falling off." Xochi scooted until the door handle dug into her side. Bubbles took her hand. "Are we okay?"

Bubbles looked soft-focus in the yellow streetlight, her hair the palest apricot, her skin a finer satin than her coat. Xochi leaned in and kissed her. It was a long kiss, a little world. Bubbles tasted like whiskey and smelled divine. Earlier with Dylan, Xochi hadn't noticed her new piercing. Now the skin around it was sensitive and each movement of Bubbles's tongue produced a ticklish little sting. In accord, they stopped and laughed.

"Now we can smoke," Bubbles said. She grabbed the back of the driver's seat for balance as she bounced back over the gear shift. She lit two cigarettes at once, handing one to Xochi.

They smoked in peace, listening to the rain on the bus's roof.

"Even besides the age thing," Xochi said, "there's Pallas."

"Ugh." Bubbles shivered. "You're right. I didn't think of that. I should have." She pursed her lips and sent a smoke ring out the window to meet the rain.

"Bubbles?" Xochi asked. "Is it weird that I kissed you?"

"Not at all," Bubbles said. "It was lovely."

21

The Whole of the Moon

Peasblossom had been uneasy all day. After a dinner of brown rice and tuna and a nice romp with Anna before the girl went to sleep, Peasblossom was restless.

He found Nora curled in a bed with a book, as usual. Reading impaired her hearing almost completely, so he didn't bother meowing. He placed a velvet paw on her cheek.

"What is it, Your Highness?" As a rule, novels made Nora uncooperative, while poetry made her dreamy and unproductive. Nonfiction was easiest to manage, depending on the time of day and how much coffee she'd consumed.

He leaped from the bed to her night table and nosed a small heart-shaped box.

"Now?" Nora asked.

Peasblossom meowed assent.

Once, after a breakup, Nora had thrown the three I Ching coins obsessively for an entire afternoon until Peasblossom finally pounced, stilling them with a frustrated paw. For the first time since the substandard boyfriend had departed, Nora laughed. She threw the pennies five more times, urging Peas to stop them, and read his fortune from her dog-eared *Book of Changes*. It had been remarkably apt. Now, once or twice a year, the cat asked Nora to consult the oracle again on his behalf.

Nora sighed and got out of bed to retrieve the notebook she kept for this sort of divination.

Peasblossom formulated a question in his mind: *What action, if any, should I take to protect Pallas and her governess from the Waterbabies?*

Nora threw the coins. The cat stopped them six times. She recorded the resulting lines and found the hexagram in the index. As with most I Ching readings, there was an initial text representing the recent past or present and a second text related to the future.

Meditation was first. As usual, the hexagram neatly summed up the cat's current state—resting, attempting to regulate his worry and formulate a sensible plan for moving forward. The changing line in the first reading formed the second hexagram.

"Your hexagram is called *Grace*," Nora said. She read, brow furrowed. "'A situation of perfect balance requiring an exquisite sense of timing. Follow established protocols to embrace a fleeting moment of shimmering Grace.' Does that mean anything to you?"

The words buried themselves deep in his mind, jackknifing into a starlit pool. Nora read the full text of the hexagram, but Peasblossom was already formulating a plan.

His destination wasn't far, but his bones still ached from the earlier trek to North Beach. He looked at the clock on Nora's dresser. Muni ran to the Avenues until midnight. There was time, if Peasblossom hurried. Headbutting Nora's thigh in farewell, the cat leaped off the bed and down the hall, through the cat flap, and into the dark street.

The bus pulled up just as Peasblossom reached the corner. The cat entered at the back door as other passengers exited. He sat under a seat and counted stops. At 40th, he disembarked. He'd only visited the Moonlit Garden once in his youth, but the fierce gatekeepers hadn't allowed him to enter. Peasblossom had always been more of a thinker than a fighter.

At the end of the block, Peasblossom found the small Spanish bungalow, owned by a famous sculptor, and approached the storied garden and its legendary occupant with a confidence he didn't feel.

"Ssstop!" hissed the guards when Peasblossom reached the gate. The cats were the same two he remembered, bulky tuxedos, both female, with immaculate white bibs and hard green eyes.

"I'm here to see Moonlight," Peasblossom said.

"Fuck off," hissed the larger guard. She was the older of the two, possibly the mother of the slightly smaller cat. Peasblossom bowed, using the gesture to pull the scent of the cats to the roof of his mouth. He tasted their relation, letting their mock-orange-and-eucalyptus musk settle. He recalled the I Ching's advice. He tucked his paws politely, slitting his eyes.

"Please tell your mother I mean no harm," Peasblossom said to the younger cat. "I seek wisdom only. I will abide by any condition you set."

The daughter crouched, hips swaying in time with her twitching tail. Peasblossom bowed his head, accepting the oncoming attack. Before he could blink, she had him on his back, her teeth in the loose skin at his neck—a holding bite, not meant to puncture.

"You stink of death!" her mother hissed.

Peasblossom regretted the fish he'd eaten for dinner. "I apologize. The food was tinned, an offering from my human. I am not a hunter," he said. "In fact, beyond insects encroaching on my home, I have never killed."

It was true, not even a single mouse. Nora and Anna had devised a method of trap and release that relieved Peasblossom from that unpleasantness.

The daughter released him. He stayed prone, allowing the tuxedos to sniff him thoroughly. They circled, tails whipping the air.

"Get up," the matriarch growled. "What's your name?"

"Peasblossom." He hoped his human-given name sufficed. These cats were clearly human fed, but it was a hotly political matter whether cats named themselves or took the name they were given.

"I am Gog," the older cat said, her tone approaching politeness. "This is Magog, my daughter."

Peasblossom bowed again.

"What is your business with Moonlight?" Magog asked. "She is very old and only responds to queries that interest her."

"My question concerns two creatures recently summoned to the city. Ancient child-sized beings with claylike skin and flowing hair."

Gog and Magog exchanged a meaningful glance. "Follow me," Magog said, pushing open the wooden gate.

Inside was another land, so lush it exuded its own tropical climate. Interspersed among the absurdist large-leaved plants were odd, plantlike sculptures—long, thin women with mushroom skirts, hooded monks with pussy-willow legs, mantises with feathered hats. Stones were stacked in pyramids, and bowling balls were stacked like stones in large, colorful mounds. The foliage was so thickly planted, it was impossible to see the garden's perimeter or guess its shape and size.

Magog's trot was graceful, even a bit provocative. She glanced over her shoulder, friendlier away from her mother's gaze. The path spiraled to the center of the garden, opening onto a pond covered in night-blooming lilies. Orange bodies flickered under the green-black surface. Peasblossom looked around in the dark for Magog, but found only her eyes glowing from the foliage.

He approached the pool and stepped gingerly to its edge. He began to purr, a peaceful drone. The sky was cloudy, the night so quiet Peasblossom heard the hiss of the sea only a few blocks west. Time stretched until Peasblossom did not know how to mark its passing, his purring song cresting and falling with the waves. Slowly, the lilies in the pond receded like ladies-in-waiting arranging themselves to receive their queen.

The water began to move, a wisp of smoke in the pond's

black depths growing brighter. A reflection shone on the water's surface. Peasblossom raised his nose to the sky, expecting to see the moon, but the light was coming from the pond itself. Now the cat understood how the venerable koi had gotten her name.

Moonlight swam to the surface a few feet away, her scales an armor of pearls. She was the largest fish Peasblossom had ever encountered, easily twice his size.

"You must go in to meet her," whispered Magog, suddenly at Peasblossom's side. She touched the water's surface with her paw. A large flat stone sat an inch below the water. He could sit there safely without having to swim, but true to stereotype, he detested water.

Magog's unflinching gaze made retreat impossible. Peasblossom stepped onto the stone. Its surface was unpleasantly slick. He walked slowly, hoping to convey dignity rather than disgust.

The magnificent koi swam closer, breaching the surface with her blunt snout. Peasblossom leaned down to touch her nose with his own. A cool wave of greeting swam up the cat's spine. He sat up, doing his best to keep his tail tip dry. "Shall I ask my question?" He turned to Magog. Her eyes were polished jade.

"You just did," Magog said. "She is over a hundred years old, but today she is surprised. See how her whiskers twitch?"

The koi's fine whiskers, as long as a cat's, undulated just under the water's surface. Peasblossom restrained an inappropriate urge to pounce. *Nerves*, he thought. He waited, unsure how to proceed.

"You have to put your whiskers in to touch hers," Magog said, her tone almost apologetic. The suggestion brought instant nausea. Wet paws were abhorrent but bearable. Bodily submersion, barbaric. But having one's whiskers underwater? Peasblossom wanted to gag. The koi swished her tail fin slowly, a polite invitation.

Magog laughed, joining him on the stone, seemingly

unconcerned about the wetness of her paws. "I know, it's unnatural as hell, but that's how it works." She headbutted Peasblossom. For a moment, they stood nose to nose. She batted her come-hither eyes. Effective, though Peasblossom doubted her sincerity. He'd always had better luck impressing human females than he ever had with his own kind.

He lowered his head to the pond. He'd intended to be quick, to get it over with, but the only way he could stand the sensation was to move very, very slowly. Each centimeter was like the sound of metal on metal. His teeth hurt. His skin hurt. He closed his eyes.

Suddenly, contact! The koi's mind operated at a speed that was either incredibly slow or unimaginably fast, nonlinear and electric.

Cedar and Sulfur
The creatures, the bath
Fog, ravens
Motorcycles, moonlight
Forest and asphalt, water and fire
Pallas and Xochi, the creatures, the fog
The Hag, her warnings
A woman weeping
A woman, a man
A steaming hot spring
A golden tub
The beach, a bonfire
A bonfire, a bridge
Seals bobbing in night-blacked water
Long-haired children swimming the bay
A man in the water breathing like a fish
A man in the eye of a whirlpool
A man facedown in a shallow creek
A woman with golden hair and Xochi's face
Tears streaming from her eyes

A comb and a hand, golden hair
A comb dripping with honey
The moon crying honeyed tears
The silver moon reflected on water
The moonlight scales of the koi

PEASBLOSSOM SAT UPRIGHT, WHISKERS dripping. The pond was covered in lilies once more, obscuring the fish below.

He looked for Magog, but she was gone.

22

Farewell, Angelina

Xochi woke to an empty attic and quiet house. She trudged down to the kitchen. Her throat was raw from smoking, her head poorly attached—the work of some cut-rate Dr. Frankenstein. Each movement loosened the bolts.

She drank a glass of water and took out her favorite mug. There was coffee in the pot. There was always coffee; Leviticus made sure of it. A pink pastry box on the kitchen table propped up a piece of Hello Kitty stationery. Xochi picked it up, squinting at Pallas's loopy fountain pen cursive.

Hi, Xochi,

Kiki wanted a road trip, so we're driving Leviticus to LA. Be back in a few days!

XOXO
Pallas

P.S. Here are some cream puffs to tide you over, since you can never find the place without me. Have fun & don't do anything I wouldn't do. —P.

LA? Leviticus must have decided to help out Rabbit Hole after all. Xochi recalled Andi's voice, sexy and low, when she'd answered Leviticus's invitation to sit in. Ugh. And the thing with her hat? Who acted like that in real life?

Xochi added cream to her coffee and read the note again. Boots pounded up the basement steps. The door opened. Leviticus.

"I thought you were gone." Xochi looked down at her thin slip and bare toes with their chipped black polish.

"We thought you were asleep." Leviticus set a half-full duffel on the kitchen table. "Where'd you end up last night?"

"Bubbles and Aaron took me to The Stud. Now I have a hangover and possibly whiplash."

"Hold on." Leviticus rummaged in a cabinet above the sink. "Where are Pallas and Kiki?"

"Getting the car washed. I'm waiting for my laundry." He pulled a small brown bottle from the shelf. "Dandelion root. Tastes like death, but it'll save you from that hangover. It cleanses your liver. You can dilute it in some water if you want."

"My grandma made her own medicines," Xochi said. "This can't be worse than her goldenseal and eyebright. Give it to me straight."

Xochi dropped the green-brown liquid onto her tongue. *Plant blood.* That's what Loretta called her tinctures. This one was intense, with a spicy bitter tang that vibrated against Xochi's piercing like an electric toothbrush.

"Your grandma sounds interesting." Leviticus poured himself a cup of coffee and sat across from Xochi.

"She died in September. I miss her a lot."

"They say the veil thins on Solstice and Equinox."

"Yeah," Xochi said. "I don't know if I'll ever get used to her being gone."

"I'm sorry," Leviticus said. "Was she sick?"

Xochi nodded. "I'm just glad we got to keep her at home. She died where she lived." She closed her eyes against a swell of tears. Behind her lids, the children from her dreams waited. The green girl and her brother were always with Xochi now, awake or asleep. She wasn't sure what was causing the dreams, but they felt like a story she needed to tell herself. If she could just close her eyes for long enough, she'd get to the end.

"You okay?" Leviticus leaned in toward her. His expression was kind, his eyes a little sad.

Xochi imagined going to him, settling into his lap, but she couldn't even fantasize without seeing what came next: Pallas walking in, the look on her face. She shivered. Just thinking about it was a betrayal.

"So when you say *we*," Leviticus said, "*we* kept her home—who are you talking about?"

"Me, mostly. Me and her grandson—my mom's ex. The neighbors brought food and everybody pitched in, but she was sickest coming up on harvest, so it was tough."

"Harvest?"

"I'm from Humboldt, remember?"

"So you were raised by pot growers?"

"I didn't tell you that?"

He smiled. "No, you didn't. You haven't told us much, actually."

"Oh, well, I was. We all lived in cabins on this big property. I lived with Loretta. She wasn't my real grandma, she was Evan's—my mom's boyfriend. She kind of adopted me when my mom left."

Xochi thought of the day Loretta signed a school paper and wrote "grandmother" underneath. It must have been pretty soon after Xochi's mother bailed. With one hastily written word, Loretta had let Xochi know she still had someone to belong to. Later, people forgot they weren't blood related.

"How long was she sick?" Leviticus asked.

Xochi blinked. "Not quite a year."

"So all of—what? Your junior year?"

High school. It hovered in the air between them. But the truth was, if Loretta hadn't died and everything hadn't gone to shit, Xochi would be in high school right now.

"Yeah. They let me study from home for the most part. I just went in for tests."

He nodded. The dryer buzzed from the basement. "Can you hold on a minute? I have something for you."

Xochi rested her head on the table, the wood cool against her cheek. She closed her eyes, eager to see the forest children, but there was just the old version of her, a girl who no longer existed. A girl slogging through the hardest day of her life.

It was hot for September the day Loretta died. The fans were whirring. Xochi stood in the sweet spot between two of them, savoring the cool wind on her face and neck.

Suddenly, the fans stopped. A humming started—not the fans, but from the garden. Bees.

The light shimmered, turned gold. The breeze through the open window smelled like rain. Something made Xochi turn to Loretta's bed. She'd been unconscious for two days now, her face tight with pain even though they were medicating her every three hours. But now, her body was relaxed, her face unlined and smiling. Her fingers curled in the air as if there were someone on either side of the bed holding her hands. Xochi blinked once, twice, three times. The stone on the necklace at Loretta's throat glowed from within, a tiny sun. She sighed, all the remaining pain draining from her face.

Xochi opened her eyes.

A memory, not a dream. Seconds later, the girl she used to be had bolted from Loretta's room to cry in the garden. Evan had found her there. What happened next left her with less than nothing.

A HAND BRUSHED XOCHI'S back, there and gone. "Were you sleeping?" Leviticus asked.

"Just resting," she said.

"Here's your shirt." He produced Coll's Zeppelin tee, warm from the dryer. Xochi stopped herself from putting it against her face. "And this." Leviticus handed her a cassette case. "I wanted to get you a new one, but Rasputin's didn't have it. I duped mine downstairs on the good deck, so the sound should be okay."

A title was written on the spine of the case in spidery black: *Wings of Desire*. Xochi pressed the tape to her heart. "Does it have the Nick Cave carny song?" She scanned the track list. "And that other band, the song about the bells when she's dancing in the club—"

"Crime and the City Solution. It's all there." Leviticus grinned. Xochi grinned back.

A horn blared. He shoved clothes into his duffel.

Xochi looked out the kitchen window. "Is that Kiki honking? I don't see her."

"She's out front. She won't come around back to get me because her precious car will get dusty. She has rules for road trips that she's trained us to obey."

The front door opened and slammed shut.

"Leviticus? For fuck's sake!" Kiki was a perfect fifties movie star with her trench coat, headscarf, and big white sunglasses.

"Sorry," he said. "I'm ready."

"Is Pal in the car?" Xochi asked.

"She's nesting. She likes things just so in the back seat."

"I'd go down and say goodbye, but I'm not exactly dressed," Xochi said. "Bubbles wrecked me last night. Will you tell her I'm going to miss her?"

"I will. Come on, then," Kiki said. "Hugs!" She opened her arms to Xochi. She was an expert hugger, firm and unrushed.

"You smell . . . glamorous," Xochi said.

"Chanel No. 5, always and forever." Kiki turned to Leviticus. "Go on." She gestured. "Hug Xochi goodbye and let's get a move on!"

Xochi stepped into Leviticus's arms. "Thanks for the tape," she said.

He held her lightly, hand on the back of her head, a quick squeeze to her neck right where it hurt from dancing. "Take it easy," he said, and followed Kiki out the door.

23

California Dreamin'

Pallas yawned. The back seat of Kiki's convertible was as comfortable as a bed and wide enough for her to sprawl out. She kicked off her cowgirl boots and pulled the blanket over her shoulders.

When they'd decided to take a road trip at breakfast that morning, all she'd thought to bring was a change of clothes and her cat hat, but when Pallas climbed into the back seat, she found pillows, her favorite quilt, and her train case packed with a toothbrush, pajamas, knitting needles and yarn. Leviticus had also grabbed the book from her nightstand, *The Fellowship of the Ring*, but she and Xochi were reading it together and had made a pact: *no reading ahead.*

"Is she asleep already?" Kiki asked. "I guess Eve still has the power."

Eve was Kiki's shiny white car. She was big, old and curvy, with a red interior and leopard floor mats. On road trips, Kiki always wore a scarf over her hair and white cat-eye sunglasses so she and Eve would match.

"Remember the fascist fours?" Leviticus was referring to a time where the family had compared Pallas to various world dictators. "I wonder how many miles we clocked getting her to sleep."

Cool air tickled Pallas's nose as Kiki opened the window a few inches and lit a cigarette. They had a rule about never smoking in front of her, but most of them smoked marijuana or cigarettes behind her back.

"So?" Kiki said, like it meant something.

"So?" Leviticus said back. The car lighter popped again, followed by a deep inhale. Her dad was smoking, too. Hypocrite!

"All of a sudden, we're off to LA."

"Dylan asked me."

"He asked six months ago, and you said no."

"Andi's in town."

Pallas knew Andi. She played the fiddle and had great hair. She and Leviticus used to date when Pallas was little and Andi lived in San Francisco. It was the year Pallas had gone to first grade before deciding to homeschool. Most of her classmates had small families and parents who didn't date other people unless they were divorced. When she discovered divorced people usually didn't get along and lived in separate houses, she took the matter up with Io.

"Your dad and I aren't divorced, Pallina," Io said. "You have to be married to get a divorce."

"Why aren't you married?" Pallas stopped walking so she could focus on Io's answer.

"Some people want to be part of a pair." Io crouched down so the hem of her long skirt billowed around her clunky boots and Pallas's shiny Mary Janes. "They feel best when they give their love to one other person, like a husband or a wife. Some people want to be singular, but love many people in lots of different ways. Some people don't want a lover at all and like being alone. There's no one right way to do love."

Pallas flashed back to her mother in the mirror the night of Equinox, a memory she'd been avoiding. Io had been more fun recently, laughing a lot, wearing yellow. What if whatever she'd been doing with James was another way to love? A strange way. Completely gross. But still.

"Andi?" Kiki sounded surprised. "I thought that ship sailed."

"I don't know," Leviticus said. "It just feels like a good time to get out of town. Isn't that why you jumped at the chance to drive me?"

"It was that or murder Pad. He sabotaged my date last night, the shit."

Pallas was there when Pad had messed up Kiki's date with the Rabbit Hole drummer. He'd called to arrange things with Kiki, but Pad had answered the phone. "Right," Pad had said, sounding sincere, "I'll make sure she gets the message." Of course, he'd done nothing of the kind.

"I think you like that drummer about as much as I like Andi," Leviticus said.

"Yeah. But what am I supposed to do? Pad and I don't want the same things. We're not getting any younger, you know. Unlike *some* people."

What did *that* mean? Pallas rolled over again. She hoped Kiki and Pad would figure things out soon. Part of the problem was that Kiki wanted to have a baby and thought Pad would be a terrible father. Still, Pallas could picture their kids perfectly: two boys and a girl with Pad's Siamese-cat eyes and Kiki's doe-brown skin, too cute to remain unborn.

"Did you actually make her a mix?" Kiki said it like it was a joke.

"No," Leviticus said in a tone that invited no further questions. They were quiet again, puffing on their cigarettes like a pair of old men. "It was a soundtrack," he said.

Kiki giggled. Pallas almost giggled herself, the sound was so contagious. Her dad joined in. Pallas closed her eyes, listening to the familiar sound of their laughter as California slid by under Eve's wide wheels.

The front seat was silent for several minutes. Pallas was almost asleep when her dad spoke again. "I'm not sure why I'm freaking out."

"Did you talk to Io?"

"Nothing to discuss." Leviticus took a drag from his

cigarette. Had he never heard of lung cancer? "This is about me, not anyone else."

"Love isn't always about the beloved?"

"And my knight-in-shining-armor complex is never really about the fair maiden. I know that. I do. I thought I'd learned my lesson."

"But sometimes the maiden is exceptionally fair . . ."

"It's not that. I can handle fair. It's more this visceral . . . identification. It's the only word I can think of that comes close. But then I'm just romanticizing, making things all cosmic and fated to excuse a lame transgression."

"One person's transgression is another's transcendence," Kiki said. "I mean, I agree it's a bad idea. Mostly for the innocent maiden. You *are* a handful. But you shouldn't be so hard on yourself. You're almost twenty-nine. It's your Saturn return, right on schedule. Unfinished business coming back to haunt you. I'm sure that's part of it for Pad and me, too." Kiki paused to take a long drag. "I wouldn't be young again for anything, but when I think about Bubbles wallowing in her early twenties decadence, I'm so jealous. I don't know if I'm ready to grow up."

They were quiet again. Pallas turned over, her back to the front seat.

Someone turned on the radio. An old song played, something from the sixties that Lady Frieda used to cover. Pallas started to drift off with the high harmony. Kiki and Leviticus were talking again up front, but she couldn't hear what they were saying.

The song changed, another oldie. It lulled her to sleep and became part of her dream.

It was the children again, the odd fairy mer-things she'd been dreaming about all week. This time they were swimming, their wonderful hair spreading through the water like octopus ink. The high, clear voice on the radio sang about bridges and water and silver girls, and Pallas was swimming and then she was flying, her hair a silver sail through a moonlit sky.

24

Wade in the Water

Xochi sat at the window seat, curled under an afghan. The attic echoed without Pallas. She tried to feel the wings Bubbles had made on her shoulder blades, but her back was the same as always—hunched and tight. Loretta used to rub her shoulders while she studied. *Damn, girl,* she'd say. *Somebody needs to lighten up.*

Xochi had always been good at school. Honors in everything. But after Loretta had died, she couldn't bear getting up in the morning, couldn't move her body from class to class. Finally, she just stopped trying.

"Divinity in, crazy out." She said the words out loud, a prescription she wasn't sure how to fill.

She opened the cassette from Leviticus. He'd copied all the song titles and artists carefully on the liner. Next to the cassette was a folded piece of paper. It was brittle and thin, like the stuff she'd used in elementary school to trace maps. A translation of the German poem that ran through *Wings of Desire* was written in the same slanting black mixture of cursive and print on the cassette case. A few lines down, a verse caught her eye.

> *When the child was a child*
> *it didn't know it was a child,*
> *everything was soulful*
> *and all souls were one.*

"Everything was soulful," she repeated. "All souls were one."

EVAN SHOVED HIS SLEEPING bag aside. The cabin was already boiling. He pictured the seedlings frying in the greenhouse. They'd need a deep watering to deal with this bizarre spring heat. Hangover or no, there was no one to do it but him.

Back in the day, tents and buses had filled the meadow every year at harvest. Even off-season, there was always someone around looking to work. Evan's dad was famous for his hospitality and his Badger Creek green, but those days ended when his stepmother, Vangie, died. His dad lost his green thumb, and for the last ten years, he'd been holed up in the big house by the creek, head in a bottle. Even Evan's half brothers stayed away, too busy at Stanford and UCLA to bother coming home, too good to call Evan their brother. And now his grandma was gone, too, killed by the same cancer that had gotten her daughter, his stepmom.

Evan downed a few aspirin and a big glass of water. He yanked on filthy jeans and shoved his feet into socks and hiking boots. He found a T-shirt over a kitchen chair and didn't bother to eat. He did two bong hits—breakfast of champions— stashed three cans of Dr Pepper in his day pack, and he was out the door. A farmer ready to tend his crop.

Outside, music drifted down from his dad's place. Bob Marley. Vangie's favorite. It had played at the wedding and then, sixteen years later, at her funeral—and again in September for Loretta. Evan revved his four-wheeler and headed for the creek. *No Woman, No Cry.* The engine drowned out the soundtrack of his father's sadness, but the music kept on playing in his head.

XOCHI TURNED THE DOLPHIN-SHAPED knobs on Pallas's bathtub until the water was almost scalding. She'd put *Wings of Desire* on repeat, and the poem was playing again. This time, she could pick out some of the words in German.

Als das Kind Kind war. When the child was a child.

She lowered herself into the tub, willing her insides to unwind along with her tight shoulders and back, but when she closed her eyes, she was back in Badger Creek.

When they first moved in, Gina complained about the lack of a bathtub. Evan found an old horse trough and went to work, polishing it to a high shine and setting it up on a stone pedestal over a firepit so Gina could soak in a circle of ancient redwoods under the stars. The last time Xochi had seen it, it had been orange with rust, full of spiderwebs and debris.

She sat up, shook her head, grabbed a washcloth to cover her eyes. With the room shut out, everything was water and music. Xochi slid down so her ears were covered, her hair floating lightly around her head. The tub was so long, her feet barely grazed the end. The water was part of her, a protective skin. She drifted, lapping at the edge of sleep.

RIDING OUT TO THE creek always made Evan feel better. It was green now, but in a month, the meadow would be the exact color of Gina's hair. *Gina again.* Not a day went by when Evan didn't think of her. So beautiful. Beautiful like the babies they should have made, the ones she promised him, the family they'd never have.

He remembered Gina crying, asking why she and Xochi weren't enough. He'd tried to explain so many times. Xochi was already half raised, and besides, she was some other guy's kid. Evan wanted a family he could call his own.

At first, right after Gina ran away, Evan couldn't stand to be in the same room with Xochi. But after a while, he felt sorry for her. He knew what it was like to be abandoned. His own mother had stuck her thumb out one day when he was five and never came back. If his dad hadn't gotten married to Vangie, who knew where he'd be? His stepmom had made him feel wanted right from the start. When Loretta moved onto the property after his twin half brothers were born, she said to call her grandma. Evan loved being part of a big family, being a big brother. That part of his life had been good.

Then Vangie got sick. He'd been out of high school a few years, was working on hybrid plants with his dad. He'd surprised everyone with his knack for nursing. If Vangie had lived, he never would have met Gina. His dad would be okay, his life would be different. As it was, Evan took off the day after Vangie's funeral and didn't come back for almost a year. When he did, he had Gina and Xochi in tow.

Everyone was mad at first—two more mouths to feed, two more people who knew their business. But it was easy for Gina to make people love her. When she left, they all blamed him. But what was he supposed to do? If it hadn't been for the trouble with Gina's IUD, the awful infection, he would have always believed he was damaged goods when she never got pregnant. Being a liar and leaving your man was one thing. But leaving your own kid? Evan gunned the engine over the rise. A woman like that was capable of anything.

Evan braked down the hill and parked the four-wheeler. He stretched, rolling out the kinks in his neck, and unhooked the bungees holding the empty water jugs. He was right where the water's edge should have been when he realized it: Badger Creek was gone.

IT WAS DANGEROUS TO fall asleep in the bath, but Xochi wasn't worried. She could hear *Wings of Desire* like it was spinning on an underwater record player. The poem was playing again, recited over a gorgeous cello line. The words were in German, but Xochi understood.

> *When the child was a child*
> *it walked with its arms swinging,*
> *wanted the brook to be a river,*
> *the river to be a torrent,*
> *and this puddle to be the sea.*

EVAN FOLLOWED THE DRY creek bed to a clearing where a heap of boulders and logs were piled into a neat dam. Bile rose in his throat. The hijacked creek had collected into a small lake, wider and deeper than should have been possible, given what he knew about his land.

He tried to walk the pool's perimeter. Trees parted before him and the water seemed to move away, manipulated by some invisible force that could subtract a redwood or stretch a pool into a lake at will.

Evan's stomach cramped. He could smell his own sweat, a beacon shouting his fear to the world. The morning was growing hotter. The cool blue beckoned. Evan licked his dry lips and tasted blood.

He walked to the water's edge and knelt to touch the tantalizing blue, but the air above the pool was thick and impassible. The heat became unbearable. He sat down in the dirt and took off his boots and socks, peeled off his shirt. On his knees again, he knew something formal was required to enter the lake. "Please." His own hoarse whisper echoed in his ears. The water was so bright, it seemed to sing. A cool breeze blew toward him, stopping short of his burning skin. He bowed his head. "Please, let me in."

Now there was no resistance. He stroked the surface of the water the way he used to comb his fingers through Gina's hair, cool seeping from his palms to his wrists to his forearms, a pleasure made of exquisite relief. He waded to his waist and plunged into the pristine cold. He kicked and tried to rise, but his legs were too heavy. Next came the horror-movie moment he should have seen coming: something was touching his feet, pulling him down.

He clutched at his ankles and found two pairs of miniature hands.

He clawed and thrashed his limbs, but every movement seemed to add weight to his body, quickening his descent to the bottom of the impossible lake. Evan's fear ebbed and flowed with the water, peaking toward the impossible and dissolving into denial. This couldn't be real.

Evan's feet hit silt. That was real enough. They must have reached the bottom. He opened his eyes. His captors were child sized, stark naked but smooth as dolls, no way to tell if they were female or male. One of them was brown and black haired. The smaller one was greenish and pale with white hair swimming around its head like a bag of albino snakes. Both had huge eyes and wide cheekbones like the kids in the kitschy velvet paintings Vangie used to collect. They were cartoon characters. Aliens. Totally unreal.

Breathing was less of an issue than it should have been. His lungs had somehow adapted. He touched his face. Expecting what? Gills? The freaky kids weren't holding on to him anymore. He told his legs to push off, kick away, but nothing happened.

You will stay.

The words formed in his mind like letters on a page. A small hand touched his chest. His eyes were closed. He couldn't open them. Another hand rested on his forehead, calming him. Waves rocked the water around him, seaweed brushing against his skin. No, not seaweed. The movements were random, alive. It was hair. Long, freaky, snaky hair.

Evan curled into himself and tried to check out, but they had invaded his mind, digging around in his skull. They pulled themselves back in time, stomping through the swamp of weed and booze, discarding fantasy and thought, shooting straight into memory. His head began to pound as they herded his attention ruthlessly back to the months after Gina had left him.

Evan began to see a story take shape, a movie starring Xochi. There she was at twelve, a grubby kid, brown as a bear and fast as a fox. Loretta had bought her a guitar, and he'd started to teach her some chords. Xochi's little-kid soprano sounded right with his bass. She was a natural with harmony. It made him feel human again, right with the world for the first time since Gina had bailed.

The images blurred. The creatures were looking for something. Something specific. His brain itched with their probing. They didn't want seeds and stems and bars and bong hits. They didn't want him. It was Xochi they were after. And there she was again. Older now, about fourteen. She moved like a woman as she helped Loretta in the kitchen before a party, managing the work in a way Gina never could. In a faded apron, her long hair hanging down her back, she could've been Vangie, laughing as she chopped vegetables with Loretta like the old days were back.

The movie faltered and went black. Evan hurt, an unspecific pain that had no physical place to land. He imagined the two of them with headlamps and blowtorches, blasting away at his brain. Finally, they found the memory they wanted, glowing in the dark like a radioactive penny. Evan wanted to move away, take cover. The thing was toxic. Cursed. But that didn't matter to the creatures. They held it in their webbed hands. The water reconstituted it. It unfurled in Evan's head. There was no place to hide.

It was hot.

An afternoon in early September.

The day Loretta died.

Xochi and Evan had been up for forty-eight hours. It had been three days since Loretta had lost consciousness, four since she'd eaten or drunk. "Leave her be," the nurses said. "Women sometimes need to be alone to let go."

So Evan and Xochi had gone. He'd showered, eaten something, was on his way back to check on Loretta when he heard sobbing in the flower garden. There was Xochi, face buried in the lamb's ears. The last few months had bonded them. He'd been surprised to find her so tough. As strong as he was. Stronger. In all this time, he'd never seen her cry like this. He pulled her up, held her close.

His heart pounded, an underwater sound.

Was he hearing it in memory, or now, in the acid-trip present?

He'd been excited, turned on to be that close to her. Now there was only dread.

Continue.

There it was. That creepy voice slithering into his head.

Show us.

He thought about fighting, but couldn't see how. They would get it out of him in the end. The creatures couldn't be stopped.

XOCHI SAT UP IN the tub. The water was cold. She must have fallen asleep. Was she about to throw up? *Maybe the coffee was poisoned,* she thought, knowing it was crazy but thinking it anyway. She was afraid, afraid of something. She'd fallen asleep, she'd been dreaming. It was something bad, but she couldn't remember. "Fates," she sang softly, "Fates and Furies. Open, open, open up the door!"

PAIN BLOOMED AS IF it were the substance of the lake that had swallowed him. The creatures cranked a knob in Evan's brain, replaying that fucked-up day. It was afternoon. It was hot. Loretta's room droned with all the fans they'd been able to scrounge. You could even hear them out in the garden.

Evan had been walking back to check on Loretta when he'd found Xochi. She was on her knees, crying her eyes out. Not at the flower bed as he'd thought at first, but in a shaded spot behind the shed, secluded. It had been Loretta's dog's favorite place in the yard. The old wolf dog had died in the spring before anyone knew Loretta was sick. That's what Xochi was doing. Putting flowers on the dog's grave.

She was on her knees, hair in a messy braid down her back, a bunch of lavender and wild roses in her lap. He'd pulled her up. Brushed leaves from her hair. Held her, tried to comfort her. Then he kissed her. Her eyes flew open, all pupil. She was out of her mind, but her body knew what to do. When she kissed him back, she was all fire. His hands were in her hair, under her skirt, she was pulling him into her, nails digging through his T-shirt, her leg wrapped around his hip. It was fast and fierce. At the time, he thought she came. But now, watching, he wasn't so sure.

IT BEGAN AGAIN, PLAYED over and over on an endless loop— slow, fast, slow again—but the little creeps wanted more. They studied his pleasure, questioned his regret. Over and over, they made him watch. By the tenth time, it didn't seem sexy. By the thirteenth, the whole thing made him sick. After twenty, he lost count but couldn't look away. Right when Evan knew he was going to lose it, the images changed.

It was the same scene, the same day, but Xochi's colors were faded, her outline indistinct. All the energy of the memory was now focused on him. He'd been skinnier that summer, with matted dreads and bloodshot eyes. Loretta's cabin smelled herbal and witchy. The vibe was intense. Xochi had agreed to go take a shower and a nap. The hospice ladies shooed him out. He'd gone to his cabin, microwaved a burrito, gotten an hour of sleep.

He watched himself walk through the gate into Loretta's garden. He was exhausted and sad, but he'd been through this before with his stepmother. He knew how to ration his energy, when to fill up. Xochi didn't. After he kissed her, something snapped. She had been so miserable for so long. And Evan had known it. He'd known what he was doing. With his hands, his mouth. Not like her fumbling virgin boyfriend. And in that moment, Xochi would have done anything for one second of relief.

Afterward, alone in his bed, he'd told himself it was mutual. A freak moment born of grief. But the truth was, he'd been after this for a year, at least. After her. There had been an opening, and he'd taken it. Right or wrong, he'd wanted her.

XOCHI GOT OUT OF the bath, turned off the stereo and opened the windows on the west side of the sitting room. She stood wrapped in her towel in the afternoon sun, limbs tattooed in shadows of lace.

Leviticus. His name bounced around her head. She'd been strict and strong, determined not to obsess. Now, she curled into the sunny window seat and allowed the images to come: the ride through the city, the bookstore, the bar, *Wings of Desire.* Dancing at Ray's. She let herself have his involuntary smile, the effort it took him to look away, the missed chord changes, Kylen's glare. All of it. She picked up the cassette case. He'd taken the time to copy the liner notes and the translation of the poem. Had he been thinking about their day together?

Before Badger Creek, Xochi and Gina used to lay in their freshly washed underwear in front of a box fan on summer afternoons, watching soap operas while they waited for Gina's cocktailing shift to start. As entertaining as Xochi found the cheating couples and elaborate schemes, she knew she'd never live her life like that. But somehow, here she was. Last night, she'd kissed both Bubbles and her douchebag ex. Now all she could think about was Leviticus, and that went beyond kissing. Pallas would surely consider anything between Xochi and her father an epic betrayal. And even if not, what about everyone else? What about Io? As welcome as they'd all made her feel, Xochi wasn't sure free love was actually free when it came to the governess.

She replayed what had happened in the alley with Leviticus. The way they'd leaned against the wall, close but not touching, the fire that had shot from her palm to her piercing when he'd touched her hand. If Andi hadn't come out when she did—what then? Xochi shuddered. One kiss from Leviticus would end her.

EVAN LONGED FOR RELEASE, but the creatures were tireless. They pored over the weeks after Loretta had died. Xochi did nothing but sleep. Evan left her alone.

At least, she thought he did. Hard nights found him in her bedroom with its clothes-strewn floor and musky scent, female and warm. He never touched her, just sat on the floor and listened to her breathe. After an hour or so, he'd leave, knowing he'd be able to sleep. They replayed these visits three times and moved on to the wake.

It was the biggest party in the county that summer. Loretta had a lot of friends. Xochi wore a red dress he'd never seen before and started drinking at three in the afternoon. By sundown, she had a bottle of Bushmills in one hand, a cigarette in the other, a pack of guys sniffing around her, her boyfriend sulking in the corner.

She got her shit together long enough to sing the song they'd planned to start the party, but as they stood side by side on a stage lit with fairy lights and a harvest moon, Evan was invisible. Every eye was on Xochi as she sang Loretta's favorite Joni Mitchell song. Her voice always cracked on Loretta's favorite line about fear as a wilderland, and Evan waited for it to break. But it didn't. She was different up there. All grown up.

Someone put P-Funk over the PA, scratchy and familiar— Loretta's music for fall and winter, the lonely months to come. People started to dance. Evan was a coyote outside the circle of fire. Food was there in the light. Food, water, warmth. Xochi danced at the center of the flames, red dress, red mouth, raccoon bandit eyes. Bile rose in his throat as she pressed against some college kid one of his brothers had brought along. Frat boy asshole.

By then, there was a bottle in his own hand. He could almost feel its weight. He lifted it to his mouth and sucked in water, not booze. So much water. This freak show of a lake had kidnapped his creek, and now it was going to kill him.

But it didn't.

He was spinning, time flying on a circular current. Now there was air where water should be, leaves blowing in the wind. *A blustery day.* Words from childhood, a story Vangie used to read his baby brothers. Then he heard it. The mind voice. It held a single, magic word, both lock and key.

Homecoming.

It echoed in an empty canyon.

Pressure built in a place he'd once called his head.

Show us homecoming.

XOCHI HUDDLED ON THE sofa. She'd been so hot after the bath but now she was freezing. Collier's Led Zeppelin shirt lay folded on the easy chair. It smelled of laundry soap and lavender. She remembered where it had been, right on Leviticus's skin. And before that, Coll's. Her best friend. Her first love. He didn't even know where she was. She remembered the last time things were good between them. The picnic dinner in the woods, his weight over hers, rocks poking through the blanket. Sex between them had been awkward before, but somewhere between his summer away and all the messed-up things that happened after Loretta died, they had acquired a certain grace. Xochi was light with relief, his touch proof of forgiveness, erasing the mistakes she'd made those wasted weeks after the funeral. She lay there on his chest, his heartbeat the only music she wanted. The sun was setting. They were going to be late.

"Thanks for asking me to homecoming." She picked bits of the forest floor from her sweater and grabbed one end of the quilt.

"Thanks for saying yes," he said, taking the other end. Together, they shook off the leaves, moving closer and closer as they folded it into a perfect square.

EVAN WAS HORIZONTAL, FLOATING. He could feel his body again, but his limbs were weak, his resistance spent. It was October, and leaves were blowing around the yard. Xochi walked out of Loretta's cabin in a dress that made her look like a frothy blue cupcake. She sparkled with some sort of glitter on her eyelids. The same shine drew Evan's eyes to her chest, exposed in the strapless dress.

She pulled on a fuzzy sweater and hiked up her skirt to climb on the back of Collier's motorcycle, leaving Evan alone to count his abandonments: his mother, his stepmother, Gina, Loretta and now Xochi. His dad might as well be gone, too, lost as he was to his grief.

Evan went into Loretta's cabin and found the bottle of good vodka she'd used to make herbal medicine. It was empty by the time Xochi got home from the dance. He was crying when she walked in, had been crying since the bottle was half done. Xochi's first response was kindness, the last time she ever touched him willingly.

It had been an animal thing, taking her there on the table in Loretta's cabin. He'd been rough, he could see that now. And she hadn't wanted it. He could see that, too.

After that, he only came to her when he was wasted, but he found a way to do it sober soon enough, never thinking of it when she wasn't there, never planning in advance, living in the moments of sweet relief and forgetting them when they were done. Now he could see his mistake, taking silence for acceptance, despair for consent. Image after image flickered past like pages in the flipbooks his brothers used to make, cartoons of goofy cats chased by mangy dogs, cars racing and crashing, a goose landing in a lake. His lake wasn't so innocent.

After Xochi took off for good, he drove north. She'd always wanted to see Seattle. He had pictures, was going to make flyers, but never could bring himself to leave the highway for long. He drove as far as Portland before he turned around and went home.

After that, there were women, a few of them too young. Hitchhikers. Travelers. Alone in the world like Xochi must be now. It was fine at first when he was the best-looking guy in the hole-in-the-wall bar, when he bought them drinks and let them win at pool. But sometimes, later, it went wrong—a crying girl in a shitty motel who wanted something he could never figure out.

He tried staying closer to home. There were bar fights in Garberville over somebody's sister, bar fights in town over nothing at all. Anywhere else, he'd be thrown in jail. But no one wanted the cops up here. Evan would suffer another punishment. He knew that now. This was his karma, come to meet him. And it wasn't just about Xochi. It went back farther than that.

Like a time-lapse flower blooming in reverse, Xochi grew younger, dark hair fading to blond, daughter melting into mother, Gina under the stars at the fair. He could have stayed there forever, but he forced himself onward. The creatures floated beside him. He found he could open his eyes. The green one touched his hand. She was female, he realized. Beautiful the way wild things could be even when they were scary as shit. She placed her hand in his. It was so small it fit into his palm.

Show us, she said. *We will help you be strong.*

THE MEMORY HAD THE faded colors of a home movie from Evan's childhood. The cabin was clean and homey, with scarves over the lamps and wildflowers in mason jars. Gina's womanly touches were everywhere, but Gina herself was on the floor. He stood over her, a monster. He was twice her size, but she met his eyes, defiant, blood smeared on her thighs because he'd been too rough. Too rough after her female troubles, too rough too many times. There were bruises on her arms, a black handprint spanning her bicep. Her blue eyes were pale as water. He remembered the fairy princess she'd been when they'd met. She looked like a different person.

With Gina so fair and Xochi so dark, it was hard to link them as mother and daughter, but now he read it in Gina's eyebrows, her cheekbones, her hairline, her voice. Mother and daughter. He had done this awful thing to both. But unlike

Xochi, Gina knew how to say no. She'd fought, but he was stronger. He'd forced her, hurt her. Gina, his soulmate, his one and only love.

THE MOVIE REPLAYED, AGAIN and again. The creatures held him as he fought to stop it, to stop himself—moment after moment when he could have been kind, could have been soft. Could have saved them all. But the moments piled up, crashed into each other, and then it was too late. There was no evil he was safe from, no innocence left to redeem.

XOCHI SAT IN THE window seat, sun warmed and empty, calmer than she'd been in a long, long time. She retrieved the poem from the floor and read:

> When the child was a child
> It was the time for these questions:
> Why am I me, and why not you?
> Why am I here, and why not there?
> Is life under the sun not just a dream?
> Given the facts of evil and people
> Does evil really exist?

EVAN FLOATED ON THE surface of the lake, face raised to the sun. The big-eyed creatures swam in widening circles around him, stirring the lake into a circular current as they went. When they reached the bank, Evan gasped as they launched out of the water to the top of the dam they'd built to trap him.

They stood with their legs planted, crazy hair flapping behind them like capes in the wind. Joining hands, the children began to chant, one soprano, one bass, chasing each other in a rhythmic pattern of call and response.

> Noontime holds breathless the balance of day
> Stones hold this sacred water at bay

Pure as her dignity should have remained
You fouled her bright faith
Maiden's flower disdained.
Judged and found guilty
Heart viewed and found vile
We come to restore
The soul-stolen child
Double, double
Toil and trouble
Fire burn!
Cauldron bubble!

The water began to bubble as bidden, heat rising from below.

Panic rose and receded.

His limbs were strong again, his head clear. The pair watched from above, impassive, waiting. Evan understood. He could leave. Or he could stay and meet his fate. He thought of Loretta, so brave in the face of all her pain. This death would be gentler than hers, a kindness he didn't deserve.

The water swirled in faster spirals as Evan surrendered to the current's urge, lying back as it pulled him into its foaming, white-capped center. The last thing he saw was the clear blue sky, as blue as the dress Xochi had worn to homecoming, as blue as Gina's eyes.

XOCHI WOKE TO DARKNESS. She tried to remember her dream. Something about Badger Creek. Something about Evan.

She sat up, an image of him so clear in her mind he could have been standing in front of her. Long legs, brown dread-locks, green-brown eyes. She'd loved him once. When he'd gotten her the dirt bike, made her a tire swing, made her mom laugh in a way that meant Xochi wouldn't be moving for a long, long time. She'd felt sorry for him when Gina left. She heard whispers about what he'd done to make her mother go, but she'd refused to believe them, hating Gina and giving him a pass. Hating Gina even now.

Xochi sat up straighter. She'd sided with Evan over Gina. A man who hit a woman. A man who hit her *mom*. Sided with him, had *sex* with him. Maybe the invisible ropes that held her down when Evan came to her cabin at night had been punishment for her betrayal. Maybe, but it was all over now. Over and done.

Xochi considered Evan for a moment more, remembering the look on his face when he wanted her and tried to resist. It could last for days or minutes. Eventually, he always gave in.

Crazy out, Xochi thought in James's proper voice. *Crazy out, divinity in.*

"I'm done," Xochi said out loud. "I'm done with you."

When she reopened her eyes, the edges of things were sharper, the reds and blues in her patchwork quilt jewellike, almost too vivid.

It was after eight and she was hungry. She found a pair of reasonably clean jeans and a soft Lady Frieda T-shirt modified by Kiki so it hung just right. She grabbed her boots. Opening her door, she almost missed the shiny laminated rectangle someone must have slipped under it while she was asleep. Xochi laughed, tucking it into the back pocket of her jeans.

When the child was a child, her friends got her a fake ID.

25

Water Music

The fish swam nose to tail around the circular tank that was the whole of their world.

Two months before, Pallas had laid eyes on Xochi for the first time in this room. It had been a gloomy day in early February, and everyone at home was cross, most of all Pallas. The Academy of Science's aquarium was a perfect relief, the watery calm a soothing remedy for her unpredictable moodiness.

At first glance, there had been nothing remarkable about Xochi—her uniform of a leather jacket and jeans did nothing to broadcast the kindred spirit within. Still, Pallas had been drawn to her. She sat down next to Xochi, but couldn't think of what to say. Xochi spoke first.

"I love your hat," she said. Pallas's big, furry cat hat was a signature item, something she rarely left home without. In the winter, with her cold-sensitive ears, it was a necessity even indoors.

"Thank you," Pallas said.

"And that red coat—you look like a girl from a book." Xochi smiled.

"Any book in particular?" It had been a promising beginning, but a lot rode on the girl's answer.

"My favorite book," Xochi said. "I haven't read it yet—I don't think anyone's gotten around to writing it—but there's a cat girl with your exact coat who lives by the sea and communicates with whales. Definitely my favorite."

After that, the conversation flew by. They discovered a mutual fascination with manta rays, a shared preference for black licorice over red and an abject terror of the crocodile in the open pit under the suspension bridge you had to cross to get to the Fish Roundabout.

Pallas's eyes followed the aquarium's largest ray. As a little girl, she'd imagined being a ray herself, arms traded for water wings, swimming through the open sea with a long catlike tail streaming out behind her.

On her seventh birthday, she'd asked to have her party here. Kiki made Pallas a set of silken manta ray fins with a manta-headed hood, and Pad brought a boom box with Handel's *Water Music*. They'd all danced around the aquarium, moving in time with the winging rays. The few people who came in just smiled or joined them. Even the guard wasn't mad. All he said was, "Turn off the music when the song is over and eat your cupcakes outside." They'd had a picnic in the Shakespeare Garden and a ride on the carousel, too. It had been a good birthday, one of Pallas's best.

Now it was strange thinking of her entire family in this room. When Pallas was nine, she'd decided she was ready to go places on her own. When her family finally gave in, Pallas had been thrilled, but after a while, going places alone became an expected thing. People rarely came along—they had other things to do. Now Pallas's favorite places in the city carried a hint of bittersweet loneliness, like the yellowish tint in an old photograph of people you used to know.

She pulled another rope of licorice out of Xochi's pack.

"Hand me the Walkman?" Xochi asked.

Pallas and Xochi were working on an aquarium mix, taking turns picking songs. It was Xochi's turn, but she was stumped. Pallas was hunting for the headphones when the room filled with kids. They were Pallas's age, or close to it. Middle schoolers.

"They smell," Pallas whispered. Was a horrible stench next in her own personal parade of indignities? She was already moody and unreliable, slept too much, and had an occasional embarrassing blemish.

"Hey, Pal?" Xochi had on her careful face, the expression everyone wore around Pallas lately. "Did you ever go to school?"

Pallas had, for two long years. She remembered noise, mostly. Noise and bad smells. The thought of liquid yogurt in a tube would always make her gag. And then there was the reading. No one else did it but her. The adults pretended to be impressed, but it made them and the other children uncomfortable.

"When I was small," Pallas said. "I stopped after the first grade."

"Ever think of trying it again?"

Pallas startled. Last week, she'd gone so far as to walk by the French American school on her way back from getting Xochi a bagel. A girl in a fetching Madeline uniform and purple hair smiled at her from the playground, but there was no way Xochi could have known about that.

Pallas's back ached. Probably from sleeping in the car on the way back from LA. A boy tapped on the glass at a passing juvenile shark. After that, an epidemic of male glass tapping broke out in the class. Girls giggled. The guard intervened. There was no logic to the children's behavior—nothing to be gained by tapping the glass, nothing humorous to respond to. The pretty young teacher shot an apologetic smile as he herded them to another part of the museum.

Pallas sighed. Maybe middle school *was* a bad idea. She'd wait for high school. A girls' school, with uniforms and strict nuns. She leaned back, intending to share the headphones with Xochi, but something hot leaked from between her legs. She jumped up. The back of her skirt was wet. Her fingers came back red stained and sticky.

"Xochi!"

Xochi was quick on her feet. "Here." She unbuttoned the flannel she wore over her T-shirt and handed it to Pallas. "Tie it around your waist." Normally, Pallas considered this practice a fashion abomination, but bloody humiliation was infinitely worse.

"Walk in front of me," Xochi said.

Thank goodness the bathroom was empty. "I can go into the big stall with you," Xochi said. Pallas shot her a look and went into the smaller stall alone.

The bathroom was freezing. Her skirt was a mess. "My underwear is ruined," she said. Stupidly, she wanted to cry. She bit her tongue. More blood. *Great.*

"You just need them clean enough to get out of here. We'll fix you up at home." Xochi was fiddling with something—probably the vending thing with period supplies. "They only have tampons," she said. There was a slamming sound. "Scratch that." Xochi sounded annoyed. "This thing is empty. You'll have to use toilet paper for now. Fold it into a pad. That's what I always do, anyway. I never remember to bring stuff with me."

Pallas bunched up the thin industrial toilet paper, but the blood just smeared around. She wiped at her thighs. "It's too bloody for that," she said. Her stomach cramped. More blood dripped into the toilet. "I'm worried it's too much. Like, not a normal amount."

"I'm sorry, Pal," Xochi said. "I know it's a pain. You just have to plug the leak."

"All those kids are out there!" Pallas said. "Can you leave me here and go home for a change of clothes?" She was crying now, just a little, but she kept the tears out of her voice.

Xochi paced, her boots appearing and disappearing from the crack under the stall door. "Even if I take a cab both ways, that leaves you sitting here alone for almost an hour. How about I call and see if someone's home to bring you something?"

"No!" Pallas hadn't meant to yell, but there was no way she wanted the whole family talking about this. She closed her eyes, made herself calm down. Her bare knees peeked above her socks, plucked looking in the fluorescent light. "Please, Xochi. Don't tell any of them about this. I don't want them to know."

"Okay," Xochi said. "It's okay. How about this: you hand me your underwear and I'll wash them out. There's a hand dryer, so I can dry them, too. If anyone comes in, I'll hide them in a paper towel and wait till they leave. We can do the same thing with your skirt."

"But that's so gross."

"Listen to me," Xochi said. "You're always talking about the patriarchy, right? Well, this is a prime example. We've been trained to think being a woman is disgusting and shameful. We've gotta reject that. We're beautiful, Pal. We're goddesses. I am not the least bit grossed out by your blood."

Pallas had to smile a little. It was great when Xochi went fierce. She remembered something Io had told her. Aaron was saying that sometimes shame was good, like if you'd done something shitty. But Io said no—shame and remorse were different things. Shame was a tool of oppression, especially if you were gay or black or brown or different. And you could multiply that by a million if you were also a girl.

"Come on," Xochi said, her boot tapping the floor outside the stall. "Hand them over."

It took Pallas a minute to figure out how to get her underwear off without bloodying her socks and boots, but she did it. Now how was she supposed to stand up without bleeding all over the floor? She balled up some of the rough paper, wedged it between her legs, and waddled to the stall door. Xochi took the gruesome bundle without comment.

Pallas heard the sink, the soap pump, the sink again. "Almost done," Xochi said. The water turned off. The hand dryer roared like a hungry beast. After a while, Xochi passed Pallas her clean, dry underwear and went to work on her skirt.

"Don't be afraid to make the pad thick," Xochi said. "It

won't show under your skirt. And if it's not too uncomfortable, shove some tissue up inside, kind of like a cork."

"Lovely," Pallas said, but realized that might actually work a bit better than the way she had things arranged. It was only a little while before Xochi handed Pallas her skirt under the door. Pallas came out of the stall clean and dry, wearing the long flannel shirt as a sort of jacket. "The blood didn't get it," she said. "And I got cold." She looked in the mirror. *No different*, she thought. "It toughens up my outfit, don't you think? And it's long, which is good in case I leak again."

Xochi nodded. "It makes you look older."

"Thank you for doing that," Pallas said.

"Anytime." Xochi smiled.

So pretty. Pallas gazed at her own pale cheeks and wished for Xochi's golden-brown.

"Come on," Pallas said. "Let's go back to the fish. Just for a few minutes. I want to listen to our mix."

"Are you sure?"

When they'd first entered the bathroom, all Pallas could imagine was holing up in her attic forever. But now she didn't want that. Not at all.

"Totally sure," Pallas said, holding the bathroom door open for Xochi. "After you."

26

Bridge over Troubled Water

Back in the aquarium, away from the fluorescent bathroom lights, Pallas's pale face gleamed like a pearl. Xochi grinned as she marched past the middle schoolers at the pendulum exhibit with her chin up. They watched Pallas, a synchronized head-turn, unconscious of all they had in common with the crocodile and the sharks.

The Fish Roundabout was empty again. Pallas sat next to Xochi, closer than before. A school of large flat fish cut through the water like thrown knives.

Just like Pallas, Xochi had gotten her period at twelve, waking up with blood on her legs after a dream about mermaids and kissing. She was in the water constantly that summer. Collier had gone to stay with his cousins for two months instead of the usual two weeks. His parents were starting to wonder why he didn't hang out with any boys, but Xochi knew. Collier loved her and was waiting for the day she'd love him back.

In the water she imagined it, kisses and more, but Collier morphed into other creatures, other people. Xochi touched herself at night in bed, in the morning in the shower, in the deepest part of the swimming hole with the sun on her back and her face in the water, the pleasure proof she was perfect, needed no one.

In the evenings before dinner, she hunted through her mother's old things. For the first few weeks after she left,

Xochi'd worn an old nightgown of Gina's to bed, the long hem snagging over the rough spots on the cabin floor. But a year later, Gina's clothes fit. Xochi tried on her mother's soft worn jeans and flowy Stevie Nicks tops and snapped on the Western plaid shirts Gina liked over tank tops with cutoffs and sighed at the collection of wooden-soled size-six platform sandals— too small for Xochi since she'd first tried them on at ten. At the bottom of the box were underthings. Loretta looked in as Xochi tried to adjust a flimsy lace bra.

"That's too small, honey. We'll get you one that fits."

The next morning, the blood had been there. Loretta took her into Garberville, bought her three bras: two ballet pink, one white. All that fall and winter, Xochi wore them under the clothes her mother had left behind.

A PAIR OF GIANT manta rays shrugged through the cool blue, unhurried by the smaller fish around them. Pallas lay back on the carpeted dais, and Xochi did the same. It was something people did in the Fish Roundabout. Once, she'd seen a woman with a baby sitting on the floor with her back to the platform, both sound asleep. The peace in the watery blue room was contagious.

A hand slipped into Xochi's. Pallas, more reserved than any cat, had offered her paw. Xochi held it lightly, careful not to move. Behind her eyelids, dream siblings floated in the swimming hole of her youth. Hand in hand, they soaked up the sun, impossibly long hair fanning around them like the halos around the saint candles that burned day and night on Loretta's altar.

Xochi caught a fragment of another dream from when she'd been dozing in the bathtub the day Pallas had left for LA. A stone wall above a swirling pool. The green girl and her brother with wings and tails. Blowing leaves, a blustery day. The images were jerky and slow, like cold honey dripping from a spoon. Xochi considered opening her mouth and taking them in, but she knew she shouldn't. Maybe she couldn't. There was pain there. Pain and power. Whatever story the dream was trying to tell, Xochi wasn't ready to hear it. She opened her eyes.

Pallas was singing something familiar, her voice fine and high like her mother's.

III.

Hand in hand, they run the forest
Hand in hand, they stop to heal

The ache of the broken man
Is Brother's breaking
Broken blue, a desolate nest
He will not hurt Xochi again

Life, Death, Life
The way of short-lived creatures
Brother knows, but Sister is new
Unaccustomed to sorrow
She sleeps now, deep and low
Healing. Growing strong

Brother rests on cooling earth
The mudpot whispers
Sulfur and secrets
Sister stirs, magma deep
Calling Brother to dream

27

Romeo and Juliet

L eviticus tipped the driver an extra twenty for helping with
his amp and slung his backpack over his shoulder. The house
was quiet, the windows dark. It seemed like he'd been gone
longer than a week. Long legs and sneakers dropped from the
fire escape to the balcony as he reached for his guitar. Xochi. She
unzipped her hoodie and pulled out a pack of cigarettes.

"Hey," he called, moving so she could see him in the porch light.

"You're back?" She shoved the cigarettes in her pocket like
a kid caught smoking. Which, technically, she was.

"Yeah. What are you doing outside my bedroom window?"

"Oh, this is your bedroom?"

For all he knew, Xochi thought he shared a room with Io.
That was the downside of the family no-gossip policy. Xochi
would have to ask if she wanted to know something. Which,
at seventeen, might be easier said than done. Leviticus reached
down for his duffel.

"Need help?" Xochi was already trotting down the stairs
that led from the balcony to the patio behind the kitchen. She
picked up his guitar case and headed for the kitchen door.

"That's okay," he said. "I was gonna bring it all up."

He reached for the guitar, but Xochi kept it, heading for the
stairs. He followed, trying not to notice how nicely her boys'
jeans fell on her hips.

"Was this back part of the house added on?" Xochi asked.

"Yeah. They made the kitchen bigger and built my room on top of it. It was supposed to be Io's dad's office when he was in town. He recorded demos here sometimes." *Stop rambling,* he told himself. He fished in his pocket for keys. "This was the cigar room," he said, unlocking the French doors that led to the sunporch outside his bedroom. "It still kind of smells like it. There was a tiki bar in here, too."

"Where do you want your guitar?"

"The floor is fine."

Xochi laid it down carefully. "No more bar?" she asked, checking out the room with its oversized lounger, Mexican rug, and reading lamp.

"Nah," Leviticus said, putting his duffel on the chair. "Booze isn't my weakness."

"Should we get the amp?" Xochi asked.

"It's heavy."

"I'm strong."

Xochi followed him down the stairs. They each grabbed a handle and carried the amp up in one go, leaving it beside the guitar.

"So," Leviticus said, "why are you out here at three in the morning?"

She held out the box of clove cigarettes. "I confiscated them from Pallas the night of the party. Now I'm the worst kind of hypocrite."

"Pallas was actually smoking?" Leviticus tried to picture it and couldn't.

"It was theater, really," Xochi rushed to explain. "I don't think she even inhaled."

Leviticus shook his head. Pallas hated cigarettes—didn't she? But what did he know? At Pallas's age, things could change so fast. Leviticus remembered his own transition from obedient son to disowned deviant. One minute he was holding his mom's hand in church, the next he was leaning against a wall on Polk Street with Ky. Not that his own childhood was anything like what he wanted for Pal.

"I've been coming out here to smoke when I can't sleep,"

Xochi went on. "Do you mind?" She shook the box. "Out here," she said, stepping back to the balcony. "Don't want to add to the cigar smell."

Leviticus took off his jacket and spread it on the worn planks of the balcony floor. Xochi sat. She pulled her knees to her chest, tried sitting cross-legged, then gave up and stuck her feet out in front of her. Her legs were long, her movements coltish—just the sort of innocent-sexy detail that made him feel like a pervert straight out of *Lolita*.

"Innocence isn't just about age," Kiki had said on the way to LA. "It's a quality of hopefulness." She'd also said, "Don't underestimate the governess. She may be young, but she isn't stupid." All true, but numbers were truer. No matter how many times you did the math, seventeen was eleven years younger than twenty-eight and five years older than twelve. *Five years older than Pallas.*

Xochi fiddled with her lighter. Her fingernails were short, the black polish chipped. Leviticus flashed to the long red nails of the woman he'd been sleeping with at Dylan's. He'd planned to hook up with Andi in LA, but she'd set him straight the first night.

"You know I don't care what you do the second you're out of my sight," Andi said, heading out the door after Kiki's drummer. "But when you're with me, I need your undivided attention. And you, my friend, seem pretty divided these days."

"You have another one of those things?" He knew it was just an excuse to sit there with Xochi. His willpower was total shit.

"Really?" Xochi handed him the cigarettes and lighter.

"A week in LA will do that to you." He inhaled the sweet smoke, light-headed and tired. Xochi looked tired, too. She yawned, proving him right. A flash of silver caught the moonlight.

"Wait." He leaned closer. "What's that?"

Xochi clicked the tongue stud against her teeth. "Oh, this? I got it on the Equinox. I went out during the party and ran into James. One thing led to another . . ." She stuck out her tongue.

James? On the Equinox? James had been at Eris Gardens that night for some secret tryst with Io. He must have gone to his shop immediately afterward and opened just in time for Xochi to show up. Leviticus hadn't noticed it during their excursion through the city, but even then he'd been careful not to look at any part of her for too long. Certainly not her mouth.

"Do you like it?" he asked.

"I'd never even thought about it," she said. "My nose, maybe, but not my tongue. James was talking about Persephone, and I kept thinking about how she was punished for eating that pomegranate seed. Something about it spoke to me."

Persephone and pomegranates. Leviticus began to see how James managed to impress Io when so many others had failed. Leviticus's money had been on the butch lady poet who sent Io sonnets or the dandy photographer who'd been after her for years—anyone but James. Aside from being a super freak with the whole modern-primitive piercing thing, he looked like somebody's dad. Old school. Or, no—just old. At least forty-five, maybe fifty. An old man with a pierced dick—something Leviticus knew because he'd seen photos. Huge framed photos at a gallery in New York, images he'd never be able to unsee.

Xochi's words drifted back into his thoughts, rewound and stuck. "Wait, so one thing led to another? You mean the piercing?"

"Yeah," she said. "What did you think I meant?"

"Sorry. Nothing. Don't mind me." Leviticus dragged on his cigarette to shut himself up. "Rabbit Hole did me in. Dylan says hi, by the way." Why did he say that? The image of Dylan and Xochi was not a happy one.

"Send him my love," she said. "From me and Bubbles both." She met Leviticus's eyes and held them, a lapse into flirtation that was surely against her governess code. Her cigarette had gone out. She groped between them for the lighter. He reached it first and leaned in close. As always, she smelled so good. The ones who smelled edible, the ones you wanted to roll in, to inhale—those were the ones you had to watch out for. He shifted position to put a few extra inches between them. It helped.

"So, how did the album turn out?" Xochi leaned back against the door. "Aaron said you were going to help them finish?"

"That was the plan."

"What happened?" Her voice made Leviticus want to lay down someplace soft.

"Business as usual. I'm not used to it anymore, the whole rock-and-roll lifestyle."

Xochi laughed. "I thought this *was* the rock-and-roll lifestyle."

"What, us? Not even close. Those guys are hard-core. Hedonists all the way."

"But so are you guys."

"What makes you say that?"

Xochi was silent. Her clove cigarette crackled as she inhaled. "I've been curious about paganism, for one thing. I was surprised to find out most of you are atheists."

"What gave you that idea?" Leviticus enjoyed the improvisation of talking to Xochi. He could never predict what she'd say next.

"Io said something about your beliefs not being literal, like you don't believe in actual gods and goddesses. That it's more about celebrating cycles in nature, something like that. So maybe 'atheist' isn't the right word?"

"I think of myself as more agnostic. Like, there could be some sort of deity, but probably not. I like this one word of Kiki's— *numinous*. Like, the goddess is in everything. Everything is inherently divine. Good stuff, bad stuff. It doesn't matter."

"Right," Xochi said. "Hedonism. Everything is just naturally divine, there are no distinctions, so you can do whatever you want. It's the whole Aleister Crowley thing you guys are into, right? 'Do what thou wilt shall be the whole of the Law'? It's the family motto, isn't it? Painted on the mantel and everything. Basically the definition of hedonism."

"I'm not gonna defend Crowley," Leviticus said. "Aaron and Ky had a thing for him, like, eight years ago. That's when they painted the quote, but what you're talking about is only part of it. The rest is done in glow-in-the-dark paint, so you have to turn the lights out. The whole thing goes, 'Do what thou wilt shall be the whole of the Law. Love is the Law. Love under will.' What do you think of that?"

Xochi's brow wrinkled. Leviticus leaned back against the door, crossing his feet in front of him. The sky was cloudy as usual, with a ring around the almost-full moon.

"It's equating love and will, I guess. Saying free will is different from simple desire."

Simple desire. The words burrowed into his skull. He imagined reaching out to raise Xochi's chin so he could see her eyes. "It's a lot of work sifting the bullshit to figure it out—what you will, what you truly want."

They were silent, staring at the moon.

"What if you want two different things?" Xochi's voice was almost too quiet to hear. "Things that cancel each other out?"

Leviticus put his cigarette out with the sole of his boot. "I don't know," he said. "Trial and error, I guess. Experiment. Make mistakes. I don't know. I'm working on that one myself."

Xochi put her cigarette out under her shoe and dropped both butts into the box, not littering. She stood and held out her hand.

Touching was a mistake, but refusal would be rude. He couldn't remember which was worse.

Her hand was surprisingly small but strong. Toasty warm. He was so tired. That was the problem. It was hard to think. He brushed a finger over her palm. Pheromones rallied, miniature cupids with arrows aimed to maim: eyes, throat, groin. A man's vulnerable spots.

Her lips were chapped and slightly open, and it seemed there was no way out but through. She took a step forward and held his eyes for a long moment before she kissed him. He cupped the base of her skull and pulled her closer. Her hair was soft and fine. She was tall, fit him easily, her breasts pressing against his chest. *No bra*, he noted, the thin cotton of their two worn T-shirts the only thing separating skin from skin.

You could tell everything about a woman from kissing her—how she'd have sex, how she'd love. How it would end. Men weren't like this. All you could tell from kissing a guy was how he gave head. That, and how he wore his loneliness.

Xochi's kiss had a hint of things to come, but was complicated by the piercing, a formal dance with a structured form and strong timing, bringing them together to tease them apart. She pressed against him, woodland-animal sounds escaping the cave of her mouth. Her back was hot under his hands. Her skin was so smooth. *No bra strap. No bra.* His brain fast-forwarded to the end of the kiss. He would take her hand. They would go to his room. He'd pull at the fly of her jeans, opening the buttons one by one. His hands slid to her waist. She pulled away.

He opened his eyes. She was breathing hard. *Artemis after the hunt.* But who was the prey here?

He'd thought it was her, so young. Vulnerable. Dependent on them for her livelihood. Which was why he'd stayed away, committed never to be that guy—that sleazy, selfish, gross older guy. But here he was. That guy for sure, led by his dick no matter what he'd decided. If she hadn't stopped, they'd be in his bedroom right now.

But she had.

This was her world. Her experiment. She'd gotten her data, and now she observed him, gaze intelligent and calm.

"Hey," she said.

"Hey."

"I should get back."

He watched her go. Strong legs, excellent hips. Gorgeous. She reached the attic fire escape and turned back to him before she climbed into the window.

"Good night," she called. "Sweet dreams."

28

Love Is a Battlefield

After the revolution of last night's perfect kiss, Xochi expected some equal and opposite aftermath, but the kitchen was the same as ever, with newspaper strewn across the long yellow table and coffee bubbling in the pot.

Pallas banged in through the back door. "Good morning, mole rat," she said, pulling Xochi out to the patio. "You look tired. Did you drink?"

"No." Xochi blinked in the innocent sunshine. "Of course not." Pallas passed Xochi her heart-shaped sunglasses. *Ah.* Xochi rubbed her temples. *Much better.* All night, her thoughts had spun round and round, replaying the scene on the balcony. By sunrise, the bed was spinning, too.

"Last time you were this squinty, Bubbles had you out drinking all night," Pallas said, collapsing into the wicker chair next to Xochi's.

"Who was drinking all night?" Leviticus emerged from somewhere in the garden. Xochi's mind bloomed with pornographic images.

"Xochi." Pallas threw her legs over the side of the chair, admiring her newly pastel toenails.

"I wasn't!" Xochi said.

"She has days off, you know," Pallas said. "They corrupted her while you were away."

"Did they?" Leviticus rested his hands on the back of

Xochi's chair. She longed to move her head against his hand like an attention-seeking cat. *Inappropriate,* her inner governess snapped. This had to stop. Pallas was right here.

"Did you have coffee?" His voice was low, just for her. She shook her head. When he went inside it was easier to think.

Last night on the balcony, a philosophy formed around desire had made perfect sense. In the moment, kissing Leviticus felt a hundred percent right. Now, in the too-bright morning, Xochi could see she was a hundred percent fucked. Even so, she had to smile. *I kissed him,* she thought. There was an undeniable satisfaction in taking charge.

"Here you go," he said, like it was any normal day. He managed to pass the cup without touching her, but his hands were shaking. He was nervous, too, then. How did people live like this? How did anyone manage to work, go to school, bathe? Xochi'd spent half an hour in the shower and hadn't managed to wash her hair before the water went cold, distracted by the showerhead's other powers. Not that it helped.

And there was Pallas, so happy that her dad was home.

Xochi was a traitor. Selfish. Just like Gina after all.

"What are you thinking about?" Pallas asked. Xochi'd read somewhere that pubescent girls were unusually intuitive. Hopefully that was a bunch of new-age crap.

"World peace," Xochi said. "Pizza." Pallas rolled her eyes.

Peasblossom appeared from somewhere in the yard and rubbed against Xochi's ankles. "You're here again?" She ran her hand along the cat's back.

"He showed up a little bit ago," Pallas said. "Meowing for cream. My dad is such a pushover."

"He was hungry!" Leviticus said. Pallas snorted.

"Hey," Kylen shouted from the lawn. "Lev! Come over here, man."

"Duty calls," Leviticus said, standing up.

What was going on in the garden? Kylen was not only outside in the sunlight, he was dressed for martial arts with loose pants and a kimono-style shirt. Pad was beside him in plaid pajama bottoms, a hoodie half zipped over his bare chest. Leviticus was wearing sweats and a faded Cocteau Twins shirt. They were all barefoot, which on Leviticus was somehow unbearably sexy.

"What are they doing?"

"Ass-kicking practice," Pallas said. "They think I need to learn self-defense. Because I'm, like, turning thirteen soon and *becoming a woman*." Her eye roll was epic. "According to my dad and Ky, every woman should know at least ten ways to incapacitate an enemy." Pallas adjusted the strap of the leotard she wore under a loose Indian print tunic. "Hence: ass-kicking practice. Kylen is a black belt."

"Of course he is," Xochi said.

"Come on, kid," Kylen called. "Right here by your dad."

Your dad. Side by side, Pallas and Leviticus looked so much alike with their strong brows and high cheekbones. She kept her eyes on Pallas as Ky led the group through some warm-up exercises and basic holds.

"You need to get in tune with your fierceness," Leviticus told Pallas. "I know it's there, kid. I have the scars to prove it."

"I was three," Pallas said. "Completely uncivilized, thanks to you people and your lax parenting."

"Maybe you've gone too far in the other direction." Leviticus tugged on her ponytail. "Ever think of that?"

Seeing them together helped. Leviticus was Pallas's father. Her *father.* Xochi's *boss.* Fuck free love. This was a bad idea. The very worst.

The screen door slammed. Kiki and Io came out to the patio to recline on twin chaises in the sun. Peasblossom leaped up to curl at Io's feet. If Xochi could paint, she'd want to paint Io, lying there with the cat in the sun.

Xochi sat on the sidelines as Pallas drilled with her dad, but every time she was supposed to escape from a hold, she giggled and went limp. Kylen put a hand on Pallas's shoulder and told her to stop. "Yo, Xochi," he called, "how hungover are you?"

"I'm not," Xochi said. Kylen squinted at her from across the yard. "I'm not!"

"Fine," he said. "C'mere." No politeness, no "please." She was too tired to argue. She drained her coffee and did as she was told.

"Were you watching the hold I taught her?" Xochi nodded. Ky leaned closer. "Model focus," he whispered. "And don't take any shit."

"Okay." Xochi handed Pallas her sunglasses.

"Shoes, too," Kylen said. "You could hurt somebody with those things. What size are they, anyway?"

Xochi rolled her eyes. Yes, her feet were big. His tone was teasing, at least. She took off her sneakers and socks. The grass was springy and sun warmed under her feet.

Xochi stood with one foot forward, one planted behind her. In the move Kylen had been teaching Leviticus and Pallas, the attacker grabbed the victim's wrist. Xochi held out her arm for Ky.

"What are you doing?" Kylen said. "Make me earn it."

Xochi started again, arms at her sides. Kylen grabbed her wrist and Xochi pivoted, the move he'd shown Pallas, but instead of moving in, Ky just stood there with a weird look on his face, her wrist trapped in his surprisingly strong hand.

Kylen knows things, she remembered Pallas saying. *All he has to do is touch you.*

Xochi faltered. She willed herself to think of anything but Leviticus's mouth, his hands, the balcony, moonlight. "What?" she asked snatching her wrist back.

"I could ask you the same thing." Kylen's voice was normal, but his eyes told a different story. Xochi stepped back a foot, hopefully out of laser range.

Leviticus sprang up from his spot on the lawn. "Anyone want more coffee?" The look on his face confirmed it: Kylen knew.

"Xochi?" Kylen said, with a scary raise of his perfectly

sculpted brows. "Can Leviticus get you something from the kitchen?"

She made herself meet his eyes. "No, thanks," she said. "We're doing this now, right? To show Pallas."

"Sure we are," Kylen said. "Get in position." His voice was cold. He gripped her wrist again, harder this time. They went through the hold till she got it right.

The moves got more complicated. Several times, Xochi landed on her ass, but she got better with each repetition. In the end, they both were panting.

Kylen turned away to drink some water. Xochi sat on the lawn, putting her shoes back on. She was hungry. *Pizza.* Two huge cheese slices and a large Cherry Coke. In a neighborhood far, far away from here. She would eat and think. She'd figure this out.

"If you're done, you have to bow to her," Pallas said. "You told me that's the rule."

Kylen turned and extended a hand to help Xochi rise. Xochi ignored it and got up on her own. Facing her formally, Kylen bowed, all politeness. Xochi mirrored him. "*I'm* done," he said to Pallas, "but she's not. We have to give her a test."

"You're kidding, right?" Xochi hated the squeak in her voice.

"It's one thing to know the forms," he said. "It's another to use them when you're not expecting it. So . . . how about this. Xochi, bend down to tie your shoe. Lev, you come up behind her and let her have it." Kylen looked slowly from Xochi to Leviticus with a mean, toothy smile. "We'll watch her, Pal, and see if she makes any mistakes."

Mistakes? Xochi'd already made a colossal one, and Kylen wasn't about to let her forget it. She turned to Leviticus. His eyes were wide. She glanced at Kiki and Io. They were reading magazines, seemingly oblivious.

"Can't we do this another time?" Xochi said.

"No time like the present," Kylen said. "Right, Pal?"

"If Xochi's tired . . ." Pallas said. "Not that she can't take my dad, because I bet she can."

Pallas was so sweet. This was about her, no one else. And Leviticus and Kylen were right—Pallas needed to learn to stick up for herself. Especially if she ever went back to school.

"No," Xochi said. "Let's do it." She bent down to tie her shoe, waiting for Leviticus to grab her. She both dreaded it and longed for it. *Shit.*

Where was he, anyway? Xochi tied and retied her shoelace.

"Lev, wake up!" Kylen said in an irritating singsong. At least in this position, no one could see Xochi's face. Her mind wandered. No—not to last night. She replayed scenes from *Wings of Desire.* Trapeze flights, library angels.

Hard hands gripped her arms, and just like that, Xochi was gone.

Sister runs the forest
Pacing a five-point buck.
Man-shaped, a horror looms
Grasping hands trap her

Black-beaked fury rises
Swan-crowned Medusa
Bite! Beat! Fight!

Buck legs falter, antlers fall to loam.
Skin slips, pelt to Brother
Calls his sister home

The forest breathes, in and out
Wingless, Sister shakes
Feathers fly to down

Moth-pale, she greens
succulent to fern

Fern to clover, as green as
The grass beneath
Xochi's feet.

Xochi blinked, silent in the acid light of the open yard, unclenching her balled fists.

Pad was on his knees at her feet, doubled over in pain.

Pad, not Leviticus.

It took her a moment to understand what happened.

"Oh my god! Pad, I'm so sorry!"

"Just a flesh wound," Pad said, giving his best Monty Python impression. "Who knew you were such a badass?"

"Me," Pallas said.

"And me," Kiki called.

"I knew," Leviticus said. "Why do you think I choked?"

Kylen stared at Xochi. She found it easy to meet his eyes now. There was a new expression there. Not respect. Was it fear? "Where'd you learn to fight like that?" His voice was quiet, finding Xochi's ear alone.

"You tell me," Xochi said. "You're the one who's supposed to be psychic." Did her voice have an underwater quality, or was it just her hearing?

"Have some water," Pallas said. "Are you all right?"

"Just hungry," Xochi said. "Okay if I take a walk and get some food?" Asking Pallas for permission seemed suddenly strange.

"Duh. My dad brought presents from LA," Pallas said. "See you later?"

"Have fun," Xochi said.

"Xochi . . ." It was Leviticus again, his hand on her arm, but Xochi shrugged him off and kept on walking out of the yard and down the driveway and into the street.

29

The Hanging Garden

Wind rattled the needles of the sentinel pines as the gate clanged shut behind Xochi. The scents of cedar and sulfur blew into the garden, a sudden gust. Peasblossom leaped to the top of the picnic table, scanning the treetops in the neighboring yards. As he suspected, only Pallas's garden was affected.

The cat reviewed the past five minutes: Xochi's sudden familiarity with the fighting ballet of a Siamese cat, Pallas's family seemingly unaware of the charge in the air and the unlikeliness of Xochi's sudden mastery, the circling crows cawing overhead, now two dozen or more.

Peasblossom dropped to the lawn. Sinking his claws into the ground, he felt the tension of the trees, anticipation in their thick-sapped veins—the hawthorn waking from its century's drowse, the lilacs tittering behind their buds, the palms hissing for heat and blood.

Xochi's newfound capacity for violence hinted at the Waterbabies' strength and reach. The cat ran to Pallas's side, but she appeared to be unaffected. Her scent was normal. No forest perfume, no feral mark. Only excitement at her governess's triumph.

Peasblossom twitched, his pelt suddenly tight. Xochi's performance had been deeply strange, as was the family's reaction. He recalled the narcotic mist the morning of the Waterbabies' arrival. The Hag had been right. These were powerful beings from a younger world with motives the cat couldn't guess at.

A crow landed beside a faded garden gnome—an elder, judging by her feathers—with a great glossy beak. Head cocked toward the garden gate, she gave the cat a meaningful look before taking flight in that direction. Her fellows followed, midnight silk in the pale blue sky.

Peasblossom meowed his frustration. After today's performance, it seemed clear that Xochi was the sole focus of the Waterbabies' attention. Even so, Pallas was involved and possibly in danger. Xochi had not been in control of herself during her exhibition. Her eyes had been closed, her breathing slow, as if she were at rest instead of moving with swift and deadly precision. Pad was lucky he hadn't been seriously hurt.

No, there was no getting around this. The image from the koi pond of the drowning man and the crying woman made no more sense than they had before, but Peasblossom was sure they were connected to Xochi. The wind was wailing, the crows were involved, the trees were interested. A breeze blew in from the sea, salted with anticipation. Something was happening. Something was coming.

Peasblossom slipped out of the garden. He was a cat, after all. Curiosity always won.

30

Tangled up in Blue

Xochi walked, her vision tunneled. She remembered it now—Pad and the garden—but in a removed, omniscient way, like watching TV through a wavy glass window in a dream.

It was crazy, the way she'd lost control. She'd never hit anyone in her life. Not when playground kids chanted that horrible racist rhyme: *Chinese, Japanese, dirty knees, look at these*—pulling their shirts away from their flat chests in a parody of breasts. Not when a girl pushed her down in middle school for some imagined infraction or when a gang of boys chased her with a *Screw* magazine and forced her to look at the centerfold. And when things were at their worst in Badger Creek, when she'd really needed some superhero moves, Xochi had been as lifeless as a wax dummy in the museum at Fisherman's Wharf.

Then there was the green girl and her brother. *Your dreams are a treasure map*, Loretta always said. *When you learn that internal alphabet, you can finally steer your own ship.*

What *was* Xochi's internal alphabet? There were the two children now, always connected, never alone. That was pretty obvious. Eris Gardens was webbed with the wordless bonds between people, a history Xochi would never share. The little siblings were company, a fairy-tale family that was hers alone. The forest was a symbol of lost memory, spirituality, childhood. *Once upon a time, two children walked hand in hand into a dark wood . . .*

But what about the fighting? That hadn't been a dream, especially if you asked poor Pad. For the first time, the dream-reality boundary felt breached. Every day, Xochi saw people on the street who lived between two worlds, talking to people no one else could see. Before today, those dreams had seemed harmless. Now she wasn't so sure.

She felt for the rectangle of the cigarette box in her pocket. She knew the contents without looking: empty except for two butts. One hers, one his. And no lighter. Was it lying there on the balcony? Or had it ended up in Leviticus's pocket? Xochi imagined herself in the small dark space beside the lighter, a sleeping Thumbelina waiting for the brush of his hand.

She sighed. She was a mess. There was a word for this, a Xochi and Gina word she hadn't thought of in months. *Regressed*—a term her mom picked up from her childhood bouts with social workers and used when she and Xochi played hooky and stayed in their pajamas all day watching cartoons together like a pair of six-year-old truants. *Oppositional defiant* was another, reserved for the few times Xochi took a stand and refused to do something Gina wanted. Mostly, they'd been a team. Right up until they weren't.

Xochi stopped to get her bearings. She was crossing Van Ness, heading toward the Tenderloin. It didn't matter where she went, walking always did her good. She would find a corner store and buy cloves and a lighter. Then she would find a coffee shop, order herself a double espresso. She would knock the sludge from her brain with caffeine and nicotine. She would figure this out. She unzipped her jacket and walked faster, slitting her eyes against the wind.

PEASBLOSSOM HADN'T VISITED THE Tenderloin in years. Now, trotting along after Xochi, he found its smoggy piss-rich scent instantly familiar. His first memories post-milk and post-mother had been made just a few blocks away in a shabby art deco building on the corner of Eddy and Taylor.

Peasblossom had no memory of his cat family. He'd been taken away too soon. At first he was all pelt and stomach, longing for touch as much as nourishment.

He knew the men by their heartbeats first. Ron's was loud and steady as he bustled around the apartment in predictable patterns of morning, noon, and night, while Eugene's rippled songs of lost keys and late auditions at all hours, filling the house with excitement.

Peasblossom began to know that while he belonged to both of them, he had originally been a gift from Ron to Eugene. "You're twenty-four," Ron had said. "Old enough to take care of something."

"I take care of you," Eugene said, pulling Ron to him, tussling him to the bed. The salt and summer scent of them pulled trilling purrs from Peasblossom's kitten throat.

"He likes it when we fuck," Ron said.

"Cats are sensualists." Eugene nodded, pulling Peas onto his own beautifully furred chest. "He needs a name. He's old enough now. We can't keep calling him Kitty."

"I was thinking Puck," Ron said.

"Puck was Oberon's!" Eugene snorted, farted, laughed. "This one belongs to the Fairy Queen."

"It doesn't leave you with any very dignified options," Ron said. "Not that Her Highness is dignified. But still—Cobweb, Mustard Seed? I don't think so."

"What else?" Eugene said. "Peach pit? Apple core?"

Ron threw a pillow, missing his target. "What about Peasblossom? I'm pretty sure Peasblossom is the other one."

And so it was. Peas pounced on socked feet as Eugene and his actor friends ran lines for auditions, batted Ron's pen as he corrected papers. Some days were lonely window-looking days, others festive with the apartment full of people laughing and talking, inhaling the sparkling dust that helped them defy the gods of sleep.

Peasblossom smelled Eugene's illness before the humans detected it. Days went by when Ron and Eugene forgot about their cat. Peas punctured the box of kibble himself, rationing the food. His litter box became a horror. He learned to slip out the window and down the fire escape to a patch of earth in the alley. The traffic on the street frightened him. The rats were cunning and stank horribly of trash. This went on until the day Nora arrived to take him away.

There was a worry about Peasblossom and Eugene's illness. There was a cage. There was the moment in the lobby when the elevator banged and a car backfired and a siren went off and the latch wasn't tight on the cat carrier. Peasblossom burst out of his small swaying prison and fled.

Alone on the streets. Cars everywhere. Crows everywhere, voices harsh and taunting. Humans, unwashed or toxically perfumed, an old man crying on a street corner. Ron crying in the elevator with Nora only moments before. Ron! Peas tried to locate his scent, to find his way home.

He slunk between parked cars and against buildings until a pocket of quiet made him stop. On the side of a stoop there was a space under the stairs that was dry and unoccupied. A desiccated rodent lay scentless in the corner. Peas curled as far from the corpse as he could. Hours passed, terrifying sounds giving way to longer stretches of silence. Suddenly, there was music. A voice, singing clear and high like bells from the cathedral tower he could see from the kitchen window. *Nora?* He stood up. Another voice. *Ron!*

Peas ran from his hiding place. Ron scooped him up and held him tight. Nora rubbed his cold ears and sang until the moon rose and the stars came out and Peasblossom stopped trembling.

XOCHI'S FEET KEPT PACE with a slideshow of images: Leviticus—his lips, her lips. His hands. His breath, his racing heart. The scent of him swooned through her, mingling with the forest scent of the green girl, the animal musk of the running buck.

She opened the door of the corner grocery. It was familiar, she realized, close to the mildewed hotel that had been her first lonely home in the city. She bought a lighter, red to match her sneakers, and a fresh pack of cloves. She walked another block, but the coffee shop wasn't where she remembered it. She walked to the next block and there was Mitchell Brothers with its garish blue stucco, improbable mural of life-sized whales, and XXX marquee.

A tall redhead lounged near the entrance. "Hey," she called, "you got a light?"

Xochi stopped. She produced the lighter, attempting gallantry, but couldn't get a flame to appear.

"Let me." The redhead stepped closer. Her eyes were a smoke-rinsed gray and a diamond sparkled in her left nostril. Her skin was free of makeup, lightly freckled and absolutely flawless. Xochi handed her the lighter. Without thinking, Xochi pulled out her own cigarette to be lit. The redhead did the clove first.

"Thanks," Xochi said.

Pocketing the lighter, the redhead looked Xochi up and down through fox-brown lashes. "They'll hire you," she said. "You're gonna rake it in with that whole gangly 'who me?' thing you've got going on."

"Oh, no—I'm not here for that," Xochi said, taking a drag of her clove. "I was just walking by." She tried to imagine herself in complicated lingerie and heels, sexy and graceful. A girl who belonged with Leviticus. She'd call herself Lola. Or Anaïs, after the French erotica lady Kiki kept telling her to read.

"Pick a tomboy stage name," the redhead said. *Pretty and also a mind reader.* "Nothing overtly sexy. And wear simple things. Feminine, but not frou-frou. Think Katherine, think Audrey. Most girls come in without thinking at all. You need a strategy. A niche. Focus on the old guys, play the nice girl and you'll hardly have to do a thing."

"Is that what you do?"

"Me?" The redhead laughed. "Oh, no. Can you imagine?"

She smoked in small staccato puffs. "Why do you think I'm telling you this? It's nice, actually, meeting someone who's no real competition. My customers don't want sweet. But their friends might, their business associates. I help you, you help me. Most of these girls, they act like this is their *life*. They have their cliques, their jealousies. But we're not here for our health. We're at work. We're *colleagues*. If we were men, we'd certainly have figured that out. But women aren't socialized for that, are we?"

"No, we're not," Xochi said. She thought Pallas was a fast talker, but this redhead had her beat.

"Auditions are Monday nights at seven," she said, "but you should go inside and take a look. Girls are free. Go on." She smiled, indulgent. Possibly the bossiest person Xochi'd ever met. "At least until the rain stops."

"It's not raining," Xochi said.

"No, but it's about to."

A car pulled up and the redhead got in.

Just as she'd said, it started to rain.

XOCHI WALKED QUICKLY PAST the men in the lobby and pushed through heavy swinging doors into a large, dark room. A woman, naked save a pair of strappy gold heels, was hurrying off a wide stage flanked by a set of brass poles. Xochi found an empty row in back. An announcer's voice filled the room.

"Gentlemen, let's give a warm welcome to the seductive, sensuous, sexy Sasha!"

The dancer was everything the DJ had advertised. Men near the stage placed money at her feet, and soon, more men rose from their seats to do the same. By the end of her second song, Sasha was naked except for her thigh-high boots. The next dancer was also beautiful, with breasts smaller than Xochi's, generous hips and a mischievous grin.

Xochi unzipped her jacket. Another dancer came onstage. She was short and muscular. A gymnast. She slid into a handstand, lowered slowly into the splits. It was like the Olympics, only sexy.

After a while, Xochi began to notice the activity around her in the audience. Two rows ahead, a woman in lingerie leaned over a businessman. "Would you like some company?"

The man pulled a bill out of his wallet and she lowered herself onto his lap. After a few minutes passed, she asked, "Want me to stay?"

He pulled out another bill, positioning her so her back was facing him. He gripped her hips, guiding her movements. Xochi looked away, but this was going on all around her. *Lap dancing*—Bubbles had explained to Xochi that it was how regular dancers made money at the club.

All around her, women gyrated on men's laps. What happened if the men ejaculated? And what if there was a customer like the creep outside the bar that night? Did the dancers have to sit with guys like that?

Xochi pulled on her jacket to leave. She felt—what? Scared, maybe. Definitely embarrassed. It was just so weird seeing this private thing done in public. So weird it was actually someone's job. But the dancers were gorgeous. Watching them was like an endless Christmas morning, unwrapping gift after shiny gift. She found herself frozen, distracted by the pink-wigged woman onstage—not so different from the men here after all. Her stomach rumbled during a break between songs. Blondie's was around the corner with its huge slices of pizza. She'd leave after one more set.

The next dancer walked onstage in darkness and took her place at the brass pole, back to the audience. Xochi recognized the opening notes of a dreamy Led Zeppelin song. The dancer swayed. Her hair was up in an elegant knot, her black negligee cut low in back. Her slow movements drew attention the way a whisper can trump a scream.

Back still to the audience, she removed the stays from her hair. It fell to her waist, a dozen shades of gold. She reached for the pole with a languid hand, floating around it like she was made of dandelion fluff.

Finally, she turned to the audience, the reveal of her face more dramatic than the unveiling of her body could ever be. Three men placed bills on the stage. Two more rose to do the same. A man in front of Xochi sat up straighter. She could see it in the side of his face—the desire to hold the delicate blue-eyed woman, protect her, buy her things. A collective longing saturated the darkness, stole the room's air, but Xochi knew not one man considered leaving.

There was only one person Xochi had ever known who had this effect on men.

Only one person who had this effect on her.

THE SMOG-STUNTED TREES WHISPERED their warnings as crows gathered overhead. The fire escapes and power lines were black with them. Peasblossom hunched under a Volkswagen bug in front of the theater. Suddenly, Xochi burst from the entrance of the strip club, ran out to the curb, and vomited. The cat's muscles readied to follow her around the corner, to see if she was all right, but the wind paused, a message to wait.

A barefoot woman in a silk robe ran out to the sidewalk, craning to see down the block. She looked up at the crows, eyes a startling Siamese blue.

"Where did you go?" the woman said. It was a whisper, but the wind brought it to Peas like a gift, wrapped in ragged loss.

"Hey, Misty," a doorman called, "you okay?"

Peasblossom went to her, brushing against the woman's ankles. He had an impulse to lie on her bare feet and protect them from the rain. She bent down, touched the cat's fur. "Where did she go?"

The full impact of her scent was an answered question, a quest fulfilled.

Like Nora and Anna, like Pallas and Io, Xochi and the bereft cat-eyed woman were related by scent, by flesh, by blood. This woman was Xochi's mother.

31

Fever 103

X ochi was halfway up Buena Vista when her legs started to cramp. She'd been riding around the city all day, first on the cable car as it climbed through Chinatown and down to the Wharf, and then on the bus, crossing the city from downtown to Land's End. When the sun came out she'd gotten some pizza and sat on the beach, but she was too stunned to eat it.

The second half of Buena Vista was steeper. A light rain glittered on the parked cars. Xochi pulled up her hood, thoughts of her mother lined up like panhandlers in the park. Xochi always gave people money when she had it. But she had nothing for Gina. Not anymore.

She pictured Gina standing at the front door of Eris Gardens. The image stopped her. Gina's need was endless, her taking as effortless as breath. Xochi had already screwed up her almost fairy tale by kissing the goddamn prince. Gina was the last thing she needed.

Sand rolled inside Xochi's shoes. At the beach, she'd bared her pale feet and rolled up her jeans, wading in up to her calves. The freezing water hadn't fazed her. She felt the ocean in her cells, an evolutionary connection she shared with the mammals who'd chosen waves over sky. Suddenly sleepy, she'd found a protected hollow between dunes to close her eyes—just for a minute.

Waking under the stars, she wasn't even cold. She'd been dreaming, of course, of the green girl and her brother soaking in a pool of mud, a hot chocolate brew. The dream was earthy, replenishing. She had been wrong before. The dreams were good, a healthy part of her that was strong and fierce and pure.

Now, inside the house, three glasses of water gulped down, the dirt and misery of the day hardened on Xochi's skin. She took to the attic stairs as quickly as she could. She would decide what to do about Gina tomorrow. She would shower for as long as the hot water lasted. She would slip into bed and sleep until Pallas woke her.

She opened the attic door and started peeling off sticky layers of clothes. She was down to bare feet, a tank top and jeans when she saw him.

Leviticus was asleep on the sofa, more beautiful than ever in pajama bottoms and an old T-shirt. A fire burned low in the fireplace. His guitar leaned precariously against the easy chair and there was a book propped open on his chest. Glasses she'd never seen before were on the cushion beside him.

A log cracked in the grate. Xochi moved on autopilot, clearing cups from the table, putting away Pallas's knitting, moving the guitar out of harm's way. She retrieved a book from the floor: *Herbal Medicine for Children*. Pallas was sick!

Xochi inched Pallas's door open, mindful of its creak. A humidifier gurgled on the bedside table. Pallas slept peacefully. Her forehead was damp and cool. Xochi smoothed the wispy curls around her face. She looked like both her parents, with Io's forehead and coloring and Leviticus's cheekbones, long eyelashes and full lips, but there was something in her face that was uniquely hers, as if the combination of genes had exploded into a soft light below the surface of her skin.

When Xochi had first arrived in the city, she'd spent three lonely weeks walking around admiring the people of San Francisco, but the only person to catch her eye and smile back was Pallas. Xochi knew a kindred spirit when she found one. Pallas was part little sister, part fairy godmother. She made Xochi laugh, but also made her think. She didn't deserve Xochi's evasiveness, her distraction. *Do what thou wilt shall be the whole of the Law?* Aleister Crowley obviously didn't have kids. Kids changed everything, canceled all of it out. Unless you were like Gina, kids came first.

Back in the sitting room, Xochi avoided looking at Leviticus. He'd been worried enough about Pallas to watch over her. Since he was sleeping, she'd take over. She certainly wouldn't be creepy and watch him as he slept.

She went to her room and showered quickly. Changing into a slip and flannel shirt, she looked in the mirror. What had the redheaded stripper said? Something about each person's kind of sexiness. Gina had always known how to wield that particular weapon, but she hadn't passed it on to Xochi.

Gina. Xochi realized she'd been thinking about her like nothing had changed. Like she was mythical, a captive in some distant underworld. But no. She was in the city, drawn here by maybe the same force as Xochi—looking for a place pretty enough to heal and crowded enough to hide.

Xochi considered makeup but rejected it. The redhead was right. She was better natural. The slip was tight, the fabric thin. *Too obvious. Totally wrong.* She found a clean T-shirt and a clean enough pair of jeans.

Back in the sitting room, Xochi added a log to the dying fire, careful to close the metal curtain that kept the sparks inside. Leviticus stirred, turning over and curling into himself. Xochi went to her bedroom and pulled the quilt from her bed. She laid it over him. His face softened. Step by step, she backed away.

"You covered me up," he said, not quite awake.

"You looked cold."

"Wait! What time is it?" He put on his glasses and looked at his watch. "Shit! I slept through her Tylenol." He pushed the blanket away.

"It's okay. I just checked on her. Her head is cool and she's sleeping great." Xochi sat on the ottoman in front of the sofa. "What happened? She was fine this morning."

He pulled the quilt around his shoulders. "Her temperature went up to 103. I was about to take her to emergency, but it started coming down."

"Is there something going around?"

"Io's sick, too. And Kiki."

"I should have been here."

"It's okay. I'm kind of glad you weren't." He rubbed his eyes and saw her face. "No! I mean I'm glad I had to do it myself, not hand it over like I usually do." He exhaled heavily, running his hands through his hair. "You know how I said we moved to New York when Pallas was a baby? That's not exactly how it happened. I blew it in London. Io left me." Leviticus paused. The humidifier hummed in the next room. "I followed her to New York. I didn't deserve it, but she took me back. Things were okay for a while. But after we moved here, I did it again. If it wasn't for Kylen, I wouldn't be sitting here right now. I don't know why Io forgave me a second time. But she did. Then Kiki came back from college and was always babysitting, trying to give us a break. And Pad was around, and he was so good with her. He knew all kinds of stuff from raising his sisters. Aaron, too. So Io and I both had a break. But I realized it tonight—a break is one thing. After a few years, it's something else."

He took off his glasses, massaged his temples. He said he'd messed up, but not how. He didn't need to. Xochi knew the need to flee your fate, the thing at your back worse than the dark shoulder of the road, the stranger in the car. His hands shook. She reached out to steady them. They were cold, fingertips calloused, palms soft. There was a tattoo on the inside of his wrist she hadn't noticed before, a number: "24:20."

"What's this?" she said. She ran her finger over it. There was a scar there, above the tattoo. Suddenly, her question was about that, too.

"My name," Leviticus said. His voice caught. "Chapter and verse."

Xochi shook her head. "I don't know what that means."

"Lucky you," he said. His smile was sad. "It's a Bible verse. The book of Leviticus. It was my first tattoo. So I wouldn't forget where I came from." Xochi gripped his wrist hard, like it was bleeding. She pressed the pain away, feeling it fade as his hand warmed. She raised his wrist to her lips. Moving from the ottoman to his lap was effortless. She blinked and she was there, straddling him on the sofa.

They kissed and kissed, her lips raw from the stubble on his face, her hands tracing the shape of his arms, his back, his chest, pulling his shirt over his head. Her body was alive with purpose. His hands were on her back, her breasts. He was kissing her collarbone, his tongue lighting a path from her neck to her ear. His hand was on her stomach, moving down. Small, bright sounds escaped her mouth to float in the firelit room. Xochi arched against his fingers, suspended in honeyed geometry, cell after cell of kaleidoscope sweetness. Once, with Collier, there had been a hint of this, but Evan had made sure it died, vodka soaked and ruined like her blue homecoming dress. After that, when Xochi could sleep at all, she dreamed of wandering through a bombed-out city trailing hacked-off body parts and bits of soul.

Now desire cast a spell calling the pieces back. Her lips were hers as they brushed his earlobe. Her teeth were hers as she bit his neck. Her blood hummed with heat, furred yellow bodies gathering, incited. Their numbers doubled, tripled, moon-veined wings fluttering in mutiny against their virgin queen, swarming out of her mouth and nose and belly button as she came, her face buried in the perfect scent of Leviticus's neck.

As the pleasure receded and her body reset, her mouth followed the curve of his bicep, lazily tracing the tattooed outline of an outstretched wing, a yellow eye, a taloned foot. An owl, a large, noble owl with a ribbon in its beak. Greek characters flowed down the ribbon in blue: "ΠΑΛΛΑΣ." She recognized the symbol for pi. *It's a "P,"* she realized. *P for Pallas.*

She was back in reality, straddling his lap with her messy

hair and ragged fingernails and unbuttoned jeans. Leviticus looked as stunned as she felt. But there was something else, a little smile. Because he knew how to make women do this. It was probably one of the things he did best.

Xochi was surprised at how easy it was to disentangle her limbs from his. When she was on the opposite side of the sofa, she understood she'd been wrong. Like an art project she'd done once in school, pressing paper against paper, an image transferred from one to the other, her arms and legs and hands were fundamentally altered, imprinted and changed. She buttoned her jeans and hugged her knees to her chest.

Leviticus was lifting up the quilt, hunting for his shirt. Xochi imagined taking his hand, leading him to her bed. Reading every single word tattooed on his skin. He pulled his shirt back down over his head. "Are you okay?"

"I'm fine." Her mind groped for something she couldn't quite place. *Cigarettes.* When had she started smoking so much?

"Is there something I can do?"

You've already done it, she thought. "No," she said. "I just need a second."

"Can I use your bathroom?"

Xochi nodded, thinking for a split second of her messy room, but that was the least of her problems now.

"Don't go away."

Don't go away? Where would she go? She was trembling again. How had this happened? She saw herself straddling him, their bodies in rhythm. She saw the strip club, women gyrating in the darkness, her mother's back in the spotlight, pale hair cascading down.

She saw the guitar propped against the side table. She took it and strummed. The tuning was slightly off. Humming to find the right notes, she fiddled with the pegs, higher on one string, lower on another. She strummed a chord, satisfied.

"Thanks for the tuning." Leviticus sat on the opposite side of the sofa. "I didn't even know you played."

"I haven't in a while." Every time she'd tried in Badger Creek, Evan found her. She'd trained herself away from it so well, even in this house full of music, she'd never thought to mess around at the piano or pick up a guitar. But it felt so good, stretching her fingers to shape the chords, the notes vibrating against her belly almost like she'd never been away.

"Xochi?" His tone reminded her of Bubbles that night in Aaron's van. If only there were whiskey and cigarettes this time to help the medicine go down.

"Are we going to talk about it?"

"We should."

She kept her eyes on the fretboard, noodling around. "You start."

"Okay. I made a list."

"You did what?"

"I was sitting here thinking about you."

"What about me?" A smile tugged at her mouth. *Stupid girl.*

"What to do about you. So I made a list. Pros and cons."

"Let's hear it. Cons first."

He paged through a slim black notebook. "You know the first one," he said. "I keep thinking about her with Ky this morning. That girl needs to wage some serious teenage warfare. It would be different if she had friends her own age. But she doesn't. She only has you."

"Which makes me a traitor."

"I don't know what it makes me, aside from a shitty father. An asshole, I guess. A creep."

"She loves you."

"We all love each other."

The way he said it, Xochi knew he meant her, too. He was so earnest, sitting there with his list and his glasses, handing her the keys to the castle. Xochi wanted to take them, but she couldn't.

"So what's next?"

"You sure you want more?"

"Pallas is the deal breaker. But go on. I'm curious about this list of yours." She gave his ankle a little shove with her foot.

"Well, I have a policy. An age limit. You fall well under the minimum."

"Which is what?"

"Five years younger. So twenty-three."

"All right," Xochi said. "That's bad. Or it *sounds* bad. I get that. But age is relative, isn't it? I might be less experienced than you, but I'm not convinced you're more mature."

"I'm sure you're right. A mature person probably wouldn't be in this situation in the first place." Leviticus took a drink of water, then handed the glass to Xochi.

"We're both in it," Xochi said. She drank some water, wishing again for a cigarette. "What's next?"

He didn't look at the notebook this time, but right at her. "Just . . . the way it is with us." His hand twitched. He wanted to touch her. She could feel it, a feather against her cheek. "It's intense. I put it in the pros column, but I was thinking. I wouldn't wish myself on a beginner. You don't deserve that."

Xochi tucked her feet under the cushion separating them. "You're making a lot of assumptions. I get that you don't want to be an asshole, but it's not your job to decide what I deserve."

Leviticus looked down at his hands. "There are some things you learn with time. And you said it yourself, you work for us, live in our house. In principle, it seems wrong."

Xochi exhaled, suddenly exhausted. "I get that we can't do this. I'm not saying we should. But I don't know if age is as big a factor as you seem to think."

Leviticus sat on his end of the sofa, not answering. He retrieved a throw pillow from the floor and held it to his chest like a shield. The fire hissed, coming back to life. Xochi picked up the guitar and started to strum.

"We agree on the most important thing," he said.

"We do." Xochi nodded. "Pallas comes first." She found a chord that reminded her of a song one of the strippers had danced to. She hummed the melody to herself, picking out the notes.

"'I Put a Spell on You'?" Leviticus asked.

"Yes." Xochi laughed. Leviticus rolled his eyes, a move stolen straight from Pallas.

"Good taste," he said, smiling.

I heard it today, Xochi wanted to say. *In the strip club where I found my loser mom.* She tried the chords again, but couldn't get the rhythm right.

"It's heavier," Leviticus said. "Like a regular blues, but in three. Or like a waltz with a heavy accent on the one."

"Here. Just show me."

He took the guitar and began to play, slowing down and stretching the notes like taffy, his voice making it hard not to touch him again. When the song was over, he offered her the guitar. She shook her head. It was all she could do to stay on her own side of the sofa.

"Don't stop playing yet. Okay?"

"Okay."

He leaned back and got comfortable, guitar resting in his lap. He ran through snippets of blues songs, union anthems, Irish ballads, singing where he knew the words and humming when he forgot them. Sound filled the space between them, a substitute for touch. Xochi curled up in the corner of the sofa. Hot tears dripped from her eyes, a benign process unconnected to distress. The damp spot they made on the pillow smelled sweet, just like honey.

The songs shifted to moody lullabies—Nick Cave, Marianne Faithful, Tom Waits. Leviticus played until the fire burned out, until the room got cold, until the sun rose and Xochi fell asleep.

IV.

Sister rises from the mud
Greets the golden moon
A song trills the forest
Deep cold water

She finds a bowl of moonlight
Hot kisses glacial cold
Everything is pleasure
Seismic, Sister shakes

In the city Xochi cries, love not
Birdsong. Sister's mouth opens
On her tongue, a sun-furred queen

It is time to return to the city
To find the woman in the moon
Heat deep, Brother rises

His tears taste like Sister's
Golden, broken and sweet

32

You're a Big Girl Now

Pallas pulled Io's cashmere sweater tighter around her nightgown. Her fever had left her hollowed, but in a nice way, like she was a wind chime or a shell. She sat at her mother's dressing table, fiddling with the tops of perfume bottles as Io braided her hair.

"Your face is changing," Io said, a finger against Pallas's cheek.

She'd certainly gotten taller. And heavier. Earlier, when Leviticus had come to check on her, he'd given her a piggyback ride to Io's room, panting by the time they'd arrived. She knew she was too big to be carried now, but it was nice that her dad did it anyway.

Io leaned over and dabbed perfume behind Pallas's ears. Pallas longed to slip her arms around her mother's narrow waist, to bury her face in Io's long, wavy hair. But she stopped, afraid of the metal she might feel through her mother's shirt.

"I got my period," Pallas said.

Io paled. "When?" she asked, too casually.

"A few days ago. After I got back from LA."

"Did you . . . know what to do? Do you need anything?" Io was starting to look weepy. Xochi had tried to explain why Pallas should tell her mom. It was important somehow, she could see now.

"I got blood everywhere, but it turned out okay," Pallas said. "Xochi was with me."

Io met Pallas's eyes in the mirror. "If you ever need any-thing or just want to talk, you can come to me. You know that, don't you?"

"Mom?" Pallas said. "Please don't tell anyone else. I mean, Kiki is fine. And Bubbles. But none of the guys. Not even Dad. Okay?"

"Of course. Girls only. You wouldn't want . . . a moon ritual, would you? Some girls do them."

Pallas smiled. "Probably not. I've never been a very good witch."

Io laughed. "Not every witch is woo-woo." She kissed the top of Pallas's head. "Are you sure you don't want to come for sushi? We can bundle you up and take a taxi."

"No, thank you. Pad's spaghetti sounds better." Also, she wanted to give her parents time alone. In the few moments Leviticus had stayed after unloading Pallas onto Io's bed, there had been a gentle playfulness between the two of them, like a cat and dog making friends through a fence.

"All right, then," said Io, holding out her hand. "I can't carry you, but may I escort you to dinner, my lady?"

Pallas held out her hand. "You may."

33

Age of Consent

Xochi woke in the dark, the embers of her dream already dying. One final image lingered—Gina as a jewelry box ballerina, dancing on a strawberry whipped cream cake. The clock read 7:15 P.M. She'd been asleep all day.

She turned on her reading lamp to find a battered guitar case on the floor beside her bed, a rolled piece of paper tucked into the handle. Xochi leaped for it, carefully unfurling the thin parchment paper. Written in a slanted hand between cursive and print, it read:

> *Dear Xochi,*
>
> *I'm so sorry for the mixed messages I've sent. I hope you're not confused or hurt. I don't want to lose your friendship or your trust. Please accept Prudence as a token of my sincerest admiration. Be good to her and think of me when you play.*
>
> *Leviticus*

THE PREVIOUS NIGHT COURSED through her body. Xochi let herself imagine a hotel room, a stolen night with Leviticus. But how much could possibly be enough? They'd have to check out eventually, and then what? Back to Eris Gardens?

Xochi pulled the guitar from the case and held it against her body. Memory filled in its curves: Xochi handing the guitar to Leviticus, his smile when she'd tuned it. Evan used to look like that when they played together. He'd been so sad after Gina left, but when they sat on Loretta's porch with their guitars, he would smile at Xochi, thoughts of Gina faded to a minor moon.

Wait a minute. Xochi was supposed to be thinking about unrequited lust, but here she was, back on the farm. She climbed into bed, laying the guitar down beside her, tuning pegs on the pillow. It smelled like incense, probably the scent of Leviticus's bedroom.

Xochi must have seemed like such a bargain to everyone at Eris Gardens—no past, no problem. She almost laughed, imagining the moment her Trojan horse of a mom showed up to loose her dysfunction cannons on Eris Gardens. If Ky thought he had a reason to hate Xochi now, just wait until her whole messy past rolled up in tight jeans and a tube top, ready to rumble.

And what about Xochi? She'd certainly created some drama of her own. And was it mere coincidence that her subconscious produced Evan when she thought about Leviticus? The parallels came together—two handsome musicians, two absent blondes. It meant something, but Xochi wasn't sure what. There were differences, of course. Gina and Evan were nothing like Io and Leviticus. No, the common denominator was Xochi.

She read the letter again, this time noting its formal tone, clearly meant to distance her. Message received. She'd keep the guitar, though.

She got up, walked to the bathroom, and stood in front of the mirror. Tired eyes looked back at her, black in the weak overhead light. She touched her breasts. They were small for her frame. It was fine to be tall and have hips if you had big boobs to match. Then you were statuesque. Her hand went to her belly. Even when she held her breath, it curved outward slightly. She touched it, imagining what Leviticus felt. The skin was soft, the flesh squishy. An image presented itself: Andi, her shirt lifting when she hugged Leviticus with her toned arms and six-pack.

Xochi splashed her face with water. Her skin was washed out from winter, but it would turn brown with some sun. Her cheekbones were high, but her cheeks a little too round, her nose "cute" rather than beautiful. Big dark wide-spaced eyes and long lashes were her best features. She also had nice lips, full and small. A rosebud mouth—that was what Gina used to call it.

Xochi was attractive. She knew that. But it was a soft kind of pretty—pleasant, but not interesting. Nothing like Io. Entire magazine spreads were dedicated to her atypical, birdlike beauty and perfect ballerina body.

Xochi thought of Gina onstage, her thinness resembling Io's. Was she onstage now, flying around the pole? Or was she at home, an apartment somewhere in the city? Did she have another man now? Another kid? No, not likely. Gina had never wanted that. She hadn't even wanted Xochi.

Back in her room, Xochi buckled the guitar into its case. She picked up the note, the ivory paper and black ink reminding her of Leviticus's tattoos. She folded her regret away with his words, smaller and smaller, a postage-stamp secret burrowed in her underwear drawer. Avoiding the mirror, she pulled on pajama pants and headed downstairs.

THE KITCHEN WAS NOISY and crowded. Pallas sat perched on a stool at the counter. Pad wanted her to eat garlic bread for her immune system and Kylen was teasing her about drinking wine for her health. Xochi stood in the doorway, trying not to look like she was searching for Leviticus.

"Hey, Xochi," Pad said. "Can we feed you?"

"Sure! That garlic bread smells great." Xochi joined Pallas at the counter. "How are you feeling?"

"So much better. I should be back to my old tricks by tomorrow."

"Right—reading philosophy, writing letters, knitting. You know, you're a Victorian spinster trapped in a twelve-year-old's body," said Kiki.

"Kiki, you seem better." Xochi hoped she sounded casual. "How's Io?"

"She says she's better, but Lev took her out for sushi to seal the deal."

Xochi shivered. Furred husks rose in her throat, wings turned to dust. She poured herself a glass of wine. When she looked up, Kylen was staring.

"Bubbles and the boys are going to a party," Kiki said. "Why don't you go with them, Xochi? It's a wild scene. You should experience it at least once."

A party was the last thing Xochi wanted. "I shouldn't. I don't want to leave Pallas."

"I really do feel better." Pallas was working on her second helping of garlic bread. Her cheeks were pink and her eyes were clear. "Don't stay on my account. I'm just planning to read and go to sleep."

"You trying to get rid of me?"

"It's developmentally appropriate for you to go out at night, Xochi. Teenagers need to socialize!"

Aaron frowned. "Why did I think you were, like, twenty-two?"

"We've been all through this," Kylen said. "The governess lied about her age."

"She told me she was seventeen the first day we met," Pallas said. "Maybe you guys never asked her. You know what they say about assuming, Ky. But in this case, it's just made an ass out of you."

"Why did I teach her that?" Kylen tossed a piece of dry spaghetti at Pallas and missed.

"It's just easier for people to think I'm older," Xochi said. "That way I don't have to explain why I'm not, like, finishing high school and applying to college right now."

"Why aren't you?" Aaron asked. "You're smart enough if you can keep up with Pallas. She's pretty much a genius."

"I might go to college someday. I mean, I hope. I'll be eighteen in September."

"Right," Pad said, grinning. "No more jailbait."

"Offensive!" Bubbles called from the sink.

"Really?" Pad looked confused.

"Think about it," Kiki said. "Bait. Like young women are *asking* for unwanted attention."

"When you put it that way . . ." Pad said, "I humbly apologize." He bowed to Xochi.

"I don't think you're sorry enough," Pallas said, aiming a dishtowel at him and snapping it. The resulting chase spanned the entire first floor of the house.

"Take it easy in there," Kiki called, shaking her head.

"Xochi, you have to come out tonight!" Bubbles was adorable in her ruffled apron, but not an efficient dishwasher. She'd been scrubbing the same pan for ages. "So I'm not the only girl again."

"Don't worry about Pallas," Kiki said. "I have some sewing to do, so I'll be home. If she's not feeling well again I can work upstairs."

"I'm staying home, too," Aaron said.

"You might as well just go," Kylen said. "I'm sure Io and Lev would appreciate a quiet house when they get back from their date."

Something writhed in Xochi's belly, larval monsters ready to explode.

"Pretty please?" Bubbles tilted her head and batted her lashes.

"I don't know . . ." Maybe it would be better to go out, put some distance between her and Leviticus.

"You're coming; it's final." Bubbles hugged her, dripping dishwater down Xochi's neck. "It's nice having another girl around to play with. Kiki and Io have gotten so serious in their old age."

"It had to happen sometime," Kiki said. "Anyway, watch me celebrate after I finish this collection."

"Are you going to do a fashion show when it's done?" Xochi loved Kiki's creations. She and Io dressed in them almost exclusively. Pallas said Kiki's aesthetic was a cross between Victorian England and 2025.

"I am," Kiki smiled, the slight gap between her front teeth making her almost too-perfect beauty rakish and sexy. "I'm making a piece for you, too, you know. And Pallas. You two are going to walk in my show."

"Have you *seen* me walk? I mean, like, down the hall?"

"Don't stress. You're gonna love it."

"Hey, Pallas," Xochi said, "want to read together before I go out and do my socializing? I kind of want to know what's going to happen to Mr. Frodo, if you don't mind. Think he'll make it out of that forest?"

"He's the protagonist, and there are two more books to go. He'll be fine." Pallas brought her plate to the sink and rinsed it.

"Come find me when you two are done," Bubbles ordered on her way out of the kitchen. "I'm loaning you clothes."

"Don't make her too sexy, Bubbles," Pallas said. "Remember, she's only seventeen."

"Not when I'm done with her," Bubbles called back. "You'll need a chaperone just to look at her."

34

Little Green

otorcycles revved and faded as people left for the party. Pallas snuggled under the covers and closed her eyes.

What was that noise? She got out of bed and peeked into the sitting room. It was empty and unusually dark, the pinkish gold of the streetlight gone. She thought of Ky and how streetlights went dark whenever he walked past them. She'd been small enough to ride on his shoulders when she'd first noticed it. She'd decided it was his hair, so black it absorbed all the lights.

Pallas sat at the window seat, staring out at the fog. At first, it was like the flowing dress of a dancer, a costume from a black-and-white musical with feathers on the hem. Little by little, the fog cleared. Pallas blinked once, twice, three times. A small, exquisite green-skinned girl stood on the fire escape.

Pallas should have been scared, but she wasn't. She wasn't even surprised. She knew this girl. She'd been dreaming of her for weeks.

She put her hand against the window in greeting.

Friend?

The word popped into Pallas's head like it was her own thought, but she knew it wasn't. The green girl lay her hand against Pallas's from the other side of the glass. Pallas glimpsed pearly nails and silvery webs between the fingers before the merchild's tiny hand disappeared behind her own.

"Friend," Pallas whispered.

The girl placed her other hand on her heart, so Pallas did the same.

A strange sensation stirred in Pallas's chest, little folds of meaning that aligned themselves into a perfect origami crane: *Xochi.*

How do you know Xochi? Pallas said, but not with her voice.

The green girl closed her eyes, so Pallas did the same. A movie played on the pink backs of her eyelids: *two girls, candles, a bathtub. Pallas and Xochi sleeping on the carpet. A sister and brother leaping from the tub.*

The potion! Pallas recalled the goosebumps on her arms as she and Xochi had circled and chanted.

Did we create you? Pallas asked. Her hand shook, sweaty against the skin-warmed glass.

You called us.

Us? Pallas asked.

Next to the green girl, her brother appeared. He was taller than his sister, with hair as black as Kylen's. He bowed his head, his mouth turned up in something like a smile.

We must find Xochi, the green girl said.

Pallas wanted to tell them where she'd gone. It felt like the right thing to do, but how could she be sure? As if she'd spoken her fears, the green girl grasped her brother's hand, standing at attention. They spoke together in a dream-voice singsong.

> *We want only to help her, to heal and protect her.*
> *We love her and honor her, we cannot forget her.*

The pair of them stood waiting for Pallas's decision.

Her dad always said that her brains lived in her entire body, not just her head. If she listened to her gut, nine times out of ten, she'd know what to do.

She stepped back from the dream children. Planting her feet, she looked them in the eyes, each one in turn.

She took a deep breath and opened the window. "Xochi's not here," she said. "She went out. But you can wait if you want to. It will be a while. She won't be home till late."

Alarm filled the children's eyes.

You need to find her now? Pallas asked.

The green girl's hair spiraled round her head in affirmation.

The party was at a warehouse, Pallas knew that much. There had been a flyer on the mail table in the front hall. Like just about everything she read, the words were stored someplace in her brain. She just had to find the way back to them. Color usually helped. The flyer was yellow . . .

"I've got it!" Pallas said, this time out loud. "If I make a map, can you follow it?"

The girl's eyes remained worried and confused. Pallas understood. She held her hands out across the sill. The green girl's skin was slick and cool, the way Pallas thought a dolphin's might be. She closed her eyes, sending the girl a picture of the way to the warehouse several times to make sure she wouldn't get lost.

Thank you. The girl bowed her head and set Pallas's hand on her chest. Pallas sensed life there but not exactly a heartbeat.

She bowed. "My name is Pallas. I will help you any way I can. But can you tell me, is something wrong? Is Xochi in trouble?"

A wave of worry passed between the brother and sister. The green girl began to speak, but it was her brother's voice Pallas heard in her mind, earthy and sweet, the way clove cigarettes smelled.

> *You called us here; we answered the call.*
> *Debt-bound we follow; we try to mend all.*
> *We want only to help her, to heal and protect her.*
> *We love her and honor her, we cannot forget her.*

"BE CAREFUL," PALLAS SAID. "This city is beautiful, but it can be dangerous."

"I will be safe," the green girl said, speaking aloud as Pallas did, her voice almost too high and sweet to hear. "I am not alone." She clasped her brother's hand.

Pallas blinked. Her eyes must have stayed closed a moment too long, because when she opened them again, the window was closed and the brother and sister were gone.

35

Funtime

Walking between Bubbles and Pad, Xochi felt the eyes of the people in line. She met their curious stares, secure in her glamorous armor. Back in Kiki's room, Bubbles had laced her into a black satin bustier with a pair of red velvet shorts. Kiki had done her makeup and loaned her a cropped military jacket and tall black boots. In the bedroom mirror, Xochi was a lion tamer, a cabaret dancer, a completely different person.

"Who *is* that?" Xochi asked, not realizing Bubbles was right behind her.

"The girl you're about to be," Bubbles said. "Any second now."

As THEY WALKED PAST the people in line shivering in their scanty outfits, Xochi realized the girl in the mirror hadn't been her future self, but the girl she could have been. A girl raised by Gina. She might not know how to interpret dreams or have a library card, but she could rock a pair of hot pants and knew how to walk in heels.

Kylen strode ahead of them, bypassing the line and breaching the velvet rope that kept most people out. A muscled doorman held it open, waiting for Xochi and Bubbles and Pad. When they were inside, he pressed a stamp to each of their wrists in turn: "VIP."

Inside the warehouse, the music was bassy and loud. Xochi's eyes adjusted to the phosphorescent dim of the cavernous space, the white concrete walls and floors translucent purple in the blacklight.

It was a "gallery/party/performance space," according to Bubbles, where a group of artists lived and worked. "It's an intense scene," she'd warned Xochi earlier. "Super druggy and kind of wild. But the DJ's supposed to be awesome." On every wall, massive photographic prints showed details of hundreds of modified bodies, close-ups of tattoos and piercings, some in places that made Xochi cringe. Disembodied, flesh and bone took on new identities, some abstract, others morphing from flesh to sea creature to flower.

"Who did these?" Xochi yelled, her lips against Pad's ear.

"Alice somebody. From New York," Pad shouted back. "Io and Leviticus used to hang out with her."

A pair of girls glared at Xochi from across the room. Hair ponies headed straight for Pad. "Incoming," Pad said. "Gotta bail." Xochi gave him a shove, a head start for his getaway, but he caught her arm and pulled her back so his mouth was close to her ear. "Please do watch yourself, love. These parties are on a whole 'nother level."

Gripping Bubbles's hand, Xochi followed her deeper into the building, a long rectangle with a high, bare-beamed ceiling. Away from the massive speaker stacks, the music wasn't quite so oppressive. Bubbles pulled Xochi into the dancing crowd.

She fought the impulse to bolt, letting the heavy rhythm pound into her body. A dandyish girl in a skimpy tank and skintight jeans held the hips of a voluptuous Latina with dark ringlets and lavender eyes. A regal drag queen with perfect makeup shimmied with a short guy in leather pants. Two Mohawked boys rocked out with a topless hippie girl, her long brown hair fanning out around her face. Xochi closed her eyes. For a long, tranquil while, her brain was Leviticus- and Gina-free.

Thirst tickled her body out of the rhythm. She looked around for Bubbles, but found herself alone in the gyrating crowd. A keg was the only option for something to drink. Xochi swallowed the cold amber beer and followed the flow of the crowd to a platform on the far end of the building. Some sort of performance was happening on a stage to the left of the DJ, but Xochi wasn't close enough to watch. Seeing a door labeled GIRLS, she waited in line and took her turn, willing herself not to think.

The crowd was thinner when Xochi came out of the bathroom. She squeezed her way into a spot close to the stage. A man, naked and heavily tattooed, hung above a platform by thick metal hooks threaded through the skin of his chest. She checked the faces of the people around her, but no one was alarmed. She made herself look again.

His waist was unnaturally small, bound in a wide leather belt. His hair was dark and threaded with silver. It flowed back from his head as he leaned into the tension between gravity and his flesh. Xochi's examination reached his face. It was James! She expected to see blood dripping from the wounds in the skin above his pierced nipples, but there was nothing. This was less a crucifixion than a display of an unusual piercing done some other strange night and long since healed.

Remembering their conversation, Xochi wondered—what was he releasing now? What divinity would fly in to fill the void?

Xochi exhaled. She hadn't realized she'd been holding her breath.

"Not into pain?"

Xochi turned. Red hair fell in loose waves around starry gray eyes lined like a silent film star's over a nose dusted with freckles, sparkling with a diamond stud. Xochi recognized her from somewhere.

"Excuse me?"

"Pain," the redhead said. "You had quite the look on your

face. But we've already established you're the sweet and innocent type."

The redheaded lighter-stealing stripper! Of course. The
way she was talking to Xochi, it was like they were still having
a smoke outside Mitchell Brothers. "Not physical pain," Xochi
said. "Emotional drama is more my style."

The redhead leaned closer. She smelled like jasmine and
fire. "Elaborate, please." Her voice was clear, creating a pocket
of quiet in the loud room.

"Love. Hate. Sex. Fate," Xochi said into the seashell of the
girl's ear. "You know, the basics."

"The basics are the best." The redhead seemed to have
made a decision. Taking Xochi's hand, she led her away from
the stage. "Come on," she said over her shoulder. "I bet you
could use a drink."

Xochi pictured the girl in the mirror. What would she do?

The redhead stopped at an unmarked door and unlocked
it with a key from a thin chain around her neck. Candlelight
revealed a windowless room with a mattress on the floor covered by a floral tapestry, a stack of old leather suitcases, and
a stuffed clothes rack in the corner. There was a small bureau
and a wooden crate beside the bed. The rest of the room was
bare.

"You live here?" Xochi asked.

"Yes." The redhead pulled a flask from behind a pillow and
took a long drink before passing it to Xochi.

"Um, I'm Xochi, by the way." Xochi took a sip from the flask.
Tequila, but nicer than the stuff she and Collier used to pinch
from Evan's dad. She sat on the floor opposite the bed and
leaned against the wall, legs stretched out in front of her. She
felt for the square edges of Kiki's cigarette case in her pocket.
"For luck," Kiki had said when she'd tucked it in. "And now
you don't need a bag."

"Is it okay if I smoke in here?" It seemed to Xochi like smoking was all she did these days.

"I'll join you." The redhead kicked off her shoes and shifted to a cross-legged position on the bed. Xochi passed her the cigarette case. The girl turned it over in her hands before extracting a cigarette and handing it back.

"I'm Justine." Xochi loved the husky break in her voice. "And I know this cigarette case. Doesn't it belong to a stacked, leggy seamstress?"

"You know Kiki?"

"I do. And I know who you are, too."

Xochi was beginning to understand why Pallas hated her family's notoriety. She waited for questions about Io and Leviticus, comments about being the babysitter. Justine leaned back against the bed without any apparent discomfort at the growing silence.

The music thumped. Xochi could hear the crowd getting drunker. She was drunker herself. She took another swig from the flask and passed it back to Justine.

"Okay," Xochi said. "I give. How do you know about me? Io and Leviticus, right?" Their names flowed together—a couple, no matter what he said.

Justine laughed. "Sort of. I'm a friend of Pad's. You came in with him and Bubbles and Ky, and I recognized you from the other day. The adorable new nanny at Eris Gardens has been gossip for weeks. I'm guessing that's you." She got up to light a stick of incense.

What was Xochi supposed to say to that? She took another swig. *Fuck it,* she thought. She was here to have fun, not freak out. This girl knew Pad? Great. She smiled. "So, tell me about our Irish friend. All the dirt you've got. I need ammunition!"

Justine became animated as she detailed Pad's history of outrageous seduction and scandalous indiscretion, but carefully navigated around her own relationship with him. Drunk enough to ask, Xochi was cut off with a wave of Justine's manicured hand.

"Pad and I are old news. Ancient history. But"—she raised

her red eyebrows"—what about *you* and Pad? I'm sure he hasn't been able to resist all this." Her gaze swept up Xochi's legs to her breasts, landing on her eyes.

"Pad and me?" Heat rose along the fault line of Justine's appraisal.

"Keeping it a secret?" Justine blinked, her long lashes performing a sweet reveal of her gorgeous eyes.

"Nothing to keep," Xochi said. "I didn't ask for it, but I think I've got myself a big brother. Overprotective, but his heart's in the right place."

"And is he right?" Justine leaned forward.

"About what?"

"Do you need to be protected?"

Xochi's brain veered to Eris Gardens. What were Io and Leviticus doing now? She took another drink and set the flask on the floor between her and Justine. She closed her eyes. The green girl as swan-haired Medusa appeared, framed in gold, fixed like an image from a tarot card.

"I don't know," Xochi said. "I used to think so. Now I'm not so sure."

Justine lay back on the mattress. Her dress slid up her leg to reveal the grass-green snake tattooed around her thigh.

Xochi leaned forward. "Wow. It's incredible. That must have hurt."

"It was a rite of passage for me. This city changes you."

"Why a snake?"

"It's not just the snake." Justine raised herself to her elbows. "It goes up and sort of slithers around to my back." She sat up, her dress riding higher. "In the Bible, snakes are about temptation and evil. But way before the Bible, they were symbols of wisdom and healing. Do you want to see the rest?"

Justine pulled her dress up to her thigh to show Xochi how the snake twisted around her leg. She turned toward the wall and unzipped her dress. The snake wound around an enormous tree. Planted at her tailbone, its tallest leaves reached the back of her neck. It was hung with all kinds of fruit, real and imagined, with one more vivid than all the rest: a perfect apple, bloodred.

Justine lifted her hair away, an invitation to touch. Xochi was tentative at first, her finger shaking as it traced leaves and branches and trunk, following every line and curve of the drawing. Justine's jasmine scent was strongest at her neck. Xochi leaned closer, her mouth an inch above Justine's pale shoulder. Her lips rested there, and then her tongue took up the tracing, her piercing sparking along the tattooed branches. When she reached the apple, she didn't think; her teeth just sank into the bright-red center of the forbidden fruit.

36

Femme Fatale

The warehouse was even more crowded when Xochi and Justine returned to the party, lips swollen, makeup smudged, hands entwined. They danced, scandalous with tequila and lust. Finally, Xochi surrendered to her sore feet and pulled Justine to the sidelines. They collapsed on a sofa. Justine blew on Xochi's forehead, her breath deliciously cool. Xochi took the last sip of her gin and tonic, but what she really wanted was water.

"Need anything?" Xochi asked. Justine nodded, leaning in for a kiss. When Xochi pulled away, Justine's eyes were already open. Had they been open the whole time? Other eyes were on her, too, sliding away as Xochi stood up. Walking took more concentration than it should have.

There was a line at the bar. The hairs on the back of her neck rose. She turned around: Kylen.

"What the hell?" he said.

Xochi blinked. He was so beautiful tonight. Black kohl lined his eyes. His hair was pulled back into a French braid that ended halfway down his back.

"Dude," Kylen said. "Justine is a menace. Like, a social disease."

"Since when do you care?" Xochi swayed. She was drunker than she'd realized.

"I just don't want you to bring that shit home. It was hard enough getting rid of her the first time."

"Whatever," Xochi said, the caricature of a bratty teen. And why not? Tonight was the first time she'd actually *felt* young in ages.

"Whatever?" Kylen shook his head. "That's all you got?" He didn't sound much more mature than Xochi. "Fine, then. Have fun."

BACK AT THE SOFA, Justine's eyes were closed. Hopefully, she'd missed the little scene with Kylen. She reached into Xochi's pocket for another cigarette. They sat in silence, smoking and watching the crowd. The music changed from hip-hop to a pounding techno that made Xochi's head ache. She stared at the photo on the opposite wall. This picture was less stark than some of the others, almost sepia toned, a close-up of a typewritten piece of paper that was probably a tattoo. "I think that's Leviticus!" Xochi said.

"I think you're right." Justine ran her finger along Xochi's arm. "People say Pad's better looking. But Leviticus? Way hotter, if you ask me. He pretends to be modest, but he knows it. How could he not? And he's got the perfect setup—a rich wife who pays the bills and doesn't care who he sleeps with."

Xochi was dizzy. She downed the rest of her water.

"Of course, what happens behind closed doors doesn't quite live up to their shiny rhetoric."

"What do you mean?"

"You must have noticed."

Xochi flushed.

"I see you have." Justine laughed like they were sharing secrets at a slumber party. "He likes us young, doesn't he? At least he's got good taste." She pushed Xochi's hair behind her ear, caressing her neck. Despite Justine's words, pleasure dripped down Xochi's spine. "It's not about us, though, is it? It's all about the two of them, no matter who they're using to act out their sad little drama. Io may not want Leviticus for herself, but she certainly doesn't want anyone else to have him, does she?"

"Wait. So you and Leviticus were . . . together?" Xochi tried to imagine it. Was she missing something?

"Don't worry about me. I'm fine. I mean, it took a while. After I finally got over it, I felt sorry for him." She leaned in closer, her hair tickling Xochi's ear. "I can see it in your eyes. I don't want you to get hurt," she whispered. Her lips touched Xochi's again, lightly this time, pulling her closer, burning the words into her body until Xochi understood: She was nothing to Leviticus. Just another girl. Just like Justine.

Justine kept talking. "He's so hung up on Io. The rest is distraction, games to pass the time. I knew that, but I couldn't resist. You know guitar players—great hands." Xochi flashed to Leviticus's precision with her body, the laughter in his eyes. "You can't blame him," Justine said. "You never get over your first love."

37

Stella Blue

B lue wasn't sure how long she'd been standing at the black marble sink. Melly and Kim had wanted to party, so here they were—another back room where the old guys kept the drugs. Duncan was better than some of them. All he wanted was a blow job to get all three of them high. As always, they did rock-paper-scissors. As usual, Blue lost.

At least Melly was right about one thing: Duncan's drugs were very good. This was her favorite feeling, a Goldilocks high where everything was just right. She fluffed her hair so the curling iron waves would spring back up, but it was hopeless. Turning to leave, she spied something in the window. Two little kids! The poor things were naked and alone, and here it was past midnight. She stumbled for a second, but managed the latch just fine.

"Come on in, you guys."

They must be hippie kids with all that long hair. She knew what that was like. Their parents had probably left them on a freezing school bus while they were off dropping acid at a Dead show. Shivering, the two kids plopped down to the slate floor, one after the other.

Now that they were inside, she noticed the kids looked kind of weird. They had the longest hair she'd ever seen and one looked sick and greenish. When she put her hand on the sick kid's shoulder, it was ice cold.

"You guys should take a hot shower." She smiled to reassure them. "Check it out, this bathroom rocks."

She showed them the tiled stall and turned on the water, adjusting the temperature till it was nice and warm, but not too hot. Sometimes kids had a hard time figuring out stuff like that. She'd hated bathing in strange bathrooms when she was little.

The two kids bowed their heads to her, like they were saying thanks. Maybe they didn't speak English. Or maybe they were just shy. They stood there, waiting for her to leave before they got in.

Checking herself in the mirror, she wiped the smudged lip gloss from around her mouth and reapplied it carefully. There, now. Good as new.

"Take as long as you want," she said, fixing the hem of her miniskirt. "I'm locking the door. There are some sketchy people at this party, you know? You guys should take off after you warm up. It's not the best place for kids."

38

Fates and Furies

X ochi followed Justine to the back of the warehouse and teetered upstairs in Kiki's high-heeled boots. Justine took her keys out again and unlocked the door to a large room. The walls flickered blue with the light of several aquariums. A huge TV stood in the corner playing a black-and-white war movie, the sound on mute. In the back corner of the long narrow space was a bed. It was dark, but Xochi could see a man sitting on the edge. Someone sat behind him, rubbing his shoulders.

A black leather sofa beckoned. Xochi slid her hand from Justine's and sat down as a door at the back of the room opened, releasing steam and a buoyant giggle, too light for the thick air.

Xochi closed her eyes. She tried to remember how much she'd had to drink, counting tequila shots and gin and tonics. Way too many, that was all she knew. Another mistake in a series of mistakes. How long before everyone in the house knew about her and Leviticus?

"Duncan," Justine called back toward the bed. "Come meet my friend."

Duncan's smooth face contradicted his silver hair and tired eyes. He wore his jeans and T-shirt like a twenty-five-year-old. "Hello there." He smiled. His teeth were crowded and yellow, a hint at the real creature inside. Xochi knew she should answer, but she didn't. It seemed absurd, like exchanging pleasantries with a crocodile.

"Xochi lives at Eris Gardens," Justine said. "She's the nanny. But I have a feeling she has some other duties at night."

Xochi saw herself fleeing, running through the party like a deer in the forest, not stopping until she found a place that was empty and fragrant and green, but she was too tired for that. Too tired and too wasted.

She closed her eyes for a moment's peace in her dream forest, but it was gone, replaced by a steaming swamp. Reptile country. Heat flooded her limbs.

"Let me guess," Duncan said, sitting down next to Xochi. "Wild night? Justine certainly is a handful."

Xochi rested against the cool leather and closed her eyes again. The fog was thicker now. The green girl and her brother lifted their faces to a hot tropical rain. Heat rose to Xochi's face. Alcohol seeped from her pores. She wished she were home, naked under her own cool sheets. Duncan reached over her, handing something to Justine.

When she raised her head and opened her eyes, Justine's arm was clamped above the elbow by a rubber tube. She gave Xochi a long look and pierced the tender crease of her arm with the needle. Duncan did the same. Xochi sat between them, strapped into the roller coaster for the duration of the ride. Justine's hand opened, the syringe dropping to the arm of the sofa. A spot of blood bloomed in the pinprick wound, but Justine didn't seem to notice. She leaned back, hair covering one eye as the rest of her face melted into dreamy softness.

Xochi lit the last cigarette in Kiki's case. Justine took it from Xochi's fingers, dragged, and passed it to Duncan. She sat up and opened the hinged lacquered box resting on her lap, then withdrew a syringe. She gazed at Xochi, leaned in to kiss her, then stopped and waited.

This was a test.

Xochi turned to Duncan. He took another drag of her cigarette and returned it. Xochi smoked, putting her lips where his had been. His and hers and Justine's.

39

No Big Deal

Kylen leaned against the wall, enjoying the view at the bar—buzzed hair, brown skin, short and muscular. In addition to being easy on the eyes, it seemed that Mike the drummer wasn't exactly straight. He looked back at Kylen, gave him a nod.

A few yards behind Mike, Kylen spotted a familiar leather jacket. What the hell was Leviticus doing here? He hated this kind of crap. "Lev," Kylen called, making sure the syllables cut through the techno drone. He strode through the crowd toward Leviticus and grabbed him in a hug meant to confirm or deny his suspicions. With people he was close to, one short touch was usually enough, but Leviticus was onto him.

"Nice try." He thwarted the hug with a rough but friendly block.

"Doesn't matter." Kylen grinned, wide enough to show his pointed incisors. "It's obvious anyway."

Leviticus rolled his eyes, a move copped from Pallas. "How's your night?"

"Pretty good." Kylen gestured toward Mike, heading back with their drinks.

"I always liked that guy. Guess he finally lost the girlfriend."

"That's what I heard."

Leviticus looked tired and bummed. Kylen felt a pang. He

wouldn't be happy about Xochi and the Demon Spawn. Hopefully he hadn't seen them sucking face.

Mike made it back through the crowd to join them. "Hey, Leviticus."

"What's up, Mike?" Leviticus grasped his arm. "How's Buffalo?"

"Cold. Wish I could move out here. One of these days, maybe. How's the family? Last time I was at the house, it was friggin' nuts."

"Right, last Equinox," Kylen said. Mike had had the girlfriend then, but it hadn't stopped him from making eyes at Kylen all night.

"You know that redhead? I think she lives here now," Mike said. "I saw her earlier making out with some girl."

Leviticus was instantly on edge.

"You guys might know her, actually. I think she came in with Bubbles and Pad?"

Swoosh, Kylen thought as Mike's little guillotine decapitated his plans for the night.

Lev's eyes went dark. He turned to Kylen. "Did you see Xochi with Justine?"

Instead of meeting his gaze, Kylen stared at Mike's drummer's arms—muscular, tattooed to the wrist. *So pretty. And leaving tomorrow. Fuck Leviticus and his bullshit.*

"I saw her," Kylen admitted. "Like an hour ago. I told them to get a room."

"Where is she now?"

Mike piped in, a total gentleman—not what you'd expect if you saw the guy onstage. "When I was looking for the bathroom, I saw her and Justine heading up some stairs. The sign said 'private,' but Justine blew right by it. They both looked kinda wasted."

Damn. No matter how much Xochi irritated Kylen, Duncan's room was no place for a kid like her, especially not without some nunchucks or a can of mace. Considering the way she'd fought the other morning in the garden, she might be fine. But she wasn't sober. And aikido was no match for the games Justine and Duncan liked to play.

"I'm sorry," Kylen said. "I'll take care of it."

But Leviticus was already heading for the back of the warehouse.

"Need company?" Mike asked.

"Absolutely. Lev's not much help unless diplomacy is required."

"I promised Io," Leviticus said, pushing through the crowd. "No fighting. All men are brothers and all that."

"Yeah," Kylen said, "brothers who need to get their asses kicked."

"I'm in, man." Mike hurried to catch up. "I hate that Duncan guy. He hit on my cousin once. She was, like, fifteen. That brunette looked young, too."

"She is." Leviticus gripped Kylen's shoulder, an admission and a silent truce. Kylen winced: *Xochi's eyes, unguarded and surprisingly wise. Her face, illuminated in firelight. Serious, intelligent, sincere.* And beautiful? That didn't even come close to the way Leviticus saw her. Kylen couldn't deny it now: Xochi had been family since the day Pallas brought her home. He should have protected her.

40

Acid Bath

One of Justine's superpowers was a certain immunity to drugs. She could get loaded enough to have a little fun, but a part of her always stayed sober. This internal governor was a heavy burden for thrill-seeking, pain-insensitive Justine. Entertaining herself was no easy task.

Xochi had been promising at first, but things had turned predictable. There were only so many ways this sort of thing went, so Justine and Duncan made a game of it. Justine undid a button on Xochi's jacket. Duncan unbuttoned Xochi's shorts. Justine undid another button. Duncan fumbled with her bra . . .

The doors on both sides of the room burst open at once.

Finally! Something interesting.

In one corner was Team Eris Gardens, with an assist from a punk drummer Kylen must have lured away from his harpy girlfriend.

In the other corner were a pair of psychedelic devil children straight from hell. Justine had seen *The Exorcist* at least twenty times. The little devils that shot out of the bathroom resembled poor demon-fucked Regan midway through the movie—still pretty, but full-on possessed.

The water in the fish tanks bubbled and hissed. One of the lids blew straight into the air, bursting into a fine glitter of plastic and glass. Justine hit the floor, grabbing a pillow to shield her face. The next lid blew, exploding into larger chunks that whizzed through the room. Duncan swore, clutching his crotch. His hands turned red. He ran to the bathroom, blood spilling down the front of his designer jeans.

The baby junkies on the bed whimpered like dogs. The demon children ignored them.

Justine backed into a corner and made herself invisible, an ability she'd developed as a defense mechanism and honed into a weapon. In the corner, you never knew what you might hear. Tonight for example, she'd been able to piece months of accumulated low-level gossip into a narrative believable enough to ignite this big juicy drama. She should become a spy. Or an assassin.

The brown demon hovered over Xochi, hands on her chest. Little perv. In the space of time it took Justine to blink, it decked and straddled Leviticus, hands wrapped around his pretty neck. Kylen went to pull the thing off, but couldn't touch it— no matter how he struggled, his hands stopped inches from the creature's hide. So much for Mr. Wizard. Apparently, his witchy woo-woo shit meant nothing in the face of an actual magical force field.

"Wait," Kylen said to the green demon. "It's not what you think. Tell him! Please!"

Kylen was foolish or wasted if he thought begging would work in a situation like this. Justine always laughed at the part in *The Exorcist* when the priests did their "power of Christ compels you" routine. She giggled. This was all so absurd. Kylen was practically in tears, the wimp.

The fish tank above her sloshed a warning. Water dripped down her neck. She looked up and the little green demon held her eyes. *Do not mock*, it said. The heroin suddenly kicked in hard, like she'd done a second shot. The high pushed into her body, hitting bottom, surging back up. Justine was dizzy, and hell yes, scared.

Instead of a floaty, sensual bathtub high, Justine was in dark, cold water.

Chemicals exploded into her bloodstream, panic drugs her own body was making in a frantic attempt to stay alive. She waited for her shitty life to pass before her eyes.

Nothing came. She floated in a bath of nothingness. How long had it been? She tried to struggle and couldn't. She wanted to cry, but her body was gone. She was shrinking, down and down and down, melting in the water. Then *BAM!* She was back, the bath turned acid, every cell exploding with pain.

The green monster's face loomed in front of her. Its voice invaded her head.

Change your ways, Fire Hair. Before you are truly lost.

Justine opened her mouth to cuss the creeper out or scream bloody murder—she didn't know which—but the green demon had resumed her place next to Xochi like the near-death Sunday school lesson had never even happened.

Straightedge moralistic little bitch, Justine thought, but she scooted as far back as possible into her corner, shaking. She kept her eye on the green one. *Her*, she thought. Of course the female was the scary one.

THE GREEN DEMON HELD out its hands, and Kylen took them.

Justine crossed her fingers that she was a head-spinning puker. Something foul and gooey would serve Kylen right. But no. The dark one let go of Leviticus, bowing its head to Ky.

"Will he remember this?" Kylen asked, looking down at Leviticus.

He will not, the green monster answered, and hell if the sound didn't happen right inside Justine's head again, like mind reading or telepathy. The green demon touched Leviticus and Xochi in turn. Then the two little monsters actually held hands, like kids on a field trip forced to take a buddy. Together, they moved toward Justine. She bared her teeth and hissed, but they passed by her corner without a glance.

She peeked around the dresser to see what was happening. She blinked once, twice, three times—and the devil children were gone. No more than five minutes had passed and the world had shifted back to normal, with Ky banging on the bathroom door for Duncan and drummer boy talking to the jailbait triplets on the bed.

Xochi was still passed out on the sofa. Leviticus knelt in front of her. He took her head in his hands and pressed his forehead to hers. He adjusted her clothes and pulled her up. She swayed, he caught her, picked her up and carried her out of there princess style, like they were in some TV movie.

And that was that. No more demons. No more drama. Duncan probably needed stitches, but fuck him. He could take a cab.

Justine sighed.

Monsters were real. And love stories.

She'd need to think about that, but not tonight.

She got up, glass crunching under her feet, still shaking.

Duncan kept cash in a compartment in his desk. She took a modest stack—no more than she'd need for a taxi, a hotel room, room service and a manicure. She'd stay away a night or two and come back after this mess was cleaned up.

41

Definitely Clean

Leviticus handed Xochi a helmet and his leather jacket. "Can you get on the bike?"

He's mad at me, Xochi thought. Wasn't she mad at him, too? She climbed onto the back of the motorcycle, surprised she could manage it.

He gunned the engine. "Hold on."

It was all he said until they got to Eris Gardens. Inside, she headed for the attic stairs, but he stopped her. "You can't go up there with Pallas. You're too wasted."

His tone was neutral, but his words made a small rip in Xochi's soft pink cloud.

He rolled up his sleeves and moved around the kitchen. Xochi unzipped his leather jacket but didn't take it off. It smelled so good.

The kettle was making a comfortable sound, like a kid blowing bubbles in milk with a straw. The kitchen was so cozy. Xochi lay her head on the table.

"What's up, Edie Sedgwick?"

The Andy Warhol girl? But wait, didn't she overdose? "That's not a nice thing to call me right now."

"Really? Why not?"

Leviticus reminded her of Pallas when he was prickly. Like father, like daughter—and she'd let both of them down.

"I know you're mad," she said.

He didn't look at her when he answered. "I was, but what's the point? You can't talk to heroin."

Heroin. Justine hadn't called it by name. Xochi hadn't asked. She'd known, of course, but it was easier to pretend she didn't. Naming things made them real.

Leviticus put the coffee down in front of her. "Drink it." He opened a drawer and pulled out a pack of cigarettes. They weren't supposed to smoke inside, but he lit one off the stove.

"Just say it," Xochi said. "Whatever it is." She wanted one of his cigarettes, but the way he looked, there was no way she was about to ask. "I think I need water. I drank a lot, too."

Leviticus emitted a low growl and got up, fishing around in a high cupboard. He took out a large plastic Batman Slurpee cup.

"Xochi—" His voice caught. He wasn't just mad. He'd been scared. "That guy Duncan? He's dangerous. Forget hedonism—those guys make Rabbit Hole look like choir boys. And did you see those girls on the bed? They're not much older than Pallas."

Neither am I, Xochi thought. *Not really.* But with the sickness and caretaking and dying and burying, the funeral and the wake, the breakup with Collier, the broken aftermath of her and Evan, leaving home, Eris Gardens—the last year could count as ten.

"I'm sorry." It was all she could think to say.

"Did they use a clean needle?"

"I don't know." Xochi felt sick. She pushed the water away.

"A new one has two caps, a skinny orange one over the needle part and a clear cap by the plunger. Can you try to remember?"

Xochi thought back. At some point, she'd closed her eyes. But they were open at first. She pictured the syringe in Justine's hand. There had been an orange cap. Maybe the clear one, too. "I think it had both," Xochi said.

Leviticus bowed his head and exhaled like he'd been holding his breath for a long while. His eyes were dark and sad when he looked back up. "All I know is I never want to see you like that again. Those people are not your friends."

"I know," Xochi said. "I'm not stupid."

"Then I have to ask. Why?"

"I don't know," Xochi said. "I was just scared, I guess."

"Of what?"

The memory was like a movie starring some other girl. Xochi watched herself straddling Leviticus on the sofa, mouth hard on his, his hand down her pants. "It was that," she said.

He shook his head, confused.

Of course—he couldn't read her mind. "When we fooled around. Sorry to sound so high school, but I don't know what it's called. When you do it to a guy, it's a hand job."

Xochi knew there was a version of her who would be mortified by this conversation, but it was hard to remember why. *If you can't talk about it, don't do it.* That was what Loretta had always said about sex. Maybe it was a good rule for drugs, too.

"Okay." Leviticus put his feet up on the chair beside her like he'd done the first night at the bar. "Go on."

"I felt stupid. Like some dumb groupie." He started to deny it, but she stopped him. "Not that night. Afterward. Then Justine—"

Xochi paused, trying to fit Justine into the puzzle. Justine, the strip club, Gina. Justine, Eris Gardens, Leviticus. Justine's mouth, the photo of Leviticus at the warehouse, the note he'd left with his guitar.

"Your note didn't help," she said.

"What do you mean?"

"It was so . . . final. And like, I don't know. Eloquent, I guess." It was ironic how ineloquent she was searching for the word. "Like you've done this before. Justine told me a bunch of stuff about you and her and Io. It made the note seem even worse."

Leviticus groaned. "I wrote that thing ten times and couldn't get it right."

"It's not just us," Xochi said. She thought of telling him about Gina, but didn't. "No matter what I do, it's not working."

"What's not?" His voice was so soothing. She wished he'd keep talking. But he wanted her to talk. How could she explain?

"I don't know. Me. The way I am."

They were silent. The clock ticked on the stove. A wind chime trilled in the yard.

"Come with me," Leviticus said, getting up from his chair.

"Where are we going?"

"Just come on."

42

Running to Stand Still

The white noise of the filling bathtub threw Leviticus a line to calm. Xochi sat on the chair he kept for visitors—usually Ky, who liked to bug him when he was reading in the tub. She struggled with the zipper on her boots, then finally gave up and let him do it. Looking up at her, he noted the smudged lipstick, the bite marks at her neck. It had been a long time since he was jealous. It was just like he remembered, an old friend you never really liked.

"I'll be in my room, right next door. The towel on the rack is clean."

"Don't go," Xochi said, a note of worry in her voice.

"I'll be right outside. I'll check on you in a minute."

Alone in his room, he lay back on the bed. That night at dinner, Io came clean about James. She'd been discreet—classic Io—but for once he was relieved. He didn't need to know the details. It was enough that she was happy.

He imagined the things Justine must have said to Xochi, embellished versions of the trouble she'd tried to make when Pad had brought her to stay at Eris Gardens. Justine might have been the first, but she wouldn't be the last. Even without her connection to Lady Frieda, Xochi was the kind of shiny and young people like Justine coveted.

"Hello?" Xochi called. "Leviticus?"

He knocked on the bathroom door.

"Come in." She was huddled in the tub, knees to her chest. "I feel kind of nauseous."

Leviticus put the wastebasket next to the bathtub and got a washcloth from the cupboard. He knelt beside the clawfoot tub—not as impressive as the one in Pallas's attic, but deep enough that Xochi was almost completely submerged. She closed her eyes as he washed the smudged makeup from her face and scrubbed her back. When he reached her arm, he turned it over to see the mark where the needle went in, backlit by a faint bruise. Reflexively, he rubbed the inside of his own arm where the black scars would always feel different from the rest of his skin.

"We're alike," Xochi said.

"Yeah, we are. I'm sorry."

"Don't be."

"I don't want to hurt you. Or take advantage." He picked up her hand and held it.

"Then don't," she said, taking her hand away.

He got up, sat in the chair. He reviewed what he knew. Xochi was wise, but inexperienced. A runaway, like him. Someone had hurt her. That was clear. And sometimes, she wanted to hurt herself. Leviticus knew this story. It was his own.

"Leviticus?"

"Xochi?"

"Come here."

"Xochi, you're high, it's not right . . ."

"Come over here." Her voice was husky. She was going to be serious trouble when she figured out seduction for real.

"Not a chance. I have a policy about that, too. No sex with anyone who's too high to operate heavy machinery. It's served me well for many years."

"So far, your policies seem pretty flexible," Xochi said, a challenge and an invitation.

She was right. If he'd followed his own rules, he wouldn't be here with her right now. And what about Xochi? Would she really have landed in Justine's sights if he'd just left her alone in the first place? He shook his head. "Not this time."

"Well, then, what?" Xochi sounded impatient, more like herself. "What now?"

"I don't know about you, but I'm tired. And my neck is killing me. Who knew you were so heavy?"

"You didn't need to carry me out. But thanks for coming to get me. It got so crazy in there. Ky—did he hit Duncan?"

"He might've. I left it up to him. I just wanted you out of there." She was getting cold, starting to shiver. He turned on the hot tap and went to his room, rummaging around in his dresser. "Here." He laid an old T-shirt and some boxers on the lid of the hamper. "There's a sweatshirt if you want it, too, on the hook behind the door."

It was a long time before she came out, long enough that he started to worry. When she opened the door, he was in bed reading. She stood there, so ordinary with her scrubbed face and damp hair. Too beautiful. She rolled her eyes, seeing he wasn't going to make it easy by telling her what to do. She closed the bathroom door and slid into the other side of his bed, letting out a long, relieved exhale.

"Leviticus?"

"Yeah?"

"Do you think it's safe to go to sleep?"

He looked up from his book at the girl in his bed. "It should be," he said. He reached over, touched her cheek. "Everything's going to be okay."

43

Night Bird Flying

Peasblossom had been plagued with insomnia since his audience with the koi. He rolled over, cuddling the backs of Nora's knees.

Tap, tap, tap.

Was someone at the door? Nora's digital clock read twelve-fifteen. The sound continued. The cat ignored it until he couldn't.

Something was entering through the cat flap.

In the hall, hackles raised, Peasblossom was shocked to see a small gray bird perched on the top of Anna's purple rain boot. Bending its neck sideways in a gesture of greeting, it made a sound that perfectly mimicked a motorcycle kicking to life. It flew a few steps toward the front door, perched on Nora's backpack, and made the revving sound again, followed by an excellent facsimile of a Siamese cat's meow.

"You're a mockingbird, I take it?"

The bird revved and flew to the doormat, cocking its head. It whistled a sharp two-note call, a human sound used to summon a taxi, and jerked its head toward the cat door.

Peasblossom approached slowly, careful not to alarm. "Did Moonlight send you?"

The bird whistled affirmation and hopped to the doormat.

"After you," Peasblossom said in deference to their predator-prey dynamic. "I will wait for a respectful interval and follow." He spoke simply, unsure of the bird's understanding beyond its ability to mimic. The bird cocked its head, eyes beaming amused intelligence. It hunched its shoulders and flew, head bent like a charging bull.

On the stoop, Peasblossom flexed his whiskers to take in the night. The mockingbird, perched on a wire above, wolf whistled as a taxi turned the corner and parked in front of Peasblossom's building. The driver got out, opening the door for the elderly man who lived next door, leaving the back door open as he carried the neighbor's walker with one hand and helped him inside with the other. The gray bird flew down to the roof of the taxi and made a soft kittenish meow.

Peasblossom had been at the intersection of fate and folly enough times to know what action to take. He slipped into the cab and slid under the passenger seat. The driver got in and took a long swig from a water bottle. A burst of static came from the radio. "Hey, Ben, pickup at the O'Farrell. It's Misty. She asked for you."

The fur on the cat's spine rose a quarter inch. *Misty.* The bouncer had called Xochi's mother by that name. A chill ran seismically through Peasblossom's pelt. The O'Farrell must be the theater that housed the strip club, the one on O'Farrell and Polk. The driver rolled down his window a few inches and tuned the stereo to classic rock. A high-pitched echo of the Hendrix guitar riff playing in the cab spilled from the wire overhead before the mockingbird took flight. Peasblossom made himself comfortable as the driver put on his turn signal and headed for the Tenderloin.

The moment Xochi's mother opened the taxi door, Peasblossom once again noted her scent's resemblance to Xochi's.

"Hey, Gina," the driver said.

Gina. The woman's real name.

"Hey, Ben," Gina said. The two were silent after that. Ben turned up the radio and they both sang along.

"'Tiny Dancer' reminds me of you," Ben said when the song was over. "Every time I hear it."

Gina smiled from the back seat. They rode in silence for several blocks.

"You're quiet tonight," Ben said. "You okay?"

"Just tired."

When the taxi stopped, Gina pressed some bills into the driver's hand. She opened the door. Peasblossom tensed. Getting out could be tricky.

"Night, Ben," she said, leaning in to extract a large bag. Peasblossom slipped out, using the bag as cover.

Date palms rattled in the distance. He wrinkled his nose: chuparosa, jasmine, overripe trash. He was in the Mission, somewhere near Dolores Street.

"Drive safe," Gina called through the driver's open window. "There's a bunch of crazies out there tonight."

"Are they tipping?" Ben asked.

"Mine were." Gina grinned.

Peasblossom hurried to relieve himself in a stand of bushes, hoping to follow the woman into her building. Charm should do the rest. But, like many things related to his aging body, the process took too long. When Peasblossom reached the lobby door, it was shut, his dreams of an elevator shattered. With any luck, Gina would live on a lower floor. He trotted to the back of the building, eyes on the fire escape. All the apartments were dark. Finally, light blazed in a sixth-story window. Groaning, Peasblossom began to climb.

44

Then She Remembers

Gina dropped her bag in the coat closet and shucked off her good leather boots and designer jeans. Some girls came and went from the club in sweats and sneakers, but at thirty-four, Gina couldn't afford to be careless.

She turned the radio on low and opened a window to the cool night air. She was getting past her fears of open windows and evening walks. High up in the building, invisible in her little nest, supported by her own honest labor, paid for in cash, life felt almost normal. She poured a glass of wine, rolled a joint and ran a bath. She was about to pull off her T-shirt when she heard something. Did someone new move in with a baby? A blue-eyed cat sat in the window, tail puffed up, eyes all pupil.

"Hey, handsome. Did you have a fight?"

The cat meowed like it understood.

"The window's open, you know. You could come in. I'm not feeding you, now. I'm just offering some sanctuary. I know what it's like to be on the run."

The cat meowed again, its voice rising at the end, a frustrated sound, but it stayed where it was. Gina made a show of ignoring it. Funny how alike people and animals were. When things were tough, even kindness could be hard to take. Well, either the cat would come in or it wouldn't. She was going to take her bath.

Gina lowered herself into the tub and lit a joint—Mexican,

sadly, not Humboldt green. She yawned. This weed was stronger than she thought. She couldn't remember ever being this
relaxed. She closed her eyes and floated. The apartment was so
quiet. Had she turned the radio off?

She tried to get up and found she couldn't. Fear bloomed
in her belly, instantly calmed by the sensation of little hands in
her hair. Her eyelids fluttered open, only to close immediately
against what she saw. There was no one else in the apartment.
No way was there a pair of big-eyed preschoolers standing at
the edge of the tub. She must be dreaming. But that was wrong,
too. She never dreamed of children. She avoided her triggers
as best she could. Even her worst nightmares obeyed this pri-
mary rule in her life. But now forbidden thoughts crowded to
the surface, and there was nothing she could do.

Images came first: silky hair, big brown eyes. Next, the
smell—café con leche and cinnamon toast. She waited for her
body to react, to reject the poisonous guilt sure to come next.

But nothing happened.

A slideshow began in her brain.

Memories that had been out of bounds for years slid noise-
lessly past: A dark, sexy boy slouching outside the 7-Eleven
where Gina worked, plaid shirt buttoned up to his neck. A
valentine with *te amo* written a hundred times. Both of them
naked in the summer heat, singing with the radio to Gina's
huge belly. Manuel burning rubber on the way to the hospital.
Xochi's birth, hazy from the drugs Gina told them she didn't
want.

After the hospital, a blank spot, a movie with a missing
frame. Gina knew what was supposed to be there—her with
a new baby in a rented room, greasy hair and zits from the
hormones, all alone. The day, months later, when she ran into
Manuel's sister in Safeway. *Where is he?* Gina had begged. *This
is your niece,* she'd pleaded. But Josie refused to look at the
baby. Manny was in jail, she said in her cold bitch voice. Josie
wouldn't say more because Manuel asked her not to. He never

wanted the baby in the first place. There was no point in asking their family for help. They all knew Gina was a trailer-trash whore. Now the family had bigger problems, and Gina's brat was not going to be one of them.

Gina had been called a whore before, and worse, by jealous girls and jilted boys. It sucked, of course, but she was never ashamed the way they wanted her to be. Josie's words were different. But Gina didn't cry. She picked up her baby and walked out of the store with her head held high, a single mother with a daughter to raise and a life to lead.

Xochi's childhood zoomed by: ugly suburbs, shitty jobs, credit-card trips to Disneyland she'd never pay off, the cardboard moving boxes gathered at yet another liquor store, the interchangeable guy with the truck volunteering to do the heavy lifting. So many times, this apartment, that condominium. A house for a brief moment of normalcy, then boxes again and another crappy cracker-box apartment. On and on her mind raced forward, night after night in bed alone, one-night stands, hot and sweet in the moment of conquest, always ending in her own coldness if they liked her too much.

Evan had been different. Handsome, gentle Evan. There were no games, only tenderness when he cried in her arms that first night in his tent at the fair. And if the vast pot growing empire he'd bragged about was ten drafty cabins in the middle of green nowhere, for once Gina didn't care. She loved him. She thought about giving him the baby he wanted. But what about her? She was already three years older than Evan. A baby guaranteed nothing. His fantasy of baby-makes-three would pass, and Xochi would grow up and move on and the two of them would live like they were meant to.

Already, they were skimming money from the harvest profits, with Evan's dad too drunk to know or care. Gina had a head for opportunity; she had plans for their business. She imagined a modern redwood house on the southeast hill, rainy seasons spent in Hawaii. She'd make damn sure she still looked good in a bikini for that. She got an IUD when he asked her to stop taking the pill and let him think a baby wasn't in the stars for them. Then the thing got infected, and the jig was up. It made Gina so sick, she was in the hospital for a week.

Evan's rage at her lie was nothing she was prepared for. He'd never once raised his voice, and now his fists threatened to wreck her face. He ended things the day he forced himself on her when she said no, messed up from the infection, bruised from his blows. She knew where he hid his cash. She stole his dead stepmother's Buick and drove away with one thought for Xochi: *She's becoming a woman. Who the hell am I to teach her about that?*

THE BATH WAS LUKEWARM now, but Gina's skin was hot. Easing deeper into the soothing cool, she let the film reel continue to spin, surprised she felt nothing but a surface-level burning as the story unwound. The world wasn't ending. The sky wouldn't fall. Yes, the worst was true. She'd abandoned her own daughter. Facts were facts, plain and simple, summaries of actions taken. Bad, yes. Absolutely shameful, the thing she'd avoided like poison these last six years. But now, thinking about it was . . . nothing. A part of who she was, like her own skin.

Next there was LA. She'd told everyone there she was twenty-three, and no one batted an eye. Scott was forty and liked his women young. It wasn't anything Gina had done that turned him against her—Scott was a lunatic in his own right. Gina was lucky to have gotten away alive. She let it all unspool: the stinging shame of the social workers, the weeks in the women's shelter, but none of it penetrated the cool flicker of the pictures lapping at her brain like waves in a lake.

It was easy to think of her first days in the city, the shabby hotel room she slunk into every day after a humiliating search for work, the ocean blue of the mural that called her into the Mitchell Brothers, the serendipity of her audition where she danced in a borrowed costume and the DJ chose her music. When the first familiar notes of her favorite song rang out of the speakers, Gina was born again. Comforted by the money piling up in her hand each night, amazed she had to do so little to earn it, she'd found a secret eddy, a way to avoid the destructive pull of her life and float free in a cool, sheltered cove.

Cool like now, safe in this underwater cave that promised pleasant, easy sleep.

Gina drifted, danger evaded, pursuers lost.

And then she was hot. Way too hot.

She groped for the porcelain bottom of the tub, but it wasn't there.

She opened her mouth to scream, but instead of sound, there was air, or something like it. She was underwater, but she was breathing. Deep, heavy breaths.

She wanted to open her eyes, but before the impulse was fully formed, she was drifting again.

A dream.

A pair of naked, long-haired children.

An abandoned industrial zone.

Slight, pale-haired girls littered the barren landscape, broken orphans in varied stages of injury or decay. Some spat with rage, throwing rocks or pulling each other's hair. Some sat motionless, humming to themselves. Others were painted in the crude likeness of women, flat chests caved inward, fingernails caked with blood.

One was dressed like a soldier.

She stood on top of a barbed wall, automatic weapon trained on the landscape below.

The dream children approached like cautious dogs.

"Stop right there," the soldier girl said.

The children knelt at her feet in surrender.

The girl took aim. The children pressed their mouths to the ground, long hair blanketing their backs, and whispered into the cracked dirt.

Come back, dear one.
Come back to sun.
Night is over, dreaming done.

"Get out," the soldier girl said. "Or I'll blow your heads off."

Come back, come back.
All is well.
Your secrets are safe; no one will tell.

"That's right." The girl spat. "Can't talk without a head."

Gina wanted to laugh. This girl was such a little badass.

Suddenly, Gina felt cold. She blinked, for one moment back in her body, back in the tub, the whole thing just a trippy weed and exhaustion-induced dream. "Go away!" she said to no one in particular. As the words bubbled from her lips, a hand pulled her hair from behind, yanking her back down to the depths.

The strange children.

The broken foster-child blondes.

The soldier girl took aim at the cracked earth and shot, round after round until the ground began to shake, a seismic rhythm in time with Gina's shaking as her body fought the dream.

Stay, the green child cooed to a middle-school version of Gina in her sixth foster home. Blood dripped from the dirty bandages around the young Gina's wrists onto her dirty bare feet.

Tell, the brown child whispered to an entire classroom of kindergarten Ginas, one girl for every day that year's foster father drove her to school the long way. They sat at the brown boy's feet, scraped knees bare in too-short dresses. "We'll get in trouble if we tell," they said, small voices overlapping. "Is it snack time yet? We're hungry."

Where was the soldier girl? Gina imagined a whole squad

of them, platoons of teenage Ginas marching alongside monster tanks. She felt them massing at her borders, her body now shaking with the beat of their boots.

The bathwater was cool again, light against her skin. She sat up, blinking.

Stumbling out of the bathroom, she dropped naked onto the clean sheets of her soft bed. She was wiped out, so sleepy she could hardly lift her head at the sound coming from somewhere in the room, near the window. Glancing up, expecting to see the cat, she saw a silhouette against the blinds of a tangle-haired child, reminding her of Xochi at five with hair past her butt, so snarled it took a full hour to comb.

That weed must have been laced, she thought, and fell into a state much deeper than sleep.

45

When a Sinner Kissed an Angel

Io sat up in bed, shivering in the still-dark morning. After the last year's fast from meat, wine and sex, she found herself embracing a state that was not quite solitude, but rather, singularity. Her time with James had reinforced the feeling of being both more connected to all living things and progressively less attached to anything specific. She no longer needed the reassurance of touch to understand the feeling she had for her family. She mourned the loss as she embraced the open place it made in her soul.

Given Leviticus's need to bond through sex and tendency to romanticize his lovers, she'd been afraid of what would happen when she ended their physical relationship, but they'd become closer than ever. Finally, last night, there was a change. He was struggling, she was sure of that, but reaching toward something now, away from the past he'd been so afraid to release. When he hugged her good night, his thoughts were elsewhere, not following her up the stairs like a loyal dog. And she was glad of it. Happy for him, happy for herself. She was so light, walking up the final flight—freedom increased, fear defeated.

Why, then, was she awake before dawn, bewildered again by this anxious unrest? What impulse led her away from her own wing of the mansion, through the basement and up the spiral staircase?

Her bare feet slid over the wood floor of the sunporch leading to Leviticus's bedroom. The sky was cloudy, pink at the edges with the first hint of dawn. She touched the heavy wooden door with the tip of her index finger. It swung open without its habitual squeak.

Her intake of breath cleared the sky, illuminating Leviticus's bed. He was not alone. Xochi was there, lying beside him. Both were asleep.

A trick of the sunrise cast a halo over their dark heads. A pair of orthodox icons, so beautiful Io couldn't take her eyes away until the ocean winds blew fog at the sun.

Was this the portent of the last months' insomnia? Or was something else coming, something she expected even less than the perfect harmony she'd just witnessed between her daughter's caretaker and the father of her child?

Io stepped backward out of the room and hurried down the stairs.

Jealousy. She'd been foolish to think herself immune. Returning to her room, she searched through the bottom drawers of her bureau for running clothes, long disused. Throwing them on, she hurried downstairs in her socks and dug through the coat closet till she found her running shoes. Grabbing the first hoodie she touched in the front hall—Pad's, by the smell—she zipped it over her slender body, grown even thinner this year. Closing the front door as quietly as she could, Io raced up the hill toward Cole Valley.

46

Angel of the Morning

The sky paled from rose to blush. Pallas wondered if the green girl and her brother had found Xochi. Beneath the siblings' clear love and concern, Pallas had sensed a river of fear, cold and full of sharks. Now, after hours of waiting, her whole body was composed of worry. Like nesting dolls, you could open any part of her and find another worried little Pallas inside, and another inside that.

She opened her closet, fingering her many dresses, ironed to perfection, hanging by sleeve length and color. She passed them by and pulled down her jeans from the top shelf. Before Xochi had come, Pallas had never worn them. Xochi had insisted. "Play clothes," she'd said, picking out a pair of dark, straight-legged Levis and some black high-tops. "Like the *Sound of Music* kids meets the Ramones."

Pallas pulled the jeans over her hips. They were stiff, but Xochi said they'd soften with wear. She laced on the shoes. She couldn't stay in the attic alone, not one second longer. It was a cold morning. She pulled on a sweater of Xochi's and found her cat hat in its usual spot.

The only person in the house who might be awake was Io. Pallas shivered down the servants' stairs, her sneakers silent on the treads. Her mother's door was open, her room empty, the bed uncharacteristically unmade. All Pallas wanted was to lie down in the patch of sunlight that fell over Io's pillows, pull the Io-scented covers over her head and sleep the entire day, but her worry was too big to let Pallas rest.

She debated where to go next. Pad had been the first one home, long before anyone else. She knew because his motorcycle was the loudest, with its distinctive lionlike roar, but he might not be alone. Ky had gone to the party with Xochi, too, so he was the next logical choice, but the most inviolable rule of Pallas's childhood was to never, *ever* wake Kylen before noon.

One the other hand, it was Saturday, Pallas and Leviticus's day together. Pallas's dad was an incredibly hard sleeper, but he didn't have a specific rule about waking him. In fact, when Pallas was younger, waking Leviticus had been her special job. Back then, he was always sleeping, missing band practice and running late for meetings and gigs. Sending Pallas in had been the final and most deadly weapon of whoever needed to wake him. Using the sunporch as her runway, she'd barrel into his room and leap onto his bed. Any technique was fair game. She'd bounce and bop him with pillows, tickle him, sing show tunes. If that didn't work, she'd use her feet and strong legs to push him bodily out of bed.

Pallas exhaled, her breath ragged in her chest. She was probably worried for nothing. Leviticus would tell her so as he lumbered out of bed, making his bearish morning growls. She'd wait on the sunporch for him to get dressed and snoop around to see what he was reading. They'd go out for an early breakfast and a ride to the beach and stop at the bookstore on the way home to visit Peas. Xochi was fine. Just out late. She might have met a friend or even a girl or boy she fancied. Or maybe she was with the green girl and her brother, doing something magical. She'd come home soon and tell Pallas all about it. She definitely, definitely would.

Pallas stopped, in the kitchen now. She sniffed. Someone had been smoking inside, but who would do that? She padded downstairs to the studio. It was ridiculous how isolated her dad's room was from the rest of the house. You could only reach it by going down to the basement and up a curling wrought-iron staircase in the studio, or from the stairs outside that led to the balcony and sunporch. Pallas trudged down and then up, her stomach gurgling for answers and breakfast.

The sunporch was toasty warm. Morning lit the garden, but something was strange. It was the trees—they were black with crows. More soared above the carriage house and perched on the power lines. An unusually large crow landed on the balcony outside the French doors. It met Pallas's gaze. She'd never been so close to one of their kind. The bird bobbed—or was it bowing? It cawed three times and lifted off, soaring into the silver sky.

Pallas was suddenly woozy, her insides congealed like the wet wool stuffing Kiki had once removed from a teddy bear Pallas left in the garden overnight. "He's septic, love," Kiki had said. "We have to operate."

Pallas wished for some sort of operation now, some emergency that would stop her from opening her dad's bedroom door. Because somehow, some way, she understood what the crow was trying to tell her: *Stop! Go back! Flee!*

But she couldn't. And she wouldn't. The crow had known that, too.

Moving forward on button-jointed limbs, Pallas approached the door. This part of the house was modern, made in the sixties. Leviticus's door was fashioned from a wide plank of redwood, a cross-section slab from a single gigantic tree. Pallas used to count the rings. "Barbaric!" she'd say. "Elder murder!" The doorknob was brass. She turned it, hoping to find it locked, but it was never locked. It opened easily, swinging on hinges that were quiet for once—not that the squeakiest hinge had a prayer of waking Pallas's dad.

She tiptoed in. At first, there was only his back and the covers. He rolled over.

Someone was in the bed with him.

A T-shirted back, dark hair. Andi?

But Leviticus never had people overnight at Eris Gardens. He slept over at other people's houses—Pallas knew that. If she asked where he'd been, he always told her. Unlike everyone else in the family, neither of her parents ever brought anyone home to spend the night. In Io's case, this was because she never dated. Pallas wasn't sure why her dad kept that part of his life separate. She'd never thought to ask.

Leviticus shifted. Pallas stood absolutely still.

The person in bed beside him shifted also, coming to rest with her head on his chest as if they slept cuddled together every night of their lives. Leviticus pulled her closer, deep in his dreams, swimming in a sea where Pallas had never existed.

Pallas's limbs were loose, a marionette with cut strings. She fell to her knees, head in her hands, a dramatic gesture she'd scoffed at in plays and movies. But now she understood. She raised her face as the sun shone in the window above the bed.

Xochi and Leviticus were yin and yang, two sleeping animals of the same species, natural as a pair of deer in a woodland glen. The room swayed with the music of their mingled breath. The crows stopped cawing and the wind chimes stopping chiming as even nature whispered to protect the sweetness of their shared sleep.

Pallas could not remember leaving the bedroom, but now she was in the sunroom. She opened the balcony door. The wind rose, suddenly cold. Pallas shivered in Xochi's sweater. Her dad's leather jacket was on his reading chair. She pulled it on, slamming the French doors behind her.

47

Meet Me in the Morning

Cold hands yanked Xochi from the warm epicenter of Leviticus's bed. "Wake up!" The voice sounded like it was coming over a bad phone connection from someone else's dream.

Opening gluey eyelids, Xochi found herself on the sunporch outside Leviticus's closed bedroom door opposite a glowering Kylen. He shoved a pile of clothes at her. "Get dressed. And don't you dare wake him." Kylen's tone made it impossible to disobey.

Xochi tried to pull a pair of jeans over the baggy boxers she'd put on the night before. *Still on*, she noted, wondering if she was sober yet. She yanked off the shorts, not caring what Kylen saw, nearly tripping as she tugged on her jeans.

"Are you happy now?"

"Shh! Just. Get. Dressed."

She sat in Leviticus's chair to lace her sneakers, then zipped her hoodie to her chin.

Kylen marched her down the stairs. "We'll talk about it over coffee. Come on. Right *now*."

Again, the tone. Xochi moved her feet even as her brain struggled to catch up and got on the back of Kylen's motorcycle. They rode through the deserted streets and parked at a diner in a nondescript part of upper California Street.

Kylen was silent as they were seated in a booth in back.

Xochi snatched the cigarette Kylen offered her with a shaking hand. "Where'd you get my clothes?"

"From your bedroom floor."

Xochi tried to picture Kylen in her room gathering her things and couldn't. The diner was empty except for a man at the counter in a glittery pink chiffon dress and basketball shoes eating chocolate pie and an old woman dressed in a proper wool suit, heels, gloves, and a hat like she was on her way to church. *Okay*, Xochi thought, *if this is a dream, I'll go along.*

"So, uh, why were you in my room?"

"I was looking for you, Einstein. When you weren't there, I had a good idea of where to find you and figured you wouldn't be wearing much."

Xochi's face went hot. She put her hands on her cheeks. Her skin was taut and parched. She switched from coffee to water, remembering the gin and tequila from last night. She was unaware of any side effect from the drug. Even in her head, she wasn't saying its name. *Heroin.* The word bounced around her brain but found nowhere to land. There should have been remorse. Horror. But there was only a pleasant detachment. Maybe she was still under its spell.

The food arrived and Xochi pushed it away, lighting another cigarette.

When the waitress was out of earshot, Kylen finally spoke. "So, kid, tell me about your freaky little watchdogs."

"What?" A giggle burst from Xochi's throat, slightly hysterical.

"Listen to me. My best friend could have died last night. I don't care if you're embarrassed Leviticus caught you drugged out with Duncan's hand in your bra. You did it, so own it. I'm talking about those fey-ass bodyguards you invited to the party. Start talking."

"Kylen, don't get mad, but you sound crazy."

"Fine. You were too high to remember Thing One and Thing

Two. But how about the pot farmer with the dirty dreads? Remember him?"

Xochi jumped up, knocking over her water glass. Kylen caught it without missing a beat.

"Is he here? In the city?"

"Calm down." Kylen was using the commanding voice that had made her get dressed and get on his motorcycle. Xochi sat still.

"Look at me." His eyes were surprisingly soft. Fierce, but in a way that made Xochi feel like he was on her side for once. "You're safe. He's not here."

"Then how?" Xochi said. "How did you know?"

"They told me. Little Green and her brother."

"Wait, what?" Xochi grabbed her water and gulped. *How did Kylen know?*

"You do remember—I can see it in your face. You have to tell me, Xochi."

"I . . . I dream about a girl and—"

"And her brother. The Waterbabies. Yes. Them! That shit last night? With the aquariums and the glass and Leviticus on the floor? Also them."

"But—" *Waterbabies?* Was that what her dream children were called?

"Dude," Kylen said. "Shit like this happens. Trust me, they're real. Fey as fuck, but corporeal. Not. A. Dream."

"No way." Xochi shook her head.

"Tell that to Pad," Kylen said. "I knew something was up from the night we played with Rabbit Hole. I saw them in your weird little head. And now they're here in the flesh. For you. They say you called them."

"So they . . . talked to you?" A sharp pain gripped Xochi's forehead. She closed her eyes. *Duncan's room. Leviticus. A small being with impossibly long dark hair.* "What did they say?"

"The green kid showed me some stuff."

Stuff? Xochi resisted the urge to stand up and run away.

"They were pretty quick flashes, but I got the gist."

The gist. Xochi closed her eyes again, trying to find an internal place to rest, but there was only a slithering, carsick darkness.

"Xochi? I know I've been kind of a dick to you. But you have to believe me about this. I'm worried. I want to help."

If this were a fairy tale, Kylen was the wolf who befriended you in the forest. But wait—that was "Little Red Riding Hood," not a good-wolf story. And Kylen *was* good, more or less. He may not have liked her, but he loved Pallas and Leviticus, and they loved and trusted him.

Xochi's tear ducts stung, too dry for her to cry. Something whispered at the edge of her understanding. She was so tired. She could have used another week of protected sleep in Leviticus's wide bed. Another year.

She closed her eyes and caught the snatch of a dream, an image of a lake where one didn't usually exist, a swirling whirlpool, a man floating in the center. She remembered the clear picture she'd dreamed up of Evan the day Pallas went to LA. The feeling of closure. How happy she'd been afterward. How free.

"Evan is dead." her words hit the bottom of a dry well, clattering like bones.

"Dreadlock man? Yeah."

"The Waterbabies—*killed* him?" The word tasted like burned foil in her mouth. Her fillings hurt. Her head pounded. Her dream children, innocent, naked—they were capable of killing?

"Yes."

Even before Kylen answered, she knew it was true. She'd called them with that bathtub potion. *Fates! Fates and Furies! Open! Open! Open up the door!*

They knew her need and came. Xochi touched her face. "Why am I crying?"

"He was good to you," Kylen said, "when you were a kid. They showed me that, too. At first, I wasn't sure why."

Xochi was dizzy. Kylen grasped her wrist—too hard, but it helped. The room stopped spinning. "You grew up with him, and he was good to you. You—"

"I loved him." The words left a greasy film on her tongue.

"What that asshole did to you was unforgivable," Kylen said. "He deserved what he got."

That day. The day Loretta died. Xochi took out another cigarette, but her hands were too shaky to light it.

"He deserved it," Kylen repeated. "He was a defective piece of shit." He took the cigarette from Xochi, lit it, and passed it back.

Evan used to tell a story. When he'd been a child, his father had kept a python. One day, it had escaped. People would see it around—high up in a tree, curled on the hood of someone's car. But no one had ever been able to capture it. Xochi slept with her windows shut for years after that.

She had to focus to bring the cigarette to her lips. The nicotine weighted her, made it possible to stay in her seat. "There's something else," Xochi said. "Something I did."

"I saw it, okay?" Kylen sat, patient and solid. "Silence isn't the same as consent."

"I know." Xochi closed her eyes. *A lake where the creek should be. Evan floating, eyes to the sky.*

"You don't know. That's the problem. We all want attention. We all need to be loved. It takes a special kind of evil to take advantage of that. Do me a favor, okay? Imagine it was Pallas."

"I'd want to murder him."

"That's right."

"Yeah, but Ky? That's hypothetical. This is real. Life and death. I don't believe in capital punishment. What kind of things are they if they go around killing people?"

"It's not like that. It's about balance. What they showed me was not an image of suffering. I wish I could explain it to you." He waited for the waitress to refill their coffees. "Okay, it's like this. Imagine you're a kid playing with clay. You make a guy, a family, a house. But in the end, it's not right. So you smash it all together and try again. This time, you make a dog. The essential stuff that made the guy and the family and the house are all there in the dog, but it's a better creation. Later, you make something else. It doesn't matter. Nothing is ruined. It wasn't meant to be permanent in the first place."

"Yeah, but in *this* world, in this reality, he's dead. No matter what Evan comes back as, right now, his dad is alone on that property with no one to take care of him."

"That's why I'm telling you this. Those guys may not be malevolent, but they're dangerous as hell. They were right about that asshole, but they almost made a mistake with Lev."

"He was fine last night." She remembered Leviticus rubbing his neck, teasing her about being heavy.

"I'm guessing you were pissed at him. The bigger one, the brother, he touched your forehead, and a second later, he had Leviticus on the ground and his hands on his throat."

"Ky, oh my god! I'm so sorry."

"No, dude. That's on me."

"But I'm the evil temptress here, right? Isn't that why you're mad at me?"

Smiling transformed Kylen's face almost completely. He shook his head.

"Listen. Last summer we were all out to dinner, talking about John Lennon. And Bubbles was like, 'Why does everyone pile on poor Yoko? It's not her fault the damn Beatles broke up.'" Ky did a spot-on Bubbles. "So Pallas pipes in and goes, 'It's obvious—blame the outsider, blame the woman. Misogyny 101.' That's what I did to you. Lev gets caught up with relationships. They mess with his head. I didn't want to have to go through that again."

The whole time, Ky had been worried about Leviticus? A memory surfaced, drug fogged but real. Leviticus in the doorway of Duncan's spooky blue room, tears in his eyes. Duncan's cold, sweaty hand fumbling with the front clasp of her bra.

She shook her head, trying to erase the Etch A Sketch image of herself, a drugged-out damsel in distress on that horrible sofa. She ground her cigarette out in the ashtray and picked up her coffee. It was time to start using her brain.

"Okay," she said. "I'm having a hard time believing this is an actual problem we need to solve, but it seems like I've summoned a pair of otherworldly creatures that are going after people from my past. Also from my present. Maybe it's all true, but it feels so . . . unreal."

"Exactly. Your brain does not want to process all this weird stuff. I'm guessing your hangover isn't helping."

"Can I just . . . tell them to go home?"

"I don't think so. It seems like . . . they have to accomplish something, you know? I don't think they'll stop till they do."

"Accomplish what?"

"That's what we have to figure out." Kylen's attention zeroed in on her, a hawk circling its prey. "When Leviticus was on the floor, the dark-haired one did something to make everyone forget. But while he was doing that, the green one put her hands on your heart. Do you remember?"

"No," Xochi said. Even as she said it, she realized she was lying. "I mean, I'm not sure."

"Think." Kylen's voice was so calm. It made Xochi want to sleep. "Close your eyes. What do you see?"

The voice trick. He was doing it again, pulling out all the stops this time. It was pointless to fight him.

"My room," she said, "my old room in San Leandro. We lived there for the first half of second grade. The green girl— she was going through my things, searching for something. She found a music box. There was a locket inside. I wanted to grab it, but I couldn't move. I started to cry. She was sorry, though. So sorry she'd upset me. I've never felt anything like the apology she made. The next thing I remember clearly is Leviticus picking me up like a sack of potatoes and carrying me out of there. Before, when she was touching me, I was sober. But when he picked me up, I was so wasted again. I think they did something to make me forget."

"Xochi, come on." Kylen's voice was hard. "Whose picture was in the locket? I hope it's not someone who fucked you over. Or worse, someone you love."

What if it was both? "I thought you were psychic," Xochi said. Her tone was bratty and false. "You probably know already. We were touching the whole time on the motorcycle."

"I was driving," Kylen said. "You want me to crash? And okay, if you must know, I only get a flash of what's on your mind. If I focus, sometimes I can see shit that's about to happen, like a tarot reading without the cards. If you can't remember what the green girl found, fine. Give me your hand." He held her eyes until she dropped them. She kept her hand in her lap.

"What do they want from me? Why are they here?" she said. The words were strange in her mouth, like lines she'd memorized for a play.

"Can't you feel it? They want to heal you. They have to. Xochi, they're protectors of children. That much I got. You're not a kid anymore, but whatever's in that locket is keeping you a victim."

"I'm no victim." Xochi stood and pulled on her hoodie. *Wait*, she told her body. But it wouldn't listen.

"Don't be like that. You can't take this on alone. It affects all of us."

"I don't see how." Xochi imagined a small blue box, the kind for a wedding ring. She put the locket inside and closed the lid. "It sounds like these Waterbaby things are connected to me. If I'm someplace else, so are they." There was the dry well with Evan's bones at the bottom. She dropped the box and listened for the thud. *There*, she thought. *They can keep each other company.* "So," she said in an underwater voice, "you should be happy. You never liked me much anyway, right?"

OUTSIDE, THE MORNING WAS glaring and cold. Xochi searched her pockets for bus fare, for cigarettes, anything that might sustain her, but there was only Loretta's hummingbird necklace. *Necklaces, lockets, wells full of bones.* It was like a creepy nursery rhyme. Was this her life now? She fastened the twin hummingbirds around her neck. She needed all the luck she could get.

48

Roller Girl

The morning was frigid and clear, with a lavender sky and sliver of moon. Synthetic fluff filled the empty bag of Pallas's body as she walked on boneless legs down the hill toward Haight Street.

The neighborhood was peaceful. No buses, only birds. The wind carried a delicious bakery smell—a warm, sugary respite, a siren donut song. She searched her dad's jacket for change. The hand-warmer pockets had a quarter and a penny. The left inside pocket was empty. The right had nothing but a piece of folded paper.

On Haight and Masonic, a girl on roller skates barreled toward her. It was Peasblossom's girl, Anna. Pallas had seen her zooming around the neighborhood for years, but they'd rarely spoken. Anna spun in a circle and stopped cold, balanced on the tips of her rubber stoppers.

"Hi!" she said.

"Hello."

"What are you doing?" Anna's eyes were big and dark, with long lashes like her mother's.

"I couldn't sleep, so I'm taking a walk."

"My mom lets me get donuts for breakfast on Saturdays. The bookstore opens late, so I have to let her sleep. She's like a scary hibernating bear."

Pallas flashed to her own bear-like parent, forgetting for a split second what she had seen in his bedroom. She blinked it away. The farther she got from Eris Gardens, the less real it felt.

"My mom is a morning person," she said.

"Wanna get some donuts with me?" Anna said.

"I forgot to bring money."

"No worries!" Anna pulled a ten-dollar bill from the cuff of her striped sock. "I'm loaded."

THE BAKERY WAS UNFANCY and old school with a few tables by the window in front. Pallas took off her dad's leather jacket. His scent brought her insides back, brittle and aching. Anna set a big pink bakery box on the table.

"I got a dozen, but they give you thirteen. One extra for good luck."

Pallas bit into a cream-filled maple bar. It totally helped. Whenever an image of Xochi and her dad nosed its way into her brain, she took another bite. "Ecstasy," she said to Anna as she bit into the still-warm dough. "Perfection."

"Here." Anna passed her a small carton of chocolate milk. "It's even better with this." Pallas wasn't usually fond of milk without coffee, but she opened the carton and gulped.

"So good." Pallas nodded, reaching for a cake donut covered in powdered sugar. Anna's eyes sparkled under her purple-and-pink calico bangs. "You're like a Japanese anime girl with that hair," Pallas said.

"So are you, with your cat hat," Anna said. "I love that thing. I've always been jealous of it."

"Always when?" Pallas tried to remember the last time she'd seen Anna. At the bookstore? Sometimes, she saw her on the street, roller-skating by with her headphones and yellow Walkman.

"Like, always forever. I don't want to be creepy or anything, but I kind of sort of spy on your family. Ever since I was little. You're very interesting."

Pallas pulled back. She wanted to trust Anna, but what if she was just like everyone else? "Interesting how?"

"Well, you're all so pretty. And there's so many of you!" Anna laughed. "Even before my dad died, it was just the four of us, counting Peas. Now we're only three. There's, like, a gazillion of you guys!"

"He was your dad?" Pallas knew about Ron, the man who'd died—that he was Nora's best friend and Peasblossom's person. She'd never given a thought to Anna.

"Not my bio dad," Anna said. "But like—my *father*, you know? He and his boyfriend were there when I was born. He cut my umbilical cord. They were both supposed to be my dads, but the other one died when I was a baby. I only remember Ron."

Pallas nodded. "We're not all related, either. I mean, my mom and dad are. Related to me. But they aren't together like a couple. They used to be, but not now." *A couple. That's what Xochi and her dad looked like. A couple. Lovers. A pair.*

"That's the other reason," Anna said. "Why I watched you guys. My mom used to point out unusual families to make me feel better."

"Why did you feel bad?" Pallas asked. She almost wished she hadn't. Anna's pretty eyes filled.

"People are stupid," Anna said.

"What people?" Pallas was surprised at how angry she felt.

"Oh. My cousins." Anna looked down. "They used to be like, 'Eww, gross, your dad is gay,' and 'He's going to give you AIDS in your Cheerios.'"

Pallas nearly choked on her chocolate milk. "That's horrible! And not true! It doesn't even work like that."

"Right?" Anna nodded. "We don't even see them at Christmas anymore. After my dad died, my mean aunt showed up at our house, and my mom went, 'Get. Off. My. Porch.' I couldn't believe it. I made her a medal. Like, a heroism award. Sometimes she's way too nice. But not that day. That day, she was perfect."

Pallas grinned. "I love that you made her a medal."

Anna shrugged. "She gets one if she's good. If she's bad, I write up a formal complaint. It goes both ways."

Now they both were laughing. "I have to pee," Pallas said. "I'll be right back."

Alone in the greasy, bleach-smelling bathroom, Pallas realized she'd forgotten to wear a pad last night, but there was no blood on her underwear. Her period was over, but it would be back. She thought of Xochi and manta rays, black licorice, bloody underwear. Had Xochi been lying to Pallas the entire time? There was something Kiki had said when they were driving to LA. *"What if the maiden is exceptionally fair?"* Suddenly, Pallas knew: Kiki and her dad had been talking about Xochi.

Pallas washed her hands. The mirror showed a cold, hard, sad face she barely recognized. *Fuck it,* she thought, surprised at how easily the profanity came. "Fuck it," she said out loud.

When Pallas came out of the bathroom, Anna was gone and two old ladies were sitting at their table. "She's outside," the guy behind the counter said. "She took your jacket with her."

Pallas smiled at her own relief. Of course Anna wouldn't leave without saying goodbye. She yawned, finally starting to feel sleepy.

Xochi and Leviticus. Leviticus and Xochi. She shook her head. She wouldn't think about it. She refused to care.

Outside, Anna sat on the curb in the sun, the pink box beside her. Leviticus's jacket was in her lap. Her head was down on her knees, and there was a piece of paper in her hand.

"I'm sorry," she said. "I shouldn't have read it."

"Shouldn't have read what?" Pallas touched Anna's shoulder.

"This." She waved the paper, head still down. "I wanted to give those ladies our table. So I grabbed your jacket and this fell out. I don't know why I unfolded it. It's the same with presents. I have to look. My mom says I'm a chronic snoop."

"It's okay," Pallas said. "This isn't my jacket. It's—" She stopped. "Anna, what does it say?"

"You haven't already read it?" Anna sat up, eyes wide. "Uh-oh. Pallas, maybe you shouldn't. It seems . . . private. It's about your nanny."

"She's my governess." Pallas pictured the green girl in the window. *Friend,* she'd said. It was a real memory, Pallas knew, but it had the feeling of a dream. "She . . . she's my best friend."

A sudden blast of wind tugged at the letter in Anna's hand. It pulled at Pallas's cat hat and lifted her hair. She sat next to Anna and took the paper—familiar stationery marked with a familiar pen.

Dear Xochi, Pallas read. The next line was crossed out. Pallas could make out *sorry* and *care.* The letter started again.

Dear Xochi,

I'm so sorry if I've confused or hurt you. This is a letter I don't know how to write. I hope you know how beautiful you are and how much I value your friendship.

This was also crossed out.

The letter began again and stopped.

Pallas didn't need to see the final draft. Even a dumb kid could see—it was a love letter.

"Pallas?" Anna sounded worried.

Pallas opened her mouth to speak as the wind ripped the letter from her hand and dragged it into the street. It careened along and disappeared under a passing bus.

Anna passed Pallas a napkin. Pallas hated to cry in front of anyone, but Anna made it easier with her simple friendliness.

"So I guess the whole thing was supposed to be secret?"

"I guess so." Pallas sniffed. Was it a secret from everyone, or just from her? She crumpled the napkin tight in her palm.

"I mean, the letter kind of made it sound like they were breaking up," Anna said.

"Breaking up?" Pallas shook her head. "I never knew they were together. Till today." She started crying again. "I saw them," she said to the trash in the gutter, so quietly she hoped Anna didn't hear.

"Where?" Anna whispered.

Pallas took a shaking breath. "In bed," she said. "They were asleep in my dad's bed." The tears came faster, angry little race cars zooming down her face and over the cliff of her chin. "It's so gross! She's seventeen. And he's old! Almost thirty!"

The street was waking up. People were out looking for breakfast or walking their dogs. Anna was quiet, picking at her glittery green nails. "I don't know," she finally said. "I don't really know your dad. But I've seen him. He comes into the bookstore when he's sad. Lots of people do. That's when Peas does his thing. And my mom says Xochi is great. 'Remarkable.' Such a my-mom word. I know she's a lot younger than him, but maybe it's not as bad as it sounds."

"Maybe." Pallas shredded the balled-up napkin with a jagged fingernail. "I just thought my dad was, like, honorable. He has a rule about dating younger people. Because it's not fair, he says. Because the older person has more experience and more power." She stopped. Her body actually ached, like her insides had been ravaged by a trapped animal. A tear leaked out.

Anna handed her another napkin. "Why does this change things?" she said carefully. "I mean, the rule sounds good. It makes sense. But what if they didn't mean to break it? If it wasn't on purpose or they weren't doing it to be mean—"

"But it is mean! They lied to me. They lied and went behind my back."

"Don't be mad!" Anna grabbed Pallas's hand. "I don't even know what I'm talking about. I just don't want you to feel bad."

"I'm not mad." Pallas was surprised to find herself giving Anna's hand a long, grateful squeeze. "Not at you."

Anna rested her head on Pallas's shoulder. Pallas found herself leaning into the contact. She imagined them as animals. Dogs. Horses. Anything but stupid humans. The wind rose again, whispery and mean.

"Come on," Anna said. "Let's go to my house and eat the rest of these donuts. I got us two more chocolate milks."

49

If You See Her, Say Hello

S unlight bounced between the ornate apartment buildings of Russian Hill like a sticky sugar-hyped toddler. Xochi longed for sunglasses.

She turned onto a nondescript part of Geary. The buildings in this part of town were too spread out, the trees anemic. It made the sky feel too big. Xochi tightened the drawstring of her hood, pulling it low on her forehead. Moving her body took enough concentration that she didn't have to think.

Pallas would be awake now, wondering where Xochi was. How long would it be before she figured out her governess was a total fuckup? And if she didn't? If Xochi managed to lie well enough to fool her, would that be best? Some things couldn't be undone.

Geary narrowed, and taller buildings softened the exuberant light. She was in the theater district. A phone booth, old-timey with a wooden bench and a door that closed, beckoned on the corner. Xochi followed her impulse and went inside.

Did she need to call someone? Her whole body ached to be at Eris Gardens, but according to Ky, she was a danger to anyone close to her. Xochi began to see a dividing line she'd missed before—people who came with a reasonable amount of baggage and people whose damage exceeded acceptable limits. An image of red hair and dark-lined eyes rose to meet the idea.

Justine had started out at Eris Gardens, too. Like Xochi, she'd done something to fuck it all up.

Xochi leaned against the cold glass of the booth. She should have eaten the breakfast Kylen bought her. She imagined staying, letting him help. Except if what he said was true and these scary avenging siblings *were* on some sort of mystery crusade, what could any of them do? And really, it wasn't his problem. The green girl and her brother had come for Xochi. To fix her sorry excuse for a life.

She stood and picked up the phone. She hung it up. She touched the spine of the black receiver. The booth was so much warmer than the street. She closed her eyes and followed the telephone wires between San Francisco and Badger Creek. With shaking fingers, she dialed to make the collect call, punched in the 707 area code and familiar number, the ingrained pattern a bittersweet souvenir of her old life.

The phone rang. Xochi could picture the other end of the line so clearly—a messy bedroom smelling of clean laundry, weed, and teenage boy.

"Ugh?"

Thank goodness. He hadn't lost the trick of intercepting the phone on the first ring to avoid parental questioning, even when he was sound asleep.

"Collect call from Xochi Madrid," the operator said. "Do you accept the charges?"

" . . . Yeah."

The operator clicked off. Xochi could feel Collier's happiness through the phone line. There was a sound like a puppy shaking off a dip in a lake and her name in his familiar stoner purr. "Xochi?"

Her skin rippled as if his breath came through the holes in the receiver.

"You awake now, slacker?"

"Almost." She knew he was grinning.

He must be so warm right now, she thought. How many

summer mornings had she walked to his house, climbed through his window and into his bed? "It's so good to hear your voice."

"Where are you?" He sounded worried. She should have called him before now. She let the tears stream down her face unchecked. It was the only way she could keep them out of her voice.

"Big city," she managed.

"Seattle?" Collier sounded dubious. "SF?"

"Something like that."

"What happened? You never said goodbye." The words were almost too quiet to hear, but for Collier, this was a serious confrontation.

"I'm so sorry."

"Might want to visit you, you know?" His voice was freer now. She remembered what it was like to be in his arms.

"Now's not a great time. I have to take care of something. But Coll?"

"Xo?"

"I promise, when it's settled, I'll tell you everything and you can come see me anytime you want."

"Okay."

They were silent again. Xochi had forgotten the long pauses practiced by many of the Native people she knew. With Collier, it used to drive her nuts. Now the silence was all right. She was willing to postpone the real reason for her call. How was she supposed to bring it up? But Collier beat her to it.

"So, uh, yeah, there's that thing about Evan . . . "

"I heard." Xochi tried to sound normal. Watery coffee sloshed in her stomach.

"He's dead. You knew, right?"

"Sure." Xochi swallowed hard, grateful for the wooden seat that held her up and the contained space of the phone booth. There was no way she could write Kylen off as crazy now.

"It was kind of messed up. The cause of death was drowning,

but he wasn't drinking. They checked. So how does a big guy like that drown in a shallow creek stone-cold sober?"

"Karma," Xochi whispered.

Collier was quiet on the other end of the line. They'd never talked about Evan, about what he'd done, but Collier knew something wasn't right. When Loretta died, he'd wanted her to move in with his family. They had a spare room since his sister had left for nursing school, but Xochi knew there was no way his parents would say yes. They'd always been sweet when Xochi and Collier were kids, but things changed when his mom figured out they weren't in the bedroom building Lego spaceships anymore. Apparently, Xochi had inherited a scarlet badge from Gina. The older she got, the less the women around town seemed to trust her.

"Karma, yeah," Collier answered. "It was karma, no doubt."

Xochi remembered the way his full lips got tight when he was worried. Picturing his face made the tears come faster.

"Coll, I gotta go. Thank you for talking to me. You sound so good."

"You sound weird."

"I'm okay."

"For real?"

"For real."

"Promise?"

"I promise." It was their familiar exchange, the way they'd always taken care of each other.

"Love you, Xochi."

"Love you, too."

Xochi placed the phone in its receiver and cried. She missed Collier. She missed Loretta. Evan was dead. Why hadn't Ky grabbed her leather jacket instead of this worthless hoodie? She'd had her wallet in there. She'd been saving up. Right now, nothing sounded better than the crappy SRO she'd stayed in when she'd first gotten to the city. She would check in and sleep for the next six months.

As it was, she was starving and exhausted and a total liability to her friends. It was crazy, but there was no denying what Xochi remembered now. The Waterbabies had appeared at the same moment Leviticus walked through the door, just like Kylen said. Wiping her eyes with the back of her hand, Xochi stood up. She couldn't stay in that phone booth forever.

She walked until she found a bus stop. What time was it? Eight or nine? She sat cross-legged on the bench, keeping her spine straight. She'd seen Io meditate this way. She kept her eyes open, though. It wouldn't do to sit around with them closed in the middle of the city. She fixed her vision on the wheels of a car parked across the street and quieted her mind.

Of course, there he was: Leviticus. His bathtub, his bed—so natural and right. Touching was complicated, so they didn't touch. Surprisingly, sleep was simple. Yes, she'd been drinking. She was high. But the comfort there was stronger than the chemicals she'd ingested, an antidote made by her and Leviticus both. It made her feel taller, sit up straighter. Iggy Pop's "Strong Girl" bounced around her head. How cool to be a girl as strong as an ocean. That's what Xochi needed now. A slight breeze disturbed the garbage in the gutters. Her eye caught a gray slip of paper floating above the collection of trash. A bus transfer, still good. A squeaking Muni bus pulled up. Without stopping to see where it was headed, Xochi got on.

50

Kundalini Express

For the first time since he'd left the warehouse, James could identify the bus's location: downtown, Mission bound. He'd ridden the entire route twice. After a third time, if his routine held, he'd be grounded enough to retrieve his car and go home.

For the last half hour, he'd been listening to the conversation of the elderly couple who'd just gotten off the bus. They'd spoken in Mandarin, so all he could make out were a few simple words, but in his heightened state, their connection appeared like intertwined roots. Each time they spoke, the roots curled more intricately together. He'd especially enjoyed watching them exit the bus, how the man had helped his wife disembark with a hand on her back, how she'd discreetly steadied him, the more rickety of the two, with a touch to his elbow, taking nothing away from his chivalry.

Now there were only two other passengers—a woman reading a novel in the seat behind the driver and a young girl in a sweatshirt with her hood pulled up. Unlike most passengers, who held their destinations tightly in their minds, the young woman did not know where she was going.

She folded her legs to sit in lotus position and closed her eyes. Lines of light flowed from the palms of her hands, which she held in a posture of surrender. As the bus turned onto Valencia, something in the girl's aura changed. The light shooting from her left hand flickered, glowing pomegranate red. He remembered the way long journeys were depicted in old movies, with a line traveling across a map.

He switched seats from the window to the aisle.

"Excuse me, miss."

The young woman opened her eyes. She was familiar, but he couldn't place her. "Excuse me, but I think we're coming to your stop."

Her brow wrinkled. After a moment, she said, "Wait, do I know you?"

He removed his sunglasses and met her eyes. "It's possible," he admitted, "but there is no doubt whatsoever that this is your stop. Hurry, young lady, you don't want to miss it."

51

Wilderland

Xochi stood on the corner of Valencia and 23rd. She'd recognized James as she was getting off the bus, too late to thank him. But really, thank him for what? He'd been so sure she was supposed to get off here, but it was hard to see why. None of the shops or houses on the street held any special significance.

Xochi was warm. She backed out of the sun, retreating to the shade of an overgrown camellia. She took off her hoodie. With the cool air against her skin, it was clear the heat was coming from her necklace. *Weird,* she thought, heading down the block.

At the crosswalk, she realized she'd left her hoodie behind. By the time she walked back, she was sweating again and the stone on her necklace was almost too hot to touch.

Wait a minute, Xochi thought. *Warmer when I'm close, cooler when I'm far away? And when I'm right here—right where the Hookah-Smoking Caterpillar sent me—it's red hot?*

There was nothing on the block besides closed-up bars and taquerias, a grocery store on the corner and an occult store across the street, also closed. The house behind her had a sign in the yard, hidden by some exuberant spring grass. The word "SIRENA" was printed in curly script under a picture of a mermaid. This must be the secret women's bathhouse Bubbles had told her about. Xochi climbed the stairs to the front porch, necklace hotter with every step.

The door didn't give many further clues except for a hand-printed sign: "WOMEN ONLY" and a piece of lined paper announcing spring business hours in pink Magic Marker.

Xochi left the porch and tried the narrow walkway leading around the side of the house. When she came around the corner, the amulet practically sizzled. She came to a high wooden gate with a sign: "BE AWARE OF THE DOG."

Be *aware* of the dog? She'd officially stepped off the bus and down the rabbit hole. She was contemplating standing on an overturned trash can to see over the fence, but then the gate opened. Standing in a posture of calm welcome was a massive German shepherd. It wagged its tail and grinned.

Xochi followed, closing the gate behind her. She found herself in an oasis of a backyard.

The cool green space vibrated with a sense of destination. A wet nose nudged her leg. A flagstone path wound through the trees. The moment Xochi put her foot on the pavers, her necklace screamed, *HOT HOT HOT*.

She took a step, then another. A wisteria trellis in full bloom scented the light wind. The path opened onto a clearing.

A swell of emotion surged, wave upon wave upon wave. Grief and longing and relief and reunion were a whirlpool that sucked Xochi to the ground. Gravel bit into her palms and dug into her knees. Crows cawed overhead. She touched her face. Viscous tears dripped from her chin. She stood and touched her fingers to her lips. They were sweet. Just like honey.

Near the fence were three redwood hot tubs. The center tub was smaller than the others and covered in a buzzing cloud. The dog pressed against her leg, licked her sticky fingers, and pushed her onward with its blocky head. The buzzing cloud of bees rose several feet to reveal two small, still figures. Xochi's mind reached for something to explain this improbable garden with its sentient dog and sentinel bees and Secret Service detail of crows, all obviously guarding the two otherworldly beings asleep in the redwood tub.

In Xochi's dreams, the pair's skin had been vivid, their hair a living thing, but now their skin was dull, their hair pooled on the deck behind them in two limp piles. Xochi wanted to run to them, as if they were long lost and beloved. But she stopped, remembering what they were capable of.

"Hello?" she said.

The Waterbabies didn't stir. Slowly, she approached the tub. She put a hand in the water. Tepid. She remembered the dreams of mineral pools and mud baths. She found the controls for the heater and turned them all the way up. The green girl's eyelids fluttered, but didn't open. Her tiny, perfect hand rose to the surface of the water. Xochi should have been afraid, but she wasn't. She took the little hand in hers.

A voice opened like a flower in her mind. *My brother is cold.*

"I turned up the heat," Xochi said. "It will get warmer."

YOU are warm.

Reason told her to stop and think, but she was already unlacing her boots. The bees buzzed overhead. The crows ruffled their feathers.

Naked, Xochi slipped into the water, the cool an instant relief. She touched the brown boy's hand. It was heavy, a clay thing, but Xochi sensed life in it. She touched her throat. *Loretta's necklace!* She took it off and placed it around his neck. The opal glowed. His eyes opened.

Thank you.

His voice in her head tasted of iron and made her piercing tingle. The fist that had been in her stomach since breakfast released.

Xochi.

He said her name like he loved her.

We greet you, he said, taking Xochi's hand. Xochi touched the green girl, who reached in turn for her brother, the circuit complete. The voice in Xochi's head was a textured thing,

each word connected to the next like the loops of yarn Loretta
hooked into blankets.

> *Low, low, deep and low*
> *In the heat at the heart of the earth*
> *Brother is alone and lonely*
> *It has not always been so*
> *He once had a sister, tall and fine, elder and wiser*
> *But one day, his sister was gone*
>
> *His kind must be paired to travel*
> *His kind must be paired to thrive*
> *His kind must be paired, but he is not*
> *His sister lost to mystery*
>
> *Alone and lonely, Brother sleeps*
> *Curled into the earth*
> *Knowing only darkness*
> *Heat and magma, ore and root*
> *Then, one day, a voice*

"I can't see you, but I know you're there," the woman said.

> *The human sound was pleasant,*
> *A thing of bark and soil*

*"I feel you every time I come here. Like maybe you lost someone
you loved."* She lowered her body into the hot spring and sat quietly
for a time.

> *From deep below*
> *Brother sends his greeting*
> *He sends a story, a gift of thanks*
> *He tells of a sister, elder and wiser*
> *A sister, suddenly gone*

The human sends the gift of her name: "Loretta."

"My aunt was a midwife," Loretta said. "She worked with a family who tried to have a child for many years. Finally, they were expecting, but the baby died the day it was born. We brought them food, did a cleansing in their house. Nothing helped until my aunt met a young woman who couldn't keep her baby. 'Perfect,' my aunt said. 'A match made in heaven.' When the bereaved couple saw the baby, they instantly knew: the child was meant to be their daughter."

The story runs through Brother, seismic
A new child, a second chance
The mudpot stirs
Bright flashes of fire wake the slow, liquid earth
Brother reaches for the woman, but she is gone

The next day,
He makes himself light
Rising through the earth's thick blood
To the cooler water atop the spring
Crows ring the meadow, melanite feathers sparkling in the sun

Smaller birds carpet the clearing,
Orbiting some earthbound moon
They part as Brother approaches
His steps as unsteady as a fawn's

In the center of the circle sits a Dream:
Honeybee mantled, hummingbird crowned,
Her skin a luminous fortunate green
A little sister. Precious and rare

A brother once more, he takes her hand
Together they listen. Together they feel

Together they travel, side by side
Brother is no longer alone

Xochi opened her eyes. The precious sister, the loving brother. They stood before her, hand in hand, eyes bright with hope. Tears streamed down Xochi's face. *Loretta.* She'd been taking care of Xochi all along. "You knew her," Xochi said.

I knew her. Brother's voice rippled through the water. He wiped Xochi's tears with the back of his hand. His touch brought back the September afternoon Loretta's pain had ceased, the invisible hands holding hers on either side of the rented hospital bed, the glowing stone of the necklace at her throat.

"You came when she was dying," Xochi said. "You helped her."

She helped us, Sister said. *She loved you.*

"She loved Evan, too." Xochi was still crying. "No one asked you to do that."

He hurt you. Brother's voice expanded into Xochi's chest like the vibration of Kylen's cello. *He hurt others. Others before, others after. He would not stop. He could not mend.*

Hurt and hurting. Sister squeezed Xochi's hand. *Golden and broken. Over and done. We led, but we did not choose.*

Xochi saw a peaceful moment, Evan's face in repose under a blue sky. She thought of the blue velvet box and locket. Panic flapped in her gut. "What about Gina?"

Your mother sleeps, Brother said. *We cannot wake her.*

"What do you mean?" Xochi pulled away, backing to the edge of the tub. "What did you do to her?"

Hurt and hurting, Sister's voice chirped. *Golden and broken. Guilty and shamed.* The green girl's eyes begged for understanding. Her hair twitched and rose an inch from the deck. The crows in the fir tree launched into the air, cawing and harsh. They reminded Xochi of Kylen.

Suddenly, Brother stood. He unfastened Xochi's necklace from his neck and put it on his sister. The hummingbirds looked alive on her throat, the opal a radiant egg. She climbed from the tub and stood on the deck with the air of a reciting child. When she spoke, her voice was rough with crow's music, obsidian and feathered and wild.

> *We tracked and we changed the one who betrayed*
> *Broke the spell of the blood-thief and snake-tongued maid.*
> *You called us here, and we answered your call.*
> *We found your lost mother, but cannot mend all.*
> *Too long from our home, cut off from our might*
> *Your mother lays trapped in ever-night.*
> *We came to help you, restore you and heal you,*
> *We came to avenge you, to know and protect you.*
> *But now we must ask these things of you —*
> *We cannot go home unless we do.*

Sister finished, her skin agate bright.

Her brother's eyes burned with pride. "Do you understand what we ask of you?" His voice had physical form, a tall tree in an ancient wood.

"You've been to see my mother. And something went wrong?"

"She sleeps," Sister said. "She cannot awaken. Hurt and hurting. Guilty and shamed."

"Okay. I get that, I think. She's too messed up. You guys couldn't fix her."

The Waterbabies nodded in unison, an oddly human gesture.

"And now you can't wake her up?"

Sister nodded again, raven eyes wide.

Xochi sat on the edge of the tub, legs in the water. A chemical stink pushed out of her pores—alcohol and cigarettes and drugs. She tried Loretta's breathing technique. She longed for a cold glass of water.

The slipperiness she'd described to Kylen edged at the perimeter of her brain—because although her body was here in this impossible situation, how could it be real? She noted the familiar internal rip of dissociation, consciousness separating from skin. She pictured a zipper on the surface of her soul, making it easier to leave at will. So many things didn't add up. Better to leave them behind with her vulnerable, treacherous body and just . . . float away.

A hand on her ankle brought her to ground. She saw water and the wooden bottom of the tub. She saw the soil and small creatures beneath it. Lower maple roots made a lattice that held her. The earth stretched its arms open wide.

She was here.

She was real.

She was safe.

Denial may have helped her survive before, but it would only ruin her now.

A memory rose from the mulch, branding her forehead with its protection: Xochi on Duncan's horrible dead-animal couch, Leviticus kneeling at her feet. Him holding her head, touching his forehead to hers. A kindred spirit. Family. Friend. The Waterbabies were as real as she had been last night in Leviticus's bed, last night on Duncan's couch, last year alone in a cabin in the middle of nowhere, lying dead as a stone as Evan moved over her again and again and again.

Something buzzed in her ear. *A bee.* Xochi stayed very still. The bee hovered. A scent lingered, utterly familiar. Gina's perfume. It drenched Xochi's skin and seeped into her open pores. Xochi wanted to reject it, but she couldn't; it was already part of her. Gina may have messed up a thousand different ways, but she would always be Xochi's mother.

Xochi sat up.

"I think I understand," she said. "Evan was too far gone. But Gina isn't. Not innocent or guilty. *Golden and broken*—I get it."

These two magical beings were so small and strange and brave. They didn't belong here. They'd only come for Xochi, for Loretta. She had to help them. And, like it or not, that meant she had to help Gina, too.

52

Gun Street Girl

Xochi took the bus again, her transfer still good. The Mitchell Brothers marquee read: KELLY SUMMERS: LIVE AND BARELY LEGAL! The club didn't open until noon, but men were already lining up. Xochi's stomach tightened. *Wherever you are is where you belong*, Pallas's voice chirped in Xochi's head. She'd said that before the Equinox concert, when Xochi had confessed to feeling out of place.

Pallas. She was probably so mad. And worried. But maybe Xochi could still fix things. She put her shoulders back and approached the bouncer guarding the door against the impatient men.

"Do I know you?" He looked Xochi up and down.

"I'm new," Xochi said, opening her eyes Bambi wide.

"Where's your stuff?"

Stuff? Crap. "Inside," Xochi said, conjuring her best black-and-white movie ingénue. "I went out for coffee."

"Where's your coffee?"

"I forgot my wallet." Xochi batted her lashes.

The bouncer shook his head but let her pass.

In the lobby, a woman with a huge duffel stomped toward a staircase. Xochi followed.

In the dressing room, her cover was instantly blown.

"Who are you?" Eight sets of mascaraed lashes blinked at Xochi.

"I'm looking for someone," Xochi began.

"You can't be in here. Employees only." The tall blonde was clearly the alpha. She stood, wearing her G-string and lacy triangle bra the way most people wore a full set of clothes.

"I'm looking for Gina," Xochi said. "I need to find her."

"Get lost." In her street clothes, the woman with the duffel had looked tough. Nearly naked, she looked tougher, muscled like an athlete. Xochi held her ground.

An older dancer put down her lipstick. "What do you want with Gina, honey?"

"She's my mom." Saying it out loud was a surprising relief.

"Wow." The dancer met Xochi's eyes in the mirror. Her breasts were enormous, fake and a little lumpy. She looked like an actress Xochi'd seen a million times but couldn't place. "We can't tell you anything, sweetie. I'm sorry."

"I know there's probably some sort of rule. Like, confidentiality—"

"It's not that." A dancer at the end of the makeup counter turned to Xochi. She looked too young to be working at a strip club. "Misty keeps to herself."

Misty? That must be Gina's stage name. Xochi rolled her eyes.

"What?" The girl smiled. She was gorgeous. Latina, but maybe not Mexican, with dark brown skin and gray-blue eyes. Xochi realized she'd seen her before, onstage. And after that at the warehouse party.

"Misty was a horse," Xochi said. "Not the one from the kids' book, but, like, a real horse my mom used to take care of. Kind of funny for a stripper name."

"I named myself after my cat," the tough dancer said, half transformed by a long coppery wig. "And Sasha's right." She gestured to the dancer in the corner. "Gina doesn't hang with anybody here."

The women turned back to their grooming. The older dancer glanced at the clock. "Come on," she said, pulling a robe over her lingerie. She steered Xochi out of the dressing room, back to the lobby. "How'd you get up here?"

"Said I was a new girl."

"Perfect." The dancer approached the front counter. "Can you call this poor girl a taxi? Make sure it's Ben. She's not feeling well, and I don't want some asshole taking advantage."

"Will do," the man said.

"Wait out front." The woman nodded toward the door. "Ben takes all of us home at night. If anyone knows where your mom lives, it's him. You have money for the fare?" Xochi shook her head, suddenly wishing this woman was her long-lost mom instead of Gina. The dancer pressed a ten-dollar bill into Xochi's hand. "If it's more than that, tell him Cassie will make up the difference tonight."

"Are you sure?"

Cassie smiled. "Get out of here. Go see your mom."

OUTSIDE, THE LINE HAD grown. One of the waiting customers was smoking a clove. *What the hell?* Xochi thought. "Have a spare?" she asked, using the same voice she'd used on the bouncer. The man blinked, surprised to be addressed. He pulled out his pack and handed it to her. "Take it," he said.

A yellow cab pulled up, right on cue.

"Thanks," Xochi said. "See you around."

53

Break Down the Door

Peasblossom woke with a splitting headache and an altered memory. One moment, he'd been in Gina's window, meowing a warning, the next he was laid out on a hardwood floor, waking after an hours-long, drugged-feeling sleep. The creatures had clearly outsmarted him.

Now he found himself beside the prone body of Xochi's mother. The woman was so still, he couldn't help but think of Ron—one moment sleeping, the next gone. Peasblossom gathered himself, remembering Nora's bravery as she held Ron in the last moments of his life.

Climbing onto the woman's chest, Peasblossom concentrated. There *was* a heartbeat. Slow, but present. He purred as hard as he could, pouring healing warmth into Gina's body. When she was breathing more regularly, Peasblossom left her bed to pace, bits of folklore coalescing into an absurd diagnosis: Xochi's mother was in some version of an enchanted slumber.

Glad there were no witnesses, he tried the most obvious remedy, touching his gray muzzle to her pale pink lips. For the sake of thoroughness, he applied his tongue, tasting traces of marijuana and the salt humans so strangely excreted. He yowled in her ear. He nudged her with a paw. He tickled her feet with his whiskers. Desperate, he climbed to the dresser and, in a flying leap—well executed but ill advised, given his age—landed on her chest with all the impact of his fourteen pounds. As a last resort, he bit her hand. It twitched reflexively, but there were no other signs of consciousness.

Her faint pulse troubled him. He touched his nose to her cheek. It was cold again. He climbed back to roost on her chest, purring and kneading with velvet paws.

The screech of the buzzer made his fur stand on end. Could it be the creatures? But that was absurd. If they wanted to return, they certainly wouldn't come in through the lobby. The buzzer rang again, tentatively this time. Peasblossom walked to the front door of the apartment, finding a conveniently placed chair where a human might sit to put on her shoes. In this case, it allowed the cat to stand braced against its high back and work the lever that operated the intercom.

"Hello?" The young female voice cracked on the upper syllable of the query. Peasblossom pushed the lever in the opposite direction, meowing into the speaker.

"Um, hello? Is Gina there?"

Xochi! Peasblossom pressed the button below the intercom's lever that opened the lobby door. He eyed the deadbolt, so high there was no hope of reaching it. Perhaps if the chair was closer. He put his weight against its legs to no avail. He rested and tried again.

The girl's quiet knock on the apartment door mocked the cat's lack of human anatomy. Not that he'd ever trade his sleek geometry for the gangling lope of a hairless human, but living in a world designed for their use was often maddening.

"Hello?"

He smelled Xochi's fear through the crack in the door. It was an old building. Pushing his snout into the space, Peasblossom had an idea. The gap was wide, the wood floor slippery with a hundred years of varnish. Where were Gina's keys? Most likely in her purse. The one-room space was neat and spare and seemed to contain neither object.

Xochi knocked again. "Uh, is someone in there? Who buzzed me in?"

Peasblossom meowed. Perhaps the knowledge that some living creature was on the other side of the door would keep her there.

He realized that the smaller door in the entryway must lead to a closet. A doorknob was something he could usually operate, especially the faceted glass knobs found in so many San Francisco apartments. A concerted push from an upright position was all it took.

There was the inevitable bag, an unstructured affair, thankfully without a zipper. On a plain ring were two keys. Peasblossom grasped the ring in his mouth and raced to the entry. Dropping the key ring and meowing once more, he pushed it under the door.

54

Gold Dust Woman

"Peasblossom?" The Siamese cat was the last thing Xochi expected to see in her mother's doorway. "Peas?" She crouched and held out her hand. The cat pressed his head into her damp palm and rubbed against her leg. Xochi stepped into a cramped foyer and Gina's familiar scent hit her like a Muni bus. Luckily she hadn't eaten, or the contents of her stomach would be on the floor. She stood frozen as Peasblossom slipped behind her to push the front door shut.

A gentle bite on her ankle reminded her to move her feet. It took two steps to get from the entry to the main room of the apartment. A double bed was tucked into the curve of the picture window. The morning sun made little headway through the blinds. Gina needed absolute dark to sleep. In every new apartment, the first thing she bought was a set of blackout shades. There were times they couldn't afford a two-bedroom, back when Xochi was afraid of the dark. In those apartments, she slept on the couch with the TV on mute, the flickering light providing comfort in so many ways her mother could not.

Walking to the edge of the bed took ten steps.

Gina had always been a light sleeper, but now she was motionless, her body surrendered in a way that looked wrong. Xochi turned on the overhead light. She pulled up the shades.

Gina's face registered nothing. Xochi clapped beside her ear. The cat meowed and shook his head back and forth, deliberately making the gesture for "no."

"Are you saying you tried already? Making noise?"

The cat mewed affirmation.

In the light, Xochi saw fine lines around Gina's mouth and dark circles under her eyes. Her hands rested on the patchwork quilt—a blanket Xochi recognized as Loretta's work, a present for Gina's twenty-eighth birthday. She must have taken it with her when she left Badger Creek. Gina had taken the blanket, but left her daughter, abandoned in the middle of nowhere with an angry, abusive man.

Xochi backed away from her mother's bed and went into the kitchen. She splashed her face with cold water. She remembered the box of cigarettes. She didn't have a lighter, so she used the stove. The cat followed her, wrinkling his nose. Xochi opened a window.

The kitchen was minuscule. So different from the one at Eris Gardens with its long wooden table, painted yellow after Frida Kahlo's, Io's favorite artist.

Io and Leviticus. Their names paired so easily. Maybe they weren't together, but they would always be Pallas's parents, always a sort of pair. Xochi inhaled, the clove tobacco crackling in the quiet apartment.

Pallas. This whole thing had started the night of the Equinox when she'd come home and found Pallas smoking. Xochi wanted nothing more than to rewind the past few weeks and reclaim her innocent nights alone in her narrow governess's bed, listening to Pallas's light snoring in the room next door.

She stubbed the cigarette out in the sink and threw the butt in the trash. She made sure to rinse any traces of ash from the snowy porcelain. Looking around, she could see the entire apartment was spotless. Gina was still a total neat freak.

Peasblossom leaped onto a kitchen chair with a questioning meow. At least Xochi wasn't alone. The cat was here—she wouldn't try to figure out why or how—and the Waterbabies were depending on her.

"So, Peasblossom," she said, "riddle me this. How many stupid girls and Siamese cats does it take to wake a deadbeat mother from an enchanted slumber?"

55

Sitting in Limbo

Leviticus had always dreaded the oh-shit moment of fear that came with mornings—missed appointments, unkept promises, regrets from the night before. Unchecked, he could sleep away an entire day, the one beautiful oblivion he was still allowed.

This morning was different. Awareness spread like syrup over a stack of pancakes, a lazy, welcome sweetness. He glanced down at the tented sheet. A dream scene: swimming with Xochi in a calm river, naked and intertwined.

He sat up. Her side of the bed was empty. He understood the animal need for retreat. He imagined her slipping out of bed, hungover and raw. She would be in her room in the attic, curled in her narrow bed with her piles of clothes and half-read books like a fox in a den.

He glanced at the clock. Almost ten. *Shit.* He'd lost track again, might have forgotten today was Saturday. Good thing Xochi was gone. He clenched at the thought of Pallas trekking up here to get him and finding who knew what instead. It would have been so easy to reach out for Xochi in sleep, to touch her before he remembered he shouldn't.

Sleeping next to her had been so natural. *Chemical, alchemical.* That's how it seemed with her. And here he was, romanticizing again. As always, Kylen appeared, a goth Jiminy Cricket in his head: *Was last night at Duncan's romantic, asshole?* Leviticus reviewed: Xochi nodded out, top undone, debauched. It took him years to realize that many people, most people, wanted nothing to do with the kind of escape he used to believe he needed.

Most people, but not Xochi.

He sat up and took a long breath, as close as he ever got to meditation. The movement released Xochi's scent from his chaste blankets. In all the time he'd lived in this room, no one but her had ever shared his bed. He cringed, thinking of the stupid note he'd left with the guitar—was it only yesterday? The days were melting into each other, a warning sign he'd come to recognize.

He hadn't looked at his calendar since before LA. His notebook of reminders and to-do lists had devolved into a lovelorn diary—the infamous pro-con list, bits of bad poetry, drafts of letters he wished he could write. He would die if Kylen ever got ahold of it. He should burn the damned thing. His hand went to his chest, pressing a sudden ache. *I'm lonely*, he realized.

He sat up all the way, feet on the floor. First things first. He was here, alive, with his imperfect vessel and flawed heart, an unsolvable problem—but all things considered, he was all right. He sifted through his dreams for the song of the day, something to soothe the familiar panic. *The river. The water. Loneliness. Limbo.* There it was: Jimmy Cliff. He stood and pulled on his pants, singing along to the chorus.

56

She's Lost Control

Io paid the driver. Halfway home from her morning run, she realized she was shaky with hunger. She balanced the large pink donut box as she opened the door, stomach rumbling. It had been years since she'd eaten one. They couldn't possibly be vegan, but she didn't ask the baker. Better not to know.

In the kitchen, Leviticus sat with a cup of coffee and the paper, still so like the boy she'd met all those years ago, thoughtful and handsome and unlucky in love. She wouldn't mention what she'd seen this morning. No need to embarrass him. Or herself.

Io glanced at her watch. It was ten-thirty, half an hour past the time Leviticus and Pallas always had their Saturday breakfast. "Why are you here, love?"

"Pallas never showed. I thought she was with you. She must be with Xochi." His eyes narrowed at the mention of Xochi's name. Io still struggled when it came to reading faces, but her time with Leviticus hiding under the covers from impending adulthood had been an excellent education. She'd learned so much from his sweet transparent face.

Kylen's motorcycle roared into its parking spot. He banged into the kitchen looking tired. Was he just back from the previous night?

"What are you doing here?" he said to Leviticus.

"Pal stood me up," Leviticus said. "She must be out with Xochi."

Kylen paled. Io stood, she wasn't sure why.

"What?" Leviticus asked them.

"She's not with Xochi," Kylen said. "The governess and I just had breakfast, followed by a raging fight. She bailed. No way she came back here."

Blood rushed to Io's neck and face. Her ears burned. She sat down, trapping her hands under her legs so she couldn't use them to hide. "I saw you," she said to Leviticus. "This morning. You and Xochi."

There. It was out.

"Join the club," Kylen said. "I needed to talk to her about last night and she wasn't in her room. Wasn't too hard to find her."

"It was news to me," Io said. "I don't know why I went into your room. I'm sorry I intruded."

Leviticus closed his eyes, his face pained. Io's brain, usually so busy, was still. Leviticus rose, went to the junk drawer, and retrieved a pack of cigarettes. No one stopped him from lighting it on the stove. He took a drag, squared his shoulders, and looked Io in the eye. "Pallas must have seen us, too."

The small word *us* rested in Io's left ear, a word that didn't include her. She remembered the brass bead she'd carried there for a week as a child, careful never to let it become lodged in her ear canal. She was six years old and deep in a phase of experiments and secrets. *Like right now,* she thought.

The donut she'd eaten in the taxi surged up. She made it to the sink just in time. Her senses were out of order. The vomit tasted violet, the light smelled of vomit, the water on her hands felt like oil.

Leviticus was behind her. He turned off the sink, dried her hands with a towel. He gave her a glass of water. She drank, hands shaking, but at least the water tasted like water and the light lost its acrid scent.

"Come here," Kylen said, opening his arms to both of them. He rested his chin on Io's head and hummed a soft tune to ground her. Leviticus pulled both of them closer. Io looked up to see his head resting on Kylen's shoulder, his eyes closed.

"I'm okay," Io said, stepping away.

"I know." Kylen smiled. "Dudes, this is normal. Growing pains and shit. Don't freak out."

"I'll take the far side of the park and Land's End," Leviticus said. "I know her spots."

"I'll do the neighborhood." Kylen downed his coffee and zipped his jacket.

"I'll wake the others and organize them." Io was surprised at her own calm, but she was a mother, after all. She'd endured pregnancy, given birth, raised a strong, healthy child. Pallas was sensible. She was safe. Everything was going to be okay.

57

Lovers of Today

Anna took off her roller skates and unlocked the door to her apartment. Pallas found her unmatched socks unaccountably endearing.

"Shhh," Anna said. "That's my mom's room." She nodded at a door off the small entry and led the way down a long hall to the back of the narrow flat, stepping over piles of shoes and coats and backpacks. "Watch out," Anna whispered. "We were tired last night. We just plopped everything down when we got home."

The word *plopped* applied to the placement of most things in the cluttered hall. Remnants of abandoned activity were everywhere—crayons and cardboard, teetering stacks of books. The walls were similarly haphazard, making a pleasing layered collage over faded raspberry paint. Anna's artwork crowded around framed posters and tacked-up postcards. A pair of baby shoes hung on an ornate hook; sparkling beads hung from the ceiling. Snapshots were tucked around the frame of a chipped gilt mirror.

The kitchen was at the back of the apartment, with orange walls and floor-to-ceiling art.

"Do you want anything?" Anna asked.

"Coffee?" Pallas had been drinking it more lately because of Xochi.

Ugh. Pallas wrapped her arms around herself, blinking

away the image of Xochi and her dad. There was a book she'd had when she was small, a version of Pinocchio where photographs of puppets were used in place of illustrations. There had been a picture of an old man sitting at a table in the belly of a whale. She imagined herself there, living out her days.

"We only have tea," Anna said. "PG Tips. It's English. My mom calls it crack in a cup."

"Pad and Kiki drink that all day long," Pallas said. "It sounds perfect."

"My mom won't let me have caffeine." Anna sighed, taking out a box of herbal tea for herself and the big square PG Tips box for Pallas. "She says it makes me crazy."

"I've always loved the taste of coffee," Pallas said. "My dad used to make me decaf when I was little. He—" She stopped. Tears filled her eyes. She dug her nails into her palms.

"Pallas, do you want to just hang out and watch movies all day? 'Cause I'm kinda tired," Anna said. Pallas thought of the little English squirrels Io used to draw for her with tufty ears and mischievous faces. Anna looked just like that with her spiky hair and anything-but-tired expression. She was right, though. Pallas needed to check out. All she really wanted was her big fluffy bed, the warm comfort of a late-morning nap in the attic. But she couldn't go home, not yet. Maybe never.

"A movie marathon sounds perfect," she said.

LEVITICUS HAD A FEELING Pallas wasn't at the beach, but he walked it anyway. The waves were aggressive, judgmental. He imagined finding her. He would tell the truth, of course. But what was true?

A forbidden vocabulary lapped his boots. *Faggot. Fuckup. Junkie. Whore.* He didn't use these words to describe other people who shared his struggles. Didn't even think them. *Failure. Pussy. Sellout. Fraud.* These words had become his blasphemy, their rejection a counter scripture to his father's fire and brimstone. He walked faster. *Apostate. Lazy. Not My Son.* The litany hissed from the throat of the sea. Leviticus reached the end of the beach. Gulls winged overhead, crying condemnation. He faced the waves, took a step forward. *Loser. Lecher. Blasphemer. Bitch.* The spray was the spittle of his father's rage, the stinging wind his palm on Leviticus's face.

A wave soaked his boots. Then another and another.

He listened for the mermaid's song, the promise of deep and peaceful sleep. He dropped to his knees. A sharp rock released a thin stream of blood in the foam that lapped at the sprung knee of his jeans. His mouth remembered the way heroin tasted, coming up from the blood instead of in from the tongue. The tracks on his arm whispered the things they remembered about rest and quiet and peace. That was the real siren song, his own blood's memory.

His knee seeped. He dabbed at it with the cuff of his hoodie. His wrist peeked out, the safety pin tattoo a reminder of the dark lady.

That's what the girl in London had called it. He was just a kid then. Xochi's age. Io had left with Pallas. It was hard to remember he'd ever been anyone's dad. He'd started with cutting, carving the tattoo, inking it in: "24:20," chapter and verse from the book he was named for. He carved randomly after that, but relief was fleeting. Then the girl was there, with her blue eyes and books and shaved head and her needle and spoon—a Shakespeare scholar, before meeting her dark lady.

White girl—that's what the jazz man with the amazing mouth called the pure white heroin they had in New York. Ky dragged Leviticus home that time, cleaned him up. Took him to the beach to run. "Write her name in the sand," he'd said. "Let the waves wash it away. Just let her go." In those days, they thought love for Io was Leviticus's problem.

Leviticus stood up. He found a stick of driftwood at the edge of the dunes. In the wet sand, he wrote:

Fracture for fracture, Eye for eye, Tooth for tooth

Leviticus, 24:20

HE WATCHED THE WAVES soften and erase the hateful words till the sand was completely smooth.

His face was wet.

He licked a tear from his lips.

It was sweet, just like honey.

He raised his hand to wipe his eyes, turned his wrist over.

A gull cried, an echo of his own amazement.

His wrist was clean, the skin healed, all traces of the tattoo erased.

WHEN THE KID FIRST started going places on her own, they made a green line on a map of the neighborhood: this far, no farther. The map was Ky's idea. He wanted Pal to have her freedom, but he would never trust the screwed-up world. Every night for a full cycle of the moon, he'd trace the line slowly with a finger, charging the boundary with protection. On the dark moon, he walked the boundary at midnight, spitting on every street corner and dropping a few crumbs of the snake root and angelica he'd pulverized in Leviticus's coffee grinder.

Now he had a feeling, a strong one, that an upset Pallas would naturally gravitate to this old perimeter. He rode the streets at the boundary's edge progressing inward, reaching the bookstore just as Nora, the owner, unlocked the door.

"Hello," Kylen said. He'd always been shy around Nora. Her education intimidated him. She wasn't a snob—far from it. She'd never batted an eye at the weird books he asked her to track down—sex magick, Filipino folklore, mystical cellists, world religions.

"Kylen!" She smiled like she was actually glad to see him. Kylen liked her untidy hair and glasses and thrown-together librarian wardrobe. If she were a guy, he'd be in serious trouble. As it was, she was a crush of his, one of a select group of women he admired from afar. "It's been a while. How did you like the Éliphas Lévi?"

"It was dense," Kylen said. *He* was dense, really. Not dumb, but a slow reader. At least he tried. Once, he'd asked Nora to give him all the books he'd missed in high school. She made him a stack and refused to charge him. "They're mine, from the house. If you love any of them, you can buy them to keep. Otherwise, just give them back and we'll dish. You can't know what a treat this is for me!"

That was how he'd ended up reading to Ron, Nora's roommate and best friend. He'd come by the apartment to return the books. Nora was out, but Ron answered the door. X was blasting on the stereo. They could barely hear each other over Exene's bratty wail and John Doe's thrash-twang guitar. Ron, weak and sick, had slipped on his way inside to turn it down. Kylen helped him back into his armchair and ended up staying, talking about the books. When Ron got tired, he'd asked Kylen to read to him. Kylen came back the next day. And the next.

"I'm actually looking for Pallas," Kylen said. "Have you seen her?"

"She's at my house," Nora said. "She and Anna asked if they could have a sleepover. Finally, they're friends! I've been trying to fix them up for years. She said she called home already."

"She didn't," Kylen said.

"That's not like her." Nora's brow furrowed. She took the chopsticks from her hair and retwisted it into a bun. She was always doing that. Kylen found it mesmerizing. "Is something up?"

"It's a long story," Kylen said.

"I'll get us coffee," Nora said. "Have a seat."

BACK AT ERIS GARDENS, Kylen told the family the plan he'd cooked up—both stunningly minimal and utterly evil.

Pallas was safe and sound and had lied about calling them.

Nora was game to let Pallas stew until she was good and ready to confess. Kylen knew that every minute Pallas waited would be pure hell. He also knew how stubborn she was, more like him than either of her parents.

"Shall we make bets on how long it takes her?" Pad asked.

"Monster!" Bubbles threw a balled-up napkin. They'd ordered pizza and were on their third six-pack of beer. When Leviticus went out to the patio to smoke, everyone followed. It had been a harrowing day.

"This is harder than I thought," Aaron said. "The house feels empty without her."

"It's my fault," Leviticus said.

"Yes, it is," Kiki said, kissing him on the cheek.

Leviticus chain-smoked, his brow furrowed. "Now that Pal's safe, I can't stop worrying about Xochi."

Here it comes, Kylen thought. *The goddamn million-dollar question.*

"What happened this morning, anyway?" Leviticus asked.

"Ask her when you see her, man," Kylen said. "I spent last night and this morning cleaning up Xochi's mess and the rest of the day cleaning up yours. I'm going to bed now, buddy."

He watched Lev's face. "Buddy" was old code between them, a nod to the lost-boy winter they'd lived in a tent on the beach at fifteen. Kylen had been in rough shape that year. Lev would read him Salinger by flashlight every night to help him sleep.

"Okay," Leviticus said. "But when do you think that'll be?"

"I don't know—soon? Never?" Kylen said. "You know teenagers—so hard to predict."

58

Blue Moon

Pallas lay awake in Anna's loft bed. It was late, close to morning. She'd fallen asleep during the first movie Anna had put on and slept till Nora came home at five with Chinese food, so she wasn't really tired. The day spun in her head, gathering things like the tornado in *The Wizard of Oz*: Xochi and Leviticus in bed; the mist at her window; the way the green girl unfolded Xochi's name like an origami swan in Pallas's heart.

Had the green girl and her brother ever found Xochi at the party? Had they saved her from whatever it was that wanted to hurt her? They must have. She'd looked perfectly fine asleep on Leviticus's chest.

She closed her eyes, but another paper bird unfolded in her mind: *Maybe there was a different reason Xochi was in her dad's bed.* Maybe something happened and Leviticus was taking care of her? But no! Everyone had already known about them. *They lied and cheated. There's no excuse.*

She curled into a ball on her side of Anna's bed. Where was Peas? Why hadn't he come home? Anna said he always visited the loft at night and stayed until she went to sleep. "Unless he's out," Anna said. "He may be fixed, but he still tomcats around." Nora's and Anna's voices filled Pallas's head with little quirks and jokes and ways of saying things. Nora at home was just as nice as at the bookstore and funnier. Also, very kind.

"Are you sure it's okay with your family if you spend the night?" Nora had asked.

"I called them," Pallas said, the lie cold as an ice cube in her mouth. "They said it was fine."

She and Anna had whispered in bed for hours, talking about so many things. But finally, Anna fell asleep. Pallas missed her attic. Was Xochi there alone? Or were they all awake, the whole family drinking coffee and worrying? Or worse, out in the rainy night looking for her? Tears wet Pallas's pillow. She climbed down from the loft and hurried out of Anna's room, down the hall to the living room. She huddled there in the dark. The air felt like it did before an earthquake, but inside of her. Everything was waiting. Someone appeared in the doorway.

At the store, Nora's clothes were classic cute librarian, but the at-home-pajamaed Nora was something altogether different. Her hair was in two long, messy braids, and her sleep clothes were shabby and eclectic—pink-and-black-striped leggings under baggy cutoff sweat shorts, a T-shirt so thin it might disintegrate and a bathrobe printed with bats. She came and sat next to Pallas.

"I didn't call them," Pallas said, looking up at her. "They must be so upset." She was crying now, so hard she couldn't breathe.

"Put your head down, honey," Nora said in her bookstore problem-solving voice. "Slow down, now."

"They must be so worried," Pallas whispered. "What if they called the police?"

"They didn't," Nora said. "Last I time I talked to them, they were eating pizza."

"What?" Pallas sat up.

"Pallas, they've known since noon. Kylen came looking for you at the bookstore."

"Why didn't you tell me?" Pallas didn't want to cry in front of Nora now, but tears snuck out of her eyelids anyway.

"They asked me not to," Nora said. "They wanted you to call in your own time."

"Whose idea was that?" Pallas asked. Nora handed her a tissue. She blew her nose.

"I won't name names," Nora said. "Could've been someone whose name rhymes with . . . well, now, what does his name rhyme with?" She scrunched up her nose, a face Anna also made. It was cute on both of them. Pallas steeled herself against Nora's cheering up, but then, suddenly, she gave in. She knew whose idea it was. Of course she did.

"If it was in a song you could get by rhyming it with *island*," Pallas said.

"I suppose if Joni Mitchell can rhyme *guitar* and *alarm* . . ." Nora's dark eyes sparkled.

"It's also synonymous with *rat fink* and *liar*," Pallas said.

Nora nodded. "Kylen's always been sweet with me, but I wouldn't want to get on his bad side. It was a diabolical plan. It nearly broke me. Why do you think I'm not asleep right now?"

"Did they tell you why I ran away?" Tears rose again. The neck of Pallas's borrowed sleep shirt was wet.

"Yes," Nora said.

Pallas exhaled in a loud, short huff. "What should I do?"

"Do you want to go home?"

"I don't know." Part of her longed for home. She'd never liked sleepovers and tired quickly of hotels. But also, she couldn't imagine sleeping in her bed in the empty attic while Xochi was—where? Above the studio with her dad?

"How about this," Nora said. "Anna has Monday and Tuesday off school, so I was going to surprise her and take her to Capitola tomorrow. We stay at this cute bungalow right on the beach. What if you came with us?"

"I'd like that!" Pallas said. She'd already forgiven Nora for colluding with Ky. He'd always been genius at devising horrible but just punishments. The worst part was how well he knew her. He was good, all right.

"Okay," Nora said, "but first, I want you to check in with your folks. I have a feeling they'll be fine with you coming, but I think it's best for you to ask them in person. I can drop you off tomorrow morning. I have a million errands, but we'll go right after that. All right?"

Pallas considered. Capitola was so pretty, a beach town with great pizza and a fascinating colony of pelicans. She yawned. "Sounds good," Pallas said. "Thank you. So much."

"Let's both get a few hours of sleep," Nora said, yawning, too. "I only wish Peas would come home. I hate leaving town without saying goodbye."

59

I Go to Sleep

Peasblossom woke with a start. It was dark, but morning was coming. He and Xochi had worked into the night to no avail—dressing Gina in pajamas, singing her favorite songs, massaging her. They'd stopped only to eat a hasty meal of bacon and eggs with coffee for Xochi and cream for Peas. Near dawn, they closed their eyes, laying side by side on Gina's thin rug.

Xochi's hand rested on Peasblossom's shoulder. He extricated himself carefully so as not to wake her. So much of his life was spent helping humans pass from sleep to waking, waking to sleep. With Nora and Anna, he was both lullaby and alarm clock. It was the same with Pallas when he visited her at night.

Peasblossom yawned and scratched his ear. He'd go to Eris Gardens, he decided, to see if the creatures had returned to the place of their summoning. Perhaps there was some way he could convince them to undo what they had done. Xochi had managed to give Gina sugar water with a medicine dropper, but the woman had been unconscious for over twenty-four hours now.

The cat groaned as he squeezed out the partially open window and squared his shoulders against the cold. Time was running out.

60

Tiny Dancer

How many mornings had Xochi sat like this, wondering which mother would wake up and greet her? The resentful, exacting mother who demanded chores and complained of ingratitude? The ethereal in-love mother who checked the mirror every hour and jumped when the phone rang? Or the fun young mother who wanted to play, who swore she didn't need a man?

For the first time since Gina had left, Xochi let herself remember the good things—trips to the pool and the beach, the way Gina would save stale bread to feed the geese at the park, weekend visits to the pet store to moon over animals their apartments never allowed. Xochi remembered freeways and identical suburban streets, driving around listening to the radio, killing time in the late afternoon before Gina had to work.

Looking at Gina's sleeping face, Xochi allowed herself the tiniest bit of her mother's beauty, but a sip might as well be a bottle. Memories rebelled, crowding for attention. Gina getting ready for work, the ritual always the same: a spritz of perfume, the matching bra and panty set in white or nude, then back to the bathroom, steam cleared, to put on her makeup. For this she shut the door, insisting on privacy. Xochi would press her cheek to the thin plywood, wishing for a keyhole so she could witness the mysterious process that transformed the pretty girl-mom who went into the bathroom into the sharp, shiny woman who came out.

Next came the clothes, versions of the black-and-white service uniform. Sometimes, a ridiculous costume was required, like the flared skirts and ruffled tops she wore at La Casa Fiesta or the cheerleader outfit she wore at the sports bar. After Gina was dressed, she did her hair. First, the hum of the blow dryer, a sound that always made Xochi sleepy, the patient skill required by the curling iron, the light mist of hairspray, the careful comb-out, the final dramatic flip.

After that, there were hugs and kisses, the parting sad, yet so sweet. The bedtime teenage babysitters blended together in Xochi's mind, unimportant. For hours after Gina was gone, her scent filled the apartment, promising her return.

Xochi touched Gina's hair. It looked dry, but the underside was damp, a state Gina would never have allowed given the choice. She'd let Xochi eat Captain Crunch for dinner or stay home from school whenever she wanted, but she was adamant about the importance of avoiding a chill. Xochi wore a coat on cold days whether she wanted to or not, wasn't allowed to walk barefoot in the house in the winter and never once went to bed with wet hair. Xochi remembered the tug of the brush on her long brown tangles, her scalp toasted by the blow dryer's heat. She remembered the good pajamas she got every birthday in September, the new robe and slippers at Christmas, the cute summer sleep sets after school got out.

Putting a hand under Gina's head, she pulled the damp hair from under her neck and spread it on the pillow, took up Gina's glittery purple comb and went to work. Most of the tangles unraveled easily, but some hairs near the nape of her neck had matted. Working into the tangle, making sure to protect the tender scalp she herself had inherited, Xochi tried to recall the weeks before her mother left.

Gina fought with most of her boyfriends. Sometimes the conflicts got physical, but they seemed more like battles than abuse. In the aftermath, it always felt like Gina won, even as they packed their boxes and left. With Evan it was different. Maybe because Gina loved him more. Maybe because he was angrier than any of the others had ever been. When they weren't screaming at each other, Gina was red eyed and quiet. Loretta suggested an extended sleepover in her cabin. Maybe Xochi shouldn't have agreed.

She got up and went to the bathroom. There was water in the tub. She drained it and turned on the shower. Gina used the same baby shampoo and Ivory soap as always. Xochi washed her hair and scrubbed her skin.

In her mother's closet, things were organized the way Xochi remembered: by type, sleeve length, and color. None of the clothes were familiar. She found a black T-shirt, borrowed a pair of cotton underwear, a little too small, and put on her dirty jeans.

Xochi sat on the bed beside her mom. She would only lie down for a minute. And then she'd do what she should have done hours ago: call an ambulance to take Gina away.

61

The Purest Blue

Xochi blinked. She'd fallen asleep, lulled by the familiar scent of her mother's pillow.

Gina was still unconscious. It was time to make the call.

Feeling rose, too rough to be tears. She slid to the floor and scooted away from the bed, stomach heaving, gasping for breath. When she began to cry, the sound was loud, foreign and frightening. The tears lasted a long time. Finally, she was quiet. She sat motionless, waiting to fly apart. She found herself humming old songs from Gina's classic rock station, the constants in Xochi and Gina's world of musical chair apartments and boyfriends and jobs and schools.

When they got to Evan's, his music took over. The Grateful Dead, bootleg after bootleg, Jerry Garcia's noodling guitar like a mosquito at the back of Xochi's neck.

There was no more music after Loretta died. Both Xochi and Evan lost their appetite for Loretta's blues and jazz and funk and folk. Even Xochi's own music fell flat. When her Walkman ran out of batteries, she never replaced them. The birds stopped singing. The air was still as the forest sweltered in a late September heat wave. Her room was airless the first night he came in. He sat, not touching her as she pretended to sleep. Eventually, she did sleep. Soon enough she slept through his weird nightly vigil. Then, one night, he woke her up.

A single word formed in her head, rising to meet the memory. She said it out loud.

"Rape."

It lay there, flat and dead, a thing in a book, the title of a famous picture, a scene from Greek mythology. Xochi remembered the green girl, swan crowned and deadly. She saw Evan faceup in the water, dead. She sat up straighter and said it again. "Rape."

Rape was bad. Even the word made her feel bad.

Still, it wasn't the worst thing that had happened, the worst thing Evan had done.

Xochi groped for the words he'd used to poison her. They lay in her body, hidden away. One by one, she dug them out. Some were alive, stinging and furious. Others were furred husks, missing legs, antennae, wings. Laid out one by one, she could see a pattern. Almost a plan. A look here, a word there. Innocent praise, a comment to someone else Xochi was meant to overhear. It went back years.

That morning at the diner—was it yesterday?—Kylen tried to tell her. Xochi was Pallas's age when Gina left, growing and hungry. To survive, she'd have opened her mouth for anyone. Loretta's clean, simple affection couldn't save her. It was Evan who'd felt most like home. He'd go weeks without noticing her until one morning he'd smile and see her all the way, saying something so good it shone inside her for days.

Xochi saw it now, a yoke of bright beads made of Evan's cleverness, like the pearl necklaces they used to sell on late night TV. *Buy it now for your daughter at this low, low price and add one every year until she gets married.* Xochi had scorned the teary bride with her ugly dress and poofy hair. She'd wanted the necklace, though. More than that, she'd wanted someone to smile at her the way the fake TV dad smiled at his fake TV daughter. Somehow, Evan knew. Not with his brain—even Gina used to say thinking wasn't his strong suit. But he was strong in other ways. He'd smelled it on Xochi, all that sweet unmet need. He'd watched, biding his time, his whispers hiding under her pillows, crawling into her ears as she slept, colonizing every part of her.

Hurt and hurting. Golden and broken. Evan's brokenness had been part of what made Xochi stay. *He would not stop. He could not mend.*

Of all the men who'd loved Gina, Evan was the only one Gina had truly loved back. Xochi's throat ached. There had been no Collier in Gina's life. No one like Leviticus or even Aaron or Ky or Pad. Just Evan, with his need and damage and abandonment. It was so little, so mean. Not nearly enough.

Xochi got up.

The sun was up now, streaming into the room. It was time to stop thinking about the past and start thinking about reality. She'd believed the Waterbabies when they told her she could make everything all right. But she couldn't. Now there was nothing left to do but get up and make the call.

"Show me my favorite color," Xochi whispered in Gina's ear. "Show me the ocean. Show me the sky." It was how they woke each other on tired mornings when Xochi was small. *Show me chocolate kisses*, Gina would say. *Show me black coffee. Maple syrup. Grizzly bears. Garden dirt.* Xochi only knew she was crying because a tear glistened on Gina's lips like something sparkly you'd find in a small hinged box.

Lashes fluttered, a flash of blue.

A second tear dropped, an eyelid quaked.

Eyes opened: Xochi's birthstone, sapphire, dark with sleep.

62

Heroes

Peasblossom panted in the side yard, exhausted from the Buena Vista hill. The wind changed. Hackles up, he scanned the garden. There, under the jasmine hedge—a furred shape. The cat approached it. Slowly, a large animal rose, bowing its head, a universal gesture of submission. It was a dog by the smell, pungent but clean. Not a stray, but a pet. Lost? Peas held his ground. An animal that size might consider a cat a meal.

"Excuse me," the dog said. "I don't mean to trespass."

Peasblossom took a step closer. The dog was a breedable female, German Shepherd mixed with some muscular Northern breed, Malamute or Husky. Possibly wolf. She exuded a trustworthy calm that made the cat's high alert feel foolish. Peasblossom's hackles settled. "May I help you?" he asked.

"I'm not sure," she said. "These creatures asked me to bring them here. Do you know them?" She stepped aside. Her own strong musk had masked the now-faint scent of the Waterbabies. Peasblossom rushed to their side. "They were sheltering in my yard," she said. "They were ill and very cold."

"You led them to Eris Gardens?" Peasblossom crept closer to the creatures and was instantly reminded of Gina. There was life in the two small bodies, present but fading.

"I carried them most of the way," she said. "But I couldn't get them into the house. I considered ringing the bell, but the creatures insisted on only speaking to the child who lives in the attic. The lights were out when we arrived. I agreed to wait an hour or so." Her black-lined eyes lowered. "I'm not as young as I used to be. I must have fallen asleep. They're unconscious now."

"I'll check the attic," Peasblossom said. For all the dog's bulk and majesty, Peasblossom had the advantage there. He stretched, preparing to climb. The sun was rising. The creatures' skin was dull and pale, their hair tangled in lifeless piles. The sky darkened with rain, but as it lowered, Peasblossom could see that it was not a cloud, but a flock of crows. They landed in the garden, at least a hundred strong. One flapped to the ground near the creatures.

"We must warm them," she said. Her accent was clipped, bare of embellishment. The crows' language was too complicated for most other creatures; they had to simplify for those less gifted. She turned to order her compatriots, a complicated series of clicks. "Step away," she said to Peas.

Several birds hopped into a loose circle around the unconscious pair, each grasping a lock of limp hair. They began to flap, carefully rising. A second group massed under the creatures in support. They rested their burdens carefully on the sun-warmed fire escape outside Pallas's bedroom. The crow in charge swooped back to Peas and the dog. "Come," she said, gesturing to the attic window.

"I must go," the dog said, bowing formally to Peas and the crows.

"Thank you," Peasblossom said. "I hope we meet again." To his surprise, he meant it.

"So do I," she said with an uncomfortably fangy smile.

"Come!" the crow commanded.

PEASBLOSSOM SET HIS SHOULDER to the attic window. It rose just enough to get the creatures inside. He walked carefully over the green girl, wedging himself between her and her companion, and started to push.

"Stop." The crow flew to the railing above him. "They need the sun. Find a covering."

Peasblossom blinked, unsure of the bird's meaning. The sun came out, streaming onto the fire escape. He understood now: a blanket. He scrunched through the window and dropped into the attic.

A heavy quilt lay on the sofa. Peasblossom pushed it to the floor. Grasping an edge with his teeth, he pulled, but the carpet's fibers held it back. From the window, Peas smelled the forest perfume of the siblings, stronger in the sun. Steam rose from the crows' feathers. He pulled at the quilt again. Nothing.

There was a clatter at the window. Two crows sat on the window seat, incongruous with the floral upholstery. They flapped to the cat's side and gripped the quilt in their strong black beaks. Together, the trio pulled it to the fire escape, covering the prone creatures.

"You." The crow in charge nodded at Peas. She held the top of the quilt open and gestured. As Peasblossom crept between the creatures, they shifted position like plant leaves angling toward the sun. The cat's fur crackled with static. He lay in the small space between their smooth chests and began to purr. Crows roosted on their bodies from above.

Under the blanket with the creatures, the world was small. The quilt made the sky rose gold. The air was thick with the scent of trees and plants, some familiar to the cat, others strange. Peasblossom's hours with Gina had primed him. Now he worked with effortless grace, not tiring, not rushing, purring warmth and life as if he were a great fire-fueled wheel whose spinning turned the world.

Up close, so still, the fey pair resembled normal children sleeping with innocent abandon. Peasblossom closed his eyes.

ANOTHER FORT, YEARS BEFORE, *the light blued by the fibers of the blanket that covered them: Nora, Peasblossom, Ron.*

"I wanted a kid." A tear slid down Ron's cheek.

"You have one," Nora said.

"I mean, our kid. A little brother for Anna B. We always said we'd do it when we turned thirty."

"Anna will have to be enough," Nora said.

Ron laughed. "Oh, she's enough, all right. Wish I could see her grow up."

RON'S ROOM, THE CURTAINS *closed on a cold gray afternoon, Peas purring on the man's thin chest.*

In a week, he would be gone, his body burned to ash, the ashes released in the bay.

That day, Ron was talking. He often talked to Peasblossom in the afternoons before Nora and Anna got home.

"Screw this," he said calmly, scorn tamed by morphine. He got out of bed, shaky. He put on an album, Skinny Puppy, an electronic cacophony that made the cat fold back his ears. Ron turned it up loud enough that the neighbors might complain, as they had last week when it was the Sex Pistols.

He danced, his limbs loose, a gift of the drug. "I never did this shit back in the day," he told the cat. "I just liked speed. It kept me skinny. Guess I'm skinny now." He grinned, still beautiful. He'd always doubted this, Peasblossom knew. Eugene had been angular, with pouting lips and pale eyes. Ron was short and strong with a sandy crew cut, his ordinary face made extraordinary by the green of his eyes. Cat eyes, Anna said. Green like agates, green as jade. Green as the succulent ice plants that grew in the small patch of earth in front of their apartment.

Peasblossom opened his eyes. The atmosphere beneath the quilt was balmy now. The creatures' skin had brightened. The green girl didn't stir, but her rest had a healing quality, like the change in Anna when a fever broke. Curling around her head as he had once done with Ron and Eugene in turn, washing Eugene's thick brows before moving on to Ron's bristly buzz cut, he kneaded his paws in the creature's tangled hair. His claws became electric, conduits for the story that poured and poured from the hair that was not hair, but something more like whiskers: a massive sensory organ, now sparking in the small space. A collage came together, images of feeling, pieces of a life, smearing, blurring, combining.

Peasblossom recalled the poster above Nora's writing table, a print called "Candlelight," full of yellow heat and wordless meaning. Through the scent of this new piece of abstract art, Peasblossom understood: the story of Xochi and her mother and a man, no longer alive. It shook the cat like an earthquake, swelled in his cells like a wave. He stood, quivering, fur upright, paws stinging with fire. The smell of the sea was everywhere, and sulfur and cedar and jasmine and crows and redwood forests and Tenderloin piss and candlelit prayer and beds full of love.

A crystal dropped from the cat's blue eye, a single tear. It slid into the green girl's mouth. Her hair undulated, seeming to yawn and stretch. Crows flapped as they flung the quilt away.

The green creature's eyes opened. She knelt by her companion and opened her mouth. On her tongue sat a sun-spun bee, a small winged creature of light. The garden exhaled: barely sprung lilac buds opened, star jasmine blinked to life, and crocuses stretched their throats in longing. The bee left the green sister's tongue and flew, landing on the lips of the sleeping brother. He sat up, hair reaching into the clear, sunlit air. Grasping his sister's hand, the creature stood and bowed to Peas.

63

Small Blue Thing

"Mom?"

"Xochi? Is that you?" Gina blinked. Her eyes widened. She leaped up, nostrils flared.

"It's okay," Xochi said, grabbing Gina's forearm to steady her. "Sit down. I'll get you some water."

Gina shook her head like a mare in a field. She circled the bed and sat on its edge. "I'm dizzy," she said.

Xochi handed Gina the water and watched her drink. When she was finished, Gina reached up to touch Xochi's cheek. Xochi let her mother's hand rest there for one broken second before pulling away. She stood up, backing toward the door.

"Are you all right?" Gina asked.

Gina's voice was a time machine. The room tilted. Xochi should be bleeding, the way she felt. But she'd done it. Gina was awake.

"I'm fine," Xochi whispered. "But I've got to go."

"Xochi—" Gina stopped, started again. "Something happened. How . . . how are you here?"

"It's a long story." Xochi backed up. One step, another.

"Please," Gina said. "I have no right to ask. I know nothing I say will fix it—"

"You could try sorry."

"Will you stay? Just for a while?"

Xochi nodded. Why was she nodding? She would give

anything to beam away like people did on the *Star Trek* reruns she and Gina had loved. But here she was. Staying because Gina wanted her to. There was nowhere to sit but the bed, so she went to the kitchen for a chair and sat down across from her mother.

"I'm sorry I hurt you." Gina's words were hurried, like she'd arranged them while Xochi was in the kitchen and worried they wouldn't stay put. "I had to go. I was so messed up."

"You could have called. Or written. Anything."

"I sent letters," Gina said. "You never wrote back."

"I never got them."

"He must have kept them from you." Gina was as pale as the walls of her apartment.

"I guess so," Xochi said slowly.

"Why would he do that? He was furious with me, but he loved you."

"Did he say that?" The fine lines at the corners of Gina's eyes deepened around the paling blue. "Did he actually tell you that?"

"Everyone loved you," Gina said. "You were safe in Badger Creek."

Xochi made herself exhale the stale air she'd been holding, a hoarder afraid to let anything go. *Crazy out.* The truth was a start.

"I wasn't safe."

Gina's arms were wrapped around her stomach so tight, her dancer's muscles showed through the thin sweater. "Tell me," she said.

Xochi pulled herself up to sit cross-legged on the chair. She straightened her spine, channeling Io in meditation. A breeze flapped the shades: lilac and coffee, the kitchen at Eris Gardens. It might be ruined now, but it was a place Xochi knew, a place where she was known. She'd found it all on her own, earning it with hard work and real love.

"Loretta got sick," she said. She waited, letting Gina take it in. "Cancer, like Evan's stepmom."

Gina's eyes emptied, tears washing blue down her face. Gina had never had a mother. Not even a flighty girl-mom to call her own. Loretta had been the closest thing. "When?" Gina whispered.

"Last year. Right before harvest."

"I'm so sorry, baby."

Baby. The word was a hand grenade. Gina reached out to touch Xochi's hand. Xochi snatched it away. She was shaking now, longing to bolt. She closed her eyes. She needed a dream forest, to race among the trees, a long soak in hot water.

"It sounds like there's more. I'm gonna sit here on the floor." Gina moved down to lean against her bed. "Why don't you come down, too? It's easier to talk like this."

The tone of her mother's voice triggered obedience. More than that, it triggered trust. Xochi wanted to laugh meanly at her own expense. Kylen had nothing on her mom.

Xochi slid from the chair, sitting on the floor across from her mother. Gina handed her a pillow. Shouldn't Xochi just leave? She took the pillow, hugged it to her stomach. *Not going*, she thought. *Still here.*

"Tell me," Gina said, knees to her chest. "Don't worry. I can take it."

Xochi dropped her face to the pillow. "It's bad." There it was—her kid voice, a dual plea for invisibility and attention.

"Is it Evan?" Gina's voice wobbled but held. "Did he—did he do something?"

The question hung between them. A tide rose in Xochi's sacrum, whooshing up her spine. Gina's face changed, imploded.

She knew.

The creatures. They must have spared Xochi this telling—no small gift, but Xochi would still rip it away if she could, do anything to take away the pain in Gina's face.

"No!" The sound pushed out of Gina's mouth, only to be sucked back in. "Oh no!" She dove for the trash basket beside her bed and retched. Her body heaved again and again, but after the water came up, nothing was left.

"Gina!" Xochi kneeled over her mother. "Mom?"

"I can't," Gina said. Tears streamed down her face. "I can't."

"Mom?"

"I'll kill him." Gina was sobbing now, tight heaves that threatened to crack her narrow rib cage.

"It's too late," Xochi said. "He's already dead."

Gina's head tilted back up, the chaos in her eyes receding an inch or two. "I feel like I knew." She wiped her tears with the back of her hand. "I think I did, anyway. How could I have known that?"

"The same way I found you here. It's Loretta. I think she wanted to help us."

Gina nodded. She was crying again, softly now. "I'm so sorry. I'm sorry, Xochi. I fucked everything up."

"Not everything," Xochi said. "I'm okay."

Gina smiled, her face lit by the sunlight streaming in from the window. "You look all right," she said. "You look beautiful."

"I got it from you."

They sat together in silence. The room dimmed and cooled as clouds swam past the sun. "Gina?" Xochi said. "I have to go now."

Gina inhaled sharply. She sat up straighter. "Okay."

Gina stood, a trick of light sketching a shadow on the wall behind her like the full-body halo around the Guadalupe mural in the Mission. She met Xochi's eyes, thick lashes over sacred Virgin blue. "Come back, okay? Soon."

"I'll try." She stood and turned to leave.

"And Xochi?"

Xochi looked back.

"I know there's no way to make up for what I put you

through. But if you ever need anything, I will move heaven and earth for you to get it."

Xochi held the shoulders of the little girl in her that wanted to rush into Gina's arms. *Not yet*, she told her. *Maybe never. But it's okay.*

She put her hand in her pocket. Loretta's necklace. She held it up to the sunny window. The opal had changed from dark to pale. Between the two green hummingbirds, it was sky blue, party dress blue. Blue as Gina's eyes.

"Take this," Xochi said, pressing it into Gina's palm. "Keep it until we see each other again."

V.

Cool stone, clay and bone
White as the inside of an egg
The child's nest perches
Above the golden city

"I long for our spring," Sister says
"I long to never leave."
Brother knows longing, leaving and loss
Together, they will bear it

Down below the family sleeps
Deep and low, the mudpot whispers

Together, they listen
Together, they feel
Waiting for wind
Wind and the sound of wings

64

Blackbird

The first thing Xochi saw when she opened the attic door was Pallas climbing in the window. The second thing was the birds. They were perched everywhere—on the mantel, the chandeliers, the backs of chairs, the edge of the bathtub. There were robins, finches and at least fifty pigeons. Green-and-yellow parrots had taken over the sofa. The flock of chickadees perched on the curtain rod turned their black-capped heads, giving Xochi a collective quizzical stare.

"What is this?" Pallas hopped down from the window seat. She was wearing jeans. Jeans and her dad's leather jacket. "What's with all the birds?"

"I was going to ask you," Xochi said.

The mass of feathers in the tub shifted to reveal Sister, sound asleep, her skin a healthy aloe green, her hair a cape hovering around her shoulders, a crown of hummingbirds fluttering around her head. Brother rested on the other side of the tub with at least a dozen puffed-up sparrows.

Xochi blinked at one surreal situation too many. A tired part of her had hoped for a quiet attic, Pallas asleep, the creatures already home, whooshed away the moment Gina opened her eyes.

"They came back!" Pallas said. She ran to the edge of the tub. The sparrows hissed. Hummingbirds dove at her, sword beaked and fearless. Xochi ran to pull her back. Pallas jerked her arm away. She was pissed, angrier than Xochi had ever seen her. She shrugged her dad's jacket to the floor.

Xochi willed her brain to work, grasping to recover the pieces of the apology she'd planned, her explanation about the green girl and her brother, what had happened with her mom.

"Where were you just now?" Xochi asked. It was the wrong question, clearly wrong. The birds were screeching. Xochi resisted the temptation to cover her ears.

"Where were *you*?"

Several crows appeared at the window behind Pallas and perched on the fire escape. The smaller birds made high, warning sounds. A sparrow bolted and collided with Pallas, claws trapped in her tangled curls.

"Don't move," Xochi said, reaching to free the panicked bird.

"I can do it myself!"

Xochi had expected this, of course. She'd been gone for two nights without a word. Pallas made the tangle worse, her cheeks red with frustration. As she struggled, the window went dark. Behind her, filling the casement, was a stately black bird, larger than the largest crow. Stepping forward with a strangely human gait, he flapped up to Pallas's forearm. Her eyes went wide as he hopped to her shoulder. The prisoner in Pallas's curls froze. There was a sound like garden shears cutting through grass. The sparrow flew to join its friends and a lock of Pallas's hair fell to the floor. The enormous bird hopped down, took the lock in his beak, and walked with enormous dignity, depositing it next to the bathtub.

The room was silent. Xochi followed Pallas's shocked gaze from the bird, a giant raven, to a red-headed parrot perched on the edge of a bookshelf. The bird gathered itself in slow motion and released a dropping on the shiny wood floor. The rest of the birds tittered and squawked. A second parrot puffed its feathers and released, this time hitting Pallas's knitting basket.

"That's it!" Pallas jumped up from the window seat. "Out!"

she yelled. "Every single one of you needs to get out of here right now! And no one else better poop!"

She stamped her foot and the birds took flight, an air traffic control nightmare. Xochi raced around the attic, saving breakables from the tops of shelves and closing the doors to the bedrooms as Pallas stalked around the room opening the rest of the windows.

Birds careened into one another and the furniture. No one could find the way out. A yellow songbird clung to Pallas's back and several of the sparrows were perched on Xochi's head and shoulders.

"Get out!" Pallas yelled. "Get out! Get out! Get out!" She was trapped in the middle of the rug, surrounded by pigeons. Tears streamed down her face when the crows began dive-bombing around the room like crazy stunt pilots, cawing insults.

Xochi knew she should take charge, try to wake the Waterbabies, get them to make the birds leave. She should comfort Pallas, clean up the bird poo—something! But all she could do was watch the unreal display in helpless fascination.

"I MEAN IT!" Pallas boomed, not crying anymore. "Every single bird in here needs to line up by the window in an orderly fashion, and when it's your turn to fly you will GO HOME."

Amazingly, the birds calmed down. Starting with the sparrows, they flew in groups of four or five to the window seat and did as Pallas told them. The finches and chickadees and parrots were gone. The sparrows and robins followed the pigeons. The crows remained, taking the parrots' place on the mantel, and the hummingbirds refused to leave Sister's hair.

The raven sat by the fireplace, now blazing on its own, no firewood in sight. Xochi blinked once, twice, three times. The room lost half its light.

She blinked again, and all the candles in the room were lit. The sky outside turned stormy and the wind smelled like lightning and rain.

Xochi was surprised to find herself sitting on the sofa. When had she moved? Sister's voice was a wisp of song tickling her ear. A hummingbird flapped suspended above her shoulder, singing a message. Xochi closed her eyes to focus, delighting at the barest touch of bird breath on her earlobe.

> Summoned by Athena's fire
> Brought in heat of Maiden's ire
> So must power rise again
> To cut asunder, later mend.

THE HUMMINGBIRD RETURNED TO its fellows, a proud link in a living crown. The sky grew darker. The attic door slammed shut. The candles flickered as the wind came through the open window and delivered its mail, depositing a piece of paper on the floor between Pallas and Xochi. Pallas backed away. Xochi resisted the impulse to grab the piece of paper and throw it in the fire.

"This can't be happening," Pallas whispered.

"What is it?" Xochi said, not sure why she didn't just pick the damn thing up.

"Take a look," Pallas said. "I think it's yours."

Xochi stared, not moving. She hadn't eaten or slept properly for days now. She retrieved the paper, saw the handwriting. Read the crossed-out words.

"Pallas." Xochi's voice wobbled. "What do you think this is?"

"I'm not stupid."

"I never said you were. It's just not what you think. Your dad and I are friends—"

"I saw you!" Xochi sat back on the sofa. Hard. "You were in his bed. On Saturday morning. You were sleeping with my dad."

Pallas's eyes were fierce. Her hair crackled with static. Xochi imagined her with a sword in one hand, a severed head in the other. Xochi's? The hummingbird's message was starting to make sense: Pallas Athena, warrior princess. Every fighter needed a fight. Pallas needed this. She'd needed it all along. And Xochi owed her. *Okay*, Xochi thought, *if this is how it has it to be.*

"Well?" Pallas demanded. "What do you have to say for yourself?"

Xochi made her voice as cold as she could. "Nothing." She cringed, but pushed on. "It's none of your business."

"None of my business?" Pallas stomped her foot again. "None of my business? Xochi, we're talking about my dad! My *dad*, not some random guy you're screwing around with!"

"No one's screwing around with anyone." Xochi's mild tone was sure to drive Pallas crazy. "You're making assumptions based on information taken completely out of context. And you know what they say about assuming."

The wind rose higher. The chandeliers clinked in alarm and the crows fluffed their feathers against the sudden cold.

"YOU!" Pallas yelled. "You're supposed to be my friend! And he's supposed to be my dad! It's disgusting! He's just using you."

The crows had taken wing again, but now they were working for Pallas. They flew at Xochi, their feathers brushing her arms. A claw grazed her back. Xochi's anger rose to meet Pallas's. The room narrowed. Words erupted before she could screen them.

"Your *dad* is using me? What about you? You wanted me to be your instant, live-in friend because you're too afraid to go out and make one of your own. And that's fine, but I'm not a windup doll. I have feelings, and some of them have nothing to do with you."

"Of course it has nothing to do with me." Pallas's eyes had turned from green to black. "I'm just a kid, right?"

"You are a kid," Xochi said. "You are a kid, and I'm not. I haven't been for a long time. And yes, we're friends. We are. But more than that, I take care of you. It's my job. A friend is a peer. An equal. They don't pull their punches, don't try to protect you from the truth the way an adult will. If you weren't a kid, you'd already know about this."

"I would already know what? That you're sleeping with my dad? You're a teenager, Xochi. That IS a kid. I feel sorry for you. I don't ever want to be your age if it means putting stupid sex and selfishness before the people you're supposed to love!"

Love. The word deflated Xochi's anger in an instant. She sat down, hardly registering the crow perched on the back of the sofa. "But we didn't. We never had sex; we haven't spent much time together at all. And it's kind of sad, because I've never felt this way before."

"I don't care!" Pallas said, crying now. "You lied. You both did."

"I'm sorry." Xochi shook her head. "I never meant to hurt you. It's the last thing I wanted. You *are* my friend. A kindred spirit. Someone I love."

Pallas continued to sob, licking the tears off her lips.

"Your tears," Xochi said, "are they sweet?"

Pallas nodded, her shoulders shaking.

"Mine too," Xochi said, touching her face. "Like honey."

"Why did you lie?"

"I didn't know what else to do," Xochi said. "I still don't."

Pallas sat down next to Xochi. A crow nuzzled her ear. Xochi handed her a tissue.

"Are you in love with him?" Pallas asked. "Are you in love with my dad?"

"I don't know." Xochi took Pallas's hand.

With the contact, the room came back like déjà-vu, mist rinsed and dim.

BROTHER AND SISTER SAT facing each other in the bathtub, hands clasped, eyes closed. Steam curled around their otherworldly hair as the bathwater roiled and spit around them.

Pallas gripped Xochi's hand tighter as the Raven walked toward them out of the mist, Pallas's lock of hair in her beak.

She hopped to the edge of the tub and dropped it in, regarding them with clear expectation in her intelligent eyes.

"Unicorn mane," Xochi whispered. She ripped up Leviticus's note, dropping the pieces into the steaming water.

"Love letter," Pallas said.

The water bubbled to a boil, but the creatures didn't stir.

Xochi reached into her jeans pocket and came up with lint and several long hairs from the dog at Sirena.

"Hair of wolf." She circled the tub. There was a pebble from the beach in her other pocket. "Eye of frog."

A long black feather floated into view borne on a current of mist and dropped at Pallas's feet. "Raven's feather."

Xochi pinched some soil from the potted plant on the coffee table. "Earth of bog." She sprin0kled it into the water and jumped back as it sparked like shards of mica. Brother's and Sister's hair flowed behind them: now flags, now capes, now wings.

Pallas started the chant.

"Double, double . . ."

Xochi joined her.

"Toil and trouble . . ."

The mist thickened.

"Fire, burn!"

Pallas grabbed Xochi's hand.

"Cauldron, bubble!"

PALLAS AND XOCHI FELL back onto the soft carpet, momentarily blinded by the sudden return of the sun. When they opened their eyes, the room was empty of steam and wind and birds.

The green girl and her brother were gone.

65

The Queen and the Soldier

Xochi woke on the sitting room rug. Someone was standing over her.

Leviticus.

"Hey," he said.

The last time she'd seen him had been in his bed. There was something besides welcome in his face. He held out a hand, but she didn't take it. She sat up. Someone had covered her, taken off her shoes and socks. *Pallas?* They'd talked a little before Xochi fell asleep. It was easier that way, side by side on the floor looking at the cherubs on the ceiling. Pallas told her about leaving the house, about her sleepover with Anna and Nora. Xochi told Pallas the kid-friendly version of her time with Gina and Peas. She told her about how they'd called the Waterbabies with their Equinox bathtub potion; that the Waterbabies found Xochi's lost mother; and that somehow, Peasblossom had been there to help. "Magic is real," she remembered murmuring to Pallas before drifting off to sleep.

"Good morning, love."

Wait. Io? Xochi stood, too fast. Dizzy, she reached for Leviticus, but he wasn't there. Io sat on the sofa. Leviticus was settling into the easy chair. The clock said eleven-fifteen. She'd only been asleep a few hours. Pallas's bedroom door was shut.

"She's crashed," Leviticus said. His eyes told Xochi he wanted her to join them. She sat on the sofa opposite Io.

"We're sorry to wake you, but Pal will probably be up soon." Io's voice was shaky. She wore an oversized sweater and leggings. In her braided pigtails, she looked like she was Pallas's age.

"We wanted to talk before that," Leviticus said.

Xochi noted the collective pronoun—the royal *we*.

She sat up straighter and forced herself to look at Io. "I'm the offending party, so I guess I should start."

"Xochi, no!" Io said gently. "This is our fault."

"We put you in an impossible position," Leviticus said.

Oh no, Xochi thought. *This all just sounds wrong. Almost dirty.* She fought the perverse desire to laugh.

There were dark circles under Leviticus's eyes. His voice was hoarser than it had been after the concert. "I keep thinking about what you said, about being the hired help and being friends with Pallas? It's like you got the worst of both. I mean, we pay you. At least we do that much. I had to check with Kiki to be sure. But we've left everything else up to a twelve-year-old."

"It was selfish," Io said. "I knew Pallas needed more of me. We gave her you instead. I never thought how it might affect you."

"I love taking care of Pallas." Xochi was suddenly aware of her greasy hair and day-old clothes.

"I was a mum when I was your age," Io said, "but that was my choice. You came to us needing a home, not knowing anyone. What real choice did we give you?"

"It's okay," Xochi said, beginning to understand what they were saying.

Io shook her head. "I'm so sorry."

"We all are." Leviticus leaned forward. "I was worried you wouldn't come back." He said it like Io wasn't in the room. He could forget, but Xochi couldn't.

"You don't have to worry," she said. "I have money saved up. You've all been so kind."

"Wait," Leviticus said. "What are you talking about?"

"All of us did our best." Xochi stood up. "I should be able to move out tomorrow. Tuesday at the latest. I'm sorry—I need to get some rest. It's been a crazy couple of days."

She bashed her knee on the coffee table as she walked toward her room. So much for a dignified exit. But her mind was pleasantly blank. She recalled the fluffy pink heroin calm. Maybe her body had learned its secrets, was compounding it now along with all the other chemicals that masqueraded as human feeling and thought. The door to her room was a white flag. Her bed was so close. Cool sheets, more white nothingness. Rest and another ending. It was all right. Xochi was getting used to it.

66

Lorelei

Io hated to intrude, but she'd promised Leviticus. She knocked lightly and turned the knob. The room was messy with scattered books and tapes, clothes abandoned in piles on the floor. A teenager's room, but Xochi was more than that. When Io was seventeen, she had been on her own, raising a baby. Years weren't the only things that made girls grow up.

Xochi was lying facedown on her bed. Io sat beside her and instructed her brain to stand down. The situation called for intuition—a quality Io used to think she didn't possess. It was just the way her apparatus worked—she had difficulty switching to modes outside intellect. It turned out it was the same basic adjustment she used for dance. The steps came too quickly if you processed them intellectually. You had to turn that off and simply surrender to movement in space.

Io lay back on the bed beside Xochi. The girl scooted over to accommodate her. There was just enough room for two.

"That went poorly," Io said. "One misunderstanding after another, according to Lev."

"He sent you?"

"Well, he encouraged me." Io scooted an inch closer to prevent her leg from falling off the bed. Now her hip touched Xochi's. "I meant to apologize, not sack you."

"You don't have to apologize."

"I do," Io said. "The governess business was my fault. Pallas came to us with this romantic idea and we indulged her. The correct thing was to offer you our hospitality, not put you to work. Every one of us has brought home a friend or two—it's how we got Bubbles and Aaron and Pad. If I was in your shoes, I'd be hurt and confused." Io waited for her words to settle. She hated to be rushed herself. When Xochi finally spoke, it was muffled.

"I saw my mom today."

Her mother? Io hadn't heard a scrap of that story, but Xochi's tone was telling. The rest was inferred by an orphan-hood Io could recognize because she shared it.

"How long had it been?"

"Six years." Xochi rolled onto her side, her back to Io. "She was here in the city all along."

"It's such a small world," Io said. "A strange, unpredictable little world."

"Yeah," Xochi said.

"Would you like to talk about it?" Io offered the question as a civility. She wished more people would. They often assumed that if you'd shared one thing, you wanted to spill your guts.

Xochi turned to face her. "Sometime, yes. But not today."

The girl was profoundly tired. It would be kind to let her rest, but Io knew what she had to do.

"I have a confession," she said. She scooted to the end of the bed, resting her back against the footboard. Xochi sat up and handed her a pillow. Her legs were so much longer than Io's. She was so strong and long limbed and tall. Io rolled her eyes at herself. Would she ever grow past envying other women? "I saw you," Io said. "The other morning. You and Leviticus."

"Oh." Xochi looked slightly ill.

"I don't know why I went to his room." Io's forehead wrinkled, a telegram from her body to slow down, be sure to explain. "I've never slept there myself, by the way. He wanted me to, but I couldn't. I've felt guilty about it for so long—but for me, with him, something was always missing in that department. Until recently, I had no idea what it was."

"Recently?"

"Not that it's an excuse," Io said. "But it is part of the reason for governess-gate."

Xochi giggled. Io laughed and continued.

"I've been terribly distracted. I'd forgotten how destabilizing a new romance can be. I don't see how people manage it."

"I was thinking the same thing the other day." Xochi's cheeks went red. Io could feel herself blushing, too. Any reference to James had that effect.

"The funny thing is, I'm quite taken with someone myself, but I was incredibly jealous seeing you there with Lev."

Xochi exhaled, seeming to gather her calm. That's what it was about Xochi that made her seem older—her ability to think before she spoke.

"If it helps, we didn't do anything but sleep. To be totally honest, I would have, but he turned me down."

"Business as usual there, I see."

Xochi's face told Io she'd done it again—assumed context where none existed.

"You know the Beatles' song 'It's Getting Better'? There's this horrific line about how he beats his woman and keeps her apart from the things that she loves."

"Really?"

"I know—such an upbeat song, too. But there it is, right in the liner notes. That's Lev in a nutshell. Not that he beats his women—god, no. What I mean is, Leviticus does that to himself. He keeps himself apart from the things he wants most. He's terrified of you."

"But why?" Xochi said. "I'm just the hired help." She smiled, but there was a challenge in her voice.

"You're awfully feisty for someone who came home with her tail between her legs." Io grinned. This girl was a good egg. She'd be very good for Leviticus. The question was, would Lev be good for her? Now that Io knew, the entire household could discuss it freely. The consensus was worry—Xochi was young enough to take on Lev's problems and troubled enough to welcome the distraction. They'd all been there before, especially Io herself. Still, there was a sweetness between them. If only she were a bit older . . . and not Pallas's governess.

"I guess I should confess, too," Xochi said. "Just now I made it sound like we'd never done anything, but we have. Not sex, but just about."

"Was it nice?"

"You people are insane. You know that, right?"

"Well aware," Io said. She picked at the fine brown hairs stuck to her sweater. "Oh dear. I may have gotten your bed all horsey."

"You went horseback riding?"

"At the crack of dawn. Kiki's been after me." Io had finally agreed as a way to distract herself from the urge to extract Pallas from Nora's.

"How was it?"

"Lovely." Today's horse was a bay mare, bossy but fair. Once she realized Io meant business, she was a dream. "I used to ride," she said. An understatement, but factual.

"Leviticus told me. Was it hard to go back?"

"It's like I left that part of me by the side of the road for years, but there she was with her thumb out, waiting to be picked back up."

Xochi smiled, but something had shifted. Her expression turned inward. She pulled her knees to her chest.

"What is it?" Io asked.

"I was being a drama queen in there, but I think I may have been right."

"About?"

"Moving out. I think I have to." Xochi sat crossed-legged now, eyes begging for understanding.

"Are you sure?"

"Your hitchhiking thing—it made me think. That's how I got here, you know? Hitching up Highway 101. I got a ride from this college girl and her friend. I remember sitting there, crammed in her back seat with all their stuff. For hours, all I could feel was relief. But when we passed through that rainbow tunnel and I saw the Golden Gate Bridge—I saw this image of myself. Living with roommates, going to school. Since moving in here at Eris Gardens, I kind of forgot about all that."

"Xochi, you know we all adore you—"

The girl's expression changed. "No offense, but you guys barely know me."

"Nonsense," Io said. "We knew what you were about from the second Pallas brought you home. I'm sure there are tons of things I've failed to teach her, but at least she can recognize a kindred spirit when she meets one. You're family now. Whether you live here or not, you're stuck with us."

67

This Must Be the Place (Naïve Melody)

Xochi showered and hunted through her clothes, pushing aside jeans and T-shirts until she found the loose dress she and Pallas had scored in a free box on the street. "Thirties rayon," Pallas said. "I can't believe someone's throwing it out."

Xochi pulled it over her head, the thin fabric settling around her tired muscles. She combed her hair in front of the mirror. She touched her throat, bare without Loretta's necklace. She put on a pair of striped socks and went to the sitting room for her boots, but left them where they were. She wasn't going anywhere. At least not before breakfast.

Leviticus sat at the kitchen table reading the paper, glasses askew. His arms were around her before she could speak. She let herself rest, head on his shoulder. He smelled like coffee. He'd been smoking. With her socked feet planted on the floor, the soft flannel of his shirt on her cheek, Xochi made herself stay, heart hammering against his, wondering what would happen if either of them moved an inch.

The back door slammed open and shut. They separated quickly. "Give it up, old man." Pad popped his head into the kitchen door, holding it open for Kiki. "We saw you through the window."

"Good morning," Kiki said, depositing a grocery bag on the counter. "Well, afternoon, but who's counting?"

"Good morning," Io said, coming in from the hall. "Lev, would you like some help? I can crack the eggs or something—"

"Step away from the refrigerator," Kiki said, washing her hands. "No one likes shells in their pancakes."

"Fine," Io said. "I'll need tea, then. With cream, please, since I'm so hopeless." She sat beside Xochi and leaned close to her ear. "That was a secret, by the way. My . . . situation. The love stuff. Not ready for prime time."

"Got it."

Leviticus shot them a look. Xochi smiled. He probably thought they were talking about him.

"What are you two whispering about?" Pad asked.

"Just me," Xochi said.

"What about you?"

"That I'm sorry."

"For what?" Kiki sat down next to Pad. Side by side, they looked like the world's most attractive concerned parents.

"For listening to Justine. For scaring you guys. I hate how I worried everyone. But mostly, I'm sorry for hurting Pallas."

Bubbles came into the room yawning. "Xochi! You're back!" She came straight in for a hug. "I missed you," she said. "Where'd you go?"

Aaron followed Bubbles into the kitchen, shirtless and crusty eyed, wearing cutoff Spider-Man pajama bottoms and wool hiking socks.

"Let's see your PJs." Kiki motioned Aaron over to her side of the table.

"I won 'em in a bet with my little brother. They were too short, so I chopped them."

"Next time, let me." Kiki frowned at the uneven edges.

"Is there coffee?" Bubbles moaned, laying her head on the table. "I'm dying here, Lev."

"It's coming." Leviticus set a large mug in front of Xochi.

"Why does she get hers first?" Aaron nudged Xochi's foot under the table.

"You know." Bubbles rolled her eyes at Xochi and motioned toward Leviticus.

Aaron yawned. "She's cuter than me, but I've known you longer, man. Doesn't friendship mean anything?"

"It's ladies first," Kiki said. "Some people have manners."

"Plus, he fancies her," Pad added.

"Pad!" Bubbles reached across Kiki to pinch him.

"Don't be like the governess." Pad rubbed his arm. "She's vicious, really," he complained to Leviticus. "Don't know what you see in her, man. I like my women sweet."

"Ha!" Kiki got up as the kettle began to whistle. "We all know that's not true."

"I have one word for you, dude," Aaron said. "Justine. There's nothing sweet about that. I don't care how hot she is, that chick is diabolical. I heard what she did to Xochi." Pad's face fell.

"No!" Xochi said. "Pad, it's not your fault. I should have known better. I mean, I kind of *did* know. I did it anyway."

"So did I," Pad reached across the table to pat Xochi's hand.

"We've all done things like that," Bubbles said.

"We have." Leviticus set down Io's tea and a coffee for Bubbles.

"Things like what?"

Xochi froze. Pallas walked into the kitchen. Xochi remembered their talk about the sleepover, the blanket, her shoes lined up under the chair. Maybe Pallas didn't hate her?

"Good morning, love. Welcome home." Io rose to hug Pallas, who was wearing jeans under a short, modish green dress. She also had on her cat hat and carried a small plaid suitcase.

"Going somewhere?" Leviticus's voice held no hint of challenge or alarm. He was probably great at poker, too.

"Yes, actually," Pallas said. "And since you're all here, I might as well tell you. I've had an epiphany. I've already talked it over with Ky just now."

"And?" Io asked. "Would you like to sit down?"

"No, thank you." Had Pallas gotten taller? "I just wanted to say that Xochi has been the best governess ever. I've learned so much the last few months." Pallas paused. Xochi could see this was hard for her, no matter what she might pretend. "But I realized something. I'm turning thirteen next month."

"Dude," Aaron said. "Really?" His confused face took on the same expression as the mask tattooed on his chest. Pallas and Xochi found each other's eyes in an instant. It was an inside joke of theirs, the way the mask seemed to take on Aaron's expressions. Xochi managed to stifle a giggle, but Pallas couldn't contain hers.

"Sorry," Pallas said, "you just look so funny." The laughter cleared the air, and suddenly, Xochi knew what Pallas was going to say. "The thing is," Pallas continued, "I'm getting too old for a governess."

"Pallas, you shouldn't blame Xochi," Leviticus said.

"If I were to blame someone," Pallas said, "it would not be Xochi. Lucky for you, I've decided blame is pointless."

"They didn't do anything, did they?" Aaron's forehead was scrunched. "I mean, they're crushed out and all, but weren't they, like—ow!"

"Aaron!" Bubbles hissed. "Shut up!"

"It's okay," Pallas said. "I know Xochi asked you to keep things from me in order to protect me. But it's okay, you guys. It might have worked when I was ten or eleven. Now it's too late. And it's not like anything has really changed."

"I don't think that's fair," Io said.

Anger bloomed then faded from Pallas's face. "I guess you're right," she said. "You've changed. And Pad. He's not bringing home floozies anymore, as far as I can tell."

"I'm not."

"And we've all agreed," Kiki said. "No more crazy parties."

"Does anyone else see her suitcase?" Bubbles turned to

Pallas. "Sweetie, where are you going with that thing? You just got home!" Bubbles couldn't wipe her tears away fast enough to hide them.

Pallas dropped her suitcase and knelt by Bubbles's chair. "I'm sorry," she said. "I'm so sorry I made you worry." She laid her head in Bubbles's lap.

"I'm sorry, too." Bubbles lifted Pallas's chin to meet her eyes. "I didn't see you. I didn't see you were changing. I didn't notice you'd grown up."

"None of us did," Leviticus said. He took off his glasses and wiped the lenses.

"Pal, how long did you last before you caved?" Aaron asked.

Pallas raised her face, laughing and crying at the same time. "Four in the morning. Did you guys bet?"

"I wouldn't let them!" Bubbles said.

"They did it anyway." Kiki laughed. "Pad, you owe Aaron twenty bucks and an oil change."

"I underestimated your fortitude," Pad told Pallas. "Never again."

Pallas giggled. Xochi's shoulders dropped several inches at the sound. "What about the suitcase, though?"

"I'm going to Capitola with Nora and Anna for a few days. Nora said I should ask you guys. It's okay, right?"

"Does Nora drive a blue Volvo wagon?" Aaron asked.

"I think so," Pallas said. She went to join him at the kitchen window. "Yes, that's her."

"Wow," Leviticus said. "Nice last-minute ask, Pal."

Pallas shot him an icy look and pressed her lips together.

"I'll go and talk to her," Io said heading out the kitchen door. "I want to find out where you're staying."

"When will you be back?" Bubbles asked.

"Tuesday," Pallas said. "I promise." She hugged Bubbles and Kiki joined in. She nodded to Leviticus but hugged Pad and Aaron. She stopped at Xochi's chair.

"Love and luck go with you," Xochi said, squeezing Pallas's hand.

"Love and luck go with you, too." Pallas picked up her suitcase and walked out of the kitchen.

No one stirred. Xochi strained to hear Io's and Nora's voices. A giggle rose above the robins in the garden from Pallas or Anna, she couldn't tell which.

Kylen came into the kitchen and poured himself a cup of coffee. He surveyed the faces around the table. "You guys, stop. She's fine."

"She hates me," Leviticus said.

"For now." Kiki nodded. "Not forever."

"She seemed . . . I don't know," Bubbles said. "She seemed all right. It so was mean to let her think we didn't know. She must've been miserable!"

"Dude!" Aaron said. "I just figured out who Anna is. The girl with the pink roller skates and spiky hair, right? That kid is so punk rock."

"Yeah, she's got great fashion sense," Kiki said. "I wonder if she's an artist?"

"She must be," Bubbles said. "And you know, being a teenager is hard. Pal's gonna need a friend her own age. Anna is super cute!"

"You people are mad," Pad said. "I've got five sisters, and there's nothing cute about teenage girls. Nothing at all."

"Are you insulting the governess?" Kylen said.

"The governess," Pad said, "is wise beyond her years. Pallas had a *sleepover*, people. She has a *friend*. Mary Poppins here deserves a freaking promotion."

"I think I just got the opposite of a promotion."

"Oh, no," Kiki said. "Did Pallas just fire you?"

"Dude, she fired all of us!" Aaron said.

The kitchen was silent. Crows called from the backyard. Leviticus stood, stretched and started mixing the pancake batter. Kiki sent Pad to the garage for the box of grapefruit she'd gotten at the farmers' market. Bubbles put her feet up on Aaron's lap and pilfered the Sunday *Chronicle*.

"Shove over." Kylen sat next to Xochi in Io's empty chair.

"Sitting by me? That's a first."

"Don't let it go to your head."

Xochi picked up a section of the paper and sipped her perfect coffee. "You want to go the movies later?"

"What, with you and Romeo?"

"Who said he's going?" Xochi said.

"Am I invited?" Leviticus asked.

"Yes." The word hung in the room for a lone moment.

Pad sat down with a fresh cup of coffee. "I'll go. I've seen almost everything, though."

"You pick, then." Xochi handed him the movie listings.

"Aaron, we should go, too." Bubbles said. "You need a mellow day to get over your cold."

Xochi reached for the comics, but Kylen intercepted her. He held her wrist. His eyes clouded over—his premonition face. "Hey!" Xochi pulled her hand away. "Mind your own business."

"Afraid I'll tell you your future?" Kylen smiled. Were his incisors more pointed than normal? *At least half coyote.* That's what Loretta would have said.

"I just want to be surprised."

"Oh, don't worry," Kylen said, handing over the comics. "You will be."

THE END

Acknowledgments

If AUSTIN WELLS HADN'T invited me to join his 2008 NaNoWriMo class, this book would not exist. I will always be grateful for his friendship and for helping me find my calling.

Thank you to my agent, Hannah Fergesen, for her vision, ambition and fierce feminism and to my editor, Amara Hoshijo, who completed our trio of weird sisters with her editorial magic. The stunning cover and interior of *All of Us with Wings* is the work of Soho Art Director Janine Agro and artist Whitney Salgado. Thank you to Alexa Wejko, Virgo publicist extraordinaire and to everyone at Soho for agreeing to publish my book.

In the years it took to write *All of Us with Wings*, I was lucky to find some excellent compatriots. Thank you, Kathe Izzo, for the accountability and encouragement. Thank you, Sherry Okamura for making me write that play and reading the very first draft of this book. Thank you to Don Babb, the first real writer I ever knew and to Diane Babb, my second mom. Thank you, Laura Fay Golston, for loving this story and reminding me who I wrote it for.

Thank you to the Squaw Valley Community of Writers and my cronies from Group Six, with extra thanks to Yeo Wei Wei and Louise Marburg and her tarot deck.

I'm grateful to Hedgebrook for the radical hospitality and to Ruth Ozeki for her continued generosity and for connecting me with wonderful freelance editor Molly Schulman. Hedgebrook also brought Brownyn Jones into my life. Thanks to all of you for your help.

Thanks and love to my Portland writing community and to Christine Toth for over twenty years of friendship, inspiration, and kitchen-witch hospitality.

Muchas gracias to Las Musas marketing collective. I am honored to be in your coven.

I'm not sure how I ever did without Tehlor Kay Mejia. Her belief in *All of Us with Wings* and unique personal stardust pulled this book into the light. To my favorite top-secret debut group—I see you chicas out there cutting class behind the school. Claribel, Nina, and Tehlor, can you please report to the assistant principal's office?

My forty-year friendship with Talese Babb provided the best education in pretend-playing a writer could wish for. I can't wait to see our books whispering to each other on the shelves! To my aunts, uncles, and cousins—the scenes with the family joking at the kitchen table are all for you. To my mom, Anita Johansen, who read every single draft of this book. Her belief in me helped me believe in myself. To my father, Patrick Smith, who never got to see this day, but who would have loved it most of all, and to Nana and Grandpa for teaching me the meaning of home and unconditional love.

To MK Chavez whose friendship has been one of the great gifts of my life and to Connor and Sayre Quevedo—our found family inspired so much of the family in this book.

My daughters and my little cousin Jamie grew up with this book and lent their various charms to my writing of Pallas. When I started, Angelika was too young to even look at this book without a chaperone. In the end, she became my most trusted editor and advisor. Thank you, Jelli, for your patience, insight, and brilliance. My oldest daughter, Luciana, has always been my truth-teller and taste accountant. Thank you for encouraging me to work even when it conflicted with your personal interests and for bringing Berwin into my life. Every debut writer should have access to a stress relief Corgi.

Thank you to my own furry muse, Stella, who has been by my side for every word of this novel and to the Siamese cats I have known and loved.

And finally, thank you to my husband, Carl, who listened to the world's longest bedtime story even though there were no car chases, moved my enormous lucky desk seven times, never stopped believing I'd be published, never stopped loving and supporting me, and still makes me laugh every single day after twenty-eight years. The luckiest day of my life was the day we met.